THE
SHADOW
REGENT

THE
SHADOW
REGENT

CHAD CORRIE

DARK HORSE BOOKS

Published by
Dark Horse Books
A division of Dark Horse Comics LLC
10956 SE Main Street
Milwaukie, OR 97222

DarkHorse.com

Library of Congress Cataloging-in-Publication Data

Names: Corrie, Chad, author. | Burgess, Dan, illustrator.
Title: The shadow regent / writer, Chad Corrie ; cover art, Dan Burgess.
Description: Milwaukie, OR : Dark Horse Books, [2023] | Series: The Wizard
    King trilogy ; book three
Identifiers: LCCN 2022022320 (print) | LCCN 2022022321 (ebook) | ISBN
    9781506734033 (trade paperback) | ISBN 9781506734040 (ebook)
Subjects: LCGFT: Fantasy fiction. | Novels.
Classification: LCC PS3603.O77235 S53 2023 (print) | LCC PS3603.O77235
    (ebook) | DDC 813/.6--dc23/eng/20220725
LC record available at https://lccn.loc.gov/2022022320
LC ebook record available at https://lccn.loc.gov/2022022321

First edition: March 2023
Ebook ISBN 978-1-50673-404-0
Trade Paperback ISBN 978-1-50673-403-3

1 3 5 7 9 10 8 6 4 2
Printed in the United States of America

ALSO BY CHAD CORRIE

PROLOGUE

Gurthghol kept his eyes shut, concentrating. Not that there was anything to see in the midst of the Void anyway. There was just an empty blackness for infinity. It was the one place even the two Cosmic Entities, Awntodgenee and Nuhl, feared to tread, having formed the cosmos to escape it. And yet, even as that cosmos swelled in size and dominion over the desolate, benighted expanse, it was gnawed on from every angle. The very substance of reality was crushed and torn into the most basic of components, which were further brought out of existence.

The Void was the place where all things met their end and the original state of reality. And he, the god of chaos and darkness, was its prisoner. The only thing keeping him alive was Vkar's throne. It had the power to sustain him for as long as was needed. And right now he would use it to the fullest extent. His father had crafted it to overthrow the old order—to topple and destroy Awntodgenee and Nuhl—but had failed. Gurthghol had thought he could finish the task but fell short himself and now suffered his fate.

The black chains encircling him and the ancient white marble seat had been formed from part of Nuhl and as such were alive in their own way. He could feel them biting into him like jagged metal, irritating him just enough to annoy and perhaps eventually drive him mad, but not enough to do any real physical harm. This was all part of the torture. He was to remain seated in the throne, chained in the midst of the Void, until his captors came to finish the job or he helped things along on his own.

But he wasn't about to surrender. He'd been so close—had tasted victory at hand and would have attained it had he acted bolder at the first. In his mind's eye he relived the final battle between the Cosmic Entities. They had stood across from him, actually willing to face him in direct conflict, and he gladly gave it to them. The throne had tapped into their very essence and was siphoning it from them and into itself—just as Vkar had created it to do.

He had felt their fear. They were seeing what a god could do. They were witnessing the end of their age. And had he been faster to act, the cosmos would have been freed. But he'd just come off of his battle with the upstart human wizard Cadrith, who thought he could take out the entire pantheon on his own. But Cadrith himself wasn't anything but a puppet deluded into thinking if he did Nuhl's bidding he'd be able to seize even greater glory.

In the end a simple goblin did Cadrith in, wielding what Gurthghol now understood was an ancient wonder created by wizard kings of old to weaken and even defeat a god. It sucked all the fight out of the wizard, returning him to his former lich state. And from there it was an easy thing for Gurthghol to send him off to Mortis.

While he'd delighted in the victory and took that confidence into the next fight, Gurthghol now realized that same confidence had made him too sure of himself. If he had just shut up and concentrated on unraveling the two entities, they wouldn't have been able to take him. He would have prevailed, and the pantheon, Tralodren, and the rest of the cosmos would have been safe and himself hailed as their champion and savior.

He willed himself to tap deeper into the throne. He'd learned some things while seated upon it millennia ago, following his father's death. Then he'd taken it by sheer coincidence of necessity. His daughter had been corrupted by Nuhl and turned against her family. Once she slew Vkar, the throne was left vacant and the cosmos in peril. For the throne wasn't created to remain empty. And the longer it did, the more the cosmos suffered destruction.

Gurthghol had found himself racing for the throne before he knew what he was doing. He took his seat and saved the cosmos, but the cost was high. Trapped on the throne, he could never leave lest the cosmos shatter. But he'd learned some things while its prisoner—saw some potential for future glory for the gods as well as learned more of the throne's hidden nature. It not only augmented the power of the one seated upon it but could also drain the Cosmic Entities of their power. And that's when he'd caught a glimpse of his father's grand plan. A plan he supported more eagerly now than ever before.

And he could still do it. The pantheon could still win. The cosmos could still be liberated. If he could just get free of these chains, he could finish where he left off. For the chains not only kept him on the throne but subtly leeched enough of his own power and essence away to keep him below his full strength. The throne would then have to supplement what lacked, which kept it weaker as a result. The chains also served as an anchor to the Void. He couldn't leave, no matter how hard he tried. And he'd done nothing *but* try since being deposited into this yawning ocean of nothingness.

Once more he latched on to the throne's core, taking a firm hold with his mental and spiritual hands and attempting to pull it up and into himself. Nothing. Same as the last time . . . and the time before that.

He snarled as he swelled his chest and arched his back.

Nothing. The chains held him fast.

Enraged, he bellowed his hatred into the Void. But even this was in vain. The sound was consumed as soon as it left his lips, leaving only a muffled anger in his ears.

He would be free.

He would prevail.

CHAPTER 1

Twila watched the Chimera lead the Tularin down one of the main hallways in Anoma, Gurthghol's grand palace. She pushed herself into the shadows of the hall, further cloaking herself as the two incarnates passed. This wasn't that hard, since the palace, like much of Altearin, had plenty of shadows to spare. And her nature as a Lady of Darkness further augmented her efforts.

One of the many strange beings to inhabit the plane of Altearin, Chimera were as tall as Tularins but with goat legs, a humanoid torso, a snake-like tail, and a lion's head with ram's horns. Like the Tularin, this one had wings, but his were more bat-like; the Tularin's were covered in white feathers which matched his platinum hair. Gurthghol had often used Chimera in various guard duties, and this incarnate was allowed his heavy plate armor and spear. The Tularin, by contrast, wore only a white robe with a golden sash around his waist and a long sword strapped over that.

Tularins weren't commonly called upon to fight, as they were more often seen as administrators and messengers between the gods. Even still, they were a rare sight on Altearin. Unlike the other gods, Gurthghol didn't keep any in attendance, making Twila all the more alert as to just what sort of tidings accompanied this particular visit. Long aware of the workings of the palace since finding her way into and up the ranks of Gurthghol's harem,

Twila knew this was something of potentially great importance. Something she wanted to be sure she was able to use to the fullest possible advantage.

Neither of the incarnates spoke. Each was taken with their duty: the Chimera to seeing this new messenger to his purpose, and the Tularin to delivering his message. Such dedication was impressive but not uncommon among the incarnates. The titans and titan lords, however, were another story. She waited until the pair were well down the onyx-paneled hall before following after them, making sure to keep clear of the occasional sconce or torch along the way.

Keeping to the shadows was easy enough, as was making sure she remained quiet. Being twice their size didn't prove as detrimental as one might have thought. The palace was built for titans, and most who inhabited it were used to the size difference between titan, incarnate, and others. It was the stealth where she had to be mindful. This was still the residence of Gurthghol—the ruler of Altearin—and most of the guards probably wouldn't take too kindly to someone attempting to sneak through it. She followed them to a closed door at the end of another hallway, where the Chimera turned back to the Tularin.

"He's in here," Twila heard the Chimera say in his native Entropis, which apparently the Tularin understood. "I'll let him know of your arrival."

"Thank you," said the Tularin in the same language as the Chimera entered the room.

Twila knew it was a library—one of a handful in the palace. But just who was awaiting the Tularin's message wasn't clear.

If this was a diplomatic message from the pantheon or another god, then it would have been delivered to another god. But Twila knew Gurthghol was on Thangaria with the rest of the pantheon. So why send this Tularin? The only other persons of rank in the plane under Gurthghol would be Erdis, Shador, and Mergis. And she knew both Shador and Mergis weren't in the palace, so that just left—

"Erdis will see you now." The Chimera emerged from the library.

Wasting no time, Twila tapped deeper into the cosmic element of darkness and enveloped herself fully into the hall's flickering shadows, hurrying to a special spot in the hall's wall that, when pushed just right, allowed a slender opening to appear. Sliding inside, she made her way through the winding tunnel until coming to rest at the end of another stone wall. Here again, if you knew how to push the right stones, you could silently create another opening that would take you into the library itself. It was one of several such secrets she'd collected through her efforts. Some from friendly palace workers or members of the court, others from Gurthghol himself. All had served her well.

And no sooner had Twila stepped into the back part of the library then she set her ears and eyes upon the two incarnates speaking at the front of the room near the door. Being an incarnate himself, Erdis and the Tularin were the same size, meaning Twila would have to listen extra carefully to catch all the details. She wasn't about to try to get any closer, staying within the cloaking darkness as much as possible.

"Welcome to Altearin. I'm told you have something important to relay." Erdis greeted the Tularin in Entropis. His robes were a rich mix of teal, white, and dark blue, which complemented his olive complexion.

"And you are Erdis, Gurthghol's chamberlain?" The Tularin kept to the same language, no doubt honoring the preferences of his given audience. Erdis often didn't speak Entropis, from what Twila knew. The official language of court and for much of Altearin was Titan.

"I am." Erdis' oval head was shaved save for a brown ponytail at the back, allowing his pointed ears to clearly be seen. The high forehead made his faint features stand out. His thin lips were almost nonexistent, and his nose was so flat it nearly blended into his face. She used to wonder how his people managed to breathe, but somehow they'd found a way to thrive, like all the other chaotic incarnates, of which the Kardu, his people, were a part.

"Then the pantheon has sent me with a message for you and the two viceroys."

"And you have my word I will inform them as soon as we finish speaking here," said Erdis. Twila had no doubt of that. The Kardu had a long record of integrity and loyalty to Gurthghol and his duties.

"The pantheon thought it right to inform you of recent events at Thangaria . . . and of some new challenges Altearin shall be facing in the future."

"Go on."

"As you may be aware, Nuhl, one of the two Cosmic Entities, recently sought to use a human wizard named Cadrith Elanis as a pawn to bring about the end of the pantheon and the world of Tralodren, which they created. Gurthghol and all the other gods decided to make their final stand against the assault on Thangaria, where, millennia prior, Vkar saw his end by Nuhl and another agent."

"Yes, I am keenly aware of that," said Erdis. "As are all of those who have a hand in keeping this realm governed."

Twila was too, of course. She made it her business to stay informed on all important matters of state and the lives of those from whom she received such information. It could be tiring work but was well worth it—especially in times such as this.

"And were you aware of Gurthghol's plan to reclaim his father's throne?" The Tularin's question gave Erdis pause.

"Vkar's throne," Twila whispered in surprise.

She, like just about all titans, knew of it. How could you not know about the most powerful item in all the cosmos? But it was always out of reach—to both god and divinity alike. Gurthghol himself had seen to that. But now to have him laying claim to it again was truly something of note. Even more so since he never shared the matter with Twila—or rather she hadn't been able to discover it through her normal channels and methods.

"Is this the pantheon asking or you?" asked Erdis.

"I make no accusations. I simply want to make sure you receive all the information I was sent to convey." The Tularin's reply lightened Erdis' features.

"Then yes, I had an idea that was what he was about. One doesn't take a small force of warriors to Galba for a simple chat. I had my concerns about him breaking the pact between them, but it was not my place to try to stop him from his decision, even if I had my doubts." He sighed. "Did he succeed? Is that what this is about?"

"Gurthghol reclaimed Vkar's throne and used it in the battle with Cadrith and Nuhl on Thangaria."

"And won?" Erdis was as surprised as Twila.

"Yes. With the throne and some help from a goblin, he was able to put an end to Cadrith and the threat Nuhl posed through him."

"A goblin?" Erdis was clearly intrigued. "The throne of the first god of the cosmos wasn't enough to take out the threat?"

"The goblin had a scepter that helped weaken Cadrith, allowing Gurthghol to make quick work of the former wizard."

"That sounds like a rather powerful scepter. One, no doubt, the other gods will be interested in now as well, assuming Gurthghol hadn't claimed it for himself."

"No, he didn't. And he didn't end his fight with Nuhl once Cadrith had been defeated. Instead, he pressed on and sought to destroy both Awntodgenee and Nuhl in their true forms."

"He did what?" Erdis barely managed to soften the shout.

"He sought to use Vkar's throne like his father before him, seeking to destroy the Cosmic Entities. He claimed it was the only way to finally be free of their threat over the pantheon and the entire cosmos."

"I knew he was seeking something bold"—Erdis lowered his head in what Twila could only assume was a form of mourning—"but to take on the Cosmic Entities? It's madness." His eyes locked on to the Tularin's. "Did—did he survive?"

"None of the pantheon know for certain," said the Tularin. "But he was taken captive and, it's assumed, will meet his end in time."

Erdis hung his head once more with a heavy sigh.

Twila could feel the weight on her own shoulders. And then there was the pang in her heart. She'd grown rather fond of Gurthghol. Her repeated efforts to raise herself in his favor and in rank in his harem had brought them closer in some ways than she'd expected. And yet, even as this all set in, her mind was racing. This opened up so many avenues to explore . . . *if* you had the right means to explore them, that is.

"I've been sent to let you and the twin viceroys of Altearin know as soon as possible so you can make the proper arrangements and prepare for spreading the news to the rest of the realm."

"But he's not dead. You're sure of that?"

Twila inched closer, intent on not missing a single syllable.

"I can only share what I've been told," said the Tularin. "And when I left, none of the pantheon were sure if he lived or died. But my understanding is he will not be returning anytime soon, if at all. You and your viceroys will have to work through what comes next until additional arrangements can be made."

"*Additional* arrangements?" Erdis raised an eyebrow. "Like having the pantheon try to take command of Altearin? This is still Gurthghol's realm—whether he's here or not. As long as he draws breath—"

"I will leave those matters to you and your viceroys. They are not of my concern. And I have spoken what needs saying."

"What about Vkar's throne?" asked Erdis. "What happened to it?"

"It was taken along with Gurthghol."

"So now they have the throne as well—I'm sure that hasn't pleased the pantheon."

"I believe it was said that what has happened has happened and cannot be changed."

Erdis snorted. "Sounds like Saredhel. So then the rest of the gods are going to be busy, I take it."

"There is much that needs to be done. And they are even now in another council seeking to be about it."

"Which gives us time," said Erdis with a dismissive nod. "If you're finished, you may go."

"And you will tell Lords Mergis and Shador this news?"

"You have my word. As soon as you leave, I'll send out messengers and summon them to the palace. *Discreetly* summon them to the palace. We don't need to raise too much concern until we've decided on the best course of action."

"Then I will leave you to it." The Tularin took his leave, closing the door behind him.

Once alone, Erdis hurried to a nearby desk and began searching for some ink and parchment. He was so engrossed in the activity he never saw the shadowed figure of Twila stealthily tread to the hidden portion of the wall and slip back inside, closing the secret door behind her. If she could beat Erdis' letters, she'd have a leg up on any competition. But she had to be wise as well as rapid; what came next needed to be delicately and decisively implemented.

• • •

Thick clouds cloaked Altearin in a purple covering similar to perpetual twilight. No stars nor any other light filled the dark canopy for miles. Yet even within this darkness, Shador didn't feel secure. He'd taken to his keep outside the realm's capital and surrounded it with his Swarthinian honor guard.

The Lord of Darkness paced before the large fountain in his courtyard, thinking. The heels of his boots clicked on the flagstone like anxious hooves. Dressed in a purple-trimmed black robe with a pure-black cloak, he blended in with his surroundings. He'd left the hood down, leaving his clean-shaven face and deep violet eyes visible to anyone lurking about. Like the rest of the Lords of Darkness, Shador had an unusual skin tone. The dusty grayish-purple grew more gray in the light and a deep purple in the darkness.

He'd fortified himself as soon as he'd encountered Rheminas' emissary in Haven. It had taken him years to recruit and carefully cultivate his cult until it was sizable enough to undertake his desires. And all that had been extinguished in mere moments. But what was worse than losing his worshipers was knowing it wouldn't have happened if the gods hadn't been privy to his actions. Which also meant the destruction of the cult was just a prelude to the real assault.

He'd taken careful study of others who tried rising above their station through the use of Tralodroen cults and thought he'd done everything right. He'd even built into his cult the desire to keep things secret and hidden, promoting himself as a divinity able to share power and wonderful secrets with those he found worthy. It was mostly lies and ritualistic jargon he made up as things progressed, but it had worked well enough, and the cult's ranks swelled.

They'd finally grown in strength and influence to such a point that he was starting to gain the ability to infiltrate and affect the administration of governments and even the faint edges of the major religions in the region. And that was what he wanted: the ability to act on Tralodren without being seen by the gods or their allies.

Because Tralodren was far from just the jewel of the pantheon, as the gods would have all believe. No, it was also a treasure cache waiting to be exploited—both of items and of people.

The titans had once ruled the planet, as had the dranors after them. And each left forgotten wonders behind one could exploit if cunning enough to find and engage them.

And this was to say nothing of the potential one could gain in taking some spirits of their own—just like the gods did—whenever their followers died. While Shador hadn't yet figured out how such a thing could be done, he was sure it was achievable and kept building his cult with as many young and healthy people as possible to allow more time for solving the mystery.

But none of that was going to happen now. The gods knew of his actions and had little love for those who were pulling others away from their worship or even playing on their private planet. The pattern for retribution was simple enough: send in a Galgalli after the cult and then follow up with the main offender. Except it got even more challenging when the culprit was part of the administration of one of those gods. Here it could possibly fall to the offended god—in this case, Gurthghol—to deal with the matter over the Galgalli. And given that the agent who'd so recently slaughtered his followers wasn't really a Galgalli but a mere human instead, things weren't as cut and dried as they normally would be.

But even while Gurthghol might have been a more hands-off ruler in many things, once word reached him one of his trusted officials—a viceroy too, no less—was working his own will on Tralodren, Shador was sure Gurthghol wouldn't let it stand. And Shador was certain that was just what was going to happen when he'd earlier received word from Erdis about needing to meet with Gurthghol for some task on Tralodren.

He was sure Gurthghol was calling him to his final judgment but quickly discovered it was to fight with another entity called Galba instead. But once Galba sent those he'd assembled back to Altearin, he only heard the rest through snips and pieces while deciding to flee the city. There was talk of a battle being waged on Thangaria. By who or what wasn't clear, but if it took Gurthghol's attention, it bought him some time. But that wouldn't stop the inevitable. And so he remained holed up in his keep, racking his brain for some way out of this mess.

He stopped his pacing, shifting his gaze to the nearby fountain. It was a lavish affair: a lifelike rendering of four barghests howling atop a large rock. The rock was of rough basalt, the barghests formed out of polished onyx. The creatures were once native to Umbrium but had arrived on Altearin with the creation of the realm. They were large tailless dogs that grew about waist high to a titan with powerful jaws and claws that made quick work of anything that got in their way.

Streams of water flowed from their open mouths, filling the fountain's basalt-ringed pond built around the rough rock. In the past the sight was a restful thing that helped soothe him during trying times. But that peace today was elusive.

Reaching into the pocket of his robes, he pulled out the silver necklace given him by the high priest of his now-defunct cult. The large circle of lapis lazuli at the center of the silver pendant shimmered in whatever light it captured. It was easily dwarfed by his larger palm, making it appear as some child's trinket. The necklace was said to enhance one's access to magic—or in Shador's case, the cosmic element of darkness. And having such an increase in ability would be an immense boon in the days ahead.

All that trouble and planning and plotting . . . Yet it had been worth it. And all he had to do was show up to collect his prize. That was the beauty of using guises. They got you through the Grand Barrier around Tralodren, allowing you to take a form that further cloaked your actions from any curious eyes. But the best part was that things could be brought into and out of Tralodren. The barrier only blocked divinities and gods from coming and going in their true forms. Anyone or anything else wasn't hampered. This meant Shador could go and pick up whatever his cultists offered him, and none would be the wiser. Yes, it was a wonderful situation, until recent events . . .

The sound of a descending Swarthin pulled him from his thoughts. Though half the size of Shador's fifteen feet, any gap in height was easily overcome by aid of the other's wings. Like the rest with him, the bat-like darkened incarnate wore dark brown brigandine armor with short swords on his belt. Each also kept a crossbow slung over their back. A bandoleer across the chest kept more bolts at the ready.

"Someone is approaching from the east," the Swarthin said in Stygian, the language birthed in the ancient plane of Umbrium—the former plane of darkness.

"Just one?" Shador asked in the same tongue.

"There isn't any sign of anything else for miles."

Shador slid the necklace back into the hidden pocket of his robes. "Are they on foot?"

"No, they're mounted on a black stallion and keeping to the road, pressing hard for the keep."

"A messenger?" Perhaps the pantheon wanted a parley. That could buy him more time.

"They carry no banner, my lord."

"Keep watch, and when they get closer—"

A sudden flurry of motion near the large barred gates stopped Shador in midspeech. "What do you think you're *doing*?" he shouted at the handful of Swarthin lifting the thick wooden rail holding the doors shut. "I said to keep the doors barred!"

"Urgent messenger, my lord," one of the Swarthin lifting the wooden bar grunted. "They had to speak with you at once."

"And so you just disobey my orders?" Shador yelled, throwing back his cloak over his left shoulder, revealing his sheathed sword.

"No," said a new voice in Stygian, "he obeyed *mine*."

Shador spun on his heel, taking note of the black stallion making its way through the small opening barely allowing it inside. Already the rider was looking to dismount. As she did, Shador only grew more uncertain.

"Twila?"

Now free of the horse, it was clear the figure was indeed a woman. And she was definitely a titan, sharing his height and build, but her black cloak and hood hid the rest of her person from further scrutiny.

"Were you expecting someone else?" She removed her hood, revealing her short black hair, along with a face and manner that were hard to forget.

"Close the gates," Shador ordered. "And this time *keep* them shut."

"You rode all the way here?" He eyed her carefully, trying not to miss a single detail. Her complexion was slightly lighter than his own but still helped to blend her into the darkness.

"I didn't want to draw any attention using the portals," she replied, "and I thought if I used other methods you might mistake me for someone else before I could properly make myself known." It was clever thinking that reminded Shador again of part of what had drawn him to her in the first place.

"And it looks like I was right." Twila scanned the courtyard. "Are you preparing for a war?"

"And why wouldn't I be?" He didn't share her levity. "The pantheon wants my blood, and I'm not yet ready to surrender it."

Twila raised an eyebrow and turned up a corner of her lips. "You seem pretty convinced of that."

"It's pretty much what's in store, given the last I've heard." He watched Twila draw near.

"And just what *have* you heard?"

"Something about a battle back on Thangaria—a threat to the pantheon," he said, half watching the flying Swarthin returning the wooden bar across the gate with a thick thud.

"That's it?" Twila was clearly amazed.

"*What?* I had some other pressing matters on my mind. And as the other Lords of Darkness were expelled from Tralodren in the first fight with Gurthghol, I haven't spoken with him since."

"But you still had time to raise the troops," she added. "You must have known something."

"Just what I told you. I let Mergis see to most everything else. The preparations allowed the perfect opening and cover so I could secure this place."

"And you're supposed to be a viceroy of Altearin?" It was the first time in a long while Shador actually heard some disappointment in Twila's voice.

"There's something greater than Altearin at stake here," he attempted to explain. Instead his words only birthed a blank look from his longtime lover.

"You're right," she finally said. "Nuhl returned to try to destroy the pantheon. Tralodren would have been next, I guess."

"Nuhl . . ." The name wasn't something you spoke lightly. All knew of its history and desire for destroying anything and everything it could. And while it had tried and failed once before in taking out the pantheon back in the days of Vkar and Xora—the first god and goddess of the cosmos—none really imagined a second attempt was possible.

"Did it win?"

"No, but it did create some interesting developments."

"I don't have time for your games, Twila. Just spit it out."

"The threat to the pantheon has been eliminated . . . but so too has Gurthghol."

"What do you mean?"

"He's gone, and Vkar's throne with him."

"*What?*" Shador lurched forward, grabbing hold of Twila's arms with a death-like grip. It was almost too impossible to believe. "Tell me everything."

"After you and Mergis summoned those other lords to Arid Land Gurthghol won against Galba. And after besting her, he reclaimed the throne."

"Why would he break the pact and take up the throne again? He hated it from the beginning."

"He wanted to use it to destroy Awntodgenee and Nuhl."

Shador paced for a few steps, attempting to wrap his mind around everything. "He couldn't succeed. He must have known that."

"From what I hear he thought he'd finally found a way to be done with them both for good."

He spun back around, facing Twila's still-unreadable features. "But he wasn't."

"No. He was taken prisoner instead—at least that's what the story was when I left the city."

"But he defeated the first threat then—the reason for the battle on Thangaria?"

"Oh yes. He even had some help from a goblin," said Twila.

"A goblin," Shador snorted. "Is that right?" He'd had plenty of opportunity getting acquainted with them during his exploits on Tralodren.

"Not just any goblin," she continued. "He had a scepter that weakened the human wizard whom Nuhl had been using for its attack, allowing Gurthghol a greater advantage."

"Weakened him even with Nuhl's backing?"

"That's what I hear."

Now this was something *very* interesting. Nuhl's original agent had bested Xora and Vkar in the past. The whole pantheon had apparently summoned their best forces to face off with another such agent, leaving one to assume victory wasn't going to be so easily won. And yet one goblin with a certain scepter could change the whole dynamic . . . What would it do to any other god—even one that now sat upon Vkar's throne?

Twila's smile was dripping with mischief. "You can see why I spared no expense in letting you know."

"And where did you hear all this? I know you weren't at the battle on Thangaria."

"I have my ways. But it's genuine and vetted, rest assured."

"And where is this scepter now?"

"So far it's being kept on Thangaria."

"And they're in another council, no doubt, to deal with all this," he mused.

"The last I heard." Twila was clearly enjoying watching Shador gather all the loose threads.

"So then I might have some time. But we'll have to act quickly."

"What do you have in mind?" She flirted with her violet eyes.

"Something bold and daring," he replied, brushing a hand down Twila's soft cheek. Already he was feeling like his old confident self again. No longer fearfully lurking but now confidently plotting.

"I like it already," she purred.

Shador wasn't saying the half of it. If he could get all the pieces to line up, he could soon find himself in the best place he'd ever dreamed possible. Forget about what his ambitions had been before. With Gurthghol gone and the gods locked in debate, he could see himself rising to some *incredible* heights. And the best part was if done right, the pantheon couldn't do a thing about it.

"Let me guess," said Twila. "Does it involve a plot to take Gurthghol's throne and finally rule like you've always wanted?"

"Not an open plot, no. We need to be tasteful in our coup—discreet and honoring of our beloved lord and master. And it has to be something that smacks of legality so the rest of the pantheon can't come after me once I've risen to the challenge."

Twila ran a hand through his short dark hair. "And here you were worried they might be coming to do you in."

"And they still will be once this current crisis has passed. Even if things go well, there will still be some calling for retribution."

"Then it sounds like you're still going to need an inside person," she said, placing a hand on his chest. "Someone with connections and ways to help sway the others more fully to your cause."

"Someone who, no doubt, will want to share in any success."

"It's only fitting, I would think," Twila purred. "If we *are* truly to be partners in everything."

Shador nodded in thought. "Too bad. You were so close." His comment caught Twila off guard.

"To what?"

"Being his favorite," he replied, referring to the past dealings between Twila and Gurthghol as she worked her way through the ranks of his harem. While others might have been troubled by the action, Shador knew the truth. It was never anything serious and just part of the game they both played: attempting to gain greater place and power. Though now with Gurthghol's absence, he was looking forward to having Twila more to himself.

"I think I'll have something to compensate the loss soon enough." Her dark eyes again flirted with his.

"I wouldn't have it any other way." He brought her close, face to face—holding her taut with his arm.

"Then let's get started."

CHAPTER 2

Thangaria, former seat of a planetary empire, once more was quiet. The clamor of battle that had rocked its foundations over an hour before had ended. The gray shroud of atmosphere draped across the sky set a fitting mood for all below.

The survivors rounded up the dead. All those whom the gods had assembled on the floating chunk of rock to face the former threat went about the dreary business with a solemn sternness. Those who'd fallen wouldn't be returning to life. Nuhl was the opposite of life, and its failed vessel shared the same nature. All those killed by the former lich turned upstart god would have had their spirits erased from existence. Once their bodies had been destroyed by rot or fire, they would be nothing but memory. All who took up arms knew that possible fate, but their sacrifice would not be so soon forgotten.

If one could look past the debris and the fallen—gloss over the sight of the patches of blood and burn marks scattered across the barren rock and stone—Thangaria would have appeared as it had for countless centuries: a faded monument to the once-great glory of the mighty Thangarian Empire. But Khuthon, the god of war, knew better than to try to look past what it really was: a crumbling shrine to fallen glories and past battles—some fresher than others.

But it still made for a safe-enough place to gather in council. And since the fall of Vkar and the shattering of his empire these councils had been far and few between. But in the last few days the council had gathered more frequently than any of the gods would have once thought possible. And yet there seemed even more business that needed attending than ever.

"I still think we should have waited," Khuthon told Ganatar as the rest of the fifteen gods entered the council chamber.

Khuthon didn't bother changing from his armor. Most of the other gods didn't either. They also kept their weapons at hand. Both were offenses that once would have barred a god from visiting Thangaria, let alone attending a council, but they'd taken many liberties of late.

"It was the right thing to do," said Ganatar. "Altearin needed to know their lord's fate." His porcelain face glowed with a faint white aura like the rest of his body, illuminating the chamber as they entered and highlighting his snowy hair, mustache, and connecting goatee beard.

"And we could have told them more still once other things had been decided," Khuthon argued. "Sending off that Tularin with only the faintest grasp of—"

"We can't change what's done," said Ganatar, "and we have plenty that needs our attention right now."

Each of the gods took up their respective seat. Aerotripton, Drued, and Panthora, the shortest of the pantheon, had a place at one end of the long table closest to the doors and opposite the head of the table, which led to the granite steps of a dais and the three titan-sized golden thrones upon it. Two thrones flanked the central one, which stood a step higher than the others.

Dradin would take the throne to the right of Ganatar, who took the central seat. Khuthon joined the rest of his siblings—Asorlok, Olthon, Asora, and Saredhel—on the left side of the table's head. Opposite them sat the other gods, their children—Causilla, Endarien, Rheminas, Shiril, and Perlosa.

While the council was getting seated, Khuthon ran through the final parts of the recent fight, processing things again in greater detail, hopeful of remembering everything closely for later study. He'd originally planned for something grand and glorious—a conflict that hadn't been seen in millennia—but the gods had hardly taken part in it thanks to Gurthghol's sudden arrival with Vkar's throne. And like the rest of the pantheon, he couldn't help but note the empty throne on Ganatar's left. It was reserved for the head of the Dark Gods, the now-absent Gurthghol.

Already, that absence was weighing upon the pantheon. For as odd as it might have sounded, the god of chaos and darkness did much to bring order and stability to the proceedings and the pantheon itself. After all, it was he who'd formed the council to begin with and who brought the gods together for their first meeting, calling for the creation of Tralodren. Such an action, he thought, would bind them all together in a more productive way. And he was right. They just proved as much by banding together to save Tralodren from destruction. And if Gurthghol's presence and participation had brought a sense of purpose and unity to the pantheon, what did his absence foreshadow?

"If everyone is ready." Ganatar peered out across the rest of the gathered gods with his powder-blue eyes. He'd put aside his helmet but left on his golden plate armor and black cape. Upon seeing there were no objections, he added, "Then I call this council to order."

"We've already sent the Tularin to Altearin," Ganatar continued, "but there's still much we have to work through."

"Agreed." Khuthon began directing the conversation, mindfully working all the various threads of his plan through the loom of the forthcoming discussion.

"And where do we start?" Endarien's yellow eyes circled the table. He'd placed his hawk-faced helmet on the table like the others had done with their helms, letting his shield and spear rest opposite each other against the back of his tall chair. The weapon's sparking and cracking white tip didn't seem to bother anyone. Khuthon always imagined both Endarien and his mother, Olthon, must have been uncomfortable sitting for periods of time, given their wings. But yet he'd never seen or heard either complain.

"We need to keep a level head, for one," Ganatar advised. "Moving too rashly won't serve any good or interest."

"But do we even know what happened?" Causilla had changed her attire for the council. It wasn't a total surprise. She wasn't really at home in weapons and armor. Khuthon was amazed she'd even brought a weapon, let alone donned armor, for the previous battle. She now wore a cream-colored gown with golden sandals and a rose sash tied about her waist. She'd also pulled her curly brown hair into a ponytail and let it drape over her right shoulder. A pearl necklace and earrings provided the finishing touches.

"We survived," said Rheminas. "And now we tally our losses."

"It's too soon for that," said Khuthon, launching off of his son's foundation. "We need to prepare."

"For what?" asked Asorlok, amazed Khuthon would even make such a suggestion. The god of death seemed more thoughtful than normal. It wasn't entirely out of character but did make Khuthon pause to polish his reply.

"For the new reality before us and what new threats will most certainly arise," he continued, running that next thread through the loom. Everything needed to run smoothly. He couldn't raise too much resistance too soon.

"Nuhl and his champion are defeated," Olthon calmly stated. "We've had our battle, Khuthon. Now it's time to deal with the aftermath."

"Exactly," he replied. "And that means dealing with Gurthghol's demise."

"And avenging his death," Rheminas added, making his coppery hand into a fist.

"A wasted effort." Asorlok found Rheminas' yellow eyes with his own piercing blue orbs. "Gurthghol isn't dead."

"But we all saw him being taken by Nuhl." The very pregnant Asora voiced everyone's amazement. Her white gown was seemingly stretched to the point of bursting due to her plump stomach. And to think just moments before she was ready to fight in such a condition. Maybe Khuthon was having a greater influence over his wife than he knew.

"But he hasn't crossed over to Mortis." Asorlok's eyes narrowed, making his hawkish nose seem even more so. Khuthon hadn't been expecting that, but he could still adapt things to his favor.

"Are you sure about that?" Drued's charcoal-gray brow wrinkled. He'd placed his double-headed axe next to his helmet. His brown beard was threaded with silver and twelve braids he'd capped in gold.

"Yes." Asorlok's steady gaze stilled the dwarven god from any further questions.

"Then maybe he escaped," offered Endarien, a small sense of hope in his voice. "Maybe he even made his way back to Altearin."

"Or maybe he's playing us all for fools." Rheminas raked his fingers through his orange beard. "We all saw him with the throne. He could have just used this whole battle as an excuse to reclaim it for himself."

"Why?" Causilla gently pushed back against Rheminas' rising conspiracy. "He'd never take up something he never wanted in the first place. Maybe, instead, we should just take what he said at face value: that he believed a sacrifice was needed to defeat the threat."

It was just what Gurthghol had told them before he was taken by Nuhl. It was even the premise of their own actions and preparations against the recent threat. Even so, Khuthon still wasn't sure what to make of the matter—he doubted any of them really knew, not even Saredhel, who first proposed it. And that was saying nothing of how they all had first launched Endarien against Cadrith, the original threat, thinking it was the sacrifice they had to make as a whole. And that had dearly cost them the last of Vkar's essence, a loss only compounded by Gurthghol's actions.

"Or he's hiding something," Rheminas continued, his words chilling the air.

"Unless you're making an accusation"—Ganatar leaned forward on his throne—"I'd remind you that Gurthghol has just conducted a selfless act in order to save all of us *and* Tralodren. We don't need to sully his deed by casting baseless claims."

"True enough." Khuthon gave Ganatar a small nod. Endless talk on conspiracies and other matters outside his objective wasn't helpful. He needed to keep steering things in the proper direction, guiding his words along with the others' thoughts. Those threads were nearly all aligned. "But it'd still be wise to send someone to check on the status of his realm."

"And we just sent a Tularin." Olthon frowned at the thought, marring her fair features.

"But not in an official capacity to really search things out," Khuthon replied. "Delivering a message is one thing. But to have the authority to make inquiries and search other matters out as they arise—"

"I believe the word you're looking for is *spy*." Dradin's green-eyed gaze locked hard upon Khuthon. The god's short white beard added a paternal demeanor to his words.

"Confirmation." Khuthon quickly reclaimed the conversation. "Tularins have some influence and respect but nothing like an official delegation would have."

Perlosa's pale lips curled into a cold smile. "And just who might you have in mind to lead said delegation, Father?" She always knew how best to rankle him, but he let it pass.

"I'd be the best candidate should the need for any type of confrontation arise." He kept his voice and manner measured.

"And why would you think there'd be a need for confrontation?" Olthon's green eyes were like jade daggers.

Khuthon's simple smile didn't blunt them one bit. "I've learned it's best to be prepared for anything."

"Including an *invasion* of Altearin?" Olthon pressed.

"Do *any* of you know for certain what's going on or what we face?" He suddenly fixed his sights on Saredhel. "Do *you*, Saredhel?"

The bald goddess' solid white eyes were unreadable. "There is much in transition at the moment," she answered in her normal serene manner. "The more time I have to sort through the matter, the clearer things will become."

"But can we wait?" Khuthon let the full weight of the question have its intended effect.

"I think the real matter here is why can't *you*?" All gathered found Shiril. Her often-silent presence in councils past made her words even more arresting. This was the second time in as many days she'd been so engaged. But whether this was a new pattern was yet to be seen. "Are you so hungry for another war that you're willing to make one yourself?" Shiril didn't pull any punches as she kept her silver gaze focused on Khuthon.

"Got some fire in you, haven't you?" Rheminas chuckled to himself. "I like that."

Shiril ignored him. "Haven't you learned *anything* from today?" Silence fell as her words sunk into the other gods' heads and hearts.

Khuthon quickly recalibrated his thoughts, wondering if he was going to need to stand against another he wasn't planning on facing in the upcoming verbal fray. He gave her a hurried once-over, making sure his previous reading of her still stood. Black haired with a brown complexion, she resembled more the Lords of Earth she ruled over than the rest of the gods.

And yet while there was indignation, there wasn't a direct threat to anything Khuthon was planning. She was upset—they all were to various degrees—but her momentary challenge had been more rebuke than outright resistance. She wasn't someone who'd stand in the way—not in the end. Changing his tone, but not his outlook, Khuthon took to his feet. It was time to make his move.

"Today has been a trying one for all of us," he began, attempting his most statesman-like voice and manner. "We've faced an old foe—one who destroyed the very planet whose ruins we're meeting upon today—and won. But that victory hasn't come cheaply, and it falls to *someone* to at least make sure all is well in Altearin. We owe that much to Gurthghol and we can't have rebellion fermenting in these delicate times."

Perlosa rolled her eyes at her father's rhetoric. Asorlok peered down at the table, shaking his head softly. The others were more courteous, at least allowing Khuthon their attention. All except Rheminas, who tried snatching fleeting glimpses of Shiril when he could. It was supposed to be subtle, but Khuthon didn't miss it, even if the other gods and Shiril herself did.

"We need order," Khuthon continued, sending a deferential nod Ganatar's way. "Order in the realms as well as here."

Dradin leaned forward. "And what are you proposing, exactly?"

"To keep order we need to keep the pantheon and do so in a balanced way." He slowly approached Gurthghol's empty throne as he spoke, letting the tension of the moment build. "And right now that balance is lacking." He stopped at the base of the dais and turned so he could face the others. "And it's also clear to me everything we're discussing or will discuss is tied into one common element."

"And that is?" Drued was unmoved.

"We need a new head of the Dark Gods."

"But Gurthghol isn't dead," Panthora interjected.

"No," said Khuthon, "he isn't, but we can't afford to have the position remain empty while we await his possible return—*if* he ever should return."

"What happened to putting yourself forward as an *ambassador* to Altearin?" While there wasn't a hint of sarcasm to Causilla's question, it was still punctuated with a sharp-enough point. Khuthon was impressed. Maybe there was more steel beneath that alluring veneer than he knew.

"You just want the seat." Olthon brought the thought already in everyone's mind to the fore. She wasn't surprised—saddened at how rapidly her brother had made the play, and maybe a little disappointed. But that was to be expected . . . and countered.

"It has to fall to one of the Dark Gods." Khuthon searched out Rheminas and Asorlok, the only other Dark Gods besides himself. "Who are just as welcome to put in their bid." Though the Dark Gods were the smallest of the three factions of gods, they still held some sway in various debates and matters, but now, without Gurthghol, the faction was further diminished in influence. But the seat still had clout.

"And given I once held the seat before—"

"*Very* briefly before," added Olthon.

"Maybe so," he acknowledged, "but I *did* have the seat."

"And now you want it again."

"*Is* there another bid?" Ganatar examined Rheminas and Asorlok in turn.

"Not from me," said Asorlok.

"No," said Rheminas.

This didn't surprise any, for none—including Khuthon—thought Rheminas would upstage his father. And no one thought Asorlok was ever interested in it. He, like Shiril, tended to keep more to himself and his own plans and ways.

"So you'd really have us vote on replacing our brother's seat when it's still unclear what his current position is?" Dradin's words made clear he wasn't fond of the notion but still realized they were all stuck with following formalities and protocols. "I would think there'd be other matters that need discussing first. Like what to do with that scepter, for one."

For a moment Khuthon considered Dradin's staff. He'd never seen him without it close by or in hand. There was always the faintest of whispers circling the glowing green crystal globe at the center of the rune-covered angular curve of gold that crowned the wooden shaft. It was assumed and believed such whispers were the secrets of the cosmos Dradin could call upon when needed. Khuthon had never been able to prove that entirely but often wondered at times—like now—just what he might be hearing in those whispers.

"You're going to need a leader of the Dark Gods for any votes going forward," Khuthon reminded Dradin along with the rest of the council. "And once we know what happened to Gurthghol—and if he wants to reclaim the position—I'll gladly return it."

"Forgive me if I find that a little hard to believe." Olthon's response didn't surprise him. Mildly offended him, but didn't surprise him. After all, she knew him maybe better than most, which made it all the more important to keep to his script.

"I'm merely helping to keep things from falling apart," he returned. "Once we have a united council, we can vote on and discuss the rest of the matters before us."

"Very well." Ganatar sighed. "If it will get us on to other matters. All who are willing to allow Khuthon to become leader of the Dark Gods in Gurthghol's absence—on the condition the position reverts to Gurthghol upon his return—raise your hand."

Rheminas' hand shot up first. Asorlok's rose second, followed by that of Drued, who grumbled something into his beard. This was followed by Aerotripton and Shiril. Five. Only two more and he'd have the majority, counting himself. Asora's hand ascended next. Her other rested on her bulging stomach. Khuthon noticed her normally relaxed face was lined with some growing unease and discomfort. For a moment he was tempted to immediately stop and inquire. But it was only for a moment. This was the more important matter—and he was within arm's reach of securing it. Next came Endarien's hand. Seven. And with Khuthon's it made for an even eight—the majority.

"It seems we have a new leader." There was neither joy nor disappointment in Ganatar's announcement. But it didn't matter. Khuthon had won what he'd wanted.

"Until Gurthghol returns, that is," Olthon quickly added.

"The babies are coming." Asora's words pierced through Khuthon faster than any sword.

"*Now?*" He was less than pleased by the news even as he hurried to her side.

The Tularins who had been keeping watch over the door to the chamber flew to her aid, seeking to offer what comfort they could. As the honor guard of what remained of Thangaria, they had the duty of serving the gods, and they'd do no less at this moment than any other.

"*Babies?*" Endarien wasn't the only concerned one around the table. "I thought she was having only *one* child."

"As did we," added Perlosa, watching the Tularins assisting Asora to her feet—Khuthon aiding where he could.

"Sometimes the best-kept secrets are the ones hidden in plain sight," Saredhel dryly mused.

"Yes." Rheminas stared hard at Saredhel. "Seems to be a lot of hidden things about these days."

"Look who's talking," Asorlok quipped.

Before any more could be said, Ganatar rose from his throne. "In light of the present situation, this council is adjourned until Asora has recovered enough to return. Her delivery will give us all time to tend to our realms, providing us all a better understanding of what needs to be done upon our return."

It was a suitable decree given the circumstance. But had it come any sooner, Khuthon's plans could have been stymied. As it was, he'd achieved his victory and was able to shake up the pantheon once again with the forthcoming birth. Everyone would be too busy to focus on it to do much of anything else. And this, in turn, would leave him free to solidify the rest of his agenda. He couldn't have wished for anything better if he'd planned it all himself.

Descending the dais, Ganatar asked, "Do you need any help returning to Bios?"

"No." Asora shook her head. "The labor isn't that great yet."

"Then go in peace and enjoy this time with your family. At least *something* good shall come out of today's darkness." Turning to the others around the table, he added, "I'll send word again soon." He vanished in a flash of golden light. The rest of the pantheon and their possessions followed in various bursts of colored light until it was just Asora and Khuthon who remained.

Khuthon brushed Asora's cheek with the back of his hand. "I'll join you shortly." Even in her labor she was such a lovely sight. He didn't think he'd ever truly grow tired of it, though this hadn't stopped him from exploring new views in times past.

Asora took hold of Khuthon's wrist while it was still near her face. "I'll be waiting. As will they." She released his grip and vanished in a flash of white light. Free from their need to aid Asora, the Tularins turned their attention on Khuthon.

"I wish to be alone."

"Of course," said one with a bow. Both flew from the room, closing the large doors behind them.

Khuthon let the shrine-like stillness of the place rest upon him like a mantle. Moving back to Gurthghol's former throne, he reflected on how well things had flowed into his hands. He'd learned long ago to never let a crisis go to waste if you could use it to your advantage. Just hours before he'd been preparing the battle plans for the pantheon's last stand,

and now here he was, newly elevated as the head of the Dark Gods and given a higher rank and greater voice in the council.

He'd been able to figure the actions of the others almost perfectly, and the drama birthed by Asora's labor only added to the ease by which he claimed his victory. Whether or not Gurthghol returned wasn't important. If Khuthon knew anything, it was that Nuhl and Awntodgenee weren't ones to be so kind in terms of punishment and retribution. If Gurthghol wasn't dead yet, he would be soon enough.

Having reached the throne, he took a seat with deep delight. While he had thought about taking the position for a while, he never saw a way until now. It was unlikely Gurthghol would ever relent, and Khuthon wasn't about to challenge his brother directly. But with the added authority his new position afforded, he could make bigger steps for greater vistas of power and standing in both the pantheon and elsewhere.

He let himself rest in the golden chair, savoring the feel of it and noting the new view it gave of the room. A room he had no doubt he would be seeing more of soon. There was still much that had to be done—and even more that was already going on behind the scenes. As much as they might have tried to put on the display of proper protocol, he knew the others were already at work with matters in their own realms and probably elsewhere, Khuthon chief among them.

Thinking on such plans, his right hand started glowing with a blood-red aura. He slashed it through the air in front of his face. A red gash spread like a bleeding wound until a two-foot-wide opening hovered across from him. Two dimensional in nature, it resembled a pool of blood, reflecting a slightly distorted image of Khuthon before another form took its place. This shape was humanoid and, suddenly aware of being seen by the god, brought himself to attention.

"We have nearly recovered from the battle, Majesty," Torgin, the gigantic commander he'd put in charge of his forces for the previous battle, informed him.

"How did the others fare?"

"Not as well as us, but seeing as the fight didn't escalate as much as we'd first thought, that isn't too much of a surprise."

"I suppose not." Khuthon imagined an alternative reality wherein he and the rest of the pantheon would still be in the middle of their conflict with Cadrith and maybe even Nuhl—and then Asora starting to go into labor in the midst of it all. Perhaps things had worked out better than they knew.

"You've earned your rest," he told Torgin, "you and all the men. All of you are to return to Kratos, where there will be much to celebrate."

"As you command, Mighty One." Torgin brought his right fist over his heart in salute. The bloody viewing pool faded, leaving Khuthon once again alone in the council room. Taking a moment more to enjoy the throne, he sighed. Other duties called for his attention.

He rose and vanished from the chamber in a flash of red light.

CHAPTER 3

Before there was the realm of Altearin, there were the planes of Umbrium and Anomolia—both of which were destroyed when they were merged into Gurthghol's new realm. And as one could imagine with such an act, there were those who didn't take too kindly to having their lives disrupted and their whole reality reforged into some new vision they had little say or control over. Chief among these discontents were the Umbrians.

Named after the plane of Umbrium they once called home, these humanoid darkened incarnates seemed to have been crafted from pure darkness. Every part of their being was a deep black. It was just another mark of pride they used as proof of their direct siring from the cosmic element of darkness. With such a grand pedigree, they scoffed at the Lords of Darkness, who thought themselves masters of the cosmic element. Such arrogance was humored for a time when the titan lords arrived on the plane under Vkar's orders, but since the rise of Gurthghol and the creation of Altearin, any such tolerance was replaced with open contempt.

The titan lords might have shared an ancient birth line, but they were only freshly arrived into the ways of darkness, while the Umbrians were its children. This was made all the more apparent when the Lords of Darkness sought to adapt to the new realm of Altearin by embracing pockets and blending of light. Such a thing was an abomination to those who were now forced to either live an adulterated existence or seek to preserve their old ways and lives however possible.

Not surprisingly, most Umbrians fled to the deep recesses of darkness, underground, or other benighted areas and regions. This often meant focusing on the areas ruled by the Lords of Darkness, since such areas were the most light-diminished places in the realm. It was a far cry from the freedom they previously enjoyed, even with the original rule of the titan lords back on Umbrium. But it allowed them a place away from prying eyes and perchance brief moments of bliss where they could pretend they yet were the sole masters of an unblemished Umbrium.

And such were the ways and mindset of those who called the city of Ulan home. The ancient metropolis was massive, housing a million inhabitants deep within the depths of Altearin. The very rock had been worked into the colossal walls and giant towers protecting the city. The gates reinforced with wrought iron were the very essence of their ancestral homeland. All of it was devoid of light. For the Umbrians, like Lords of Darkness, could see in the dark as if it were day.

Behind the walls the streets were filled with people; the shops, taverns, and other spaces were crowded with dark-clad figures—all of whom blended in with their dusky surroundings like shadows with night.

Each of these watched the procession of guards leading a figure easily twice their size down the main street and straight for the palace. The guards' long black halberds helped narrow the height gap between them, while their suits of pitch-black chain mail with matching open-faced helmets let the titan know they were willing to give him a fight if allowed the excuse. None who viewed the scene had a kind expression for this new arrival, and more than a few muttered curses under their breath.

The soldiers guided their prisoner up and into the palace, winding through the aged corridors until coming upon their prince's throne room. The large double doors were easily the same size as the guards' prisoner and were a mixture of onyx and black walnut panels, reinforced with more wrought iron. The two guards at the lead opened the doors and moved inside, alerting the one seated on the throne of their arrival.

Rilas, prince of Ulan, was bedecked in a fine black tunic, pants, and boots. A sable-colored cape draped around his shoulders, while an onyx crown studded with black diamonds and pearls completed his attire. As in all Umbrianic cities, the prince was the highest ruler—the Umbrians never having taken to a king or queen, thinking a prince or princess regal enough for their needs. Rilas' throne was a blending of wrought iron, black walnut, and midnight-stained silk. It rested upon a dais of dark marble, which brought him eye to eye with the titanic prisoner.

"Why have you brought me *this*?" Rilas sneered at the hooded titan.

"He was found outside the walls saying he wished to speak with you." The captain of the guard spoke in Stygian, the only language any spoke in the city. The only *true* language any child of darkness *could* speak.

"And what would a titan want to speak to me about?" He attempted to peer into the other's hood. Even on the dais the additional height netted no advantage.

"We've gone to great lengths to keep ourselves as far *from* you and your kind as possible," he continued. "We have *nothing* to speak about. You've wasted your time by coming here."

"I don't think so," the titan returned in a strangely accented Stygian. "And neither does my master, who sent me."

"I'm more interested to know how you found us," said Rilas. "Ulan has been hidden for centuries, and yet you come strolling right up to our gates. So how did you do it? Who sent you and why?"

"My master showed me the way," said the titan.

"And who is your master?" Rilas' interest in the matter was piqued enough to inquire further. If the accent could be believed, this wasn't your average Lord of Darkness, perhaps not even your average titan lord.

The other extended a golden-skinned hand from under his black cloak. In it was a steel disk with some sort of design carved in relief. "His emblem." The titan handed it to the captain of the guard, who in turn brought it to Rilas.

"No Lord of Darkness has golden skin." Rilas watched the titan during the captain's approach. "Who are you?"

"My name is Bron. I'm a simple servant doing his master's will."

"Bron." Rilas tested the name aloud. "Not a common name among the Lords of Darkness—assuming it *is* your real name."

The steel disk found its way into Rilas' hand. Crafted for use by a titan, the object was closer to the size of a saucer, larger than the impression he'd had of it in the titan's grasp. The emblem, however, was quite easy to make out: a silver amphisbaena ouroboros with both heads facing instead of devouring each other. The background was purple. Both the two-headed serpent and the emblem it formed were easily identified. They were part of an empire that still held parts of the cosmos in its death grip.

"You know the mark, I trust?" Bron asked as the captain of the guard returned to the titan's side.

"You won't find too many who don't." Rilas raised his gaze. "Especially among the Umbrians. But an old emblem doesn't prove anything."

"It should prove I'm not on the Lords of Darkness' side."

"Which is why you're still standing before me, but you've shown nothing else." Rilas wasn't getting any of this. It made no sense. Why would this titan come all this way to see him? He had nothing to offer, and the titan, as far as Rilas could tell, had nothing to offer him. It was a waste of both their time and possibly even the titan's life.

"Gurthghol has been removed from his place in the pantheon and Altearin." The words caught all off guard. "You'll hear about it shortly through your normal channels of spies."

It took Rilas a moment to regain control of his jaw and tongue. "Even if what you say is true, you still haven't shown me why I should let you keep talking." Rilas did well in hiding the surprise from his voice.

"My master has foreseen some great changes are about to take place for you and your realm—the pantheon too—and would like to take advantage of the situation," Bron continued. "Many who already know of Gurthghol's removal are working to secure a place in the new order. My master has foreseen the rise of Shador, the current viceroy over the Lords of Darkness, as taking that place."

"Shador." Rilas spat out the name like a soured wine. The Lord of Darkness had been a viceroy for some time. He was better than some of his predecessors but still an enemy holding court and supposed power over them. "We've no love of him nor his kin—*or* Lords of Chaos for that matter. And he'd be wasting his time; the pantheon would rise up to stop him."

"Not if what my master says is true."

"And why's that?"

"Shador already has a plan to keep them back from Altearin, allowing him free rein over the realm." Rilas didn't believe it but let the titan continue, curious to see how far he'd take his wild tale. "But that isn't my master's main point of interest. In the process, Shador will be seeking to lay hold of a certain scepter to use in securing his power. My master wishes to stop him from claiming it and take it for himself."

"And all this concerns me *how*?"

"By taking the scepter you'll be given an opening for your own plans to succeed." Rilas could sense the smile in Bron's voice. "My master is seeking to rid the cosmos of the current order in favor of a new one. And you"—Bron jabbed a golden finger at Rilas—"have the opportunity to join him as an ally."

Rilas studied the emblem again. It didn't seem too old, but it also wasn't freshly forged. But it was still an echo of something long since passed. A faint shadow of something that had no real meaning anymore.

"Everyone knows your so-called master's long since left the cosmos." Rilas raised his head. "I don't know who you are, but I've humored you enough." He motioned to the guards. "Get him out of my sight."

Bron stood firm. "Gurthghol is gone, and Shador shall arise. If he's allowed to gain the scepter he seeks, the Umbrians will just exchange one master for another. But should you side with my master and the new order to come, you'll have your freedom." The guards pulled hard upon the titan, forcing him to turn to leave the room. "When you're ready, simply speak your agreement to the emblem, and I'll return."

"*If* you do return, you'll find a cell in my dungeon waiting—"

Rilas stopped upon witnessing something truly wondrous: somehow Bron had managed to collapse in upon himself. He didn't fully know how to comprehend it. One moment Rilas was chastising him, and the next the gold-skinned titan was condensing in upon himself as if his body was being compressed by two massive hands. A violet aura glowed around him as he rapidly grew thinner and thinner until he was gone—completely removed from reality.

The guards sought their prince for answers. He had none—not yet. This was all for some purpose, for sure, but whose? The Lords of Darkness? Were they trying to bait him into some foolish action and then close the trap, dooming him and the city to destruction? Or was what he'd just heard—as far fetched as it sounded—actually true? And if so, what then? The best course of action, it seemed, was to sit back and wait. If what was spoken did come to pass, then that was one thing. As to the actual offer . . .

Rilas dismissed the guards. "Go. And double the guard around the walls. I don't want any more unexpected visitors. And make a search of where you found him—we need to know if there are any more surprises in the area." The others departed as ordered, leaving Rilas to his thoughts and the emblem resting on his lap.

• • •

Mergis strode into the dimly lit audience chamber of Gurthghol's palace. His short white hair made him hard to miss. The Lord of Chaos was the second viceroy over Altearin, a rather high position that saw him and Shador share rule over about half the realm each. Though there were other factions among various other incarnates who sought their own autonomy, the viceroys' command was basically uncontested. After Gurthghol, the next most powerful were the Lords of Darkness and the Lords of Chaos. These titan lords ruled very much like minor lords in their own right, which Gurthghol allowed. Each was even tasked with various administrative duties—both to keep them occupied and to keep the rest of Altearin in line.

Mergis wasn't the first to hold his position. There were others throughout the millennia, but he was always eager to make sure he was the longest serving. This meant he was ever listening to those he ruled over—both covertly and overtly—ready to cease any hint of anything that might disrupt his established command. While it was perhaps odd to think of a Lord of Chaos so concerned with keeping the status quo, he was doing nothing less than Gurthghol himself, who despite being the god of chaos and darkness desired and enforced a form of order across all he ruled. And these last few days had much to keep one busy in the area of maintaining that control.

Recent events had been both rather rapid and confusing, to say the least. There were a lot of wagging tongues about, and plenty of information to accompany them. Information that was equally far fetched and troubling. There was news of a war in Thangaria—which he'd been able to verify since he'd sent some titanic warriors there to help fight in it. And then there was talk of something taking place with Gurthghol. What it was, exactly, though, he hadn't a clue. When he'd received the summons from Erdis to appear at the palace, he was hopeful he'd get some answers. It wasn't wise to allow too much speculation to run wild.

Mergis wasn't alone in his visit. With him were two of his most trusted advisers and assistants: Lagella and Cirgin. Lagella's rich purple skirt matched the short-sleeved tunic draped over it. Her long brown hair was left free flowing. Cirgin's tunic was a light brown, the same color as his boots. His pants were a deep purple. Since this was also a courtly call, all three had donned the regalia marking them as titan lords: a half cape, silver cuirass, and bracers. Each was also crowned with an amethyst diadem specially designed for and by each of the three titans.

Mergis himself wore a rich burgundy long-sleeved tunic over a pair of finely crafted black pants with pale silver stitching forming the Black Sun—Gurthghol's crest—in a vertical pattern up the outside legs. Deep brown boots finished the outfit. It was simple but clean enough to showcase his place amid the rest. He wore no weapon nor any jewelry outside an onyx ring marking his place as leader of the Lords of Chaos.

The audience chamber was one of two side chambers flanking the main throne room. Rectangular and rather large, it had walls lined with wrought iron sconces burning with flickering tongues of plum-colored flame. Opposite the trio of titans was a black walnut door, which granted access into the main throne room beyond. On either side was a red hydra. Carved of solid red agate, the statues were lifelike in every detail. Even coiled up, they were easily the same height as the approaching titans. Above their fat coils, each had eleven serpentine heads that studied every part of the chamber. Arched above these heads were their tails, capped with scorpions' stingers.

"Odd that we're the first to arrive," said Mergis, his amethyst eyes taking in the statues' finer details. "Shador is usually fairly prompt about such things."

"Let's hope Gurthghol notices," said Lagella, the corners of her lips creasing with a faint grin.

"For what purpose?" The graying temples of Cirgin's red hair matched the streaking in his thick mustache.

"It's always wise to garner favor with Gurthghol," she replied.

"And to show up Shador and his bunch," added Mergis.

A round of soft chuckling followed them as they stopped before the two statues and waited for the doors to open. In the strange light Mergis could almost imagine those fat coils slowly moving, that pointed stinger carefully swaying as each head stared down their approaching prey. Though Mergis had only seen a hydra once in his life, the sculptor of these statues had captured nearly every detail to perfection.

"How bad do you think it was on Thangaria?" asked Cirgin.

"You know as much as I do," said Mergis. "But we're still here, so it couldn't have been too bad. I'm more curious to see what became of the matter with Galba on Tralodren."

He and Shador had been asked by Gurthghol to send some of their best titan lords with Gurthghol for some sort of confrontation. He wasn't privy to all the details, but from what he could recall of his own history, Galba had never been an enemy; the two instead were allies in many things.

Lagella raised an eyebrow. "Isn't that breaking the pact they'd made?"

"Maybe, but he was the one who made it with her in the first place. So I suppose he can rewrite it when needed."

Being Lords of Chaos, none was too worried about altering deals or pacts. All things changed over time. To believe otherwise was foolishness—even more so if one tried to stand against the change. In some ways the recent flurry of actions was a rather welcomed event. Everything had started becoming a little too mundane for even Mergis' endurance. This was just the sort of thing to spice it up and maybe even work out some greater benefits and boons in the process.

"Once we're done here, I'm going to need a report for the regions," he continued. "I've been hearing talk about some pockets of Anarchs trying to stir things up. We don't need that after all this."

"You think—"

Cirgin was interrupted by the sound of doors opening.

Behind the thick wood wasn't another titan lord, nor even Gurthghol, as Mergis was expecting. Instead, the regally garbed Erdis stepped into the chamber.

"Is he ready for us?" Mergis' question slowed the Kardu's step and furrowed his brow.

"I'm afraid not." Erdis' tone was solemn.

"Then when will he be ready?"

"I don't know," he replied. "He isn't here."

Lagella exchanged a glance with Cirgin.

"I didn't expect the pantheon would take so much of his attention."

"He isn't with the pantheon."

"But you sent a summons saying Gurthghol wished to speak with Shador and me at once."

"I know." Even under Mergis' stare, Erdis remained the calm, professional figure he'd long known him to be. "I regret having to use such deception, but it was the only way to make sure you both arrived without having anything sensitive leaking out among others."

Mergis crossed his arms. "And just what sort of sensitive things are we talking about, Erdis?"

"Gurthghol and the future of Altearin."

"Go on."

Erdis sighed. "I was hoping to speak to both of you at once, but it appears Lord Shador hasn't taken my summons as seriously as you."

"I guess some of us just know how to show the proper respect." Lagella flashed some teeth that had Mergis questioning if she wasn't flirting more than driving a dagger into Shador's back. Whatever her intention, Erdis remained unmoved.

"So what exactly is this all about? And where's Gurthghol?"

"He's not here, as I said."

"Then where is he?" Mergis didn't like this back-and-forth. There was a certain part of the court etiquette he was expected to maintain, he understood, but this wasn't it. Things needed to be out and in the open— especially now.

"I don't know." Erdis' words chilled the air. "No one knows."

"What do you mean, no one knows?" Cirgin nervously half chuckled.

"Gurthghol is gone." Erdis was matter of fact. "I've been informed by the pantheon that he was taken captive by Nuhl after the battle at Thangaria, and no one knows where he is or what's become of him."

"Is this a joke?" Cirgin was far from amused.

"It's the terrible truth," Erdis solemnly continued. "Nuhl took him and the throne he reclaimed from Galba. He was using it, I'm told, to try to destroy the Cosmic Entities."

"How did he think he'd succeed?" Cirgin blurted.

"I don't know," said Erdis. "But Vkar's throne is a wonder of the ages, and he might have known or seen something we don't."

"And yet even using Vkar's throne he failed?" Mergis said to himself more than anyone else.

"From what I understand, yes."

"Then he's dead for sure," said Cirgin. "If Nuhl has him—"

"He's its prisoner," Erdis hurriedly interrupted. "He's not dead."

"But the original threat has been dealt with?" asked Mergis.

"Yes. Nuhl's agent was destroyed, and the threat with him. The pantheon survived, as did Thangaria and Tralodren."

"And there won't be any reprisals?" Mergis worked his way carefully through everything, making sure he saw all the facets of the situation.

"Not that I was told of. The pantheon is in another council and will most likely remain so for some time."

"Giving us time to act," Lagella muttered to herself before realizing she had spoken aloud. "For whatever the pantheon will do next," she quickly told both Mergis and Erdis.

"And you're sure Gurthghol isn't dead?" Again, Mergis would have everything in the open—nothing in nuances.

"The last I heard, he wasn't counted among Mortis' ranks," said Erdis.

"So he could still return." Lagella was neither relieved nor saddened.

"That would be the hope." Erdis nodded.

"But not that likely if Nuhl really does have him." Mergis burst whatever bubble of hope had been swelling in their midst.

"So then what do we do in the meantime?" Cirgin sought Mergis.

"That is what I summoned both you and Lord Shador here to discuss. Word will get out as the warriors return from Thangaria, and a god's absence can only be covered up for so long. We need to stand together during this time—to decide how best to keep things together until Gurthghol's return."

"Which could be never," Mergis continued his bubble bursting.

"I'd prefer to not surrender all hope just yet," said Erdis.

"And I assume this all came through a Tularian messenger?" asked Mergis.

"Yes, not too long ago. He would have spoken to all three of us, but only I was in the palace at the time. I trust you can keep this matter between yourselves until I've been able to speak with Lord Shador? It's better to have such things coming from the leadership, speaking with one common voice, than the cacophony of the masses."

"Of course."

"I'm sure Shador will reach out to you once he's been informed," Erdis continued. "You two will need some time to coordinate things. And then we can all make the final decisions."

"I'll do my part," said Mergis. "You have my word on that."

"I hope so. Gurthghol wouldn't want to return to anything less than something as close to what he left as possible." Mergis wasn't sure about that, but he wasn't going to argue with the Kardu.

"Then where does that leave us?" Lagella cautiously inquired.

"That's for us to decide," replied Erdis. "But we need to be unanimous in our efforts—whatever they may be."

Mergis was already starting to lose himself in his thoughts. Everything was rushing over him so rapidly it was hard to latch on to any one thing, yet there were so many wonderful options now bobbing about his mind. If Gurthghol *was* truly in a place none could find, let alone free him from—even if found . . . Oh yes, this could definitely spice some things up nicely.

"I'll do my part. I can't vouch for Shador and his bunch, though. But I'm willing to work with them to figure something out."

"Good." Erdis nodded. "Now if you'll excuse me, I have a few other matters that need my attention."

"Of course." Mergis gave a small nod and stepped aside, clearing a path for Erdis to pass. "I won't keep you from it."

Mergis and the other titans watched Erdis make his way from them, not speaking again until he'd reached the door on the opposite end of the room through which they themselves had entered just moments before.

Once he was gone, they kept their voices low.

Cirgin went straight to the point. "What do you think?"

"We can trust Erdis," Mergis reminded them. "He's nothing but loyal to Gurthghol."

"But is the news he's hearing accurate?" Cirgin continued.

"If it came from a Tularin, it can be trusted," said Lagella. "They don't lie. And it's not like Gurthghol to pull stunts, and he isn't one for court intrigue either."

"No, he isn't," said Mergis, thinking. "But we do have an advantage over Shador at the moment with this news."

"Then we should use it. You don't really trust him *not* to take advantage of this, do you?" Lagella was stating the obvious.

"No less than he'd be a fool to think *I* wouldn't," he replied. "But *we* have some time to plan and prepare."

"But to do what?" Lagella studied Mergis carefully, no doubt trying to read his intentions before he shared them. She'd gotten good at it over the years but still wasn't able to anticipate his thinking entirely, for which he was thankful—especially at moments like this.

"We have a rare opportunity for some real freedom." He grinned. "We need to be wise in how we use it, or we could lose it just as quickly. You'll both need to gather the other lords." He raised his voice just loud enough for the others to hear him. Though Erdis had departed, he knew most walls had ears in the palace, and he'd keep them deaf for a while longer. "Have them gathered at my keep by the end of the day. Let them know it's urgent."

"Even the Anarchs?" Cirgin's mustache bristled with his sneer.

"Yes. They'll especially want to hear what I propose."

"Which is?" Lagella inquired softly.

"You'll see." Mergis had shared all he would for the time being. He had to be sure he had everything thought out before revealing too much. But what he had envisioned so far was in quite some detail. He just needed a unified force behind him in carrying it out. And if he could get all or most of the Lords of Chaos on his side, he could push forward an agenda without any real opposition.

"Get everyone possible," he continued, following Erdis' path from the room. "And don't be late."

• • •

Rilas walked the long, dark corridor in silence. It was empty except for the occasional door or patrolling guard. This part of the palace wasn't much used but was still preserved and kept watch over, though with a lighter force than in the rest of the city. There wasn't much trouble to be expected from the old tomes and scrolls that resided behind the doors the Umbrianic prince was passing.

Coming to rest before a doorway on his left, Rilas put his hand to the wrought iron handle and shoved the door inward. Behind it was the smell of dust, old parchment, and dry leather. In keeping with their ways and nature, there was no light, but that didn't hinder anything from being seen, nor did it prevent an older sage seated at a table from reading from the hills and valleys of scrolls and books before him.

"Well?" Rilas approached the table.

The sage lifted his head in greeting. "I think I've made some progress." He was dressed in a black open robe over an iron-gray tunic and deep brown pants. His full black beard swallowed much of his face. Rilas had sought the sage early that morning, handing him the seal his titanic visitor had left, along with the titan's description. Now evening, he'd returned for some answers.

"Is the emblem real?" Rilas stood opposite the sage.

"It's of some age," the man said, retrieving the object from where it rested within arm's reach. "But it isn't as old as something from the proper time period."

"So it's a fake?" He watched the sage examine the metal disk.

"If it is, it's incredibly well done." He handed it to Rilas. "You'll note the slight wear on some of the surfaces—fine things here and there, really—but enough to show it hasn't recently been created."

"So an old forgery . . ." Rilas returned the disk to the table with a small clunk. He wasn't interested in trying to pry anything further from the object. He'd done all he could already and come up empty. It was what brought him to the sage in the first place.

"Perhaps. Or perhaps it's just an old reminder from another age. The crest *is* accurate—from the records we have on hand."

"What about the titan?"

"Yes, the golden-skinned titan. The notes were old, but I found some texts that confirmed them. Golden-skinned titans were either titans of the first generation or titan lords—Lords of Space."

Rilas pondered the first option. Could that really be possible? A titan from the first generation surviving into the present day? It could explain the connection to the crest, but it wasn't plausible. The emblem had come much later—well after the passing of the first generation from history and all of existence.

"I'd lean more toward a Lord of Space myself." The sage's words fished Rilas from his thoughts.

"It would also explain his disappearance and how he probably got here in the first place," added Rilas. "But why would he have come to

Altearin—and *here* of all places? What's his game, and why has he chosen *us* to play it?"

"I'm afraid I can't answer those questions, only say that the Lords of Space aren't known to travel outside their plane for almost anything. And it just raises more questions about the crest."

"Such as?"

"Why would a Lord of Space supposedly be in service to the very one who was said to have once tried to remove all the Lords of Space from the cosmos?"

Rilas nodded, recalling his history. It had happened so long ago, though, it could just as easily have been myth. So much of what took place before the coming of the pantheon was left to the shadows of legends and myths. It made things easy to exaggerate, distort, and use to various advantage . . .

"I'm sorry I couldn't tell you anything more."

"At least I know more about who I'm dealing with." Rilas retrieved the disk from the table, making ready to leave. "As to what he *really* wants, that remains to be seen."

• • •

Mergis peered out across the gathered throng of titan lords, mentally counting every olive-skinned face crossing his view. The audience chamber of his personal residence could barely hold everyone. Even so, having them gathered to his private keep was the best option. It was the most secure and best suited to host the gathering. He'd made sure it was richly decorated, befitting the topmost ruler of the realm under Gurthghol, but also that it paid homage to their historic roots. This was achieved mainly by means of the mural of Lords of Chaos and other denizens of Anomolia, the ancient plane of the cosmic element of chaos, that wrapped around the room in a fat stripe.

"You did well," he told Lagella, who stood beside him. "Both of you," he told Cirgin on his opposite side.

"Some were actually interested in what you were planning," said Cirgin, "but others were just bored and wanted something new to look forward to."

Mergis chuckled to himself. It would be impossible to take offense. How could you when you knew it was the very nature of those bound to the cosmic element of chaos? Had things gone a different way, he might have been just like them, but Gurthghol had helped steer his future with an invitation into the viceroyship, and now the god of chaos and darkness was helping steer his future again with his recent absence. He supposed it was fitting.

"I am surprised the Anarchs are here." While Mergis was wise enough to leave most things be, he often kept a closer eye on the Anarchs. Thankfully, they were a minority among the Lords of Chaos but were often known to be rather unpredictable. And right now he could do with as little of that as possible.

"Not all." Lagella watched a few of them among the gathered bodies, clearly not that impressed.

"But enough," he countered. "And that will help make a good showing."

While the group didn't include all the Lords and Ladies of Chaos across Altearin, these were the ones who mattered—the ones who had higher ranks and places of influence over others. They also were closest to the capital, allowing Mergis a steady base who were supposedly more loyal and invested in the capital and the general governance of the realm. This made what he had to do next all the easier. The more control he had over what followed, the better he could mold things in his favor. Those not with him were few, and thankfully any influence lost because of them would be minimal. He'd carry the majority, which was the most important thing for now. The rest he could smooth over in due course, when everything else had been dealt with.

"I'm pleased to see you were all able to come so quickly," he began, bringing the murmuring to an end. "I'll be to the point. Gurthghol is missing and might possibly even be dead."

The room erupted in an explosion of excited voices.

"Naturally"—he endeavored to be heard over the noise—"you can see why I've summoned you."

"So is he dead or not?" asked one of the Anarchs, this one more wild eyed than the others. Mergis didn't know his name. Perhaps he was from farther out of his usual circle. There were plenty of titan lords across Altearin, after all.

"I don't know—no one does . . . But what *is* known is that he won't be returning to Altearin for a time . . . possibly ever. And as such, we need to act. Because I was told this news by Erdis before he could pass it on to Lord Shador, we have a unique opportunity before us.

"With Gurthghol absent from the throne, the reins of power will fall between Erdis, Shador, and myself. If we can act quickly enough and keep a unified front, I'm confident I could secure a more senior role in upcoming affairs, giving us more freedom to finally take greater command of our place and lives."

"So you want to be in charge now, is that it?" This came from the same Anarch. Mergis wasn't sure if he was approving or disapproving of the idea.

"I want to give us greater freedom to return to the lives we once had before Gurthghol took Anomolia from us. But that won't happen if Shador steps in to make his own bid, or if we leave things without an appearance of order, leading the pantheon to appoint someone else over us instead."

"And what about Erdis?" asked a fair-looking Lady of Chaos from the crowd. "You think he's just going to let you have your way?"

"He'll be brought around easily enough," he assured them. "Outside the palace he wields little influence." And that, for the most part, was truth. Though chamberlain, Erdis was really more a manager, not anyone of any great power—not outside the palace and official places of power. And the further one got from the palace, the weaker his sway. No, he needed Shador and himself more than they needed the Kardu.

"So what would you have of us?" asked another lord. Mergis thought he recognized him as a lesser person of rank from the outer rim of the capital's reach. Since he rarely directly interacted with those outside the city, having his own administrators take the lead, he drew a blank on the other's name. He made a note to fix such things for the future. If he was going to rule with a stronger, wider reach, he'd need more interaction and improved relationships with the population.

"To support me in my bid for sole rule over the realm. If we act fast enough, we can call a meeting of all the titan lords before Shador knows what's happening and bring it to a vote. I'm confident we could bring more than enough Lords of Darkness over to get the majority."

"And why would Lords of Darkness vote for you?" The question was posed by Melinda, a richly garbed Lady of Chaos whom he'd known more intimately in times past. It was a good question, and thankfully Mergis had a good answer.

"I have a plan." The words didn't engender much confidence; instead he noted more than a few foreheads furrow in doubt. "Trust me," he hurriedly added. "It will work. I just need to know you're all behind me and can get others to support the effort."

"And if we are and do, what then?" asked a gruff-looking titan he thought was named Quain.

"I'd be able to put on the face of order and control for the pantheon and have a legitimate rank over Shador to keep the rest of the Lords of Darkness in their place. All the while you'd be truly free to live your lives like our forefathers did. And the longer Gurthghol remains away, the greater chance we have of regaining more of our old ways. We might even be able to finally separate Anomolia from Altearin."

"Bold words," Quain snorted, "but can it be done?"

"If I have your support and we move fast enough, I believe so," said Mergis. "But we do need to move swiftly. So what would you decide?" The room again was awash with murmuring and discussion.

"Get some parchment and ink ready," he told Lagella in a low voice. "We'll need to craft a letter for Shador and his side."

Lagella excused herself from the room.

Cirgin watched the other lords, his face a stoic display. "How long are you going to let them talk?"

"Patience. I can't be too hasty, or some might suspect something is off. Things will find their level soon enough." The murmuring increased as they waited. Discussions spread from person to person. Soon enough they'd form larger clumps and, with them, consensus. And when that happened, Mergis would move in and hammer out the final details of his plan.

"Let's hope so." Cirgin continued his stoic staring. "'Cause if word gets out before you're ready, things could quite easily go in a different direction."

"They'll back me. They just need to think it's their own decision, not something they're being channeled into. And the more convinced of that they are, the better for what lies ahead."

"So then we wait," returned Cirgin, flatly.

"We wait."

CHAPTER 4

Mortis was quiet. It was always quiet. All sound, all air—even breath—was absent. It perplexed nearly everyone who arrived in the realm over the millennia. For though sound seemed to be swallowed up as soon as it fled its source and breath was no longer needed to survive, a sense of life still somehow remained. A feeling of order and structure of a sort that infused a sense of purpose to the unending graveyard stretching for endless miles in all directions.

And Mortis, as Asorlok had intended, was little more than a massive graveyard for all that had died across the cosmos. It was part of his plan to continue seeking things out and keep track of them as they passed from life and, in many cases, reality altogether. All life, all things—ideas, actions, worlds, stars, and any and every piece of reality—eventually found their way into decay and death of some sort. And when Nuhl's touch finally prevailed, the object or creature faded from reality, never to return.

It wasn't the desire of Asorlok's patron to create the realm in the way Asorlok had, but it was allowed as a sort of trophy hall to show off its achievements. Another sign that, as far as Nuhl was concerned, it was winning over Awntodgenee. For eventually Awntodgenee would weaken—as all life did—and in time fall into Nuhl's clutches, perhaps even ending up in Asorlok's graveyard as it passed.

Asorlok didn't try dissuading his patron from its thoughts but looked at things from a more distanced perspective. And with that distance he could see the two entities balanced for all eternity. Their constant back-and-forth would continue until they themselves sought to end it and, in so doing, destroyed themselves in the process. It was a bleak thought, he supposed, as he knew that eventually such a thing might very well mean the end of everything else in the cosmos as well. But it was a thought he sometimes revisited after events like the one he'd just experienced on Thangaria. One could say it helped to keep things in perspective. But in truth, it only served to remind him they were birth pangs of a time to come when he alone of all the pantheon would be left to see it.

The god of death surveyed the unending expanse under the eternally gray and uncertain sky. Somewhere between twilight and sunrise, life and death. He spied the crumbled columns of ancient buildings once the centerpieces of wondrous empires, noted the petrified trees which represented majestic forests lost to time alongside the clumps of storied statues and faded works and cracked artwork, rusting and crumbling into the dust blanketing the ground—the very ashes of stars and planets.

He wouldn't have been here, nor would the pantheon—nor would much of anything else as he'd known it—if not for his father. Vkar's desire to have revenge on his enemies called him to cross Nuhl and Awntodgenee's decree. Had Vkar not intervened, all soul-possessing spirits would have faded into nothingness upon death. That was how it had been up until Vkar's time and so would it have remained had he not acted. But in making all soul-possessing spirits immortal, Vkar changed the rules and showed the true extent and reach of his desires as he rose in his newfound power. Physical bodies might be able to be killed or pass on, but their spirits and the souls possessed by and intermingled with them would remain.

Asorlok doubted if Vkar knew the full extent of his decree. He'd originally been seeking a way to make his enemies suffer in the Abyss, but what he did, on such a cosmic scale . . . well, not even Asorlok himself knew the full of it. But he did know how enraged it made Nuhl. It was the main thing that stoked its ire so hot against Vkar. It also brought changes to Mortis, which became the focal point for all the spirits making their transition from their former life to their new eternal one.

Yet when Vkar and Xora were killed by Sidra, their spirits never graced Mortis. And that was because they simply were taken out of existence entirely. He didn't want to admit it at first, but the longer he searched, the more he finally accepted the truth: Nuhl had had its way. It had entirely destroyed Vkar and Xora, denying them the very afterlife he'd created for so many others.

The irony wasn't lost on Asorlok, and most certainly it was intended as a final form of vindictive vengeance. Both of the Cosmic Entities had wrestled with Vkar for so long and on so many things—it was no surprise that when they finally found a chance to act, they did. And recent events with Gurthghol brought all of those thoughts and memories once more to the fore.

Gurthghol had only been removed from them for just a few hours, but already Asorlok's gnawing doubt and rising anger at his inability to make sense of what was going on and what had happened brought him back to the same place, both mentally and physically. Was Gurthghol really gone? Asorlok had told the others he didn't sense him pass—and that was true—but one didn't have to pass if one was entirely erased from all reality. And if Nuhl had done it once before . . .

He'd been walking since his return from the council. Walking and thinking and moving ever closer to a copse of statues. His black cloak and charcoal-gray robe helped him blend into the scenery, while his tanned skin and bright blue eyes made an interesting contrast to the cold stone as he drew near.

The statues were dark gray and stood the same height as himself. Taken together, their lifeless eyes and dusty details could easily have been overlooked. These were a handful of many statues covering the realm. But closer inspection revealed distinct differences and other unique characteristics easily seen by a god that marked them as the most influential titans from the now-long-dead Thangaria.

Asorlok found himself contemplating the fading face of Adon, the first ruler of the titans. His attire was savage—almost barbaric—but that was far from how he lived. Adon raised the titans from their simple beginnings and set them on the course of greatness while siring a dynasty that would eventually give rise to the gods.

Born before Vkar, Adon and his sons after him were not part of Vkar's decree. As such he and all of his generation—along with the second and third generations of titans that followed—were forever lost.

Asorlok and his siblings should have been like them, their time and place long passed and themselves forgotten, save in the faint memory of myth. Instead, they were growing stronger and adding to their numbers. If Vkar's ascension was enough to upset Nuhl, then certainly the entity would be even more upset when it learned of the new gods born into the pantheon. While Nuhl and Asorlok didn't often commune as they had millennia before, it wouldn't have surprised him if Nuhl had known of the upcoming birth already, and this had been one of the main reasons it had returned to try to destroy the pantheon.

And if Asora was going to have more than one child, he could definitely see Nuhl's fear of a new threat in the future. Why Asora and Khuthon kept the number of children secret he didn't know, but he supposed it had been done at Khuthon's urging. He tended to share some of the same worries of perceived threats as his son and perhaps wanted to keep Asora safe from any possible harm . . . or keep things cloaked long enough to use the knowledge to his advantage. Asorlok supposed there was that too. If the recent threat of the destruction of Tralodren and the pantheon itself wasn't enough to get his family into a flurry of activity, the disappearance of Gurthghol and the birth of new gods would do quite nicely. Khuthon claiming Gurthghol's position over the Dark Gods would only be icing on the cake.

In the grand scope of things Asorlok wasn't really too concerned about all of it. He was, after all, the most well placed of them all. All would have to pass through his gates in time, and there was even the possibility, as long as the cosmos survived, that he would too—continuing his duties as Nuhl allowed. He really had nothing to lose in the short run, but in the long run—that was another matter entirely.

He shifted his attention to the statue of Vkar, his father. Standing with crossed arms over a sturdy chest, the stone captured the stubborn and definite nature of the Eternal Emperor quite well. A titan who made himself a god, defying the place created for him to make his own mark and way in the world and then the cosmos at large. Gurthghol took after him in many ways, from the long mustache and hair to even the same facial features. They were so close in appearance that if one looked at just the right angle you'd think they could be twins—apart from Gurthghol's strange eyes and plum-colored skin, of course.

"Ever the defiant one," he addressed the stone. "Gurthghol learned that very well from you, didn't he? And, like you, he's not here, and I don't know if he's alive or dead. Not that you'd care, I suppose. Though you *are* setting a bad precedent." Asorlok scanned the open area to his right. "Two dead gods is hard enough to deal with, but now a third . . ."

He pivoted on his heel to the statue of his mother—the first goddess of the cosmos. Xora was the first true god, since she didn't get her powers from the throne, and she had passed that freedom on to her children.

Xora was a sight to behold, just like he remembered. Equal parts strong and beautiful, she was the iron behind Vkar more than most would care to admit. For while Vkar was a visionary and powerful in his own right, Xora was the enforcer of that vision and will—"the Sword of Vkar," as some once called her.

"So should I consider him dead, or are Nuhl and Awntodgenee having some sport with him first? Or have they locked him away or done something worse to him?"

"Gurthghol will not be making a visit to Mortis." The sound of a strong, familiar voice spun Asorlok around in a flash.

"Then he's alive?" He observed the dark mass hovering like an ink stain in the air.

"For now." There was a genuine disappointment in Nuhl's reply. "But in the end he shall come to you."

"And the throne?" He raised an eyebrow.

"Out of the reach of anyone else that would seek to do us harm." He wondered why Nuhl had appeared to him. It had been years—decades even—since their last, more direct, communication. Their interaction had grown from a steady discourse in his youth to an empty silence in these current times. The sudden reversal was quite the surprise . . . and slightly troubling.

"I couldn't help but notice how you appeared to stand against me just a short while ago. You and your family and the forces you tried to marshal in opposition."

Now things were becoming clear, as were the implications. "It wasn't *you* but your *pawn* we stood against." Asorlok spoke the truth. According to his pact he was free to stand against others who sided with Nuhl, as all of them had with Sidra, but not allowed to confront Nuhl directly. He couldn't see where he'd crossed that line with his recent actions on Thangaria.

"He was doing *my* will." Nuhl's voice grew low, accompanied by an agitated shifting of its dark shape. "I've given you a great opportunity, Asorlok." Nuhl's voice evened out as it continued. "You will get to see the close of every age, the end of all things, and be allowed to learn all the secrets of death you can possibly receive. We had a pact—"

"And I intend to keep it."

"Then you have a strange way of showing your loyalty."

"It was no different than when Sidra attacked Vkar. You can't expect me to not at least stand with my family in times of trouble. Some bonds are too strong to forsake."

"But in death all bonds break; and families fall, as does all else before me." Nuhl's words chilled Asorlok's spirit. "If you are to see all I have promised, then you have to decide where your loyalties lie."

"They're quite clear." He hoped Nuhl would believe him until Asorlok could believe himself. Recent events had muddied the waters too much for any clear thinking. All he could see was the gray, like the very realm around him.

"As displeased as I am with your actions, I'm even less pleased by the birth of these new gods." Asorlok was amazed by just how well he'd been able to predict Nuhl's mind on the matter. Even after all these centuries of being more or less left to himself, he was still well attuned to his patron. "Your kind should be dying out, not making more to plague the cosmos."

"I was as surprised as you that she was carrying more than one child," said Asorlok. "We all were."

"Yes . . . more gods that would never have been had Vkar not overstepped his place." Asorlok heard cracking in the statues behind him but remained focused on Nuhl. "But the time will come when you will all pass away," Nuhl continued as more cracking and the sound of falling pebbles tickled Asorlok's ears. "And then things can finally continue as they should." The sound of something like a great many bones and tree limbs being broken in a staggered fashion finally caused Asorlok to look over his shoulder. Where had stood the statues of Vkar and Xora now rested a pile of rubble that was quickly disintegrating into a fine powder.

"And you will join them, Asorlok, if you should fail to live up to our pact." Nuhl's words faded with its form. "Decide where your loyalties lie, and do so quickly. I won't be as forgiving should you defy me again." The warning was devoured by the realm's deafening silence.

Asorlok stood in place for what seemed like hours, until his thoughts were jarred by the voice of an approaching human—a Telborian. He was dressed in bone-colored robes with a red sash tied about his waist: the garb of an Asorlin.

"I bring news," said the priest. "Asora has given birth to three children."

"Three . . ." Asorlok weighed the possible repercussions in his thoughts. Those he could easily see, at least. One always had to allow for the unexpected in his family—however best one could.

"Two girls and one boy."

"That must have made Khuthon quite pleased." Asorlok's attention was still drawn toward the distance—the ever-expanding grayness of his realm. The house of death where shadows of life still lingered. Shadows and uncertainties.

"And yet it won't be long until we'll be in debate over what to do with them. And now Khuthon just happens to have a greater voice in that as well." He shook himself free from his reverie, taking in the much shorter human. "Was there anything else?"

"No, my lord." It was then Asorlok noticed the Telborian taking note of the mound of powdered stone beside his god. He was visibly amazed and confused but held his tongue.

"Then you may return to the city. I'll follow you shortly." He didn't even see the priest go. Instead he moved his feet while his mind wandered elsewhere. He now knew part of Gurthghol's fate, but there was still a lot more to wade through and resolve. Nuhl's recent appearance made that quite clear, maybe more than he cared to admit. It had to be done, one way or another, and right now that path of resolution took him to Sooth.

• • •

Sooth was usually a place for those given more to pondering than to taking action. Cloaked by a constant cover of clouds laced with a myriad of vibrant patches of colored hues, it was a world where none could see the heavens above nor the world below.

Cloistered in her private study, Saredhel was focused on the unrolled parchment laid across her desk. One didn't need the light radiating from a collection of candelabra stationed on tall stands around the table to see the parchment was old. The once brilliant and brightly colored inks scrawled across the vellum in a mixture of images and text had faded to dullness. But to those who knew what they conveyed, a great deal of insight could be gleaned.

She didn't share the scrolls with anyone else—including her family. They all knew she had them, but that was it. None asked her anything about them, and she never gave anything other than a faint outline of what they covered. And for all these years, that had sufficed. And yet, even after all these years, she remained confounded by the hidden truth and meanings expressed upon them. And though some at times might have wanted to learn more of what she had at her disposal, none dared try to take the Omnian Scrolls from her.

They had once belonged to Xora, the wife of Vkar and mother to most of the pantheon. She had in turn taken them from where Omni, the second ruler of Thangaria and Saredhel's great-grandfather, had kept them for safekeeping. Said to be the first true seer, Omni saw things he believed would come after his lifetime. And since he died before Vkar's decree, he was forever lost to oblivion. Dismissed by those who came after him as nothing but fever dreams, his scrolls were left to collect dust in the crypt of the old palace on Thangaria. And there they had remained, rotting away, until Xora retrieved them. Being a Lady of Time, she wanted to be sure nothing was left to chance when Vkar rose to power.

In short order, Saredhel was at her mother's side, learning more of the scrolls and their encrypted messages. Since then, many things that were predicted had come to pass, but there were still more on the horizon, some of them more deadly and quite devastating. Such was the case with the matter of the scroll she presently pondered. It was the seventh and final one, which covered the topic Omni called the Great End. He was convinced he knew the time of the final ending of all things, the event wherein all of the cosmos was to be destroyed.

Prompted by the scroll, Saredhel had actually thought what just took place with the battle at Thangaria was that end, but now she could clearly see there were too many factors that didn't line up—as far as she could discern them from what the scrolls shared. Omni never did know what to fully make of all his visions and so just wrote and drew them as he saw them, hoping he'd find a way to bring greater clarity as his insight increased. But he died before any such insight came, leaving others to draw their own conclusions.

A knock pulled Saredhel's gaze to the door on her left. The structure, like much of the room, was simple and unadorned.

"Enter."

A Lord of Time stepped inside. His pale skin seemed even more so in the candlelight, while his white hair shone like fresh snow. He wore a gray tunic and white pants. And while his garb did hold to some finer embellishments, he seemed rather plain in both dress and manner.

"I hope I'm not disturbing you, but I have news on the birth."

"How many children did she have?"

"Three. Two girls and a boy."

"Three," Saredhel repeated. "Do they have names yet?"

"Not yet but they will, I'm sure, by the time you arrive."

"An imperial presentation so soon?" She raised an eyebrow.

"No," said the Lord of Time. "She wanted something more intimate with the family first."

"Then I suppose I shall go." The Lord of Time remained in his place. "Is there anything else?"

"You have a visitor who wishes to speak with you." She was caught off guard by the comment. Sooth wasn't a place many sought to visit— whether god or divinity. In fact, if it wasn't for that short interlude in her dealings with Endarien and Asorlok, it would have been millennia since anyone outside of Shiril or Dradin had set foot in the realm.

Closing her eyes she focused on who had come all this way to see her. "Asorlok." Her brother's figure took shape in her mind's eye.

"I wasn't aware you sent for him," the titan lord continued. "I wanted to verify with you before I allowed him an audience. If you wish for me to send him away—"

"No," she said, her eyelids springing open. "He came here for a reason; it might be best to find out why."

The titan gave a slight bow. "I'll have him waiting for you in the hall." This said, he left her some more time with the scroll.

What was she not seeing?

• • •

Asorlok stood patiently by a statue of a Nanoan, thinking back to the last time he'd made a trip to Sooth and what he'd said and been told during that visit. It wasn't on the best of terms, but he was hopeful in light of other events his sister would still be open for another encounter. She was a pretty forgiving sort.

The statue was still an unusual sight, no matter how often he'd seen it: seven feet tall with twelve eyes ringing its bald head. Three eyes at the front, three at the back, and three at each side above his pointed ears. He still didn't know what his sister saw in them, but Vkar had thought them a threat when they'd sided with the Lords of Time in their ancient battle.

Making a race with such a past your favored emissaries wasn't what he would do, but who knew what Saredhel knew—what future they might have before them. Something great enough to make her shave her own head in honor of them. All he knew was that he couldn't go too far into the palace without running across one of the incarnates. Their eyes never left him alone, no matter if the Nanoans were coming or going. For how could you be free of a gaze that was ever present? Perhaps it was a fitting metaphor of time for those who sought to peer into it . . . or a reminder of what was always watching you just out of sight. Either way, it was hardly a pleasant experience.

He'd arrived in his true form and dressed for his upcoming visit to Bios: he'd donned a black robe with silver trim and a charcoal-gray cape, with silver skull-motif bracers completing the outfit. He thought it wise to make the trip a short one and do so in transition, before things grew more complicated and each took to their own devices again, as was so often the case with his family—even after the momentous challenge they'd just endured.

But the longer he stood in Saredhel's audience chamber, the more the doubts soaked in. Doubts and then fears. For what once appeared to be a wise decision now started to look like a rather foolish—even reckless—action. He hadn't felt this way when last he visited—well, not to such a great degree as now—but in that aftermath and following Nuhl's visit, things had taken on a new light.

"I didn't expect to see you again so soon," said Saredhel, striding into the chamber.

The floor and walls were covered with mosaics depicting the history of her realm from its formation to the present time. Too many for Asorlok to consider in any great length, though he supposed if he got truly bored while waiting he could attempt such a feat.

"Neither did I," he confessed.

"And in your true form too."

"I would have used a guise but—"

"But you're on your way to Bios, as are the rest," she finished his thoughts. Usually one had to have permission to arrive in another god's realm unannounced. The process was both a formality and a practical safety measure—for all involved. Yet another reason the longer Asorlok had waited, the more uncomfortable he'd become with his choice. But apparently Saredhel wasn't upset with either his presence or his form. He took that as a good omen. He'd take as many as he could get.

"I assume you heard the news?" he asked, studying the reflection of himself in her solid white eyes.

"Triplets. More than a handful for both of them."

"For Asora, you mean. You and I both know Khuthon will dump them on her lap and not lift so much as a finger until they've been weaned."

"So you don't think people are capable of change?" The question caught him slightly off guard, but he'd gotten more used to having strange questions and phrases put to him of late.

"I don't think Khuthon wants to change. And now that he has another son, he'll be busy making plans to bring him into the fold. Being the leader of only Rheminas and myself just isn't impressive enough."

"I wasn't asking about Khuthon." She stared back. Asorlok hated when she did that.

"You knew already back then, didn't you? Was it that obvious?"

"If you're referring to yourself, yes. It has been for some time . . . for those who know how to see such things."

"Is that why you contacted me for that whole matter with Galba?"

"Why are you here, brother?"

He waited a moment more, making sure he really wanted to go through with what he was about to ask. Once steeled in the decision, he made sure they were truly alone. When satisfied, he said, "I need a favor."

"An answer to your question?"

"I think you and I know they're both one and the same," he said. "Nuhl wasn't too pleased with my aiding the pantheon in our recent confrontation."

"That's to be expected, I suppose."

"Yes." Asorlok looked away from his sister's constant stare. It always had a way of making him feel she was looking more through him than at him. "But he made it quite clear I would have to make a choice going forward as to where I stand—with *whom* I stand."

"And you wish for me to make your choice easier? How?"

"I need to know if Nuhl can be trusted."

"You realize the future is not always clear when free will is in play."

"I just need a few options—a few glimpses of the future—and I'll be better able to make a decision."

"Or maybe you've already made your decision and are seeking a justification?" The question was like a fist to the heart. The most troubling part was he didn't know why.

"I just need some answers."

"You need the truth, but how will you see it when you're already wrapping yourself in a veil?"

"If you don't want to help, then just—"

"I'll see what I can discover, but it will take some time. Nuhl is tightly bound to the cosmos. Trying to pry some threads free to read won't be easy."

"I'm willing to wait." He made another quick search of the room. Not a Nanoan or titan in sight. "I trust this can remain between us?"

"I have no desire to share what I find with anyone else."

"Thank you. So what would you want in exchange?" Asorlok wasn't about to be a debtor to anyone.

Again, the goddess pondered the matter while peering at Asorlok with those pure-white eyes. "Your thoughts."

A strange request, but he was willing to go along with it. "On what?"

"These new gods. What do you make of them—of this whole event?"

"I don't see how—"

"Please, you have a different perspective than the others, and I'm curious to hear your thoughts."

Asorlok took a breath and dug deeper, beyond his most pressing consideration and the matter of their addition to the pantheon. "I guess it all seems a little off."

"How?" Saredhel's eyebrow raised.

"Like there's something there I should know but can't see for some reason," he explained. "Something *you've* never had to deal with before, I'm sure."

Saredhel remained unreadable.

"It's just a feeling really, nothing more," he continued. "And I guess I'm not looking forward to when they come of age. We don't have enough resources left to divide. And I don't think anyone is going to share their domain or other areas of control with these three."

"So it's the passing of the older generation to the younger," said Saredhel. "New life pushing out the old?"

"It's not going to be easy."

"Keeping death at bay normally isn't." Again he was slammed in the chest at the weight of her words.

"Death?" He attempted to laugh off the notion, with unease still lingering about his innards. "No one's talking about death. We're talking about a new order for the pantheon, if anything."

"Yes, the death of the old, to make way for the new. It happened to Vkar, and one day it shall happen to us too." It was Asorlok's turn for silence. "And why should that trouble the god of death so?" Again it was as if another fist had struck him hard in the gut. He kept it all from showing externally, but that might not have been where Saredhel was looking.

"I'll see you at Bios," he said, taking his leave.

"Asorlok?" He glanced over his shoulder but maintained his brisk pace. "Choose wisely."

CHAPTER 5

"**Y**ou took your time." Erdis wasn't exactly upset. Disappointed, certainly, but not in a full rage. Shador couldn't recall a time the Kardu had lost his temper.

"I came as soon as I could." Shador finished entering one of the two side chambers adjacent to Gurthghol's throne room where so much of their private court business was conducted. The rectangular room was lit by means of silver sconces whose purple flames were ever present. These lined the windowless walls, adding a strange cast to the Kardu's features and further obscuring a clear reading of his mindset.

"There's been so much to contend with of late, as I'm sure you know. But I made as much haste as possible." He stopped a few feet from the short table at Erdis' side.

"Well, Mergis was faster, and we've already spoken. So what I say now will only be between us."

"I thought Gurthghol wanted to speak with us both directly." Shador pretended to be confused, since Erdis' letter had said the summons was for a meeting with Gurthghol, not a private parley with his chamberlain. Though he already knew what was coming thanks to Twila informing him of Erdis' efforts, he still needed to put on the proper performance.

"My apologies, but I couldn't be sure who might hear, and right now these are rather delicate times." He motioned for Shador to take a seat. Erdis would remain standing. It was a tactic he often employed to bring himself closer to eye level.

"What do you mean?" Shador continued to feign confusion.

"I've been informed by the pantheon that Gurthghol will not be returning to Altearin," Erdis began. "And, sadly, he might not ever return."

"What are you saying?" He needed to make sure he used a more fearful expression. He didn't need to oversell it—just keep it real enough to be convincing.

"You're no doubt aware of Gurthghol going to Galba on Tralodren."

"Yes. He requested some warriors to help him there."

"Well, he took Vkar's throne and brought it to Thangaria and then—"

"Vkar's throne? You mean *the* throne of the first god?"

"The very same."

"But why would he take it?" While he knew the answer, it would be interesting hearing Erdis' take.

"He wanted revenge on the Cosmic Entities," said Erdis. "And, I guess, he thought it was his best way to do so."

"So then what happened on Thangaria?"

"The pantheon won, thanks to Gurthghol, but he was taken by Nuhl in their final confrontation."

"Taken but not killed?" Shador wanted to make sure he had that part right. Things might have changed since Twila shared the news.

"I haven't heard anything else on the matter and so can only hope he still lives," said Erdis. "Though as to where that might be, no one knows."

Shador leaned back with a sigh. "So Mergis knows this too?"

"I assured the Tularin who informed me I'd make you both aware. And now that you are, we'll have to work on an official policy on just how to inform the rest of Altearin."

"I'll need some time to get a sense of the rest of the Lords of Darkness," said Shador. "I don't want to drop this on their heads out of the blue.

And if there were possibly any cracks in the old order, they'd have to be repaired—or identified, in the least, to prevent them from widening."

"Agreed. And I'm sure Mergis is doing the same with the Lords of Chaos. I can see to the palace and some other matters outside it—but we need to have a united front and voice when this is announced. And it will need to be announced. We can't take too long and run the risk of rumor getting ahead of truth."

"But what do we say? How do you tell the realm that its god is gone—possibly even dead?"

"We'll have to find something," said Erdis. "I'm sure between the three of us, we'll come to a mutually agreeable solution."

"Let's hope so." He maintained an appearance of genuine concern. "I don't want to imagine the alternative." And that was true enough. Anything outside of his own agenda was truly something he'd rather not ponder, let alone endure.

"In the meantime, I trust you can keep this to yourself." Erdis eyed him with a more concerned expression than Shador was used to seeing.

"Of course," he lied. "Like you said. We can't have rumors and factions forming now."

"So how much time would you need for your internal inquiry?" Erdis began to pace slowly.

"No more than a week." Shador figured that should give him enough cover. Twila had already laid most of the groundwork. Together they could cinch up the rest.

"A week . . ." the Kardu mused. "That should be doable for myself and Mergis, I would think."

"All right." Shador took to his feet. "I'll start right away—do everything as quietly as I can—and then look to meet back with you and Mergis."

Erdis turned on his heel, facing Shador. "Then we have a plan. I'll send word for the next time and place for the meeting. Do please make sure you're more prompt this time around."

"Now that I know what's at stake, I won't waste any time."

"Then I'll leave you to it, Lord Shador."

• • •

"You're lying," the Anarch named Alarin snarled at Lagella, splattering some spit into his monkey-tail beard.

"No." She took a slow, calming breath, reminding herself they needed this wild-eyed Lord of Chaos to finish tipping things in their favor. "Gurthghol is gone, and Mergis is moving to take a greater hold over Altearin. But that can't happen unless you're willing to give him your vote."

"And why would I do that when the alternative is so much more interesting?" The madness ringed his eyes as he spoke. Lagella had wondered if she'd be able to get through to him when Alarin had first invited her into his modest estate. But now it was clear he wasn't only borderline insane but stubborn to boot.

Most Anarchs who followed their extreme philosophy—the total destruction of order so that chaos can roam completely unhindered— wound up as madmen. Those who didn't die from their dangerous experiments with the cosmic element of chaos, that is.

While she and most of the other Lords of Chaos had a more refined and balanced outlook on their agenda and goals, the Anarchs were ones to shed such obligations and rules, becoming wild and unprincipled in all they did . . . not to mention unreliable.

"Imagine the whole of Altearin in a state of division," Alarin continued, "constant chaos—eternal changes of allegiances and disruptions to the old way of things."

"No." She hurried to stem the tide lest she lose him entirely to such fantasies. "The alternative is us losing our chance to claim our own stake in the game, and leaving ourselves at the mercy of the gods. We finally have the means and opportunity to grasp at something great—something returning us to what we once had as a people."

"And what were we as a people, hmm? Do any of us know what we once were?"

"Yes, there are some among us who lived during those early times before Vkar granted all of us immortality."

"Things change. It's their nature." Alarin leaned back in his chair. "And why go back to the past when we can embrace the future?"

"Exactly." She tried a new tack. "A future that we can mold together, for the better of all of us and Altearin."

"No." Alarin wildly shook his head. "You're looking to revive the past, not embrace the future. Let Gurthghol go. Let it all go, and things emerge organically."

"I just told you what would happen if we did." Lagella could barely hold back her rising rage. This circular logic was almost enough to bring her to madness herself—even more so, as she'd had to deal with several others of the same bent over the last few hours. Mergis had her and Cirgin traveling farther afield—outside the immediate reach of the capital—to increase his chances of success.

"We need to stand against the pantheon," she continued. "We need to maintain—"

"Your order?" The two words brought Lagella to a standstill. "Hardly something a Lady of Chaos would be advocating, now is it?"

Lagella sighed. This was hopeless. "If we can't have your support, can I at least ask that you won't vote against the action to elevate Mergis?"

"Since I have no interest in the matter, that would be a safe assumption."

"And I'll give you a few gold bars to help you stick to your convictions," she added.

"Lovely." His smile revealed a few missing teeth. "I suppose I could take those too."

"Fine. I'll make the arrangements. Thank you for your time. I'll see myself out."

Relieved to have finally ended the conversation, Lagella hurried into the outer hallway and sped toward its exit. There her waiting griffin took note of her return with a curious turn of his head.

"What?" she huffed.

The griffin gave a screech.

"I know. I know. You're hungry. Just hang on, we're heading back to the keep now."

She took to the saddle and brought the beast airborne, both of them eagerly longing for their return to Mergis' keep. It was too long a day filled with too much arm-twisting, but she could console herself on having shored up support for the final vote. That was worth something.

Soon enough Mergis' imposing keep came into view. This last visit was actually closer to Mergis' lands than the others, providing a perfect end to her circuit. She brought her griffin to land on the open courtyard, where two titanic attendants and Cirgin stood ready to greet her.

"Make sure he gets a good meal," she told the two attendants as she dismounted. "He's earned it." The titans hurried to their task, taking the griffin's reins and leading him back to the stables.

"You've finished already?" Cirgin was impressed.

"Some were easier than others. How about you?"

"I got back about a half-hour before you did."

"That good or bad?"

"Good," he replied. "Most were happy to take the gold—Lords of Chaos and Darkness both."

"We'll need to be more generous with the Anarchs. They were harder to win over than reason would allow."

"And there's your problem." Cirgin's mustache seemed to swell in size with his smirk. "You were using reason."

"And gold. Lots of gold."

"How much exactly?" Cirgin appeared to be totaling some mental tally.

"Fifty bars so far." She watched Cirgin's cheeks pale.

"Which would bring us to an even one hundred, I guess."

"Does Mergis even have that much?"

"He will after he's been made regent. New taxes and other measures will fill things back up to level and beyond."

"I just don't like having to rely on the Anarchs," said Lagella, recalling her frustrating conversation with Alarin.

"That's why we bribed some Lords of Darkness. We'll be ready, don't worry. Mergis will have the votes. And we'll be right alongside him as he steps into his new position."

"Has he made the final arrangements on his end?"

"He's working on the letter to Shador," said Cirgin. "And now that we've secured the votes, things will start to move."

"And us with them." Lagella couldn't help but take some delight in the thought. She couldn't speak for Cirgin, but she wasn't about to not turn this into some sort of advantage. And she didn't think anyone else wouldn't attempt the same. It was going to be an interesting time in Altearin, but she wouldn't have it any other way.

• • •

Shador was in his private chamber reclining on a purple chaise sofa and reading some recent reports. He'd been able to get updates on the present state of the realm. And from what he saw, everything was still flowing right along—just like it always had. Though how that flow would continue once news of Gurthghol's absence arose was still hard to foresee. But so far, even with Twila working on shoring up support and Shador sending out what tendrils he could, no one was any the wiser to that absence. There might be a handful of whispers in some corners but nothing outside some wild gossip . . . for now.

A knock at his door roused him from his reading.

"My lord, you have a visitor." It was the voice of one of his Swarthin attendants.

"You can see them in." Shador rose to greet the titan ushered inside.

"I'm told you're searching for a special piece of jewelry," the titan said in Stygian, though that was clearly not his native language. Like all the titans who called the cosmos home, he had white hair and brassy skin. His red tunic and brown pants further set him apart from the rest of Altearin's inhabitants.

"And you must be the jeweler," said Shador.

"Atticus Worin at your service, my lord." The titan took a shallow bow from his waist.

"I'm expecting a big event soon and want something unique to celebrate."

"And what do you have in mind, my lord?"

"I'd like a pendant crafted to house this inside it." Shador reached into the pocket of his robes and pulled out the necklace from Tralodren. He always kept it with him—especially now.

"Of some special significance, is it?" Atticus hunched forward for a better look, absently scratching his beard in thought.

"You can say that."

"I might have something in mind." The titan returned to his full height. "Were there any particular requirements?"

"Some black diamonds are always nice. But the pendant shouldn't be too showy and should lock very well. I don't want this"—he gave the necklace a lift—"to fall out or be detected. How long would that take?"

"I have the shell of something now I could adopt, so maybe a month."

"How about two weeks, and I'll pay you double." Shador's offer raised Atticus' thick eyebrows.

"That might be possible. Though I'd need to have the necklace to ensure the proper measurements."

"It stays with me." Shador closed his fist over the necklace. "Take what measurements you need, but I keep the necklace."

"Very well . . . I suppose that can work too. If you'd please be so kind as to set it on the table." He motioned to a nearby square slab of stone held aloft by a wrought iron base. Shador pushed some of the books and scrolls resting upon it aside, creating an open space where he set the necklace. He kept a careful watch over Atticus as he picked it up and turned it around in the light.

"Unique craftsmanship. I haven't seen its like before."

"It's foreign," said Shador.

"And old. A few centuries, I'd wager."

"You have a good eye."

"I'm told that's why you sought me out." He shared a brief grin.

"Find the best jeweler in Altearin, I told them."

"And you have, my lord, rest assured there."

"What else can you tell me?"

"It's of high workmanship, but crafted from smaller hands. Incarnates, no doubt. And there's a sense of something imbued within."

"That there is. They left their mark upon it." Shador was pleased to hear the pendant was still worth his efforts. While he could sense something, it was good to have a second opinion on the matter—especially from one so knowledgeable. Though Atticus wasn't a mystic, if this common titan could sense something still resident within, then how much greater must it really be?

Shador watched as Atticus withdrew an ivory ruler from his pants pocket and measured various aspects of the pendant and chain, both hanging from his hand and lying on the table. Finally, he finished, turning again to Shador.

"I don't think it will take too long. And I just happen to have some black diamonds on hand I could work into the design."

"Excellent." Shador returned the necklace to his pocket. "Then I'll see you in two weeks."

"It shall be an honor to grace you with my work, my lord." Atticus was headed to the door just as it opened and Twila stepped inside. Clearly not sure what was transpiring, she held her peace, allowing space for Atticus to exit.

"My lady." He shared a nod in passing.

"Did I miss something important?" She closed the door behind her.

"Just going over some reports. Nothing to worry about."

"And how are things out there?" She made her way toward the table and Shador.

"You should know, you've been out there yourself. Speaking of which . . ."

"It's done. We have the Lords of Darkness behind us."

"Just like that." Shador was impressed by the speed of the endeavor, let alone its success.

"The gold helped, of course, but many were already inclined to offer their support."

"That's promising."

"Though it sounds like we aren't the only ones greasing palms. Mergis' agents have been out and about trying to bribe some Lords of Darkness to take his side in support."

"Support of what?" Shador returned to the sofa.

"The same thing we're doing, it seems."

"Really." Shador chuckled. "Good thing we have a head start then."

"And more coin to split the difference," she added, taking a seat beside him. "It took a little more than you wanted, but we brought those Lords of Darkness back in line. And I even took a few Lords of Chaos to our side."

"The ones closest to the capital, I assume."

"A few, yes, but I opted to take the more wild Anarchs, hoping they'd like the idea of bringing some change into the realm."

"And did they?"

"More than you'd think, and some even without the gold."

"That's helpful."

"Maybe. They were rather on the edge of madness, so who knows if they'll change sides again."

"So then we're really ready." Again, Shador was amazed at the thought.

"Yes. Both of us are ready." Twila stroked the side of his head. "I'm looking forward to joining you on that platform . . . and with that throne."

"One thing at a time, my dear. We can't—"

"We've been partners in all this from the beginning. I'm trusting you to remain true to your word."

"And I will. I just can't have you put forward right away. Let's secure the throne first, and then I can bring you forward as my consort."

"And coruler," Twila pressed. "I'm expecting nothing less."

"And you shall have it. I can't think of anyone better to be at my side."

"I can't wait to see Mergis' face when you're finally elevated."

"And the gods," added Shador. "When they realize they can't do anything to stop it and I've become untouchable."

"And then the real fun can begin." Twila drew closer, wrapping her arm around his torso.

"For both of us." He stroked her cheek.

A knock at the door snapped both to attention.

"Busy day," said Shador, rising.

"Messenger, my lord, from Lord Mergis," called the Swarthin behind the door.

"Mergis?" Shador hurried to the door, keenly aware Twila's eyes followed him the whole way. "Lord Mergis, you say?" Shador flung wide the door.

"Yes, my lord." The Swarthin lifted the letter overhead. "It just arrived a short while ago."

"Thank you." Shador took it and closed the door once more.

"What do you think he wants?" Twila had already come up alongside him, eager for a peek. He ignored the question but not her gaze, opening the letter closer to his chest, allowing him a better opportunity at having the first look.

"Interesting."

"What?" She tried for another peek.

"He's inviting me to an official meeting, asking to summon the Lords of Darkness, as he will have the Lords of Chaos on hand for something rather important to discuss."

"So he's making the first move," Twila mused.

"So it seems. Apparently we wrapped things up just in time."

"And you're just going to let him call this meeting?"

"Yes. The more of a lead he takes, the more rope he has to hang himself in the end. This couldn't work out any better. He probably already knows I've spoken with Erdis and wants to bring me onboard with his agenda before I've had time to work out my own."

"You sure about that? He could be out to set you up for a fall instead."

"No." He returned to the letter. "He's seeking to do things legitimately, just like I would. He wants all the lords behind him—and both viceroys on the same page."

"You think he's swayed Erdis?"

"No, Erdis said he wanted us to work together, which I believe. Though I'm sure Mergis has an idea on how to bring our chamberlain firmly into the fold."

"When does he want to meet?"

"Tomorrow."

"Then he *is* desperate."

"We'll see. Right now I have plenty of letters to write."

"I'll get you some more ink." Twila gave him a peck on the cheek.

CHAPTER 6

A festive mood permeated the entire realm of Bios. There were three new gods in the cosmos and the inhabitants of Zoe, the capital of Bios, were filled with jubilation. All about the streets and the buildings lining them, the realm's inhabitants mingled in excited airs and joyous mirth. The walkways filled with the oncoming traffic that would soon swell along the palace courtyard in time to see the new babies and their mother. For now, though, there was dancing and song, laughter, food, and drink.

This was to say nothing of the regular titans, priests, and followers of Asora from the various beings who had arrived on Bios for their final afterlife throughout the centuries. Added amid these were the Lords of Life, Animals, and Plants who had a special role in the festivities given their greater place over certain aspects of the realm. And then there were the Tularins flying and walking about, keeping order and watch over the growing throng of celebrants.

Asora, as goddess of life, ruled over a realm teeming with it. And now she had added three new inhabitants to the mix. The birth had gone well but still took something out of her. She rested inside her majestic white-tiered palace rising from the center of the city, enjoying the result of her relatively short labor. Each child had found their way into the world rather easily and smoothly. She turned her head to the maple crib beside her bed. Compared to the rest of the room it was plain and rather common, but those who rested inside were the most precious things of all.

No matter how many times she'd seen the process, Asora was always amazed by the miracle of birth and the power of the life behind and sustaining it. To know that only a short time ago these three weren't even part of the cosmos and then, in one of the most repeated miracles throughout it, they had come into being was an eternal wonder.

In a few days she'd be able to resume her normal routines and responsibilities, but for now she rested. Alone in the very same bed where she had brought forth the triplets, she took careful study of their unique features and demeanors, already noting the smallest of traits and mannerisms that would only become more pronounced and refined with years. Two girls and a boy, none of them identical, rested in their white gowns and blankets. Each had strands of red hair, yet another thing tying them together.

They were already showing themselves unique individuals and, she hoped, more prone to *her* temperament than their father's. It was a hopeful thought but she didn't know how close to the truth it might be, given what she knew of Rheminas and Perlosa. She understood each had to make their own choices and way in the cosmos, but it would be nice to have some of her children lean more toward her nature—for the sake of posterity, if nothing else.

Resting her head again on the pillow, she gathered her strength. Khuthon would be arriving soon and then Rheminas and Perlosa behind him. And then it would be time for her brothers and sisters and their families to visit. She'd requested that all not come in their true form, in keeping with tradition, but allowed the right to her husband and children.

What she wasn't looking forward to was the start of the speculation as to what these three new gods were going to become. It was challenging enough being born into such a family and race of beings. The added pressure of what was expected of them was something she'd seek to keep from them as long as possible. There would be time enough for their education and growth and responsibilities later. They needed to be able to enjoy their lives and the cosmos, to be loved and share in the wonder of their place that would eventually become clear to them. They needed to be children first, gods second.

"Asora?" Khuthon's voice shifted her gaze to the door. She smiled at the sight of her husband strolling into the room. "How are you feeling?"

"Better."

He'd changed into a dark gray doublet over a white long-sleeved shirt. His matching gray pants were topped with a black belt, complete with a silver buckle in the shape of his crest. She didn't see a sword or dagger anywhere on his person. She even peeked at the lip of his black boots and found nothing. That was a first in she didn't know how many years. The outfit also reminded her of what she'd first seen in him long ago and stirred her heart with memories and delight.

"Well, you *look* even better than I remember." He took a seat on the bed, taking in Asora's green eyes with his own. The soft brown seemed somehow softer when she peered into them.

"You clean up pretty well yourself." She'd donned a white gown for the occasion. Not too common but nothing too elaborate either. She wanted to be at least presentable for her guests but still remain as comfortable as possible.

"I thought I'd try something new for the occasion," he said, giving her a peck on the cheek.

"Well, you're doing well so far."

"Was it a long labor?"

"Not any longer than it was for the others." She knew better than to think Khuthon would have been by her side during the process. He barely was there during Rheminas' or Perlosa's births; it just wasn't his nature. And she had grown to accept that—grown to accept a great many things during their long marriage.

"But still, *three* babies—it couldn't have been *too* pleasant."

"It's over now." She rested her hand on top of Khuthon's. "And we now have three strong children to enjoy." She was careful to send a messenger sharing only that she'd given birth but not the ratio of boys to girls. She figured the surprise would keep the joy lasting slightly longer that way.

"Which must make the others just as happy, I'm sure." Shifting his focus to the crib, he asked: "Boys?"

"One boy, two girls." Asora noticed the small falling of Khuthon's mouth as she answered. It was the look he had when she'd first told him Perlosa had been born. A girl and not a boy. It was the same thing she was also trying to keep back for as long as possible by originally keeping the full knowledge from him.

"A boy and two girls." Khuthon made his way to the crib. "At least the girls aren't identical; that could have caused some trouble."

"You don't think you'd be able to tell your own daughters apart?" she teased.

"I was thinking more of the trouble they could cause when they started chasing boys around."

"They aren't even a day old yet. Let them grow into themselves first. You might be surprised by what develops."

"It'd be nice to have another son to train, though. Yet another sword arm at my side."

"And what if he doesn't want to *be* your sword arm?" Asora's question pulled Khuthon back around. "What then?"

For a few heartbeats he stood silent, possibly even giving the matter some actual thought, before saying: "You're right. Let's not trouble ourselves with such things right now. We really should name them before the others arrive. It would help add to their plotting."

"I think you've given them enough to talk about by taking Gurthghol's seat."

"I did what needed to be done." Khuthon made his way back to the bed, taking a seat once more at its foot. "We couldn't go on not having a leader. Not with what we'll be facing. And besides, if Gurthghol really *is* gone, we have to have a stable environment for bringing up the children."

It was Asora's turn to remain silent until she found the right way to steer the conversation into less troubled waters. The last thing she wanted was to get into an argument. Not today. "I figured you wouldn't be that keen on naming the girls, so I took the liberty of coming up with some names on my own."

"What are they?"

"Meesha and Talaya."

Khuthon nodded. "Those could work. But who gets named what?"

"I think I've narrowed that down too," she said, pointing to the baby on the left side of the crib. "She looks like a Meesha. And she"—Asora moved her finger to the baby's sister to the right—"looks like a Talaya."

Khuthon took in the two, tilting his head and mulling it over until at last he was forced to admit: "I think you're right."

"That just leaves the boy."

"He should have something strong for a name," said Khuthon. "Something fitting with his place as my son. He looks like he'll be an impressive one too—maybe even put his father to the test someday."

"Or he could just be a normal child too," she offered, but Khuthon ignored her, already enveloped in his thoughts of future glory and wondrous plans for what was yet to come.

"Vearus."

"Vearus?" Asora tasted the word. Something rang true about it. "How did you come up with that so quickly?"

"It just came to me."

"I suppose it's too early to start discussing how we're going to raise them?" she cautiously inquired. They'd discussed the matter from time to time but nothing was ever truly decided.

"Yes." Khuthon watched the babes as they wavered between a state of slumber and wakefulness.

The door to her chamber opened again, and Rheminas and Perlosa entered.

"So how many this time?" Rheminas made his way inside, Perlosa a few steps behind him.

"I made sure to have them tell you with the news," answered Asora.

"I wanted to be surprised," he returned.

"Three." Asora smiled softly. "You have three new siblings."

"A boy and two girls," Khuthon was quick to add.

"So I have a new brother." Rheminas made a beeline to the crib, leaning over it with curious eyes. He wore a pair of black pants and boots with an amber-colored tunic. A dagger was sheathed on his belt, but other than it, he carried no weapon.

"*And* two sisters," Perlosa chimed in, coming to stand beside her mother's bed. She was the image of cold beauty thanks in part to her pale blue-and-white dress studded with diamonds around the cuff, hem, and collar. "We trust all went as it should."

"I'm fine, Perlosa," Asora said, acknowledging the closest thing her daughter would be offering in the way of concern for her mother.

"I'm surprised you even managed to show up." Khuthon's comment brought an icy glare from Perlosa. Asora internally cringed. She was hoping they could have a peaceful affair for as long as possible. After everything else that happened, it would be a welcome respite.

"There are certain expectations we need to uphold," Perlosa returned flatly.

"Well, I'm glad you came," Asora said, managing to prop herself up on some pillows. "It's good to have the family together like this."

"Then I guess you just need to have more babies." Rheminas cocked his head over his shoulder. "So who's who?"

"Meesha, Talaya, and Vearus." Asora pointed each out in turn.

"I'm sure you're already wondering where they're going to fit in the order," Rheminas shared with his father.

"I've given it some thought." Khuthon shot a quick glance to Asora before adding, "but we don't need to discuss such things right now. They *are* just born after all."

"I don't know if the rest of the pantheon's going to feel the same way," said Rheminas.

"Oh, I think they will. For your mother's sake, at least."

"Are you going to stay and dine with your father and me?" Asora asked, looking to Perlosa and then Rheminas in turn. "You're more than welcome to. And it would be nice to be together again—even if just for a short meal."

"There's a lot that needs to be done—especially after the battle," said Rheminas. "I can't afford to be out of Helii much longer than I will be for this visit."

"We could be tempted to stay, we suppose." Perlosa's reply made both Rheminas' and Khuthon's eyes widen.

"That would be lovely." Asora didn't hold back her joy. "I'll make sure they set the table for three. I don't think I can remember the last time we even tried to have a meal together."

"For a short time," Perlosa clarified after catching sight of Khuthon and Rheminas, the brief flirtation with actual emotion once again frozen beneath her snow-white skin. "There are still matters that we need to attend to as well." Walking to the crib, she peered inside, taking careful note of each occupant in turn. "Such tiny bundles of life and power. A great blessing and curse in one. Now we know what the others felt when *we* were born."

"For right now let's just focus on how *we* feel about it," said Asora. "We've had a great addition to our family and I couldn't be happier."

"Then enjoy it while you can," said Rheminas. "The others will be here soon."

• • •

"I can't wait to see them," Olthon told Ganatar. "It's been so long since there's been any children about that I thought I'd never see any again." The two gods were joined by their own children as all made their way through the masses in Zoe's streets, taking note of the festivities bubbling about them.

"You don't think you'll have any grandchildren?" Endarien asked from between Ganatar and Olthon. He wore a white toga and black sandals for the occasion.

"It's not that," said Olthon. "It's just so fun to see them when you can. We're such a unique race in the cosmos. Seeing new life gives me hope we won't be forgotten." Olthon had decided to go with a luxuriant silver gown with a golden sash around her waist. She let her blond hair fall freely around her head, making for a more relaxed appearance.

"If we can survive what just happened," Endarien returned, "I don't think we have to worry too much about our place in the cosmos."

"Time has a funny way of making you doubt such things," Ganatar informed his son. "That and being a parent. I'm starting to understand more of what our father and mother were thinking as *they* got older." Ganatar wore a golden tunic, black pants, and boots, with a white cape draped over his shoulders. The effect was a suitable blending of regal and casual. In this guise he opted to forgo his normal glowing aura, making him blend in more with his family and the rest of the inhabitants.

"You're not that old, Father," said Causilla, giving him a small side hug. She was on Ganatar's other side, opposite Endarien. As always she was garbed in fine attire: a coral dress and light brown sandals highlighted her natural beauty.

"We're not getting younger, though," he countered. "And having that confrontation with Nuhl helped me realize it even more."

"Away with such talk," said Olthon. "We've had enough of death and darkness. Let's focus on life and light. Asora has to be beside herself with joy. Three strong babies . . . what a blessing."

As Ganatar and his family turned a corner, Asora's massive palace came into view. It was a strong structure towering over everything else in the capital. While it had a defensive purpose and place, it was also inviting and open. It had many windows on the higher levels and was covered with white marble that still gleamed as if freshly installed just days before. Each of its four corners was capped with a turret, all fitting in neatly with the elegant yet sturdy ramparts.

Along the main cobblestone road leading to the palace gate stood white banners emblazoned with a golden ankh, marking the recent manifestation of new life. Further on, above the gates, hung another white banner. This one displayed an open hand, palm out, with a golden ankh in its center. The Hand of Life, as it was called, had long been the emblem for Asora and her domain. And above this banner stood some watchful Lords of Life on a balcony, keeping sight of all below.

"Seems all the realm has made merry," Causilla observed.

"As they should," added Olthon. "Though I'm sure things will really become festive this evening after the presentation."

Asorlok materialized a short distance ahead of them. "I see you made good time," he said, not missing a step as he fell in line beside Olthon as she passed.

Ganatar greeted his brother. "As did you."

"Thankfully, Zoe has more than one portal," he explained. "Both are going to get plenty of use over these next few days."

"Hopefully she'll do well through all the protocol," Olthon mused with only a slight hint of concern in her voice.

"Of course she will," Ganatar told Olthon, cheering her countenance. "We have a very strong sister."

"Even so," said Asorlok, "I figured I might as well make it earlier than later. She'll probably need her rest after all this." He made a study of the area as they walked. "Aero, Panthora, and Drued not joining you?"

"No. They'll come later to pay their respects," said Ganatar. "The invitation was for family anyway."

"And they don't feel they belong," Asorlok concluded. "I understand."

"I wouldn't say that," said Olthon.

"But it's probably close to the truth," added Endarien. "And after what you and Uncle shared in council about their elevation, they might have a few more things to ponder."

"What was said was the truth," Olthon told Endarien.

"Which probably could have waited for later," said Asorlok, "but we can't change any of that now, can we? And here comes the rest of the brood."

Asorlok pointed to the last family missing from the list: Dradin, Saredhel, and Shiril. The three appeared out of a side street very close to the palace. Unlike the others, two of them didn't wear anything out of their ordinary garb: Dradin was in his green robes, cloak, and staff, and Saredhel wore her white skirt, shawl, and silver serpent-shaped brassiere. It was Shiril that the others took notice of. Her copper dress was actually quite elegant, which made even her brown leather bracers seem worthy accessories while complementing her brown skin, black hair, and silver eyes.

"You look lovely, Shiril," said Causilla, joining up with the goddess of earth as everyone mingled into one mass.

"It seemed right for the occasion," she returned.

"Well, it suits you," Causilla concluded, clearly pleased with her cousin. "Copper is really a nice color on you."

"Thank you." There was a slight hesitancy in her voice, almost as if unsure how to or if she really wanted to reply. "It's a special event, so I went for something a little different."

"I didn't think Asora wanted all of us at once," said Dradin.

"The sooner in, the sooner out." Asorlok came to a stop beside the palace's main gate.

"That's nothing like Asora at all," Olthon corrected her brother.

"No, but it *is* like Khuthon," said Asorlok. "And you know how he tends to dominate any situation he's given access to."

All waited until the sound of wooden bars getting removed and locks being undone filtered through the other sounds of celebration. This was followed by the opening of the gate itself, allowing the divine family entrance.

"For once it would be nice to enjoy a gathering without accusations and fault finding." Ganatar sighed as all resumed their pace. "I know recent events are still fresh in our mind, but this isn't about the council or anything else other than welcoming three new gods—three new members of our *family*—into the cosmos."

Asorlok's lopsided smirk drew the attention of the others as they walked.

"What?" Olthon inquired.

"I just was thinking what Gurthghol would have said to Ganatar's rebuke." Instantly, the gods' faces and shoulders went slack as a sullen air thickened around them.

"Asora's waiting," said Dradin, taking the lead of a now rather solemn procession.

CHAPTER 7

Asora was resting Meesha and Talaya in her arms when a Lady of Life opened the door into her bedroom. "The rest of your guests have arrived, my lady. Shall I send them in?"

"Please do."

"I hope it wasn't a long ordeal." Olthon was the first to make her way to Asora's bed.

"Not any longer than the first two." Asora smiled at her sister's company.

"And already so peaceful and relaxed." Olthon's face beamed with delight at the two infants' wondering expressions. "Let's hope they stay that way throughout the night as well."

"I take it you have the boy?" Asorlok asked Khuthon. He was cradling the child with an unusual gentleness at the foot of the bed.

"Vearus." Khuthon held up the child like some prized trophy for all to see. "And he has all the makings of being a strong youth and man."

"But of course you're not biased." Asorlok smirked. "And the other two?" he asked Asora.

"Meesha and Talaya." Asora denoted each with a slight lifting of her arms in turn.

"Three children," said Saredhel, who remained removed from the rest, taking the whole scene in with studious care. "Something to make one appreciate the recent series of events all the more."

"I take it you're going to leave the children with Asora?" Ganatar's question was tinged with somber tones as he joined Asorlok.

"In the beginning, perhaps—until they're weaned," said Khuthon. "But they'll need a strong hand to guide them soon enough."

"And a father," Olthon gently reminded.

"They won't be deprived in any way, I'll see to that."

"Can I hold her?" Causilla had moved between the crib and the other side of the bed. Happy to oblige, Asora surrendered Meesha. Causilla took the babe in her gentle arms. The child cooed and smiled in delight. "You must be so excited."

"It hasn't all sunk in yet, but yes, I'm looking forward to what the future holds for them and for us."

A flow of conversation soon followed. And as with many family gatherings, the women gathered around Asora, while the men found their way off to the side of the room. Vearus was passed along to his mother or the waiting arms of another goddess, all of whom took turns holding the baby. They talked about their own motherhood experiences or, among those who yet had no children, hopes for such experiences.

Such talk wasn't well endured by Perlosa. She eventually found herself standing behind the crib, watching the women from a distance. Nor was it relatable to Shiril, who stood between the gods and goddesses like some lone mountain rising between two seas. And so she would have remained had Rheminas not drifted her way. Curiosity was just one of the many expressions swirling across his coppery red face.

"That's twice now you've let yourself be seen, and in just as many days, no less. I was starting to forget what you looked like."

"And that was a bad thing?"

Rheminas paused. "I just don't remember you being so . . . as you are now. The dress—new?"

"It seemed fitting for the occasion."

"Yes." Rheminas took his cousin in from toe to head. "*And* on you." Shiril was slightly dumbstruck. "I meant it as a compliment," he quickly countered upon seeing her reaction. "You really do look the better for the years."

"And you look . . . healthy."

"I'll take that as a compliment too." Rheminas' yellow eyes danced with a playful mirth. "Especially after what could have been not too long ago."

"So everyone seems eager to remind each other about." Shiril's words instantly stilled the flow of discourse. Eager to resume it, she said, "I suppose it will take some getting used to—having so many new siblings."

"Not as much as you might think." Rheminas caught sight of Perlosa. She was doing her best to try not to look like she was staring at the two of them. But it was clear that was exactly what she was doing. The action wasn't completely out of character, but the sense of her being jealous was something new. "I don't see us ever being that close of a family—not in the way some are."

"Even with Vearus?"

"Even with Vearus. Father will have him most of the time, and when he comes of age . . . Well, we'll see what happens. But that won't be for a little while yet."

"Strange how more life brought into your family brings about less harmony and more division." Shiril considered Rheminas more closely as she spoke, almost as if seeing him fully for the very first time.

"Just the way it is." He added with a halfhearted grin, "You grow up and move on. These three will learn it soon enough."

"So you don't think they'll forge a new path?"

"I think they have one pretty well blazed for them already. It's not so much following it as falling into it. Like I said, they'll figure it out in the end. We both did. Just like you did with your parents."

"My situation was different." Shiril was cautious. "I was an only child."

"Maybe, but we all choose our own way in the end. That part unites all generations. A common bond we can share, I guess, if we ever need it."

"You sound like you've been spending time with my mother." Shiril's smooth face flickered with humor. It was yet another surprise. All had always seen her as serious and staid. And now, in just a matter of days, such notions had begun to crack like ice in a roaring fire.

"Was that a joke?" It was Rheminas' turn to jest. "And here I thought you were always as stoic as the rocks you lived with."

"And you nothing more than a hotheaded braggart," she returned in kind.

"Seems we both have some misconceptions to clear up . . . if you have the time."

Shiril's smile deepened. "I might."

• • •

Perlosa kept to her place behind the crib as the hours passed, using the wooden structure to deter anyone from approaching. Dividing her attention among the doting goddesses around Asora, the gods huddled in their own conversation, and the strange discussion occurring between her brother and Shiril, she kept asking herself why she was still there. She'd done her duty: shown up and seen her new siblings, made the pointless chitchat, and now should have been back to Naiada. She had much to do there but mainly just wanted to be done with the others and back to her own life. A life she'd had to disrupt in favor of this series of recent events. It would be good to return to it and get away from all this.

But then she made that commitment to stay and have dinner with her parents. What had she been thinking? She'd tried to give herself a small out when she heard the words come out of her mouth, but this did little good now. She could certainly make up an excuse to leave, true, but some part of her didn't want to. That same part that had spoken her acceptance of the invitation before she knew what she was saying. And that same part that had her thinking about what it might be like for her to have children of her own. To love them and help them grow into—she closed her eyes and quelled such stupid meanderings. When she opened them, she found Endarien standing before her.

"You all right?" His yellow eyes echoed the hint of concern in his voice.

"Fine." The last thing she wanted to do was engage in more meaningless conversation.

"Must be different having such younger siblings," he continued. "Almost like they could be your *own* children in a way."

"What do you want?" Perlosa's eyes narrowed.

"To talk. Is that okay?"

No. She wanted nothing of the sort, but when faced with having nothing left to do until dinner, she supposed it would help the time go faster than it had.

"Have you come to apologize for your failure with the lich?" Her mind immediately went back to one of their previous exchanges before the final battle on Thangaria. His foolish bravado had cost them the last of Vkar's essence, probably one of the most reliable safeguards they could have used against any further threats now that Vkar's throne had also been taken from them.

"No." Endarien seemed surprised she'd brought the matter up. Not offended, just surprised. "It's not every day we get to see each other. And given our last meeting, I thought we could both do with something less confrontational. I just thought to get caught up."

"Is that not what your spies are for?" Again Endarien was a bit dumbfounded but managed to soldier on. Every bit as persistent as he often was when he wanted something.

"You are aware I'm the only one in this room who's even *tried* to speak with you?"

"And you are aware we never asked to be spoken to."

Endarien sighed. "Don't you ever get tired of the act?"

"We are who we are." She made sure to put as much defiance into her posture and face as possible.

"No," Endarien countered. "You are who you've become. We all are, which means we can always choose to become something else if we want to."

"So you came to lecture us?"

"I came to see how you were."

"We are fine and plan on remaining so."

Endarien gave another small sigh as Perlosa's attention floated back to Shiril and Rheminas. The two were engaged in quite an animated exchange—a sight totally uncommon for both of them. "It seems our brother has chosen an interesting conversationalist."

"Some might say the same of you and me." Endarien's words gained Perlosa's full attention.

"Yes, they might."

"They might actually think you've started to let your icy wall down."

Perlosa had forgotten how impertinently Endarien could make his point while mixing in his own brand of sarcasm. It had always been something that she liked about him since they were children. That and the—stop it. Just stop it. She willed herself to remain focused on the present, forgetting the past.

"Then they would be wrong."

"I see." Endarien gave a grim nod. She was finally getting through to him.

"You asked why I came over," said Endarien with uncharacteristic sadness creeping into the corners of his eyes. "I wanted to remind you if you ever do need some help or someone to talk to—a friend—"

"We said we will be fine."

• • •

From the corner of his eye, Ganatar watched Endarien retreat to where the rest of the gods were gathered in debate. He didn't need to hear what had been said to know the result. Perlosa and Endarien had been such close friends and now barely spoke to each other. While it wasn't his place to pry into his son's affairs, it was clear Asora and Khuthon's children were capable of some surprises. All the more reason for some to wonder just what might be down the road for all of them.

"I really don't think this is the best time to be bringing up such matters." Ganatar tried steering the conversation away from where Khuthon had been endeavoring to keep it focused: on his recent ascension to the rank of head of the Dark Gods. He'd talked of little else for the last half an hour.

"What better time *is* there than now?" Khuthon insisted. "We're all here—"

"Not all of us," Ganatar countered.

"The ones that really matter are," Khuthon replied.

"There's protocols that have to be obeyed," he insisted. "And I don't think your wife would take too kindly to turning her bedroom into a new council chamber."

"Why not let Asora enjoy this moment?" added Dradin. He stood opposite Ganatar, both gods facing Khuthon. "It has been a trying time we've had to endure, and this is a bright spot we can rally around and rest in for a while. There'll be more work to do soon enough."

"Yes, much more work to do . . . like raising these new gods."

"You don't plan on having any more, do you?" asked Asorlok. He stood to the side of Khuthon, opposite Dradin and Ganatar.

"I didn't say I wouldn't try." He beamed. "But I think this is the end. Five is enough to deal with—grown or babes. As it is, these last ones were a bit of a surprise."

"We're here to help if you need it," offered Ganatar.

"Yes." Dradin nodded. "I'd be happy to help tutor them when they're of age."

"I'll keep that in mind," said Khuthon. "Just be mindful of your wives tonight," Khuthon said with a mischievous smirk. "Seeing babies tends to make a woman want to have some of her own. Well, I suppose we've kept the masses waiting long enough," he said loud enough for all in the room to hear. "It's probably time we made the presentation."

• • •

Since the time of Adon, the first titanic ruler, the ruler's children had been presented to the citizens of their capital city. It was meant as a time of celebration for the family and citizens but also showed the lineage would continue and the throne would not sit empty. Security and stability mattered a great deal in those early days. But as the kingdom grew into an empire, the presentation became a thing of pageantry and a sign of the strength of the royal family and their growing might across the cosmos.

This custom reached its climax under Vkar, who, by making all beings essentially immortal, ended the need to present a display of stability. This just left the show of favor and growth of the divine family line. Vkar and Xora had made a great spectacle out of it with their own children, and to a lesser extent their children did the same, though here too Vkar and Xora made sure they were tied into the affair. It was still their family that was increasing, after all.

Following their death and the destruction of Thangaria, the custom faded from memory. With no new children born thereafter, no thought was given to these presentations. With the birth of Asora's triplets, however, interest in the tradition was revived. But Asora wasn't given to the pageantry of old—not to the extent of the previous generations. Instead, she would simply announce the birth to the people of her realm, her family by her side.

The gods had assembled on the white marble balcony at the back of Asora's palace. It faced a massive square, giving the large crowd plenty of space to gather. Here too were many white banners with the Hand of Life with others displaying plain golden ankhs peppered among them. Asora and Khuthon were in the forefront, with Perlosa beside Asora, Rheminas beside his father. Asora had donned a fine gown of white satin for the occasion along with her golden crown, marking her as queen of Bios. In her arms she held Meesha. Talaya was held by Perlosa, who actually did a fine job of keeping her sister calm and close to her chest. Rheminas held Vearus.

Behind Asora and Khuthon stood their brothers and sisters: Ganatar, Olthon, Dradin, Saredhel, and Asorlok. Behind these were their children: Causilla, Endarien, and Shiril. All kept still, letting the cheers and accolades of the massive multitude below reverberate through the air. Their part was only to show the solidarity of the divine family, assuring all the known stability would continue for the foreseeable future.

As they waited for Asora to address the gathered throng, Causilla's hand grabbed hold of Endarien's. "You okay?" She kept her voice low.

Shaken from his thoughts, he glanced her way. "I'm fine, why?"

"I saw you talking to Perlosa earlier and wondered if you needed to—"

"There's nothing to talk about," he cut in. "She's still the same."

"I'm sorry."

Endarien gave a hurried nod and focused once more on the presentation. "I probably was a fool for even trying."

"No," said Causilla, giving his hand a squeeze, "you're a true friend for trying. She'll see that in the end."

"Maybe."

"Citizens of Bios, Lords and Ladies of Life, Animals, and Plants." Asora's raised voice brought an end to all conversations and cheers. "In keeping with the ancient custom established by our forefathers, I and my family stand before you to present the new additions to our family. I stand before you now the mother of five children. Two of them you already know, but let me present to you the other three." Lifting Meesha overhead, she continued. "Behold Meesha, daughter of Asora and Khuthon, children of Vkar, son of Enduris, son of Omni, son of Adon, the first ruler of the titans."

"All hail Meesha," said the crowd in unison. "Long life and great favor be upon her."

Asora handed Meesha to Perlosa in exchange for Talaya, lifting her second daughter overhead. "Behold Talaya, daughter of Asora and Khuthon, children of Vkar, son of Enduris, son of Omni, son of Adon, the first ruler of the titans."

"All hail Talaya," said the crowd again in unison. "Long life and great favor be upon her."

Asora turned to Rheminas, and the two of them swapped babies while Khuthon looked on. Vearus peered up at his mother and grinned. Asora couldn't help but share it. Lifting him above her head she said, "Behold Vearus, son of Asora and Khuthon, children of Vkar, son of Enduris, son of Omni, son of Adon, the first ruler of the titans."

"All hail Vearus," said the crowd one last time. "Long life and great favor be upon him."

This done, Asora handed Vearus to Khuthon, who took the babe into his strong arms. "We shall raise them well," she continued, "bringing them up in the same ways as our other children were brought up and instilling in them the understanding of their responsibilities and duties as part of this family and of the ancient order that rules over the realms and planes."

"Long live Asora," rose up a jubilant shout.

"Long live the gods," said another group of the throng, this followed by more applause, cheers, and shouts.

Back on the balcony, Olthon smiled at her husband.

"What is it?" said Ganatar.

"I'm just thinking back to the presentation of Causilla and Endarien."

"It wasn't so simple as all this," said Ganatar.

"No, Father always did like his pageantry and rituals. Do you remember during Endarien's presentation how Sidra got a bit too excited with her cake and—"

"Ran right into Gurthghol with it?" Ganatar chuckled. "I'd never seen him laugh so hard before."

"He really did love her," she added before gloom completely consumed her joy.

Instantly, Ganatar's own mirth subsided. "Yes . . . he did."

"Well, I suppose we should be off," said Dradin, breaking Olthon and Ganatar from their conversation. "It's been a long day for both mother and children."

"For all of us," added Ganatar.

"Wait a moment," said Khuthon, making his way to them through the others. He'd handed Vearus off to Asora as soon as was acceptable. "We haven't set a time for the next council. There's still much that needs to get done."

"You mean that *you* need to get done?" Olthon inquired. "Can't you even enjoy your family for one day?" Khuthon was going to say something but bit his lip instead.

"Let's take a look at the rest of our realms first, like we agreed," Ganatar advised, "see what needs to be done, and then come back for a full and complete council where we can cover everything at once."

"Fair enough." Khuthon was curt. "I'll be looking forward to the announcement."

This matter of business finished, the gods all made their goodbyes. Last among them were Asora, Khuthon, Rheminas, and Perlosa. The babies were entrusted to some Ladies of Life, who'd make sure they'd get their rest.

"Are you sure you can't stay for dinner?" Asora asked while giving Rheminas a parting hug.

"I'm sorry," he said. "Maybe we can do so later—after the council perhaps."

"Perhaps." Khuthon eyed his son. "You're up to something, aren't you?"

"Nothing that need worry you."

"It better not. Everything is almost lined up perfectly. I can't have others throwing rocks in the path now."

Rheminas' levity quickly departed. "It's nothing that concerns you or your plans, I assure you."

"You don't know all my plans."

"Should we?" Asora's question brought the whole discussion to a sudden end.

"Well, I'm hungry," said Khuthon, making his way back into the palace. "And I'm sure your mother has had a fine meal prepared."

"Take care," Asora told Rheminas, who glanced at Perlosa.

"I'm sure we'll see each other at the council soon enough." A copper glow traced his frame as Rheminas departed, fading from sight.

CHAPTER 8

When the Race Gods were brought into the pantheon, Ganatar and Olthon set aside a part of Civis for each of them. Yet while the section had been partitioned for their own rule and customs, it remained under Ganatar's ultimate authority. The Race Gods were content with this arrangement and divided the portion among themselves.

Drued received a realm he called New Druelandia—the name of both the great capital built to be an improved version of the old origin city on Tralodren, and the land over which he governed from that city. Here the god of the dwarves ruled over his people for all their afterlife. In some ways New Druelandia was a place where it was as if dwarvenkind had been reborn in a time when the Imperial Wars had never occurred. If not for the occasional sighting of ordered or illuminated incarnates or the Tularins flying about, it would have seemed as if none of them had really died and all were still on Tralodren. And that, in many ways, was what Drued wanted.

He wasn't interested in establishing himself as something incredibly great but rather keeping alive the way of life and the best of his people for all time. In so doing he'd put forth the perfect template from which to draw when seeking to guide the rest of the dwarves on Tralodren. And while he was honored to have been given such a divinely assigned task, he also was always mindful to know his place. Even if he was now a god, he was first a mortal—born into one of the many races calling the world they'd created home.

All he had came from them. Nothing of his current rank was in any way merited or created by him. He made it a custom to always remember that truth lest he forget and start thinking his station something more than it really was: a gift and a responsibility he needed to steward wisely. And he had done so for several millennia, moving ever forward toward completing his grand task and mission. In some ways he was closer to achieving it now than ever before. Soon enough he'd be able to bring all the dwarven clans and groups into one united people. His confidence only grew with each passing generation. But such thoughts weren't at the fore of his mind as he made his way into the depths of New Druelandia. Present changes to the current pantheon had set him to work on another project.

Drued watched through the haze birthed from the smoke rising from scores of forges as the smiths put the finishing touches on the still-glowing fourteen-foot golden ankhs. Laid out across the massive anvils, they were only a handful of those being worked across the great workshop nestled in the bowels of the city; the workers' gentle tapping kept their own rhythm amid the rest of the pounding.

Three in number, the ankhs had been created from the purest gold and poured into molds which the smiths had recently removed to tend to any minor matters that might have escaped their initial inspection. Each had a hole in the center where the cross beam and base met. Drued had yet to visit Asora, but when he did he wanted to bring something fitting to honor the occasion. The holes would be filled with a setting of electrum that would keep in place a massive diamond he was having cut for each ankh. They would be a gift worthy of a goddess—one ankh for each child.

"Well done." Drued walked behind the busy smiths, watching them closely. "The purest gold for the purest of life. A fitting gift." He stood out from the rest by his great size, almost three times the height of the tallest dwarf, with purple eyes, charcoal-gray skin, and wheat-brown hair. He also wore rather common attire. While still regal and of fine quality, his tunic, cape, and pants helped to blend him in among his fellow dwarves.

Upon his ascension he was made aware he could change himself into a more fitting figure, should he desire. Drued refused. Instead, he only added some small refinements to his spirit that highlighted his former natural appearance. The size increase came with his elevation—as it had with all the other Race Gods. And while he could have changed that, he decided to keep it. It was one thing that set him apart and served as a constant reminder of his charge.

"The diamonds should be finished in a day," said the finely dressed Rolland, one of Drued's retainers, whom he'd put in charge of the project.

Like all of the dwarves in New Druelandia, Rolland had the appearance of someone in his midtwenties—a fresh adult ready to live out the entirety of his years. Though the four braids in his beard would mark him as much older. In their mortal lives dwarves would make a braid for every twenty-five years lived. Most kept them in the afterlife, leaving them as they were before they died but not adding any more lest they'd have nothing but braids for beards in their now-immortal existence.

"Have them take all the time they need," he told Rolland. "They have to be perfect."

"And they will, my lord. You have my word."

As a god Drued could have simply created the objects himself, willing them into being, but there was something to be said about having them created by hand, making each unique and original. It also didn't feel like much of a gift if it took little to nothing to create them. He was still of a mind that things had greater worth if something was invested in them. It didn't seem right doing anything less.

Drued turned to Vordin, another of his court, who was standing on his left. "Did you get the final count from the battle?"

"We lost only two on Thangaria. The rest are healing nicely." Vordin's deep voice rose above the hammering. "Considering how things could have gone—"

"They shall be honored for their sacrifice and duty," said Drued. And they would. The two who had fallen had lost their existence. Neither he nor the rest of the pantheon could undo such a fate. It was horrible, true enough, but also final. He, like the rest of the city, would set them in high regard, seeing they would be remembered for the rest of time. It was only fitting. Those who were wounded in the battle would also share in the glory. For it was truly a monumental affair which they were still seeing their way through, and most likely would be for the next few councils, if not years after that.

"Let me know when they set the diamonds; I want to be here personally to bless each one." Drued began his exit of the forge, stepping between blazing furnaces and anvil stations where dutiful dwarven smiths—both men and women—continued hammering away.

"As you command," said Rolland, who remained behind while Drued faded from sight, only to appear alone in his throne room an eyeblink later.

The contrast between the two locations was instant and obvious. The silence, for one, seemed to swallow everything that waded into it. But the brilliance of the many gold-trimmed stained glass windows was what made the major difference. The workshop's forges could only provide a tinted glow, obscured by the near constant smoke flowing around their heads. Here one entered into something almost celestial.

With the light streaming, the whole chamber seemed almost alive. Painted marble statues of all the dwarven kings who had ruled Druelandia up to Drexel lined both sides of the wide red granite path, straight to the obsidian dais. In the light the statues appeared to stand at attention, ready for any command their god would decree.

His eyes fixed on his gold-and-marble throne sitting in front of a long black banner depicting two crossed silver hammers before a golden double-bladed axe. The Holy Crest was more prominent in the capital, growing less so the further out one went. It was his preference it not loom above those who lived in New Druelandia, instead remaining a subtle reminder in the background. It was the way things were in the days of old—at the height of ancient dwarven power—and would remain so for as long as Drued sat on New Druelandia's throne.

Taking his seat, he conjured an image of the three finished ankhs. They were exact copies but insubstantial, allowing him to see right through them as if they were of gossamer. He studied each closely, turning them around and observing every angle. Yes, they would be a fitting gift. The diamonds were clear and brilliant, shimmering in the light. They were flawless in every respect. The gold bodies. The electrum settings. Everything. He was so enraptured with his viewing that he failed to detect the presence of a Tularin flying his way.

"Lord Drued." She landed a few yards from his throne and behind the transparent ankhs between her and the god. Drued shifted his focus, not that surprised. Tularins were an almost common sight on Civis.

"Yes." With a gesture he raised the ankhs above the incarnate, allowing for an unobstructed view.

"Asora has presented her children to the people of Bios." Her brown face was unreadable, but her blue eyes clearly spoke of duty, as was common with her race.

"What are their names?"

"Meesha, Talaya, and Vearus."

"I assume the family have returned to their own realms."

"They have."

"Has she said if she was open to receiving any more visitors?"

"I have not heard yet, my lord, but no doubt she'll make it known when she is ready."

"Yes." Drued nodded slowly. "She'll need time to rest, after all, and I'll need time to prepare my gifts. Was there anything else?"

"No, my lord."

"Then you have my leave." He gently waved the Tularin away. She gave a bow, flapped her wings, and returned the way she'd come. Once she'd departed, Drued lowered the ankhs and continued his inspection.

"Meesha," he said aloud. White glowing letters spelled out the name in bold titanic script across the crossbar of the first ankh. "Talaya." The crossbar of the second ankh glowed with the new goddess' name. "Vearus," he said, birthing the name's creation across the crossbar of the third ankh.

He sat there considering the work. The white-hot carving had cooled, allowing the sparkling platinum that had filled the letters to shine. All combined, it worked well. It wasn't overstated and wasn't too plain. A simple elegance for a goddess who wasn't known for ostentatiousness.

"Much better," he said, admiring the final design more closely. "Now, to find the best way to present them."

• • •

"Keep a watch on him at all times. Nothing more," Panthora informed the five Tularins gathered around her wooden throne. Apart from the two seated panthers carved on its sides, it was covered with a mixture of hide and leather, like her dress and bracers. It complemented the rest of her stone-and-timber audience chamber that would have fit in with many human settlements at the time of Panthora's ascension.

Draped here and there along the walls were white banners. Her crest of a roaring gray panther's head in profile was displayed on each. The lone brazier sitting in the center of the room was the only source of light, apart from the handful of torches that flickered in the corners and near the door.

"What if his life is in danger?" asked one of the three male Tularins among their number.

"I've already provided a means for his protection." Panthora's brown skin was smooth, but her brown eyes revealed deeper thoughts flowing just beneath.

"Then we will just watch?" the same Tularin inquired.

"And keep me informed of *all* that you observe," she stressed. "The days ahead will test him, but he has to see them through."

Like Aero and Drued, Panthora had been given a collection of Tularins to help her rule over the section of Civis she'd received as her own. She called her realm Gracia. All who died while holding her as their goddess entered into it. Never one to overstep her place after the kindness shown her by Ganatar and Olthon, she sought to keep herself in a position of perfect balance between the two other Race Gods and the Gods of Light calling the greater realm of Civis home.

And as with Drued and Aero, she soon found herself ruling over an empire of her own. This one, though, was ever growing and never ending.

Not the place she thought she would have ended up in death but she, like the other Race Gods, had learned to adapt to the privileges and responsibilities of their call. And though now a goddess and easily twice her former size and that of all the people she governed over, she favored Drued's mindset, retaining her former mortal form as much as possible. This even extended to her simple dress and black dreadlocks.

"We'll do as you have said," said the Tularin before he and the others made for the door.

Panthora half watched, half pondered as they departed—the sound of their beating wings helped her sink deeper into her thoughts. She'd been focused of late on a young Nordic knight freshly returned to his home and order. He'd been through a lot—they all had these last few days. But she was confident that, like metal tested in the fire, he'd make it through stronger and better than he ever was before.

"You've put a great deal of faith into this Nordican," Jillar, Panthora's Tularian chamberlain, said from beside her throne. His white-trimmed red robe set him apart from his fellows.

"Not more than he's placed in me," she answered, not taking her gaze from the wall across from the chamber.

Jillar had remained in the room while she had debriefed the others. Always in earshot if needed, he'd waited for them to leave before taking a place beside her. The fair-skinned paradisal incarnate was seasoned in years but far from elderly. Instead, he possessed the well-mannered nature one would expect from the best people suited to be advisers to persons of power.

Panthora believed him to be the best chamberlain she'd ever had and was hoping he'd have a long tenure. He was also the most open and direct, which she very much appreciated. So much of the court life that followed the gods was unnatural to her. While she didn't oppose it outright, she never really felt comfortable with any of it. And while she always tried to strike a balance between what was expected and what was truly needed, if she could find others who could talk through the trappings of state, as it were, so much the better.

"Some might think him too young."

"Some or you?" Panthora turned his way.

"I merely express the obvious." Jillar made clear he meant no offense. "A quality I believe you appreciate."

"I do, and it's quite welcome. But you share only what you can see with your eyes. I have faith in him following his heart. He's been true there, if nothing else. And that will carry him through if he holds on in the days to come."

"A final test then," Jillar mused.

"For himself, not from me. He now knows the truth. The test will be if he can walk in it."

"And if he does, you'll have your standard-bearer." Jillar took on a more scholarly, paternal aspect he often adopted while pondering aloud. "I'm impressed with your boldness in all this, my lady. Your actions, I'm sure, will catch the pantheon's attention in short order."

"I'm not worried about that. And I haven't left him without protection—as you've just heard—or guidance, and he won't be looking to do this all on his own. If my desire is finally going to be birthed into Tralodren, he won't be alone for long. In the meantime, he needs to be watched and protected, so when he comes to the time of making the final choice he's free to do so, no matter what he might decide. It has to come from him and no other."

"If everything seems dependent on this youth, then why, might I ask, do you seem so troubled by the matter?"

"Bolder still." Panthora smiled.

"Would you have it any other way?"

"No." She grew more serious. "I just wish there was another way. He's already been through so much."

"But there isn't," Jillar completed her train of thought. "Because then you'd be stopping him from reaching his true potential and passing that final test."

"Yes." Panthora sunk back into her throne with a sigh. "Which I'm sure we've discussed far too often already."

"It never hurts to be sure before you take action. And you've never been one to be reckless in your decisions either."

"There's still that lingering doubt, though," she confided. "I thought only mortals doubted, but I've come to find it still lurks in the minds and hearts of gods too."

"The challenge of free will." Jillar nodded. "One is never sure how it will unfold until it finally does. A troubling matter in some ways, but I doubt you'd have it any other way."

"No. I wouldn't."

"Important as the matter may be, there are some others that require your attention, if I might continue in being so bold. Your paying of respects to Asora and her children is chief on the list."

"Three new gods." Panthora was still amazed when she thought of it. "I've never been asked to honor the birth of *one* god, let alone *three*. What am I supposed to do?"

"The same as you did when you were human and your friends or family had a child." Jillar made it sound like a rather simple affair—a common event.

"A god being born isn't even *close* to the birth of a human."

"Life is life, no matter where it's found. Each produces after its own kind and in like manner. To mortalkind, mortalkind, and to gods, gods. There's little difference in that. Both have a mother and father and are delivered in the same way."

"Yet one can wield the power to form planets and create whole nations of beings and the other simply seeks to live as well as they can with the life they've been given."

Jillar shook his head in what she thought might be bewilderment.

"What is it?"

"Forgive me, my lady. I just find it amazing you still think of yourself as a human when you've been among the gods now for centuries. Your dealings with this Nordican and now with these newborns . . . I know of no other god who would even see these things in the same light as you do."

"I was raised up to help humanity. I don't want to forget what it was like to be human. As soon as I stop being able to relate, then my purpose here stops being relevant." Jillar was pleased with the reasoning, if he might not embrace it himself outright. "So then what do you advise?"

"While a gift isn't needed, it would be wise to bring one and keep in everyone's good graces. With Khuthon's new position, it would be prudent to start off on a good foot as things move along."

"Let's hope Khuthon gives us a rest before moving forward on some new plan. I think we can all do with some peace for a while." It was then that the weight of what had taken place over the previous hours and days grew heavier across her shoulders and brow. She stood to her feet. "If you don't mind, I think I can do with some rest myself."

"Of course. Rest well, my lady." Jillar gave a flap of his wings and left Panthora alone with her thoughts.

For a moment she stood by her throne, dwelling on all that had happened and all that she had yet to do. After a short time she summoned a viewing portal by the wave of her hand. The flat disk of white light illuminated more of her pleasing features as she concentrated on focusing the portal on what she wished to view. Like a mist the white light of the disk parted, becoming a window. Through it she watched a young, sandy-haired Nordican moving about the grounds of the keep of the Knights of Valkoria. She could almost feel the burden growing on his shoulders, not to mention his heart.

She'd shared with him more than many of the Panians had ever known before. Such truth was needed for the days ahead, but the cleansing process that now followed would be a trying one. For Rowan had been wounded in both his spirit and his soul. And his previous adventures had taken their toll, leaving him in need of his own rejuvenating rest. And he'd get it . . . but not from the thoughts and doubts that continued to circle him like angry crows.

She reached out for the portal. Ripples reverberated from where her finger touched just above Rowan's face. "Be strong," she told him. "It's not as dark as it looks." She watched him draw closer to the keep, still lost in his thoughts and cares, before making the portal fade from sight.

She sighed.

You still think of yourself as a human. Jillar's words came back to her as she contemplated the empty chamber.

"Be strong."

• • •

Aerotripton, god of the elves, sat in his golden throne. Ten feet below him at the white marble dais' base, a collection of elven officials of the realm of New Remolos stood in respectful silence. The added elevation granted by the dais made the god, already over twice their height, all the more imposing and impressive.

Aero was resplendent in his golden-trimmed purple toga, black sandals, and golden crown. And with the large set of golden spread eagle's wings rising from behind the throne, he was every bit what his followers thought a god should be. Not much had changed in the way of his appearance from when he was a mortal. For in life one had to play the part well if respect and awe were to be earned, and the same held in his divine state if he wished to keep his hold over all who made their way to New Remolos in death.

While the capital might have been a glorious version of the city of Remolos on Tralodren, Aero knew he didn't hold the prestige of the other gods. He lacked their divine nature, having risen from mortal lineage, forever setting him apart as lesser rather than equal. Moreover, he'd even mocked and turned his back from the gods for most of his adult life, professing himself to be something of a divinity himself before losing his life. This all made his ascension even more amazing. But with such a background it was easy to create a path for others to follow, making sure it was clear who was in charge and giving everyone reason for their awe and worship.

"Colloni is on the rise, but we'll need to shepherd it in the days to come," he told all gathered. "I'll need you to be ready for anything. Galba may be gone, but the Syvani still can prove difficult."

Aero was quick to find one of the silver linings of the dark clouds that still hovered over the horizon of recent events. Galba—an aspect of Awntodgenee, he now understood—had long held sway over the Syvani of Arid Land, keeping them in shamanism. This, naturally, had made it challenging for Aero to reach them as he worked on them and the other elves across Tralodren. But with Galba's removal also came the end to their shamans and faith, and that provided the perfect opportunity to act. And he wasn't one to let such an opening go to waste.

"Without Galba the shamans will have no power, my lord." This was spoken by Astanius, one of the first of his chief priests selected to stand in his court. As in life the priest kept to his purple toga, white tunic, and black sandals. And, of course, the Imperial Star—Aero's holy emblem and crest—rested around his neck. "A simple sign of your divine presence and power will easily turn these savages to the truth."

"Perhaps, but they're a stubborn people. Some might turn to the truth, but some will also dig in their heels and refuse to take hold of my offer."

"Then they're fools," said another of the court, this one not of the priestly faction, but part of the administration.

Aero appreciated the zeal. All of his court shared such sentiments. But all of his court and all of New Remolos were Elyellium. And if he was to ever complete the task assigned him upon ascension, he'd have to reach out to the other elven nations—even more so now than previously. For the current shakeup of the old order provided the perfect seedbed for new things to spring forth.

"They just haven't had the chance to hear the truth," Aero continued. "And so we need to bring it to them. And in time all of Arid Land shall be brought into the unity of that truth. Which means we'll have to prepare for new arrivals. And that means taking on some of the land around the city for expansion and alteration into a setting they'd find suitable."

"Not grass huts and skin-draped timber frames, I hope." The husky voice of one in the back of those assembled brought forth a burst of mirth. Even Aero found himself sharing a thin grin, but quickly stopped it from going any further. Old attitudes such as that would have to be changed if he was truly going to be a success in welcoming all of elvenkind into his realm and service.

"No," said Aero, "but something to help blend the two cultures into a more unified whole. So I need to begin work right away. As soon as Barius makes landfall, we can start to expect the first arrivals. We need to be ready."

"May the glory of the First Elf cover all of Tralodren," Talos, another priest, cried out.

"So be it," went up the thunderous refrain, followed by, "Hail the First Emperor. Hail the Eternal Elf."

Aero basked in their praise as he watched a Tularin fly into their midst. His light brown skin and short white hair further set him apart from the rest of the elven audience. He landed effortlessly behind those gathered, who parted to create a path to Aero's throne.

"News, my lord, of matters on Bios," announced the Tularin. "The babies have been presented with the entire family."

"Good," said Aero. "With that out of the way, it won't be long until the next council is called. I can see about taking care of any remaining matters, and then my hand will be free to keep focused on Arid Land.

"So what are their names?" he asked the Tularin.

"Meesha, Talaya, and Vearus."

"And Asora is doing well, I trust?"

"Quite well."

"Then the council will probably happen soon enough." Finding another of his administrators, he asked, "How is the gift coming along?"

"It should be finished in a day or so."

"See that it is. It wouldn't do to have it arrive too late.

"Thank you for the news." Aero dismissed the Tularin. "And I think we're done for the time being here too," he informed the others, rising.

The assembly bowed and removed themselves from the room. Aero stepped down the dais as the last of them exited. Closing his eyes, he concentrated on the image he'd been going over constantly in his mind of late, the vision of a new and wondrous future for his people. Keeping that focus, he willed the vision to appear outside his mind, forming a transparent map in the air.

Opening his eyes, he considered the map with a pleased grin. Before him was the entire Northern Hemisphere of Tralodren. Of the lands shown, only Colloni, Arid Land, and Rexatoius stood out in a bold white. The rest were outlined in a faint glow, providing the needed perspective of the entirety of the world but keeping much of it in the background.

Mingled amid the other lands were solid white splotches in some of the seas and oceans. These marked the domains of the Aquadions, the last branch of the elven tree.

Overall, the map was an inspiring sight when viewed with an imperially inclined eye. If one could imagine all the white as part of an empire, and all in that empire worshiping Aero as their god, one could see he'd have quite an influence over not just the elves but Tralodren too. It had taken him centuries to reach this point, but now he would finally be able to bring about what he'd been working for before his ascension and had been commissioned to undertake following it: the unity of all of elvenkind.

"Soon . . ." he told himself. While he knew it wouldn't happen overnight, when that final pinnacle was reached, it would be glorious to behold.

"Soon . . ." he repeated as his thoughts drifted into the future.

CHAPTER 9

"I can't remember the last time we had dinner together." Asora sat at the end of a large table with Khuthon to her left and Perlosa at her right.

"Not all of us are together." Perlosa was referring to the absent Rheminas.

"Still," Asora continued, keeping to the brighter side of things, "it's been too long."

The large dining hall had been meant to house a sizable gathering, making the three presently seated within it seem all the more conspicuous. Even with the handful of titanic servants scattered around the room, the impression was far from intimate, but each made do. Globes of light were hung from the ceiling on spindly silver chains, bathing all beneath in a warm glow. Their dinner was a vegetable stew with bread and wine. Dessert would be some sweet pie and cheese with more wine.

"Thank you for coming, Perlosa." Asora's kind face found a confused expression washing back and forth across Perlosa's features. She said nothing, focusing on stirring her stew.

"Yes." Khuthon grabbed his nearby golden goblet. "So why *did* you decide to stay?" He drained most of its contents with one gulp.

"The important thing is she's here," Asora said before Perlosa could glare at her father. "We're *all* here. And you're always welcome to visit." Asora cast a loving look Perlosa's way.

"We will be sure to keep that in mind."

"Is everything well in your realm?" Asora asked Khuthon.

"Yes." He considered Perlosa in a manner she wasn't certain how to take.

"How about you?" Asora went back to Perlosa.

"She looks fine to me." Khuthon tore off a piece of his bread.

"We are well." Perlosa was curt. She'd never been one for small talk and, given her surprise at having followed through on showing up for a meal, didn't really know what to say or talk about. Generally she preferred remaining more private with things regarding her life.

"You sure? You look a little tired." Asora's maternal nature couldn't be hidden, even if she tried. Perlosa almost found herself wanting to embrace such sentiment. Almost.

"It has been a long set of days"—Perlosa took up her own goblet—"for all of us." She took a drink.

"Yes it has. But at least they're over."

"Don't bet on it." Khuthon tore off some more bread. "We're going to have some long discussions in the future. There's the matter of making a new defensive plan for Thangaria and then what to do about Gurthghol and that scepter too."

"Which I thought was already watched over by the Tularins."

"A temporary measure. We're going to need to review all the plans for securing Thangaria and anything we keep on it."

"Why?" asked Perlosa. "Nothing has been even close to a threat until just recently. And with Nuhl defeated—"

"It's not defeated," said Khuthon, "just deferred to another day. And the next time it comes I plan on being prepared."

"You sound like Rheminas, always suspicious of everything."

"He's mindful of his surroundings and knows that in the end you can't really trust everyone who claims they can be trusted." His eyes locked with Perlosa's. "Which I think was made clear enough during the recent battle."

"We came and fought." Perlosa offered her rebuttal, even though she knew it would really never be enough. No matter what she said or did, her father's image of her would never change. He'd always see her the same way.

"But only after enough arm-twisting to nearly rip it out of its socket." Khuthon's stare held firm.

"Would you rather we stayed away?"

"I would rather you'd be more loyal to your family, especially now. With your new siblings it won't be long until we're going to have to stand together—when they're old enough to lay claim to realms of their own. It would be nice to know that in this family we don't have any weak links."

And there it was. Bad enough she wasn't a son, but to not follow after his ways of thinking made her a potential liability, a threat constantly in need of assessing. After all, who knew what wild things his daughter might get into—or worse yet, how she might make him look to others?

"We did not know we were slated to be a soldier in your army." She kept her tone less icy than usual, but still tried to maintain as much independence as she dared.

"It's about loyalty and the future," her father continued. "We're now the largest family in the pantheon, and when the triplets are grown we'll hold the most sway over the others."

"Assuming we all join the Dark Gods," she quipped.

"*Family* ties are stronger than any other," countered Khuthon. "And when the time comes, they *will* be tested."

"Another matter for another day," said Asora, motioning for one of the nearby titanic servants to freshen their goblets. "And I doubt it will be as dark as you paint it."

"Like father, like son," Perlosa chimed in.

"And if he were here, he'd put forth a good case for it." Khuthon jabbed his spoon her way. "You need to take your eyes off yourself once in a while and look around. The cosmos is still wild and untamed. Our place in it is only assured by keeping a strong watch and being willing to do what's needed to ensure our interests and survival."

"Hardly the philosophy the Dark Gods are said to subscribe to." Perlosa didn't acknowledge the handsome titan beside her as he poured the wine. It was best just to ignore them unless needed. After all, they were no doubt doing all they could to keep such personal conversations out of their own minds and memories.

"A realistic take on it. Not that *you* hold true to all of what the Gray Gods are supposed to value."

"Maybe it's best if we talk about something else." Asora leapt into the verbal fray, pulling against the conversational reins and veering them in a new direction. She'd been doing it for so long, she was more than skilled at the task. It was actually something Perlosa admired about her.

"Has anyone recently caught your eye?"

Perlosa was bewildered by the sudden question.

"That is, if you wish to share anything about it. I know you're busy with matters of your own—"

"No. We have been busy, like you said."

"I just happened to see you and Endarien talking earlier and—"

"He was attempting to be polite." She nipped the topic in the bud.

"Oh." Asora sipped from her brimming goblet.

Perlosa wondered how many others had seen her and Endarien talking and then asked herself why she even cared if they had. There wasn't anything to be concerned about anyway—regarding either Endarien or what the others thought. So why didn't it sit well with her when Asora brought it up?

"Speaking of which," Khuthon added, making another assault on the loaf that remained at his side. "Did you see Rheminas speaking with Shiril?"

"Yes." Asora was obviously pleased. "I haven't seen her so talkative since she was a child. It was nice to see her being more social for a change. It must be so lonely at times being as cooped up as she must be."

"Like parent, like child," offered Khuthon through his full mouth. "Dradin and Saredhel are practically hermits."

"I won't go that far, but it would be nice for Shiril to have at least *one* friend. You all used to be so close growing up." Asora glanced lovingly at Perlosa. And again, for just the briefest of moments, Perlosa was tempted to return the look. "It would be wonderful to see if you could rekindle those connections."

"Some things are best left forgotten." Her words smothered Asora's pleasant expression. "And if how he treats his family is any indication, Rheminas will prove an even poorer friend."

"And he'd probably say the same about you," sniped Khuthon.

Perlosa heard her mother's small sigh before she took another drink—a longer one this time, she noted. Perlosa mimicked the action, mentally steeling herself until she was able to finally break free from this table and return to her own realm and life.

• • •

The realm of Boda was ruled by Shiril. Like so many of the realms across the cosmos, Boda had been created by a god. In this case, Shiril, who took the plane of Boda and merged it with Engimi, one of the moons of Sooth, the world claimed by Saredhel, long ago. Like its ruler, the realm was a place often left to itself. None had a strong desire to visit it or its ruler. This was fine by the Lords of Earth, who had called the plane home long before Shiril made it her realm. The less they had to contend with those outside their interests, the better.

While aboveground, the realm was a rich example of the cosmic element of earth, displayed in the varied forms of mountains, hills, deserts, fertile fields, and more, most of the activity—at least of the most important sort—happened below the top layers, in the honeycombed tunnels across the realm. It was here the Lords of Earth had built their complexes and cities, and Shiril, her official dwelling, called the Golden Womb.

In keeping with all the other vast resources Boda provided, everything in the palace was covered and overlaid with precious metals, stones, and polished rock. Its wide hallways were lit with glowing stones the size of human heads. These were embedded into the walls or affixed to ornate sconce-like structures, sharing their ocher illumination everywhere.

It was through these richly decorated hallways that Rheminas was led by a Lady of Earth. In some ways her brown skin reminded him of Shiril's. Lords and Ladies of Earth had a complexion that matched the cosmic element they strived to master, ranging from a light sand to an umber hue. Their eyes were various shades of brown or black, matching their hair. This particular lady's hair was a lighter sandy shade and kept in a shorter style. Her clothing was an interesting mix of work and casual attire, consisting of a silver-colored dress with a wide black belt and matching steel-toed boots.

Rheminas didn't know quite what to make of all he was seeing. Had he just been left to his own devices, he would have wandered the surface, never knowing anything about how much lay hidden beneath. Before he'd even gotten to the palace, he had already seen some amazing sights. Amazing because they were the last thing one thought about when the idea of Shiril came to mind. Art and fine craftsmanship you would expect from Causilla, but some of what he'd just encountered outside the palace was on equal footing with Causilla's work. And now that he'd been navigating the corridors of the Golden Womb, he had an even stronger belief there was a great deal about Shiril that none of the pantheon had any clue about.

He'd taken to his true form, a favor Shiril had granted him for their meeting. The normal protocol was to keep to guises when visiting another god's realm. It was supposed to help maintain the peace. It also made sure the god being visited was the most powerful being present should anything take an unexpected turn.

He'd decided on a charcoal-gray shirt with a cream-colored leather vest, accented by his black pants and boots. Across his shoulders was a black half cape. He wanted to impress as well as convey a slightly different impression than one might have expected. Given Shiril's recent unique presentations, he figured he could do the same.

"We will be reaching the dining hall shortly," said the Lady of Earth. One of the few times she'd spoken since meeting him at the palace's entrance.

Rheminas said nothing, continuing to observe the long section of bas-relief to his right stretching down the hallway. It presented the scene of the formation of the realm, from what he'd been able to figure out so far. All of it, though, was a mixture of stones, gems, silver, gold, and minerals, so that the skin of the Lords of Earth was composed of polished stone, their black and brown hair actually formed from pieces of onyx or jasper. The sky was a blend of lapis lazuli, blue and white quartz, and crystal. Every facet of the scene was alive and gleaming in the palace's unnatural light.

"You will find it to your left." Rheminas pulled himself from the relief and saw his guide directing him to a strong, silver-shod white marble door. "Her ladyship is expecting you." She gave a nod which Rheminas thought was to help speed him along.

Taking the cue, he approached the door, set his hand on the diamond-studded silver doorknob, and gave it a twist. There was a sound of metal gears turning inside the door itself, and then it opened into the room beyond.

"Welcome to Boda." Shiril's voice carried across the cavernous oval room that was the dining hall.

Lit by the same light sources found throughout all the palace, the chamber was massive, even by divine standards. What made it seem even more so was the fact there was only one table in all of it. And this was set for two—one chair opposite the other on the longer ends of the rectangular granite slab. Much better than having to shout to be heard and squint to see if they'd been seated at the far ends. But certainly far from what he was expecting. The chairs were crafted of brass and were rather plain when compared with the rest of the interior.

"I take it you don't host too many dinner parties." Rheminas moved into the center of the room to where Shiril stood beside the table.

"You'd be the first." Her silver eyes seemed to sparkle; her black hair was like strands of silk flowing down her head and neck. Even though she wore the same dress he'd first seen on Bios, he still found himself amazed at her natural beauty.

"Then let me thank you for having me, and in my true form too."

"I think I can trust you." She shared a grin, which was something quite unusual—even unheard of, considering what everyone assumed was her normally stoic nature.

"I see you've taken a liking to the dress."

"I thought it was a fitting choice for a dinner. And I didn't really know when I'd have a chance to wear it again."

"I'd never expected your palace to be like this." He spun his head around the room.

"You thought I lived in a cave?"

"No," he lied, "I just . . . it's just so opulent. And you don't seem like one given to such things."

"And many might think you're not one given to rational thought." The wide grin helped dull the end of the playful barb.

"Only Perlosa." He found himself hard pressed to release his gaze from her pleasant face.

"I suppose you'd like to sit down." Shiril motioned to the nearby seat. He quickly took it. There was nothing on the table. No food. No dishes. Not even goblets of wine.

"Have I come early?"

"No. You're just on time." She sat across from him. The move made the sense of formality only increase between them.

"So what are we having?"

"I thought roasted lamb would do with some potatoes."

"Sounds good." Rheminas nodded absent-mindedly. His thoughts were latched on to his hostess. Those wondrous silver eyes . . . her pleasing lips. In truth, most of his thoughts had been attached to her in some degree since their time in Bios. It was a fresh blaze that had sparked some long-dormant kindling, and those flames refused to die out.

"Have I told you how lovely you look?"

"I think you alluded to it."

"I'm sorry." He did his best to relieve the discomfort he could clearly note in Shiril's person. "It's just seeing all of this—seeing you like this—is a bit to take in."

The same Lady of Earth who had escorted Rheminas earlier made a return appearance. She was carrying a golden tray with a crystal decanter full of red wine with matching crystal goblets. He noticed a door far off to his right that had previously been hidden from sight now open and allowing the titan lady access. He wondered how many other such doors and secret compartments were still hidden across the palace—even this room.

The titaness set the tray between Rheminas and Shiril with a slight bow.

"Dinner will be served shortly."

Shiril took hold of the decanter and was about to lift it when she was stopped by Rheminas reaching over to touch her hand. "Let me."

"Usually the host is the one who—"

"Just humor me."

Shiril sat back, allowing Rheminas to stand and pour the wine into the goblets, one of which he handed to Shiril. "Might I propose a toast?"

"To what?"

He took Shiril's hand and lifted her from her seat. "To new friends and new beginnings."

"Very well." Shiril lifted her glass. "New friends and new beginnings."

By the time she'd taken a drink and set down her goblet, Rheminas had worked himself close enough to ensnare her with his arm, pulling her toward him. "And to the brightest of gems in this setting of splendor."

At this he brought Shiril's lips to his. Intoxicated by the press of her body against his own, he failed to relent for some time. When he did, the breathless Shiril could do nothing but stare back with wide eyes. Only then did the full reality of what he'd just done sink into his skull. He might have acted too soon—too rashly—and thrown everything away with the impulsive action.

But he didn't have long to contemplate. Shiril latched both hands on either side of his head and rendered an equally enthralling kiss of her own. When it was over, it was Rheminas' turn to be breathless and bewildered . . . which again was short lived. He grabbed hold of Shiril and brought her beside the table, then shoved her down on top of it even as she ran her fingers through his wild orange hair.

He was only barely aware of the same Lady of Earth arriving with a few others in tow with a platter of food and dishes between them. Upon catching sight of the scene they drew to a sudden stop and, after a quick collection of nervous glances, decided it best to retreat to whence they came.

• • •

The night in Civis had already aged, but Ganatar and Olthon were still wide awake. As much as the day had been eventful, so too had been their evening, which now saw the couple resting in bed. The fact that the husband and wife chose to live together, ruling side by side, was unique among their siblings, who had adopted distant marriages and relationships, holding the separation of their powers and dominions as more important than combining the many aspects of their lives. Ganatar and Olthon were just the opposite.

Their bedroom, like much of the palace and realm itself, was a beautiful mixture of order and tranquility. Yet here, in this most private sanctum, their surroundings were quite subdued: a collection of teak furniture lining one part of the room while the other allowed an open expanse flowing into a finely crafted balcony.

In the middle of the room was their white-dressed canopy bed. The bed's pillars were carved to resemble Tularins holding aloft the white muslin and wooden crown above their heads. The curtains around the bed had been pulled back and the plate glass doors to the balcony left open, allowing the breeze to flutter in with the light of the two moons.

Olthon delighted in its soft caress over her shoulders and wings. Naked beneath the white sheets, she rested her head on Ganatar's bare chest, her wings folded behind her.

"Your heart's calm," she said, "but I can tell your mind still isn't."

"And why do you say that?"

"You seemed . . . *distracted* earlier."

"Not *too* distracted, I hope." His hand found and then caressed Olthon's shoulder.

Ganatar's strong fingers sent an enjoyable shiver down her spine. Even after all these years he was still the only man for her. Just like she was certain she was the only woman for him. Yet another difference from their forefathers and some of their own family, but it was the best life Olthon ever had lived.

"No, but enough to tell me you're a bit too troubled about something." She softly shifted her head for a better view of his face. "What is it?"

Looking aside to his wife he was taken once more by the golden curls framing her bright green eyes. "This whole matter of the last few days," he confided. "The battle, the births, and now Khuthon looking to gain more power while Gurthghol languishes who knows where. It's just all too sudden to not be a coincidence."

"You think Khuthon planned it?" She wouldn't put such a thing past her brother—even something as grand as all they'd just endured.

"No, he's not cunning or powerful enough to bring all this about."

"Nuhl?" Olthon felt Ganatar's chest tighten upon mention of the name. Things were still too fresh in all their minds. They'd thought they'd never have to contend with it ever again. But now all knew it was only a matter of time until it returned to threaten them and Tralodren.

"I don't think so, but from what we've just seen, anything is possible, I suppose."

"Well, it couldn't have had anything to do with the triplets," Olthon teased.

"No, you're right there." She was pleased to see his disposition lighten at the jest.

"And the vote was fair for Khuthon's taking Gurthghol's seat too," she reasoned.

As much as she might not have liked it, they had all voted, and it had been done openly and fairly. And everyone had clearly seen it for what it was: a naked power grab, no matter how much Khuthon might have tried to dress it up with his concern for Gurthghol and the council's continued stability. He knew it. She knew it. They all knew it. And yet everyone still voted the way they did.

"Yes." Ganatar started drifting in his thoughts.

"We've been through a lot. You just need some rest and to get your mind onto something better for a time."

"I suppose. He won't try to take on too much at once." He rubbed her shoulder, sending another tingle down her spine. "He's not that foolish, even when he gets what he wants."

"Let's hope so." Olthon tilted her head to rest her cheek on Ganatar's smooth, muscular chest, delighting in its strong rising and falling. She was convinced he possessed the same strength as in his youth. "We could do with some peace and quiet for a while—Asora chief of all." She listened to the thumping of her husband's heart, finding a sense of growing peace and assurance of brighter days to come. "But this whole matter with Khuthon isn't really the issue, is it? You're not comfortable with the new gods, are you?"

"Have I grown that readable?"

"To me you have." Olthon reached up to put a hand on his strong right shoulder, giving a small twitter of her wings in the process. "You think it'll give Khuthon an unfair advantage, tip the scales more in his favor."

"The thought *has* crossed my mind, but if history is a good teacher, he'll have his own hands full with three strong-willed and independent children. And what's *that* speak to our future? We have some unclaimed planes, and maybe a few planets, but—"

"They might not even want any of them, have you thought of that?"

"I doubt it—not in *this* family."

"Weren't you the one who was just telling Khuthon to let his children grow up?"

"Yes," Ganatar weakly confessed.

"So let them grow. It could be nice if Asora could at least have *one* child take after her. It would mean so much to her, I'm sure."

"I'm sure it won't always be easy. Three children with little help from Khuthon will add to her burden."

"All the more reason for us to step in to help where we can."

"As long as *you* don't get any ideas about having any more children in the process," he teased.

Olthon promptly snuggled up against his head. "And why would you think a thing like that?"

"Because I know a thing or two about women and saw you and the rest huddled around Asora. I don't have any interest in having any more children. Now *grandchildren*—that's another matter."

"Does that mean you're going to stop the process altogether?" Olthon slid herself on top of Ganatar's chest, wrapping her wings around the both of them. She couldn't help but notice the playful mischief peeking out from behind his more serious façade.

"Now that would be rather excessive, don't you think?" His hands began sliding down her back and under her wings.

"You tell me," she said, raking her fingers through Ganatar's thick white locks before pulling his face toward hers, lips to lips.

Yet for all the fire the action produced Olthon could sense Ganatar still mulling over matters in the back of his mind. Desirous to free him from such things for even a little while, she wrapped her legs around his muscular waist while mimicking the action with her wings over the rest of his body. That seemed to do the trick.

CHAPTER 10

Mergis was pleased as he made his way through the press of bodies. The Viceroy's Hall, as it was called, was one of three large audience halls in Gurthghol's palace. The first two were adjacent to the throne room, with the Viceroy's Hall being on the opposite end of the palace as a symbolic means of balancing the two main parts of governmental power in the realm.

The hall was the most fitting and only logical place to announce his plans to the other titan lords and also provided him a cloak of working jointly with Shador to share whatever it was he wished to convey to the greater ruling population. The hall was also the largest venue to gather so many titans in one room—which is just what was needed for today's engagement.

In keeping with trying to satisfy the varied host who'd be gathered within it, the hall was lit only by a handful of clear glass globes hanging from the tall ceiling, their purple light providing enough illumination for each titan lord's use. The hall had been used in times past by previous viceroys for making their edicts and rulings known—more like kings of old with their subjects—but such things eventually fell out of fashion in later generations and among the Lords of Chaos most of all, who hated being tied to anything that smacked of tradition or needless repetition.

It was rare to use the hall these days, since much of the day-to-day operations were overseen by Mergis and Shador, who simply delegated matters to others to work out. Once in a while they'd meet face to face, but such times were an informal affair that had nothing really grand or impressive about it. But today the hall was filled with Lords of Chaos and Darkness.

From what he could see, just about everyone was present. That made things even easier. The closer he was to a majority, the better this would all play out. Now he just had to play his part well, and everything would fall into place. Shador had made quick work of calling and assembling his own fellow lords. Mergis was actually impressed. Even with his own advance knowledge, it had taken some effort. Maybe Erdis had managed to scold his fellow viceroy about being more timely with such matters.

He was interrupted from any further thoughts by Lagella coming up beside him. "We got a rough head count. We should be good. There's enough of a margin if anyone gets cold feet. I also have some gold on hand. Cirgin and I are ready, should—"

"We'll be fine," he interrupted with a raised hand. "As long as everything goes to plan we have nothing to fear. And everything *will* go to plan."

"Now there's something you don't see every day." Mergis' attention focused on a gathering a little ways from them, where Shador was talking with a handful of Anarchs. If memory served, these were some of the same titans who'd been absent from his original meeting with the Lords of Chaos.

"You *did* say we had some Anarch support . . ." Mergis kept his voice low.

"Yes," Lagella assured him. "I know I did what I could and brought several around in the end—as did Cirgin. And those that already sided with you earlier did what they could to convince others too."

He'd never known Anarchs to openly communicate with any Lords of Darkness as willingly as they were doing now. Just like it was rare to see so many of them looking so sane. Why Gurthghol mandated some of them be allowed to have places of rank in his kingdom Mergis would never know. Though he was the god of chaos, Gurthghol was far from one to fully embrace their beliefs. But then again the Lord of Altearin didn't play favorites with the Lords of Darkness either—the chief example was both Mergis and Shador holding equal weight in the realm.

Mergis watched Shador excuse himself from the others and make his way toward him. The smile was something trained. Mergis wondered if he even knew he was doing it. Then he realized he was doing just the same upon sight of his fellow viceroy. Yes, they really were two sides of the same coin in some ways. But not for much longer . . .

"Care to share what this is all about?" Shador finished his approach. "Your letter only hinted at things."

"I couldn't risk sharing everything on parchment," Mergis explained with as much humility as he could summon. "I'm sure you'll understand once I say my piece."

"If it was that important, you could have approached me directly. That's what Erdis did when he informed me of Gurthghol's current whereabouts. I was about to reach out to you to confer, but your letter beat me to it. That is what this is about, isn't it?"

Mergis momentarily froze. He understood Erdis would have shared the news with Shador, but just wasn't expecting the sudden way in which Shador was relaying the information. Nor the subtle innuendoes connected with it.

"In part, yes. But not everything."

"So Erdis left something out?" It wasn't clear if Shador was being honest or sarcastic.

"I think it's just better if I explain everything to everyone at once," he politely and calmly replied.

"Will Erdis be joining us?" The question needled Mergis.

"No. He wants us to speak with each other first, as I'm sure you recall him saying to you when you spoke."

"Then I look forward to what you need to share—apparently we all will." Again there was the flash of teeth and what could be acquiescence or a subtle ploy for plotting something else.

"Shall we?" Shador motioned for the two of them to ascend the black marble steps of the dais in the center of the room. Behind the dais was a long purple banner on which the Black Sun—Gurthghol's crest—was embroidered with black silk thread. The same open dark circle with eight radiating points was displayed on many such banners and even the god's throne.

"I wonder if you'd mind me speaking first?" asked Shador. "It's been a long while since we've used the hall, and I think a little ceremony is in order—to set the proper mood and context for why we've gathered. Not so much for your fellow Lords of Chaos—I know how you all usually chafe under formalities—but more for my fellow Lords of Darkness."

Mergis paused for as long as he dared, searching anew around the borders of his plans for any fresh holes. "If you must," he said with a slow sigh. "But it would be wise to keep it brief. We do have a lot to discuss."

"Of course. I won't make it too long. I'll just establish the general order, and you can take it from there."

This said, the two took their appointed seats, Mergis on the throne to the right, Shador to the left. Once they were seated, the chatter in the room faded. When all were facing the viceroys with rapt attention, Shador rose and began his address.

"As you know, it hasn't been our custom to meet in this hall for some time, but I thank you for honoring the tradition. For today is a momentous day, and it's fitting all those of rank be present to hear this news together."

Mergis was about to stand when, to his rising annoyance, Shador kept speaking.

"By now all of you know there was a great battle on Thangaria that involved the pantheon and some of our own number. But what you don't know is that because of what transpired, Gurthghol is no longer among us." As expected, the room filled with fresh murmurs and commotion.

"Please," Shador continued, raising his hands for silence. "Lord Mergis, my fellow viceroy, has called an assembly of the more illustrious of our numbers, and I, like you, am eager to hear his words. So, if you would, please, share what you have to say." And with that Shador bowed to Mergis and returned to his throne.

"Thank you, Lord Shador." Mergis took to his feet as rapidly as protocol and proper appearance allowed. "And thank all of you for coming. As my fellow viceroy was saying, sadly, the great Gurthghol was taken by Nuhl, and there's no clue of what's befallen him or *if* he'll ever return. Naturally, as soon as I heard of the matter, I acted quickly and called this assembly."

"And we've come," said Shador, motioning to the gathered multitude. "But for what purpose, I wonder?"

"To reclaim our place," Mergis informed him and the others, "and protect us against any others who would try to take it from us." It was time to get right to the heart of the matter. It wouldn't do to leave Shador too much of an opening should he get the gist of what he was about to say next. "We're in danger of losing a wonderful opportunity to reclaim our freedom and destiny. With Gurthghol gone we're free to rule ourselves once again." This stirred up some fresh murmurs from the crowd.

"I'm not talking about outright rebellion," he continued, "but a carefully choreographed effort to maintain Gurthghol's control until his return."

"A regent then." Shador acted as if mentally testing the concept, though Mergis was hard pressed to clearly discern what he was truly contemplating.

"Yes, and if we act quickly and install one, we'll have the option needed to once again live free from the pantheon." More excited voices filled the room. "We would have the legitimate cover needed to secure our true freedom," he continued over the crowd's increased muttering.

"And I suppose you have a candidate in mind?" Shador crossed his arms, clearly seeing where this was all going.

"Two, actually." Mergis delighted in Shador's genuine surprise at the comment. Clearly, he'd been thinking Mergis would strong-arm the glory for himself upfront. Which was just the reason why he sought a more diplomatic and therefore legitimate process for his desires instead. He took Shador's surprise as a good sign. It meant Mergis still had the upper hand.

"The pantheon would accept either Shador or myself as acting regent, as we were appointed by Gurthghol and have served under him for many years. He has our trust, and therefore we should have the pantheon's."

"So you'd look to be our master now instead? Is that it?" shouted a wild-looking female Anarch from the back of the room.

"No." Mergis shook his head. "I don't plan on being anyone's master, but would be willing to act the part needed to keep the rest of the gods at bay. As would Shador, I'm sure."

"And what if we don't want *either* of you?" the same woman inquired.

"Well then, you don't have to vote," Mergis shot back. "You're free to vote for another, of course, but like I said, if we want to keep the gods at bay, then you'd be better served by one of us."

"Not the most conventional solution," said Shador, "but we have a rather unconventional problem." Finding Mergis, he added, "I can see why you kept the details from me at first. But given the situation," he continued, returning to the lords, "I'd be open to the idea of a regent if it would keep the pantheon from intruding into our affairs. And I'd rather have Mergis than one of the other gods trying to run things over us."

Mergis wasn't expecting such magnanimity. Though that didn't mean he entirely trusted or believed Shador. But still, the longer things played out in his favor, the better.

"Shador and I will both stand for regent. But if anyone else wishes to stand for consideration, now would be the time to make it known. The sooner we put our regent in place, the sooner we'll be protected from anything the pantheon might be planning."

The chamber exploded with voices as all sought to discuss the matter or put themselves forward for consideration in the vote. It reminded Mergis of an agitated beehive. Things couldn't have been going better for him. He just needed to keep subtly steering things in the desired direction, and everything would be just like he'd envisioned.

"Anyone who wishes to make their case, come forward, and let the vote begin." A handful did just that, these mostly Lords of Chaos—though none from the Anarchs—with a couple Lords of Darkness in their mix. There wasn't a worthy candidate among them, but Mergis would let the farce play out nonetheless.

"You seem to have most of your lords' backing," Mergis told Shador.

"They know a true leader when they see him, which doesn't seem to be the case so much for you and yours."

Mergis returned to the other candidates. "Each of you, step forward in turn, and those who side with them, raise your hand." Each did as ordered, looking back at the others over their shoulders and being dealt a humiliating blow. Of the multitude gathered, there came only a smattering of upraised hands for any candidate. Again, it was mainly a farce, but now none could say they didn't have an opportunity to make their voices heard.

When the last candidate stepped forward with only a few hands of support, Mergis reclaimed the floor. "It seems then the vote falls between Shador and myself. So who's for me?"

At this all the Lords of Chaos, except the Anarchs, raised a hand. The former confidence buoying Mergis' plan sank. Where were the Lords of Darkness? Lagella and Cirgin had doled out plenty of gold and promises. And without at least some of the Anarchs, he wouldn't be able to carry the vote. Worse still, when he took a careful second look, there were some Lords of Chaos whose hands had not been raised. A surprised Lagella and Cirgin shrugging their shoulders didn't help any either.

He'd been expecting a sweeping victory that would put any lingering doubts or unease at rest. A clear mandate would make things so much easier, but if he had only a thin margin to lay hold of, there was always the potential for disruption and Shador trying to push his way in. His only hope lay in Shador receiving a worse showing.

"I thank you for your confidence." Mergis accepted the vote, motioning for everyone's hands to return to their side. "And who says Shador?" All the Lords of Darkness, the Anarchs, and the remaining Lords of Chaos who hadn't yet voted raised their hands. It was a clear majority. It couldn't be denied.

"Thank you," said Shador, rising with a smugness Mergis wanted to rip from his lips.

He'd stepped right into Shador's game. Mergis had been the victim of the very scheme he'd attempted himself, but since Shador didn't look like the instigator, he therefore appeared less politically motivated and potentially dominating. Now, if Mergis ever tried to challenge him, he'd be seen as the aggressor and feared as the oppressor. The coup was brilliant in its cunning and execution, he'd give him that. Mergis swallowed the bitter sentiments and put on his best pretend smile. He still had a game to play—they both did—even if at the moment he felt like punching his colleague in the face.

"It seems we have our new regent." He placed his arm around Shador in what he hoped seemed like a genuine display of unity.

"I welcome your confidence," said Shador. "And I'll hold to what was proposed: a freedom from the pantheon's yoke we haven't known since before the rise of Vkar." This brought some wild applause from the crowd.

Using the noise as cover, Mergis leaned into Shador's ear. "You played the game well, but if you take things into ruin, you'll have to answer with both your blood and spirit."

Shador said nothing, merely lifted a hand in thanks to the cheering throng. None in the room noticed one of the shadows drift from the wall and slide toward the door . . .

• • •

Rilas sat on his throne, listening intently to the other Umbrian speaking in measured tones. ". . . And then they voted him the regent of Altearin."

"All of them did?"

"The majority did—Lords of Chaos and Darkness. I saw it with my own eyes."

"So they've made Shador regent." Rilas leaned back, letting the full weight of the words resonate in his mind and heart. "And Mergis just accepted it?"

"He did. The matter is closed between them."

"But not with the pantheon, I'm sure," he mused. No, that was another thing entirely. But with the addition of three new gods into their ranks, they'd most likely be distracted for some time, allowing Shador more room to set down roots and tighten his grip.

"I knew I had to come as soon as I could," the spy continued. "Any delay ran the risk—"

"You did well. And I will see you're rewarded. If there's nothing else, you may leave."

"Yes, my lord." The spy gave a bow and exited the throne room.

Rilas stepped down the dais even as he worked some darkness between his hands. When it had cleared, the metal disk Bron had given him earlier rested in his grasp. It felt heavier than before, more important now in so many ways.

Things had taken such a sudden turn since the titan's appearance; it was like the difference between dream and reality. But part of what Bron had said had come to pass. He couldn't deny it. His own spy had told him to his face: Shador was now regent of Altearin. Naturally, such news couldn't help but bring to mind the other part of what Bron had prophesied. Could he risk such a thing knowing Shador would now sit on Gurthghol's throne?

The emblem continued to hold his focus. He wasn't able to believe what it conveyed—that the supposed titan's master still lived—but he wasn't about to throw out the only offer to possibly help secure a new place in the cosmos in several millennia either. So it was he found himself speaking over the emblem with a less-than-convinced voice.

"I accept your offer."

There. He'd said it. And as part of him had suspected, nothing happened. Rilas gave a huff and returned to his throne. This didn't change the fact he still had to contend with Shador. In some ways it might have been easier if Mergis had arisen to be regent. A Lord of Chaos he might have been able to stomach. But a Lord of Darkness assuming power . . . Taking his seat, Rilas rested the metal disk on his lap and began mulling over all the various options he could fathom at his disposal.

"I trust you believe me now?"

Rilas, jolted, spun around to see Bron behind him, speaking the same accented Stygian.

"Who are you?"

"I told you. My name is Bron."

"And why pretend you're a Lord of Darkness?"

"There are more than just *your* eyes in Altearin." Bron circled around to stand a step below Rilas, immediately reinforcing their difference in height.

"Yet you seem to be one step ahead of all of us."

"And if you want to stop Shador from getting that scepter, you'll be wise to act now."

Rilas wasn't pleased with the circular argument that was ensuing. "I'd be wiser to know who I'm really working with. What's your master's real name? Who's behind all this?"

"You already know that."

"No, I don't."

"I've given you his crest."

"An old crest from someone long dead. I want the truth."

"Everything I've said has been the truth." Bron wasn't upset, but there was clearly the sense of growing tension. "You already know my master's name; that should suffice. But if you don't think it honorable enough, I can find someone else who will."

No, Rilas wasn't liking this one bit, but if it was an avenue to get an edge over Shador and the rest of his enemies, then he'd have to play the game.

"Fine," he sighed. "I'll humor you a little longer. Tell me about this scepter."

"Gladly." He could hear the smugness in Bron's voice. "It's something created to hinder the actions of divinities and other powerful beings long enough to give the wielder time to destroy them."

"How?" Rilas leaned forward.

"Through a spell placed upon it by its creator. I won't get into the specifics, but you can see where Shador getting his hands on such an item could be problematic for you."

Rilas could easily envision just that. Shador getting anything more than he already had was *more* than problematic; it was disastrous. The whole balance of power was already shifting and would continue to do so as news of what had taken place reached the ears of the rest of Altearin.

If he had the scepter, he could at least keep Shador in check, giving the regent something to ponder before trying to do anything against Rilas or his people.

"It might even give Gurthghol pause before doing anything too," he thought aloud, seeing the potential beyond just this present threat.

"*If* he returns," said Bron.

"Will he?"

"If you want to stop Shador, your window is rather narrow. He wouldn't wait long to savor his newfound success."

"Then how do we stop him?"

Rilas snatched a glimpse of the other's purple eyes sparkling with a sardonic mirth. "By helping him get what he wants."

• • •

"So how much coin did you spend?" Mergis questioned Shador in the nearly vacant chamber.

The celebration had ended. The congratulations, favor hunting, and politicking had been intense but thankfully brief.

"Apparently less than you did."

Shador had dismissed most of those assembled, keeping those who had a place of high rank or who were tied to other matters of importance so some quick logistics could be worked out before he could consolidate his place over the palace and bring a certain Karduin chamberlain into line.

"How long did you know?" Mergis continued.

"It's not important now. We have some rather significant work to do."

"So what's your first act as regent?" Shador had left the others with vague assurances and ideas for future discussion. Nothing solid or committal, but something they could chew on for a while. But Mergis wasn't so easy to placate, wanting more concrete commitments and plans.

"I think we need some time to mourn Gurthghol first," he replied, "before we move ahead with anything else."

"He's not dead," Mergis reminded Shador.

"No, but it's best we not jump to things too quickly," he advised. "We aren't playing to just the audience on Altearin, after all."

"Who will no doubt want to speak with you once word of your recent elevation reaches them."

"Yes." Shador watched Twila draw near. "Which is why we have to do this without any hint of unrest or trouble. Anything they see as a crack will have them looking to wedge themselves inside. I trust they won't find any such place between us." He took some pleasure in the brief pause the statement caused. Already things were falling into a tighter alignment than he could have hoped for.

"I meant what I said before," Mergis returned, taking his leave as Twila reached Shador's side.

"And what *did* he say before?" Twila inquired.

"Nothing of value." He watched Mergis mutter something to the two Lords of Chaos who were waiting for him before making their departure—Cirgin and Lagella, if memory served. Each a capable lieutenant to Mergis' will. He'd do well to keep tabs on them too.

"I have the position. That's all that's important for the moment." He returned to Twila's pleasant presence.

"So then this means you'll be making a certain announcement about our arrangement soon?"

"You won't be able to wield a great deal of power right away. Not when things are still as raw as they are now. But in time, as the new order sets in and the pantheon sees there's nothing they can do, I'll be able to take the next step and bring things fully into view." Shador watched Twila carefully. "I trust you can wait?"

She tugged playfully on his belt. "As long as you don't keep me from having all the fun, I can wait . . . for a little while longer."

• • •

Outside the reality that was called the cosmos there was yet another that few, if any, ever considered. And for those who called it home, that was just fine. For the Expanse was a place that preferred to be left on its own.

Free from so much of what had taken place over the millennia with the Thangarian Empire and the rise of the pantheon, the Lords of Space and the native inhabitants had found it a peaceful plane on which to live their lives. For neither the gods nor Awntodgenee and Nuhl gave it much notice.

So it was with no fear of detection that a lone figure gazed at the vast stretch of the dissolving cosmos called the Fade. The Expanse was a place of extremes but also of great power and knowledge if one knew how to look for and tap into it. All of the Expanse wrapped around the constantly growing cosmos, swelling with it and creating a disk-like plane in which one side was always blending into and growing out of the cosmos, and the other, outer, side was crumbling away and dissolving into the nothingness of the Void.

It was the meeting between the absolute emptiness of the Void and the bulging press of the Expanse that created the Fade. This final stretch of space was where the last pieces of reality disintegrated into the nothingness from which it all first arose. The result was a hazy sea of dust and debris populated by the fade whales, who scavenged these cosmic remains for sustenance.

The figure was silent in his contemplation, letting his long white hair flutter in the breezes of oblivion. While he was confident in his privacy, he still dressed as a Lord of Space, though it was clear with even a passing glance he lacked the golden complexion and other features of their kind. His olive skin made him appear more like the gods or titans of old than anything else.

A small chunk of ground a few yards away broke off and became a floating island. Even as it drifted like some tiny iceberg into the dark of the Fade, the Void's cruel maw was fast upon it, nibbling away and leaving a trail of dust like a ship's wake. Eventually even the dust would be dissolved and forgotten.

The figure heard the sound of Bron's footsteps from behind, but kept his focus where it was. "Three new gods have entered the cosmos," the white-haired figure told Bron.

"From birth or elevation?" asked Bron, who still remained clothed as a Lord of Darkness.

"From birth and Asora," said the first. "Two girls and one boy. Too young to be of much concern at present but something to watch in the future."

"Then the pantheon will be doubly distracted." Bron was pleased with the development. "That will make things even easier."

Both drew still as a large fade whale swam out of a thicker cloud of dust and swallowed some chunks of land whole. The massive beast's white-speckled black hide helped conceal it from sight. Only its white-tipped mouth was clearly visible at times. Though why it needed help concealing itself in a place devoid of any predators was a mystery. As was how they could survive in an environment so hostile to life, much less reality.

"I take it he's seen through your disguise by now?"

"Yes." Bron lowered his hood, revealing his golden skin and medium-length silver hair. His most striking feature was his purple eyes, which further strengthened his serious nature. "But it served its purpose. He won't expose me or your plans—not now."

"So he accepted the offer?"

"Yes, my lord."

"You did well, Bron."

"I merely pointed out the obvious. If he wanted to stay in power there was really little choice."

"And what of Shador?" He watched another small chunk of material break off and float away.

"Plotting for more power, like you said. Everyone is distracted, making it the perfect time to strike."

"And keep our actions hidden. I trust you made Rilas aware of that too?"

"He doesn't want to be found out any more than we do."

"My father used to say that taking hold of power was like grabbing a wolf by the ears. What he didn't say was there was always the threat of new pups arising to nip at your heels."

"I'm confident you'll have your scepter soon, my lord."

"I have every confidence I will. You've proven to be the most trusted and accomplished of all my court."

"It's an honor to serve."

"The pieces are finally starting to fall into place. In time all will be as it should and those who side with me will enjoy the fruitful rewards of the greater things to come."

"So be it, my lord," Bron said with obvious pride.

CHAPTER 11

Everything about what he was doing grated Rilas to his core, but he continued pushing himself onward. The sooner he finished all of this, the faster he'd be able to resume his previously cloistered life away from the titanic court.

He'd taken to a private room off the main hall where he had spent some time meticulously crafting a letter along the lines Bron had instructed. He appreciated its brevity; he might have been tempted to add a few choice words of his own, but thankfully, he'd been able to restrain himself and stick to the plan they'd agreed upon. While the ink was still drying, he lifted the parchment off the table and read it over one last time.

> *Rilas, prince of Ulan, to Shador, regent of Altearin.*
>
> *I wish to congratulate you on your recent elevation. Upon hearing of it, I wanted to express my appreciation for the fact that we'll not be ruled by someone outside our realm, which I'm sure we share an aversion to. I hope we can continue to have peace between our peoples.*
>
> *It has also come to my attention we could help each other even further when it comes to a special scepter you have set your*

eye upon. I'd be open to sharing what I know about it and helping you obtain it if you so wished. I have no interest in it myself, but do share the desire of having it rest in the right person's possession. I'm sure you've already considered the worst outcome if it is allowed to be seized by another.

I await your reply.

Yes, short, simple, and to the point, even if he'd lied throughout the entirety of the letter. Hopefully, Shador wouldn't see too much into that but rather would take hold of what he offered. Bron had assured him if he did this right, Shador's desire would work for him. He hoped that was true.

From what he knew of the plan, it was a simple-enough thing. But even simple things were prone to unforeseen complications. And he didn't want any complications. Not when he was taking a risk in just sending this letter. He was openly exposing himself and his city to Shador with the message, basically bringing himself into the light, so to speak. If Shador should refuse, they wouldn't be able to remain cloaked from his notice or any future wrath or any other means of interaction. It was a risk, yes, but the reward yielded a much greater payoff.

Satisfied, he rolled the parchment, then tied it with a black silk ribbon. It was time to get this over with. He'd used a larger piece of parchment than normal, but knew it would still be rather small in titanic hands. But it was the best he could do. Too much larger, and it would be harder to transport with the level of secrecy required.

With a steady stride he cleared the space between the table and the door to the hallway beyond. Opening the door, he startled the brown-furred Swarthin standing beside it. He was one of a handful Rilas kept on hand for various tasks, including spying on other parts of the realm.

"See that this gets to Lord Shador," he said, extending the roll of parchment to the messenger. The Swarthin was quick about his task, taking the scroll and swiftly moving through the lightless corridor. Rilas watched the progress for a few more breaths and then moved in the opposite direction down the hall.

The hallways in this part of the palace were sparsely populated. The occasional guard here or there making their rounds and the lone scribe or member of the inner court made their odd appearance, but for the most part Rilas was left to himself. Taking a right turn into a more narrow corridor, he came to a dead end. Rilas knew better.

He pressed in a section of the stone. A clicking noise from behind the wall was followed by the sound of something being unhooked or released. A section of the wall, large enough to allow for a doorway, popped out from the rest of the stone. The smooth, seamless manner in which it had been blended into the wall was a long-held secret . . . as was what was behind it.

Confirming he was still alone, he took hold of the exposed door with the tips of his fingers and pulled it open. Behind it was a darkness even denser than that of the rest of the palace. It was so dark, Rilas had to wait for his eyes to adjust before entering. He closed the hidden door behind him by means of a wrought iron handle affixed to the door's middle. It clicked shut effortlessly.

The room was only about twelve feet by twelve feet, with a matching twelve-foot ceiling. A smooth shelf ran near the top of three walls of the room, with the section holding the door lacking this fixture. On top of this shelf was an assortment of skulls. They were old and formed a macabre display. While a few were smaller than the rest, the bulk of them were large titanic skulls. Claimed in battles past when there was still a plane worth fighting for, they now served as a reminder of what all Umbrians had lost . . . but also what they desired to see returned.

To those who didn't know any better, it would have seemed Rilas had stepped into some grim trophy room. But it wasn't a hidden alcove for past glories; it was a shrine to what the Umbrians held as the greatest thing in their lives: the cosmic element of darkness itself. They had sprung from it like all the other darkened incarnates long ago, but unlike them, the Umbrians held true to the wellspring of their being.

While others had turned aside to titans and the later Lords of Darkness and then Gurthghol, they were free from such fictions of these new rulers being anything better for them or even beings worthy of worship. No, Rilas, like all Umbrians, held to the darkness. He was one with it, and it with him. From it they all came and to it they would once more return when the cosmos had finally run its course.

Rilas took a knee and bowed his head. "I have sided with the enemy to win our good. I only seek to secure our freedom," he addressed the specially concentrated darkness in the room.

It never spoke but was always listening. Always watching. Many Umbrians, Rilas among them, believed that at the proper time, when all was ready, the darkness would move into action, joining them in the restoration of all the things stolen from them. Until then, they had the skulls and past memories as touchstones—a steppingstone for their restored place and power.

"Once I have my opening, I'll make sure to do right by us and secure the better future we deserve. This I swear." He fell silent, not looking to anything else—nor saying anything else—only desiring to bask in the deep darkness in worship.

• • •

Khuthon sat in highest honor in the great arena on Kratos. Here, in his realm, surrounded by various administrators, Tularins, priests from some of the monstrous races, and others from mortalkind who'd once served him in life, the god of war watched the bloody feats of combat playing out one hundred feet below. The full day's light made for fine viewing. Those assembled had been cheering the contests since dawn.

The arena was massive and made of hard granite, reflecting the strength of the god it honored. Black banners fluttered from the arena's top, while a large one was draped from the special viewing box built for Khuthon and his chosen guests. Each banner depicted a round silver shield over which two blood-red falchions were crossed. The Steel Cross was the sacred emblem of Khuthon and thus displayed prominently across his domain.

The shouts and calls were deafening at times, but Khuthon wasn't the least bit bothered. He, like those around him—with the exception of the Tularins, who tended to shy away from such excessive displays of violence as a form of entertainment—was enraptured by the series of battles. Kratos wasn't like the other realms the gods ruled. Here position and place were achieved and kept by strength and the means to enforce said strength. Anyone could advance to any rank if they could vanquish the one who held the spot they coveted.

But as often as combat was engaged, no one was truly killed. One couldn't really die in the afterlife. Thanks to Vkar's decree, every soul-possessing spirit was immortal. And so while someone might get attacked and wounded to the point of what might seem like death, they were instead instantly revived on the bottom tier of both rank and station. This produced a strong drive to take back what was theirs, and so the whole process kept in place a never-ending cycle of challenge and rechallenge, which Khuthon saw as continuously honing those who entered his realm. One could always be better, even across the lengthy span of the afterlife.

All of Kratos was run with a militant mindset, which helped enforce the ideal of cohesive unity and an ideology of purpose. It might not be the best afterlife for many, but those who found their way here soon learned their place or were crushed under the heel of others seeking to make their own way over them. Compassion and pity weren't to be expected in Kratos, nor could one be too fond of peace. For constant vigil and preemptive strike were the common ways of life.

As entertaining as the fighting might have been, Khuthon wasn't paying close attention. His thoughts were on his newborn children and what would need to be done in the future. True, it wasn't going to happen right away, but soon enough the matter of where they would fit in the pantheon was going to come up—maybe even as early as the next time they met in council. When it did, it would force all the gods to take a hard look at a process Khuthon knew only too well from having lived through it before—both with himself and then with the children who followed him and his siblings.

None of the gods would be willing to share what they had already gained, and there wasn't enough left in the old empire or planes to suit all three comfortably. Not without having to make some arrangements first. But those arrangements could cause still more trouble and discontent. And so it went. No matter how he viewed it, he knew it was far from pleasant. And this was if his children sought to be fair and not covetous. If they followed the pattern taken by the rest of the gods, they'd be taking on at least two areas of dominion, maybe more. Maybe one of them might be more esoteric, like Causilla or Dradin, but that was the deviation, not the norm.

While it might have been nice to contemplate such ideas, his gut told him they'd most likely follow in the steps of the rest of the pantheon, which meant there'd be a competition for more resources, power, and space. He was starting to understand how his father must have felt when he considered his own ever-increasing brood.

When Khuthon had been younger, he didn't have much attraction to such things. Like his forefathers before him, he craved the conquest of land and territories. But now, as the years had seasoned him, he'd come to learn the benefits of latching on to a realm while he could, perhaps even sharing it with Vearus if it came to that, and in the very least having a larger hold on things himself to stand in greater honor among the rest of the pantheon.

He was the leader of the Dark Gods now, and it was only fitting he should have such honor to go with the rank—no matter how temporary it might be. And there was the open realm of Altearin. Could he really turn back such a tempting prize? And the realm was really the formation of two planes and one planet, which he could spin off, he supposed, and give his children if needed. Yes, so many possibilities . . . but what was the right angle to get there?

The battles ahead would be more political than martial. He would need to be wise in the steps to come lest he get himself too tightly bound in a corner to do any good. He already was dealing with more than one project he wanted to keep from the pantheon. There was no sense in being too aggressive in the beginning. Better to press hard but patiently for the time being—use the current climate as much to his advantage as possible.

A great roar shook Khuthon from his pondering. The shout had risen on account of a giant who had just fallen in battle to a bloodied goblin. Normally such a sight would have been comedic, as the goblin was only a third his opponent's size. But in Kratos if one was bold enough to start a fight, one saw it through. And no challenge, once given, was refused. Such a thing would only show weakness and just invite more challenges in its place.

Naturally, the goblins were more taken with the matter than others, celebrating the victory from where they were stationed across the arena. Their green skin helped them stand out amid the other shades of flesh. The giants, for their part, didn't know what to make of it other than jeering the result. That one so small could have bested one of their brothers served to prove how weak the other was. That didn't mean he'd have to stay in such a defeated state, but any new position would have to be earned anew and with a more determined giant in the process, they knew.

"Seems you have a new captain of mining." This was spoken by a porcelain-skinned, red-haired Jotun named Korlin.

Khuthon watched two other giants carry the defeated one's body from the sand as the bloodied and bruised goblin, arms raised, continued cheering his success. "If he knows how to improve the output and quality, he'll be a welcome addition."

"I'm sure he'll be eager to prove himself," Korlin returned.

"No doubt." Khuthon's attention was directed to another giant making his way into the box. This giant was from the first stock Khuthon had created, before the race had split and formed its various groups in the ensuing millennia. He was fair skinned with black hair. His light blue eyes were fixed on Khuthon. Like all on Kratos, he appeared as he did at the prime of his life, youthful and healthy.

"I was told you wished to speak with me, Majesty?"

"Have a seat, Kala." Khuthon directed him to an empty chair beside his more ornate throne-like seat. Kala did as invited.

In his order of things, Khuthon had a special place for Kala, one of the first to find his way to Kratos, setting him apart as the commander of his mounted warriors. That place wasn't guaranteed, of course, but he'd managed to put down challengers long enough that none had dared contest his place for decades.

"I heard you had a strong son. I'm sure that made you proud." Kala had come directly from the stables. Khuthon could smell the griffins on him, but didn't mind. There wasn't anywhere else Kala would be if not seeing to the creatures or training his men. Khuthon did notice how clean his half-plate armor was. He'd no doubt even the sword at his side was well oiled and sharp. He expected nothing less from those who served him.

"He'll make a fine man one day. And I suppose his two sisters, fetching maidens in their own right."

"Just more prestige to add to yourself when suitors come calling," said Kala.

"Perhaps . . ." Another massive shout shook the arena as a new battle began. This one pitted two ogres against each other. Each was naked save for a breechcloth and armed only with a morning star. And neither wasted any time in putting it to use.

"The men have all recovered and are doing well," Kala continued. "Soon enough the battle on Thangaria will be only a memory."

"As it should be. I've already been informed of the losses, and their places have been filled." Shifting to face Kala straight on, Khuthon added, "I trust you've heard the other news about Gurthghol."

"I don't think there's anyone on Kratos who doesn't know by now. Such a matter is hard to keep to oneself."

"I suppose it is. Which is why the sooner we act, the better. I want you to take a small group of riders to Altearin." Even with his ironclad discipline, Khuthon could still see a pinch of surprise peek out of Kala's features. "You're to be my delegation."

"I'd be honored to lead it, of course, but what right would we have to enter into another realm uninvited?"

"You're to inform those of Altearin of my elevation to leader of the Dark Gods. It's fitting they should know it as soon as possible, before they could get too many ideas in their heads and before news of Gurthghol's absence blankets the realm."

Kala nodded. "I assume you wish us to scout out the land en route?"

"That goes without saying." Kala had served for so long, he was right in step with Khuthon's thinking. There were others in his administration who were of the same mold, and he always sought to keep them close at hand, but none were as finely tuned to his own mindset as Kala. "But I trust you can keep it measured, as it needs to be. We don't want to rouse too many concerns at the moment."

"Are we to look for anything in particular?"

"Tell your men to keep an eye out for anything strange."

Kala raised an eyebrow. "Strange in Altearin?"

"Things relating to Gurthghol in particular," Khuthon clarified. "I don't fully believe my dear brother hasn't left a surprise or two that might need dealing with sooner or later. And who knows what that leadership is plotting. We've already given them plenty of opening by sending that Tularin earlier. Report back as soon as your visit has been completed."

Kala stood and brought his right fist over his heart. "As you command, Your Majesty. I'll make preparations to depart at once."

Khuthon shifted his attention back to the fight as Kala made his exit. The two ogres were still holding their own rather nicely. Each seemed the equal of the other, no matter how bloodied and marred the pounding of the morning stars' spiked balls had made their bodies. But there could be only one victor—the strong—who would always rule over the weaker by the strength of that might. It was so in the arena and in life, and the sooner one embraced this truth, the better off and further along they'd be—god, divinity, and mortal alike.

• • •

Shador let his black robe hang loose. The belt kept it from falling completely open, allowing him to concentrate on other matters. He'd risen earlier than usual for the day, making sure Twila would continue sleeping for a few more hours while he took care of some business in his private study. He needed time to think things through. The first part of his plan went smoother than he'd thought possible, but that was just the start. He had much more to do. He also desired some freedom from Twila's eyes for a while.

She'd made it clear she was hungry for more of a place in all this, but it wasn't yet the time for that. Not until he had secured the scepter. Until then he had to keep up appearances—move slowly and wisely. Perhaps *too* slowly for Twila's tastes. But she'd have to keep her desires curbed until everything was secure and he was in a position where none could successfully challenge him.

While he'd taken command of Altearin, he'd still have to come to terms with Erdis. Shador was hoping he could be satisfied with running the palace and overseeing the court in many ways, like he had been already. The only difference would be they'd be working together until Gurthghol's return. In time he'd be able to subtly turn that around so the chamberlain was reporting to him as head of all, but it was wiser to give the Kardu some slack in the reins for the interim.

There was a faint knock at the door.

"Enter." He watched a brown-furred Swarthin make his way inside. He didn't look like one of his. Perhaps he was tied to the capital.

"I have a message for you."

A warding hand told the Swarthin he'd gotten close enough. "From who?"

"I was only told to give it to you directly. The rest will be made clear." The other held up a rolled parchment. Shador simply stared at both it and the Swarthin. "I was told to make sure you received it and then ask for your reply so I can return it to the one who sent me."

"And who sent you?" Shador raised an eyebrow.

"It's in the letter."

"All right." Shador straightened himself. "I'll humor you." He extended his hand.

The Swarthin placed the parchment into his grasp. It was smaller than what the titans used, but it worked. He undid the black ribbon keeping it shut and set to reading the contents. And what a strange collection of words they were. He almost didn't want to believe them—yet here they were in permanent black ink.

"Seems your prince has been busy spying on matters that aren't his concern," he said at last.

"I wouldn't know anything about that. I'm just here to deliver the message and pass on your reply."

"So you have no idea what this says?"

"No." The other remained stoic. "I'm loyal to my prince."

"Which is, no doubt, why he sent you. And where does this Rilas rule *from*? Where is this Ulan located?"

"I'm not permitted to say, only to ask you if you accept my lord's offer." There was a sense of duty that flowed from the Swarthin. Such things were hard to mimic, though it could be done—his own behavior with Mergis and others in the court being a strong example. But it wasn't something commonly feigned among the Swarthin.

"But he's not a titan, I take it? The letter is too small and the writing slightly different from what you'd normally see in such things."

"He's an Umbrian," said the Swarthin.

"I see. Then you'll forgive me if I have some trouble trusting an Umbrian." Shador tried to keep his commentary as mild as possible. What he really thought on the matter wasn't the most diplomatic. And right now this encounter was in need of the proper verbal finesse.

"Then you're turning down the offer?" He couldn't tell if the Swarthin was upset, sad, or indifferent.

Shador considered the letter again, peering through what was said in as many ways as possible. If this Rilas really did know of his plans—plans no one else knew of—then if anything, it would be wise to at least meet with him and find out what else he might know and how he came about it. It wouldn't do having his intentions exposed before he even began achieving them.

"You can tell your prince I'd be open to meeting him. Alone. It would have to be a neutral spot, far enough from his city and the capital that each of us can be assured privacy and protection from the other."

The Swarthin bowed. "I'll relay your message."

"And tell him I don't have time for games. If he means what he said, then we can talk. Otherwise, he'd be unwise to risk losing my patience— especially now that I'm regent of Altearin."

The Swarthin quietly saw himself out of the study. Once he was sure he was alone, Shador returned to the letter, reading every word slowly. If this was all true, things had taken a very interesting and beneficial turn. Only he didn't believe in coincidences—especially after all of the recent events he'd just survived. But if any of this helped bring him closer to the scepter, he needed to explore every option. He couldn't afford missing any opportunity while so much was still in play.

"Riders from Kratos have been spotted, my lord!"

It took a moment for Shador to register the news. He'd been so engrossed in the letter and his planning, he hadn't even realized how much time had passed. It was well into late morning when the Lord of Darkness had hurriedly entered the room.

"Kratos . . ." Shador let the word slowly drip from his lips. First Rilas and now Kratos. Were they connected? Or were they just another coincidence in a growing string of them?

"Griffin riders, I'm assuming." Khuthon wouldn't send foot soldiers. That might send the wrong message. And griffins were faster.

"Yes." The other kept his place by the door. "They recently arrived through a portal outside the capital and are making their way to the palace."

"How many?" Shador did his best at keeping the swirling sensation in his gut from increasing. He knew there was going to be an encounter at some point, of course, but to have it finally stare you in the face was another thing entirely. At the same time he was glad he found himself in his new position. If he'd waited any longer to claim his regency . . .

"Twenty-five in all."

Instantly, his stomach calmed. "The perfect number for a delegation. And where are they exactly?"

"About a quarter hour from the palace, I'd wager, given what I last heard. I came to tell you as soon as I could."

"And you did well. They're not attempting to be stealthy and they don't have the numbers to do any real harm. So they want to talk or make some sort of show, I suppose. Which means we're going to need a similar presentation to greet them. I trust some of our own troops are shadowing them?" He made sure to keep himself the very image of confidence and calm rationality.

"Of course," said the other. "A squad of Swarthin are doing just that."

The more he heard, the better he liked his chances. This could be just what he needed to finish solidifying his position and shoring up his base. Once again timing was seemingly on his side.

"Then all that remains is to summon Mergis and the rest of the court. I trust you can do that promptly?"

"Yes, my lord. I will inform them you require their presence immediately."

"To meet another delegation," added Shador. "Don't leave that part out. It's sure to motivate Mergis. The others maybe not so much, but they should know what's taking place. We need to be on the same page from the start. It'll make us all the stronger in our united front."

Shador waved his hand. "Tell them to meet me in the palace, and I'll share everything with them then." Shador watched the titan lord fade into darkness.

A twisting motion of his right hand sent the parchment he'd been holding into a special pocket of darkness where he could retrieve it later. This done, he made his way from the study even as he conjured suitable raiment from the cosmic element. He wouldn't have time to properly dress for his guests. Even as he faded from sight, his mind raced for the right words and tone for what he was going to tell the others and the delegation. Everything had to be just right. He only had one chance to make an impression. And it needed to be a memorable one at that . . .

CHAPTER 12

Kala was at the lead of twenty-four griffin-mounted giants flying into Altearin's thick atmosphere. True to his duty, he'd called for the best men for the mission and mounted up once leaving Khuthon's side. He knew this wasn't something to waste any time on, for it was obvious Khuthon had a deep desire to see the matter done. Kala wouldn't disappoint.

They had made use of the portal slightly farther away from the capital, allowing them to see the lay of the land en route. It also allowed others in the city to properly know of their arrival and have it look less like a precursor to some invasion and truer to the diplomatic nature of the mission. And in keeping with that mindset, they made sure to keep their flying measured and path direct. Slow and steady, with nothing to hide: the perfect example of peaceful intent.

Kala, like the rest with him, came from the first generation of giants that walked Tralodren. The others possessed fair skin and light eyes with brown or blond hair, contrasting Kala's black locks. Each wore half-plate, carried a sword at their side, and had a shield emblazoned with the Steel Cross on their back. The last two of their party also carried black banners with a red Steel Cross clearly displayed for all to see. Another mark of their intentions and purpose made visible to all they met.

"Keep a tight formation," he barked over the wind.

As the purple-hued clouds finally cleared, the giants drew closer to the bizarre sight that was the realm of the god of chaos and darkness. It was an overcast world quite in contrast to Kratos, which resembled Kala's idea of a normal planet, much like the Tralodren he'd known before his death. He was careful to take note of all he could, being mindful as well to not look like a scouting party if he could help it. It was a delicate line he was called to walk in all this, but he knew he wouldn't have been entrusted with the task if Khuthon didn't think he could get it done. And it was that confidence that kept him focused, for he wanted to validate his god's trust.

"Keep an eye out for the palace," he ordered his men. "We should be getting close."

"I don't see any escorts," said a giant on his left. "Do we just keep on to the palace?"

"For now," said Kala. It wasn't a normal practice to let strangers have free rein of your skies, but this wasn't a normal place, and these weren't normal times either. With Gurthghol missing, who knew what sort of disorder and disarray might be churning beneath them.

"Capital in sight, sir." Another giant pointed at the massive walls and buildings seemingly rushing to greet them.

"Still no escort," repeated the first giant who'd spoken.

"We head for the palace," returned Kala. "No deviations."

It was hard to miss Gurthghol's palace. It rose in the midst of the capital like some great mountain. The black stone was assembled into an unsettling shape Kala had a hard time describing, let alone contemplating. Even as he took it in, seeking a place to land and dismount, he could swear it seemed to shift and shiver ever so slightly out of the corner of his eye, as if it was molding and remolding itself just on the outside of his peripheral vision.

"We'll land there." He pointed to an open area that was like a combination of ledge and balcony on the southern side of the palace. It was the perfect spot for them and their griffins. It was also a defendable position should things take a bad turn.

Leading his men into the pattern for a group landing, Kala guided his griffin down. He steered it into a smooth encounter with the open balcony's black marble floor. His griffin's front talons clicked on the polished stone as it came to a standing rest, flapping its brown wings with a mighty gust before folding them beside its leonine body. After rider and mount had surveyed their surroundings, Kala dismounted. The rest of his men mirrored his actions.

"No swords unless absolutely necessary." He eyed a set of double doors about twenty yards from their position, also of black stone. He could discern little else about them other than they were solid and closed. "Stay ready. If we need to act, it will come quickly."

"Five of you stay with the mounts," he instructed the two standard-bearers and the three giants closest to them. "The rest come with me, block formation," he continued, stepping forward.

The rest fell into a formation of five rows of four men each, stepping in time with each other and Kala, who was part of the first row.

"Still no escorts," another from behind Kala murmured.

"Stay focused."

The closer he got, Kala could see how the doors were easily twenty feet tall and fifteen feet wide. Once again he found himself doubting his senses, as he was sure the geometric pattern carved into them was twisting and moving in subtle gradations. He couldn't prove it, but there was just this suspicion that it was moving, even if it wasn't. How he knew this was beyond him, but he was certain of it nonetheless.

The lack of an escort was one thing, but to be so close and now actually inside the palace and not meet even some sort of token resistance or greeting set him on edge. If this were Kratos, there would have been troops ready to confront them before they could land—even greeting them at the portal when they arrived. He was hoping to see some guards on the balcony or have someone rush out to meet or try to detain them. But as they neared the door, the less likely it seemed that was going to happen.

The lack of any sort of defense, or even an escort, showed either utter contempt for Kala, his men, and Khuthon, on whose behest they had come, or the general disarray that was already taking root across the realm in Gurthghol's absence. But then, when he'd gotten just a few yards from the great doors, they opened, spilling out light from lanterns held aloft by two Centaurs. As one, the giants came to a halt, hands instinctively falling to the pommels of their swords.

Of all the denizens that called Altearin home, Kala thought the Centaurs were the least bizarre. Part horse and man, they were about half the height of the gigantic commander and his men and given to shaving their heads, leaving a stripe down the middle of their scalps. He supposed it could be seen as mane-like in design but didn't really know the exact reasoning for their efforts. The ones before him were both male with fair skin, brown hair, and black horse bodies, which they'd painted with geometric patterns and other images Kala couldn't readily decipher.

Each also wore a silver cuirass. They preceded a collection of Lords of Chaos and Darkness as a sort of honor guard, and a group of well-armed Swarthin formed a circle around a single hooded Lord of Darkness in the company's midst. If these were meant to be bodyguards, they were laughable, given their height compared to the one they defended.

The only real danger would come from the titan lords, who had a couple of feet on the giants. But none of the ten gathered—five Lords of Darkness, five Lords of Chaos—carried any weapon or seemed the faintest bit interested in starting a fight. But things could change, and quickly.

He was pleased to see each of the lords was wearing their regalia, which was adopted for official purposes and encounters. Yet another indication they would treat Kala's visit as a diplomatic visit. The Lords of Chaos wore silver cuirasses and matching bracers, half capes, and diadems crafted out of pure amethyst. The Lords of Darkness were garbed in dark robes and cloaks, each with an onyx diadem studded with black diamonds.

"And what does Khuthon wish of Altearin?" This was asked by the Lord of Darkness encircled by Swarthin.

He'd spoken in Titan, which was the more common tongue for doing this sort of business. Kala spoke it well. It wasn't the most respectful way to greet a delegation, but it was practical, Kala supposed. He didn't follow things outside of Kratos enough to know who this titan might be. He didn't really need to. As long as he was able to complete the mission, that was all that mattered.

"Khuthon, lord of Kratos, has sent us to deliver a message. He has been elevated to the position of new leader of the Dark Gods." There was a momentary murmuring among the other titan lords.

"So he usurps Gurthghol's throne in the council and now seeks his seat over Altearin as well?" asked the same titan lord. The confrontational tone wasn't totally unexpected, but there was something else behind it Kala couldn't place. As if the other titan lords were together on something just eluding the giant's perception. He didn't like it.

"No," replied Kala as modestly as he could, "but he does stand ready to aid those who might need it in this time of turmoil for Altearin." It was a safe answer and kept him in line with Khuthon's wishes. He'd served long enough to know a great deal of his preferences and ways. Yet another matter while the Mighty One trusted him so.

"What did I tell you?" the same lord asked the rest of his entourage. "You see how the pantheon has already thrown away Gurthghol and, without any regard for us, sends this delegation to offer what I'm sure will soon be a convenient excuse to invade." The tone had grown harder. But for now it was just an edge in his words. Kala still saw no weapons among them. Though titan lords didn't need any actual physical weapons to cause harm. They could wield the very cosmic element they mastered however they saw fit. Kala and his men, however, weren't so blessed.

"I can't speak for the pantheon," said Kala, "just for my lord. And the Mighty One wished for me to come and tell you as soon as we were able."

"So you could spy on the realm, is that it?" Again the same titan lord addressed the other titans, as if all were sharing some sort of inside joke.

Kala managed to extinguish the few embers such words tried stoking to life, keeping his focus on his mission, which also called for getting as much information as possible. It was time to take more ground on that front.

"And who are you to make such claims?" Though the question had a point, it wasn't as sharp as it could have been.

"Shador." The Lord of Darkness pulled back his hood just enough to allow his amethyst eyes to stare hard and sure into Kala's. "The regent of Altearin."

"Regent?" Kala didn't know if he'd heard that right. "I know there should be some viceroys, and then a chamberlain, but only Gurthghol ruled Altearin."

"Until he returns I'll be keeping the realm safe." Shador was too self-assured for Kala's liking. This wasn't right. He could see the wisdom in Khuthon acting as quickly as he did. If they had come any later, this Shador might have been able to dig in his roots even deeper, making it all the harder for his lord to take action. Not that Khuthon would have ever shied away from any challenge . . .

"I see." Kala could feel the tension among his men growing.

"This is far from a rebellion." Shador read Kala's mind. "A majority vote carried the matter. Something the pantheon will appreciate, I'm sure."

"Did they now?" Kala asked flatly.

"Yes. It was fair and open, and the vote elevated me above my fellow viceroy." Shador quickly raised a hand. "With the understanding that it's only temporary until Gurthghol's return. Make sure you mention that part when you tell your master the news."

"I will. And I'm sure he'll hold you to it."

Kala tried studying the rest of the delegation. Speaking wasn't the only way to get information. But none of them provided anything useful. They were solidly beside and behind Shador and his claims. Which meant they were either fully committed or had been made to seem so by threats or cajoling. Not giving up, he tried mining what he could from Shador's cloaked features. Still nothing.

"Was that all he wanted, your master?" Shador asked, motioning to Kala's men. "Twenty-five armed giants to deliver a message?" he continued, stepping forward. The Swarthin went with him, so that he stood across from Kala with only one Swarthin between them. The bat-like incarnate did little to block them staring each other down.

"Why not send a Tularin?" asked Shador. "The pantheon managed that well enough earlier with news of Gurthghol's capture."

Kala wasn't looking for any diplomatic shadow boxing. "We didn't come for a fight."

"Then you're free to go." Shador gave a sweeping gesture as if Kala and the rest were rubbish in need of being cleared away. "And you can tell your master Altearin will be well seen to. I'm only here to keep things from falling apart. I'll make sure it remains for Lord Gurthghol—in one piece—and free from any other outside interference."

The implications were clear, but Kala pressed anyway. "My men and I have come a long way. Usually it's customary to offer a brief respite—some refreshment and—"

"Forgive me," said Shador, interrupting. "But I have no intention of letting you see or hear more than you already have. You've already seen enough to give Khuthon a fair report. He won't fault you for that. I simply ask you return to the same portal from which you came, using the exact same route."

Kala's jaw clenched. The refusal was an insult to them all, as well as Khuthon. If he wasn't intent on being so diplomatic, he would have had his sword in hand and strongly encouraged this would-be regent to reconsider his words.

"I thank you for your time, Lord Shador." Kala spun on his heel. The men behind him parted so he could pass between them before re-forming and following after him.

This wasn't something he was expecting to find, but Kala had been able to get a general gist of this new leader and could see for all his boasting, he was still weak and on some levels fearful of a coming invasion. All this, he knew, would be of interest to Khuthon. All the more reason to return to Kratos immediately. Taking to their griffins, the gigantic company departed from the balcony and returned to the purple-cast sky. He made a direct exit this time, knowing whose eyes were watching him.

"We follow our previous path," he told the others.

None said anything, and wouldn't until they reached the portal to Kratos. As they flew he worked on the wording of his report. It needed to be precise as well as concise. The Mighty One wasn't one to suffer empty jabbering and embellishment. As he flew he studied the same things he'd seen before, confirming previous observations as best he was able. He wasn't about to leave anything out if he could help it.

• • •

"Do you think that was wise?" Mergis asked Shador. The two of them joined the others watching Khuthon's delegation shrinking in the sky.

"Wiser than giving them more excuse to size up anything else," said Shador. "I can't keep them from gaining anything from their flight—they can have the terrain—but I'm not going to give them anything else." Facing Mergis, he continued, "You can see how Khuthon wasted no time in taking Gurthghol's seat for himself. It's just another small step to claim his realm too. But thankfully, we've a check to his aggression."

Shador was impressed at how rapidly everyone had appeared and taken their place in their own delegation. It actually felt like they were a united body with just enough pomp and circumstance to lend a real air of legitimacy to the encounter. And it worked on several levels, giving him a preview of what was possible for future events and encounters that would be coming, now more surely than ever.

"You think he'll make a repeat visit?" asked Myrin, an older Lord of Darkness.

"I think he'll try, but won't be able to do more than what just happened if we all keep united in our goal of a free Altearin."

"So what do we do now?" asked Cirgin.

"We keep doing what we have been doing," said Mergis. "Solidify our gains, and keep our focus on staying free from any external rule." He gave Shador a once-over, adding, "Or *internal* rule, whichever the case might be."

"I can understand your disappointment in losing the vote," said Shador, "but I have no other designs on taking or doing anything more than what I've been elevated to do." He hoped it sounded convincing; he almost believed it himself.

"I meant what I said earlier," said Mergis. "I'll be watching you."

"I think everyone will now. The pantheon most of all."

CHAPTER 13

As with many things associated with the god of war, Khuthon's throne room was an aggressive display of both strength and domination over all who sought entrance. Hard stone walls stood watch over the space they enclosed, keeping the high ceiling at bay. Sconces resembling upturned shields were pounded halfway into the stone of the walls. Lining these walls was an assortment of black banners sporting his mark, intermingled with marble statues of titanic and other warriors, weapon displays, and even a few trophies Khuthon had plundered from victories in battle.

All this paled before his throne. The red marble sat on a five-step granite dais and was polished to give the impression Khuthon was seated upon fresh blood. Here too continued the themes of hard lines and domination. Worked into the throne's back were jutting spears. The two at either end of the back were the tallest, the ones between lowering in progression and thereby crafting a valley of points behind the god's head.

Behind the throne was another large black banner, flowing from ceiling to floor and flanked by two large tapestries. Each of these expressed a pivotal time in Khuthon's life. The first displayed him taking his place as ruler of all Kratos when he came into the full power and authority he presently enjoyed. The second, oddly enough, showed him marrying Asora. It was the most subdued and peaceful-looking object in the entire room.

Khuthon kept his eyes on the doors as he awaited Kala's report. They resembled strong barricades more than a simple means of entrance and egress. Tall and wide enough to grant access to all who called Kratos home, they were guarded by two Anakim. Each of the brown-skinned, charcoal-gray-haired giants was dressed in half-plate with a long sword strapped to their side and a halberd in their right hand. In their left was a round shield, with the Steel Cross for their crest.

Just as he was about to ask what was taking Kala, the doors flung open. Both god and giant alike watched Kala stride into the chamber. He'd come alone, not even bothering to attempt to make himself more presentable after his ride. It was clear he didn't want to waste a moment. Khuthon approved.

"I see you and your men had a safe journey. Did you make sure my message was clear?"

"I did." Kala stopped a few yards from the dais and bowed from his waist. The height difference between them allowed Khuthon to loom large over the other for an even greater effect in demonstrating his dominance over the room.

"Altearin knows you are now head of the Dark Gods. But there is something else you should know: they've sought to replace Gurthghol in his absence."

"What?" Khuthon's brow furrowed and eyes narrowed. He'd been expecting many things, but not that.

"A Lord of Darkness named Shador has been elected to rule in Gurthghol's place as regent until Gurthghol's return."

"Shador." Khuthon ground the name between his teeth.

"You know him?"

"He's one of Gurthghol's viceroys—or was," he replied. "And it seems he hasn't learned his lesson from meddling in affairs beyond him." Kala was obviously lost on the reference.

"Shador started a cult on Tralodren," he explained. "Rheminas informed me before he brought an end to it. We can only allow so much before things spread too far and greater measures are needed. I see now it would have been better to start with the harsher measures and save ourselves having to deal with this."

"I would have sought to press for more, but—"

"No." Khuthon's expression lightened with his tone. "You did the right thing. And I can use this as another pretext when the next council convenes. You did well."

Kala took pleasure in Khuthon's praise.

"He said he was elected, but were there any signs of a coup?"

"No. There was nothing we could see while flying in and out."

"Did he say exactly how he came into his new position?"

"I've told you everything I was told, Mighty One. He was elected to the position and appeared to have the people of Altearin behind him."

"And you believed him?"

"He didn't give me any reason to doubt, and they made a strong show of unity as well."

"Which means he's already fearful he's going to lose his place." Khuthon was searching, checking for any weakness or opening. He had to have a strong case if he wanted to work things in his favor. There were already things in play he didn't want to risk hindering and so had to work everything smoothly and wisely. He didn't want to fight any more wars than were needed.

"What of the land? What did you see?"

"I saw almost nothing of note." Kala sighed. "Some villages and towns along the way—but all seemed as normal as possible for Altearin."

"So he's been working hard," Khuthon mused. "I wonder how fast Shador had to push everything along to be so entrenched. I told them we should have never sent that Tularin with the news about Gurthghol."

"Even the portal was run smoothly," said Kala. "And there were no additional troops assembled in any way that we could see."

"Peacefully elected," Khuthon muttered. "I don't believe it for a minute. But I don't have to. It's the pantheon who are going to have to make the final decision. I'll do my best to inform them on the matter. Was there anything else?"

"No, Mighty One. I wanted to report as quickly and accurately as I could as soon as we landed."

"You've done well, Kala. Take your rest until I have need of you again."

"I'm honored to have served." Kala brought his fist over his heart in salute and then left the god of war to his scheming.

Shador was clever. He'd give him that. But he wasn't innocent—there were still charges he'd have to answer for, and this could work out well in Khuthon's favor. Soon enough the renegade titan lord would fall, and Khuthon would be ready to sweep in and claim his spoils.

• • •

Shador had finally cleared away Mergis and the rest who had joined him in meeting Khuthon's delegation and was looking forward to a visit to Gurthghol's throne room. He thought it a fitting reward after what they'd just won: the first skirmish against the pantheon. But no sooner had he opened the massive doors and stepped inside than he was greeted by a less-than-pleased Erdis.

The Kardu seemed almost out of place amid the collection of titanic marble statues standing along the long walls leading up to Gurthghol's throne. In between these stone warriors were a series of purple banners, each with the Black Sun displayed in black.

Here the light was more pronounced, allowing a full view of the grand splendor of the place. This was achieved through a series of skylights and then some hanging globes of white light that had been arranged into various configurations via silver scrollwork, creating truly unique chandeliers.

"Seems you've had a busy day." Erdis crossed his arms. "A delegation makes its way here from Kratos, and you don't even tell me?"

"It's not like that." Shador closed the doors, ensuring what came next was as private as possible.

"No. You took the rank of regent too," Erdis continued. "Again without any consultation. I thought we had an understanding."

"We do." He cleared the distance between them. "It was Mergis who started this off by calling for a meeting—"

"Which you also kept me from."

"Mergis. Not me." He made sure to stress that point. "I didn't set anything up and was as surprised as you when I learned what he was planning. We didn't speak about any of it—he simply put it for a vote, and the lords elected me. If anything, you should be speaking with *him* about all this."

"I will in time," said Erdis. "But since you've taken over as regent, it seemed you were the proper first choice—especially after meeting that delegation."

"I trust you can understand the delicate nature of the matter," he started. "It all happened so fast. I needed to act quickly."

"Or rather, impulsively," scolded Erdis. "From what I've heard so far, you were rather blunt—even insulting. You know how Khuthon might receive that? And if he *is* the new leader of the Dark Gods, we don't need him riled up already against us. There's plenty to keep us busy as it is."

"My apologies, I obviously got a little lost in things. I should have told you about the vote sooner. I was going to relay it before the delegation, but then that turned things around."

"And you never thought to contact me?" Erdis raised an eyebrow. "You found time to reach out to Lord Mergis and some other lords but not me. Yet when I was approached with news from the pantheon I immediately reached out to both you *and* Lord Mergis. And *he* was prompt in his reply."

"You're right." Shador sighed. Erdis had him, plain and simple. He might as well own up and move on as best he was able. "I let some things slip that I shouldn't. I guess, in a way, I didn't want to burden you with too much, given the situation."

"I'm not afraid of any burden," said Erdis. "I'm only doing what I'm supposed to do."

"And that's very honorable," Shador countered gently, "but in order to keep things running as they should, there needs to be one head over the whole administration. I'm sure you can understand that."

Erdis said nothing. Shador rushed to fill the silence. "I'm not looking to do anything out of order, but with Gurthghol gone—"

"You took matters into your own hands, I know. We both know what happened, Shador." There wasn't any anger in his tone, but Shador couldn't help but wonder what the Kardu was thinking while he said it.

"Do we?" he cautiously inquired.

"A good chamberlain endeavors to be always well informed." The last comment stirred up fresh concerns, causing him to wonder if Erdis might know about his desire for the scepter or even his recent dealings with Rilas.

"Are you implying something I should be aware of?" Shador prodded as respectfully as he could.

"I serve Gurthghol," Erdis made clear. "And that means I watch over his palace and his estate. I also see to the matters of court."

"All of which you could still do while I'm seated as regent. And with a regent we can keep the pantheon from claiming the throne for themselves. This way one of our own can watch over things."

Erdis remained unimpressed. "You still need some polish if you're going to keep your crown."

"And we still need unity to make this all work," he replied. "I need a partner to hold things together. You can keep doing all you've done before. We'll work together—you and I and Mergis—like you said before. All of us will help keep back the pantheon and any other challenges until Gurthghol's return."

"I have your word on that?" Erdis' gaze was strong and stern. "And you'll keep me informed of everything else from now on?"

"Yes and yes." Shador felt safe committing to as much. He could always define the finer details in greater depth later.

Erdis appeared satisfied. "Then we might be able to work together."

"I'm happy to hear it. I hope we won't have to keep it up longer than needed. I'd like to think Gurthghol will be back soon."

"Let's hope so," Erdis gravely added. "If things go too long . . ."

"Altearin will still be here when he gets back," Shador assured him, then paused. "So I have your permission to make a joint statement in all our names to the greater population of the realm? The sooner we make things official, the better it will be for everyone—about Gurthghol's absence and the regency."

"Yes. A statement would be in order to quell any lingering confusion. I could prepare it and have you and Mergis sign it. That way it would look more official."

"If you wish." Shador wasn't sure what Erdis was going to put in it but trusted it wouldn't be anything disparaging to him or his actions. They'd already cleared the air on that front. And Erdis was right: if it *did* come from the chamberlain, it would be more official.

"Then if you'll excuse me, I'll see to it."

"Of course." Shador watched Erdis depart, pleased with how well the whole conversation had gone. It could have been much worse.

With it behind him, he fixed his sights on Gurthghol's throne. The five black marble octagonal steps of the dais led up to a black walnut chair with thick arms and sides. The back was plain in contrast to the swirling designs carved into the side panels, while a wrought iron version of the Black Sun crowned the throne's back, giving the impression that the one seated on it possessed some sort of nimbus. Behind it all was a tall purple banner with another Black Sun—this one extending from ceiling to floor. Eagerly Shador ascended the steps and took a seat. It was invigorating.

He'd just closed his eyes when the sound of the door opening filled the room.

"I saw Erdis in the hall," said Twila, with Aris, Shador's barghest, in tow. "Is everything—"

She stopped upon catching sight of him enthroned. "It suits you, really."

He couldn't help but notice how easily she had just walked into the throne room: unannounced and assuming she had free rein of both the throne room and maybe even himself. While he'd said he was open to having her join him in his rule, her recent actions—her bold assumptions—were starting to wear thin.

"Though you could have told me about that delegation." She slowed her stride as Aris trotted up the dais to sit at his master's feet.

"Seems you heard about it just fine without me," he coolly replied.

She frowned. "If we're going to be equals, Shador—"

He cut her off. "It was something for a regent to deal with. You'd have nothing to offer to the discussion."

"But I would need to be kept informed if I'm to help make decisions."

"And you will be. I'm not going to cut you out of anything, Twila."

"Except meetings with delegations from Kratos." She flung the words in his face.

"What's done is done. Let's let it be and move on, shall we?"

"Just remember who helped you get that throne." Twila smiled with all the love of a hungry serpent. "And your promise to me when you got it."

"Both are always at the forefront of my thinking," he returned with a flat grin of his own. "And this will work out just like I told you."

"Messenger for Lord Shador." A Chimera entered the throne room. Shador sighed. "What is it now?"

Aris growled as the Swarthin neared. It was clear Twila didn't recognize the new arrival, but Shador did. It was the same one who'd brought the message from Rilas earlier.

"It's all right, boy." He stroked Aris' head to calm him.

The Swarthin addressed Shador. "My lord sends his greetings."

"Looks like the congratulations are going to start pouring in now on my elevation." Shador stepped in before Twila's curiosity deepened. "Or maybe people asking when the gold will arrive. I trust you've been able to see to that."

"Of course." Twila straightened her spine with a modest amount of pride. "It's being sent out even as we speak."

"Then that's it then." He motioned for the Swarthin to approach the throne. "I don't think I'll be too long here. I just wanted a moment alone to savor—away from Mergis and the others."

"And me?" It wasn't harsh but still had just a hint of a point to needle him.

"I meant what I said, Twila. We'll get this all sorted out soon enough. Just let me enjoy this for a moment, and I'll meet you tonight for dinner so we can hash more of the details out."

She sighed. "All right. Dinner and discussion . . . and maybe a little something extra for dessert. So don't be late." She saw herself out.

Shador waited until the doors were entirely closed before acknowledging the messenger patiently standing at the base of the dais.

"So what do you have to share?" he asked the Swarthin.

"An invitation." The messenger handed Shador the letter. Once more it was written on a small piece of parchment, but it was in the same hand as the first note from the Umbrian. It was also short:

> *If you are still open to my help, then we can meet at the following location this evening—two hours after midnight. I believe time is of the essence, and we need to be ready to strike when the opportunity arises.*
>
> *I shall come alone and unarmed, assuming you will do the same.*

Below the text was a crude map, denoting just where the proposed meeting should occur. He didn't see anything out of the ordinary, though it was clearly well into the wilds outside the capital and even his keep. That might prove an issue in terms of travel time, but he thought he could both make it and keep his current dinner engagement.

"Tell your master I accept his invitation." The Swarthin bowed and saw himself from the throne room, leaving Shador to stroke Aris' ears, thinking.

CHAPTER 14

The singe hounds barked and yipped as Rheminas entered the outer courtyard of his palace. Though it wasn't so much their master's arrival that had stirred up such excitement but rather the quarter of a black oryx he'd taken from his hunt.

"Calm down," he told the four hounds as they took turns jumping up and nipping at the hunk of flesh. The mixture of black, red, and orange in their coats gave them an appearance of cooling lava. Even the charcoal-gray tips of their tails and muzzles added to the illusion.

"I told you I'd bring something back."

He dropped the quarter and stepped back. The hounds were upon it at once, digging in with jaws and claws. Rheminas retreated further to a nearby settee and watched the singe hounds devour their meal.

He didn't hunt that often, and whenever he did, it was more for entertainment—the passing of time—than anything else. He'd enjoy his dinner, of course, but he never took to such things as did his father, who'd first taught him how to hunt. He also didn't live for the thrill of battle or the clash of swords. There was a different fire that burned in his veins.

He was interrupted by a Lady of Magma drawing near. He delighted at what rested on the dark orange cushion in her reddish-orange hands. The necklace was bright bronze with an oval pendant also made of bronze set with a fire opal the size of a fig. The highly polished gem shone even from a distance like fresh magma. It was even better than he imagined it would be.

"I think you'll find everything is set to perfection, my lord." The Lady of Magma presented the cushion to him.

"And what do you think of it?" The question caught her unawares as he lifted the necklace from the pillow. "How do *you* see it?"

"It's a fine piece of craftsmanship, my lord," she gave a measured reply.

"Besides that. Is there anything else?"

She paused, black eyes seemingly pondering what exactly was being asked of her. "The fire opal gives the illusion of being alive. It has a very alluring quality to it."

"I agree." Rheminas held the necklace before his face. "Something unique for someone quite unique. You can tell all the craftsmen they did an excellent job."

"I will."

"Now," he said, rising from his seat, "I need a special matter attended to and don't want anyone else to know of it. Can you keep it hidden?"

"It would depend on what I'm asked to do." Again, her manner was measured.

"I want to have this necklace given to Shiril. Is that something that can be done? Without you attracting any attention either in Helii or on Boda?"

"I can't speak too much to Boda, my lord, as I've never been there and don't know its ways or people, but on Helii, at least, I should be able to keep the matter hidden quite easily."

"A good start." He nodded. "Those in Boda aren't given to being that social anyway, so if we can keep the tongues from wagging here we should be fine."

"When would you have me leave?"

"As soon as you were ready. I'd like to get this into her hands right away."

"Was there anything else that needed to be done or said?"

"Only that it is a gift from me," he replied, returning the necklace to the pillow.

"Very well. It shall be done." She gave a bow and retreated from Rheminas' presence.

"Yes," he said to himself, returning to his singe hounds, who were cleaning the rest of the bones between them. "A unique gift for a unique woman . . ."

• • •

Panthora made a final inspection. Nothing was out of place and all was as it should be—just like it was for her last inspection, and the one before that. She was clothed in a flowing tawny gown with a silken white sash about her waist. Her feet were shod with fine leather sandals and her wrists and neck were adorned with gold. It wasn't what she normally wore but more fitting for the occasion. Yet she couldn't help feeling as if she'd missed something.

Once again, she considered the blue velvet pouch she held in her left hand. Her gifts were still inside and the object still exuded the richness of the fabric in Bios' light. The silver-and-gold-spun ribbon artfully cinched the top of the sack. It was a pleasant gift. A practical gift. And she was sure she did right in bringing it. She'd convinced herself of this several times since her arrival. Now she just needed to present it.

She ran a hand over the top of her head, ensuring the dreadlocks were still pulled back into a collected mass at the back of her head, creating a rough ponytail. As with the other Race Gods—and gods in general when visiting another god's realm—she'd come in a guise. But she wasn't about to embellish anything in her alternative form. Instead she was as she was in life, wanting to show her true self and make her true praise known at such a momentous event.

Again willing herself to relax, she took a slow breath and held it before exhaling. She didn't know why she was so nervous. It wasn't like she hadn't seen Asora before—the two of them just spoke to each other in the previous councils and then the fighting at Thangaria had given them additional face time.

You still think too much like a human. Jillar's words echoed in her mind.

She couldn't help but chuckle at the notion. It was true. And no more so than right now, as she waited in the small room off the main hallway in Asora's palace. She was trying to do right, of course, and that was honorable, but she was thinking of herself as a petitioner coming before a god. They were both gods here. Not equal in stature, of course—the Race Gods would always be a step lower than the pantheon in many ways—but still gods, and she needed to remind herself of that more often. Especially now, as her own plans were finally getting underway and she was moving into the greater part of her purpose and charge in the pantheon.

She'd found her way to Bios easily enough and into the palace shortly after that. The city was still decorated for the celebration of new life, and the people she passed remained jubilant. The public presentation must have been something to behold. The realm—and the cosmos, for that matter—hadn't seen its like for centuries. The old court ritual must have served as a pleasant point to connect the rest of the pantheon around . . . if only for a short while. They needed more unity of late and more peace to enjoy it.

Panthora had waited until all the festivities had died down and Drued and Aero had their chance to visit. She wasn't in any rush, nor was she going to rush anyone else. By going last, she also let everyone have their full amount of time with each other. She was thinking really of Asora more than the others. She could imagine it being rather hard to balance three newborns along with the day-to-day affairs of her realm. Asora would master it in short order, she was sure, but in the interim Panthora would help provide a more measured pace so she could better manage and even enjoy this phase of her life.

She didn't know how long she'd been waiting, but it didn't matter. It wasn't about her anyway. The visit was for Asora—a new mother with new children, godlings to welcome into the cosmos—and she was pleased to do it. Who knew when she might be able to behold such a thing again. Gods were rare enough as it was, but having new ones enter reality was something even rarer still.

"Asora will see you now," the Lady of Life's soft voice informed Panthora from behind. She'd been so silent she hadn't even heard her approach.

Of all the titan lords she knew, Panthora thought the Lords of Life the most human—at least in appearance. This one even shared Panthora's brown complexion, but differed in her green eyes and brown hair. Like the gods they served, the titans stood head and shoulders above Panthora. It always gave her a sense of being a child in an adult's world. And while she was sure that wasn't their intention, it was something she could never fully ignore whenever she encountered them.

"If you'll follow me." The Lady of Life led the way down the long white marble hallway, turning a few times before stopping at a certain door.

"She's inside." The titaness motioned to the door, clearly indicating Panthora should open it.

Taking the hint, she slowly pushed in the polished teak and entered Asora's private audience room. She, like many of the gods, had several places to receive visitors. Some more lavish and grand and others, like this one, more private for less formal affairs. The room was lit by a row of clear glass windows on the wall immediately opposite the door. Inside was a square table with two cushioned chairs on either side of it—Asora rising from one of them.

"Welcome to Bios, Panthora." Asora greeted Panthora warmly as the Lady of Life closed the door to the room, allowing them their privacy.

"Thank you for allowing me the visit," Panthora began. "I'm sure you've been pretty busy of late."

"More so than usual, but these are different days, aren't they?"

"Yes, they are."

"Please, be seated." Asora motioned to the nearby chair. Panthora was surprised by how comfortable it was. Built for titanic occupants, the seat was larger than herself but not so large as to swallow her whole.

"How are the children?" Panthora rested the pouch on her lap.

"Very well. They're starting to figure out a routine, I think. That's what I tell myself, anyway. Sometimes children have a mind of their own with that sort of thing."

"Have you been able to get enough sleep?"

"For now. But thankfully I have some help with the servants. Though I don't plan on pushing them off on others—I want to raise them as much as possible. These will probably be the last children I get to enjoy. Assuming Perlosa or Rheminas don't have any of their own."

"Then I hope you get to enjoy them."

"You don't have to be so formal, Panthora. I appreciate your respect, but I consider you more family than court. You can speak freely and be free here."

"I'm not family. I'm simply—"

"You're a goddess," Asora cut her off. "And as far as I'm concerned that puts you in the same group as the rest of us."

Unsure just how to reply or even if she should, she instead shifted to the blue pouch in her lap. "I brought these for you—well, for the children, really."

She handed the pouch to Asora. "I wasn't sure what to bring but thought something for the children would be more appropriate." Asora gently loosened the ribbon and carefully opened the top wide enough for a peek inside. Panthora couldn't miss the smile that lit up her face at what she'd discovered.

"These are wonderful." Asora pulled out one of the three golden lions Panthora had placed inside. She'd made sure each was as lifelike as possible. Crafted of solid gold, they were also created with moving parts, allowing for a full range of articulation. Even their mouths could open and tails turn, allowing for a whole array of options for play and maybe later display should they grow out of such things.

"They can also roar if you speak a certain word over them."

"Really?" Asora chuckled. "I'm sure the children will love them. How did you ever think of them?"

"I just imagined what I would want for my children," she replied. "I didn't have much when I was a child but I do remember the toys."

"You had golden lions growing up?"

"Oh no, just wood carvings. We had to use our imaginations to do much of the work when at play."

"Well, they're quite lovely. And this is the only gift the children have received personally. The rest have been things for me in their name but really nothing they could enjoy or care about. But these"—she held the toy lion aloft, grinning from ear to ear—"these will be just perfect. Thank you, Panthora."

"Of course. I'm happy to do it. I wasn't sure about the lion at first but then realized if they could roar, that would be even better."

"Would you care to see them?"

"The children? Certainly, if that's all right."

"Of course it is. And it's right about the time I should probably check on them anyway." Asora went for the door. "You can follow me. They aren't that far away."

Asora moved from the room and down the same hall Panthora had previously traversed. Only this time they took a different turn and entered Asora's private bedchamber, where a crib with three small bodies resided.

"They're starting to develop their own personalities—or I'm starting to figure them out, I guess." Asora approached the crib. "It will be interesting to see how they develop as they age." She reached inside and scooped up one of the girls in her arms.

"This is Meesha." Asora handed the child to a surprised Panthora.

"And this is Vearus." She lifted the still-groggy boy. "The other is Talaya."

Panthora watched Meesha's gray eyes slowly open and fix upon her. The heat of her tiny frame made her feel like she was holding a bundle of smoldering kindling. "She has very lovely eyes."

"Yes, they all do," said Asora. "And the same hair color—for now. We'll see who keeps it all their days. I'm thinking at least one might go brown or even lighter."

"They're just so innocent, aren't they?" Panthora was mesmerized by the pleasant face staring back at her. If she hadn't known better she would have imagined this was just a simple baby. A common infant no different from any other. But this child had the ability to do things no common baby would ever do. The potential for great wonders . . . and terrible deeds . . .

"Most babies are." Asora carefully put the toy lion on Vearus' chest. He was obviously intrigued. But the extent of his investigation involved bringing the golden animal to his mouth and slobbering over it.

"I think he's going to like it," Asora told Panthora, who couldn't help but laugh. Asora joined her, and then Meesha and Vearus started giggling.

"I had no idea you'd have three children. When I heard you were pregnant I thought two at the most, but three—"

"Surprised me too. I wasn't expecting to have any more but I'm not complaining. It's almost like getting to start over in a way—see about perhaps fixing things you got wrong the last time or doing better than before." She fell silent, contemplating Vearus as he garbled something between sucking the lion's head and mane.

Panthora waited for Asora to continue, but as the silence grew, so too did her unease with it. "I'm sure you'll do well," she finally blurted. "You are a goddess of life, after all."

"One can only hope."

"Not that it's my business, but is Khuthon going to be helping more? With you two not sharing the same domain I'm sure it can be challenging in times like this."

"We're used to it." The words were flat, but Asora's demeanor hadn't changed.

"I meant no disrespect."

"And none was taken." Asora returned Vearus to his crib, being careful to remove the new toy lest he get too familiar with it for his own good. "He'll do what he can and when, but for right now I'm enjoying these three blessings as best I can."

Meesha reached up with her small arms, apparently eager for an embrace. Panthora indulged her request. It felt good. Normal. Almost as if she was a common woman. She could almost be elsewhere— anywhere—it was so universal.

"And how are things in Gracia?" And just like that Asora's question returned Panthora to her constant duties and mission.

"Well enough. I think things are back in order again, allowing me to finish up what remains."

"Yes, I think we're all going to enjoy that again," said Asora. "Just like I think we're all going to appreciate what we almost lost not that long ago."

"Have you heard anything about Gurthghol?"

"No. Last I heard there were some titan lords and Tularins looking into a few things but nothing else."

"Do you think he's . . ."

"We might not ever know." A momentary frown wrinkled Asora's brow.

"I'm sorry, I shouldn't have brought it up."

"It will be brought up at some point. We still have another council before us, after all."

"I guess you're right."

Panthora wasn't clear on just how to read the curious look Asora gave her. "When was the last time we actually had a chance to speak to one another—goddess to goddess?"

"I don't know. We've been so busy for so long it's hard to remember."

"Yes, all of us do tend to keep so much to our own realms and lives, don't we? Maybe we should start to change that. It would be good to reforge relationships—keep what was started in these trying times and use it more for good. Are you free to stay for lunch?" The question caught Panthora off guard.

"I-I suppose I could, if you'd have me."

"And what did I say about formalities?"

"I just don't want to impose is all."

"If I'm asking, how is that imposing?"

She supposed it wasn't. "Then if you'd like, I'd be happy to stay for a while longer."

"Wonderful. I'll have an extra plate placed at the table. You're the last to visit me anyway, so there's no rush. We can take our time—get caught up. Make you feel more like you're part of the family." She grinned.

"Thank you." It was really all Panthora could say. She was honestly at a loss for anything else.

"Of course. And I haven't entertained for so long—it will be nice getting back into practice. And interesting hearing a new perspective on things. It'll be refreshing having someone to talk to who isn't so wrapped up in the trappings of everything we've come to embrace. Sometimes we all can lose sight of the larger picture—no matter our intentions. And I could do with a little more grounding right now, if that makes sense."

"I think we both could." Panthora surrendered Meesha to her mother, who returned the babe to the crib and her rest.

"Then let me show you to my private dining room." Asora took the lead, as Panthora took one final glance at the dozing children. The slumbering future of both cosmos and pantheon.

• • •

"I wasn't expecting an answer so soon." Asorlok took a seat across from Saredhel.

He again found himself in Sooth, this time in Saredhel's private reading room, shifting his gaze between Saredhel and the stained glass windows behind her. They were filled with symbols, images, and people he knew had a hidden meaning and secret insight to share with any who knew how to decipher them. And Asorlok was not one of those people.

"I don't have an answer for you just yet," she confessed. "I asked you to Sooth for another reason."

He raised an eyebrow. "And what might that be?"

She reached for an old-looking parchment to her left on the desk. It was all that had been placed upon the clean surface. The rest of the books and scrolls had been left lining the walls in their various places on the crowded shelves.

"From our past dealings, I believe I have your word that what I'm about to share will be kept strictly between us."

"Of course." Further intrigued, Asorlok watched Saredhel carefully unroll the parchment across the table. It was old but still held its form nicely. He could see why, with her treating it as carefully as some newborn. And it was a fairly long roll too, if he judged correctly. About ten feet long, he'd guess, and a foot and a half wide.

"The more I sought an answer for your questions, the more I began seeing that what you sought was interwoven with what I've been searching for an answer to as well. After weighing the matter further, I've come to see we might be able to help answer each other's question together."

Asorlok noted the images and text on the parchment were scrawled in a way that was sort of orderly but still somehow foreign. "Something even *Saredhel* can't solve? Now that *is* an impressive mystery."

"More so than you know." Her milk-white eyes found Asorlok's face once more. "For I think the events of these last few days may have been part of the Omnian Scrolls."

"Really." Asorlok's eyes locked anew on the millennia-old text and images. "And this—this is one of those scrolls, I take it?"

"Yes."

He tried making a better reading of some of the text. It was old but not indecipherable. It was Titan, their mother tongue. Antiquated, but still readable. "I thought you once said it was best for us to leave them and their decoding to you. And after what you once shared about the Great End—"

"I shared only what I believed prudent at the time."

"You told us it was fated for the cosmos to end." Asorlok had been the first to accept this truth. He was, after all, tied closely to Nuhl, the very one who hungered to do just that. It wasn't implausible that such a thing was possible, even though Asorlok had no clear idea—even after all these years of being connected to Nuhl—how such a thing could come about. Though he was still of a mind it was more worst-case-scenario thinking than anything else.

"And it is." Her flat reply lifted the god of death's gaze back on his sister.

"But you weren't that clear on the details, if I recall."

Saredhel surrendered a soft sigh. "That's because I don't have many."

"But you can see the future, you said, and with the Omnian Scrolls it was clear—"

"Not as clear as you might think. The further one dives into the future, the murkier things become. And I've never seen anything more clouded than matters related to the Great End. But that's not why I've summoned you."

Saredhel gently tapped the ancient scroll. "This is the fourth scroll in the collection, and it speaks to something I believe is in our present or very near future, but I need to be sure."

"Well, if *you* don't know for certain, how can *I* be of any help?"

"The more familiar one becomes with something, the easier things can be hidden," she explained.

"So a set of fresh eyes then. But you're going to actually trust me alone with one of the Omnian Scrolls?"

"You're not alone."

"As if you'd trust anyone with them but yourself."

"If you read them for yourself, you'd understand." She signaled for him to do just that, asking, "What do you see? And how do you read it?" Asorlok began poring over everything anew, carefully considering the colorful scene the scroll conveyed.

" 'Behold, after some absence I dreamed another dream,' " he read aloud from the text. " 'And in it I beheld a strange sight. It was night and I looked heavenward and saw the stars. And as I viewed and pondered them, three of them streaked across the sky, where I watched all three fall into a lake. But they did not strike it hard, merely kissed the surface, creating many ripples—though they themselves remained on the lake's surface.

" 'These three stars I then saw were about the size of a fist and were rough diamonds that continually kept glowing pure white. And as I watched, the three of them were cleaned, polished, and cut by some unseen hand and tools.

" 'When they were finished, they were magnificent, and each was placed in its own crown. It was then I awoke and recorded what I had seen.'

"Makes no sense to me whatsoever," he told Saredhel.

"Did you study the images with the text?"

The text was actually broken into blocks around roughly drawn pictures it was meant to explain. In this case what he'd just read had shown what he assumed were three falling stars. The next displayed those three stones hitting the surface of a lake, creating ripples, yet the stones remained on the lake's surface. The next image was of three majestic crowns, each with a large diamond in a prominent location.

"They don't really help any, do they?"

"They're impressions of what Omni saw and was unable to fully explain in his words or give proper reference to in his art."

"So he was just guessing at what he saw? I thought the scrolls were supposed to be so exact—so prescient. Mother would never have devoted so much time to them if they were so open to interpretation."

"As things get closer to manifestation they often get clearer."

"Well, this certainly isn't clear," said Asorlok. "Maybe you're worried about nothing."

"Read the next vision," she advised. "That was what I wanted your opinion on in the first place; the previous vision was needed to give you the proper foundation."

"All right." He sighed and returned to the scroll.

"First, what do you see in that vision?" asked Saredhel.

"What looks like a young titanic male talking with a silver serpent in his path. In the next picture the serpent has coiled around his waist like a belt. Next is an image of the serpent coiled around the titan's head and biting into his forehead. The man's eyes are like the serpent's in this image. Then we see the titan crushing statues with his mace in a rage. Some statues are smaller, others his own size. The final image is of the serpent slithering away, leaving a fresh wound on the man's neck and him on his knees amid a field of debris from the smashed statues."

"Now read the text and share how you understand it."

"'The next night I dreamed again and this was what I saw: a handsome young male titan exploring the wilderness. He was enjoying the process when I saw a silver serpent slither up to him. At first he wasn't sure what to make of the serpent, but then it started speaking to him in comforting tones, telling him it meant him no harm.

"'In time he accepted this message and welcomed the serpent's company. And as I watched the titan explore the terrain, the serpent moved up around the young man's waist. He allowed it and kept about his business. And then the serpent grew bolder and encircled the young titan's head like some sort of diadem.

" 'This the male also welcomed, but his countenance changed into something darker and crueler than before. It was then the wilderness transformed into a great collection of statues. Some of them appeared as titans, but many others were beings unknown to me.

" 'As soon as the scenery changed, the serpent bit into the male titan's forehead, releasing its venom. When it did, the other's eyes became like a serpent's and he became enraged. Suddenly, he had a large mace in his hand and started crushing and damaging the statues around him, being fueled with a dark rage to crush and destroy. And this was what he did until all the statues were destroyed.

" 'And no sooner had they been destroyed then the serpent bit him again on his neck and uncoiled from his person. This bite was deadly and caused him great pain. Yet though he suffered, he would not die, refusing to do so until he'd made amends for the destruction he had wrought.

" 'After this, I awoke and recorded what I had seen.' "

Asorlok paused, scanning the images and text once more, searching out whatever may have been hidden amid them he wasn't seeing. Finally, he gave up entirely. "I don't know what it means. It could just be a dream—simple as that."

"No." Saredhel was resolute. "Omni was gifted with a sight that few of his generation ever knew. He could see things that were yet to come and saw it as a warning that needed sharing with others—his family—to protect them and the rest of the cosmos from harm."

"So then how do *you* read it?" he asked.

"The first vision is tied to three new bright lights from on high whose arrival sends ripples across the cosmos. This, I believe, speaks of the birth of Asora's triplets. The crown these three will receive is what awaits them in the near future when they're of age."

Asorlok considered the first vision again, taking in the pictures and text more carefully. "You got all that from this, did you? That's more than I would have seen."

"But do you see that too?"

"What difference does that make? If you've already solved the—"

"Do you see that too?" she repeated with more steel in her voice.

"I-I suppose that could be an interpretation. Three new lights in the sky coming to land in the cosmos and shaking things up. You don't need much divination there to know that's going to be the case soon enough."

"The second," she continued, "is what troubles me."

"Yes, it was rather violent, wasn't it?" Asorlok's eyes traced the silver serpent around the young titan's head. "I'm going to guess the silver serpent is tied to the Abyss or evil? The two are fairly similar in their symbols."

"I'd agree."

"But I don't know anything about the titan. Is he supposed to be literal or symbolic?"

"Did you look closely at his features?"

"Close enough," said Asorlok.

"Look again." He did as bidden, noting for the first time the other's build and appearance. And then he saw it.

"The face. It almost looks like Khuthon."

"But it's not him. He's no longer so young, and this can't be part of his life. So that would just leave his son."

"Yes." Asorlok nodded. "The red hair could be a nice fit there. But what does it mean? He's attacking statues—but of whom?" Asorlok couldn't help but recall his encounter with Nuhl in his own collection of statues not that long ago. They too were destroyed, but not by some mace-wielding warrior . . .

"Omni has told us already," said Saredhel.

"Titans," he mused aloud.

"And others," she added. "And how would you read that?"

"I already told you, I'm not a seer. None of this makes any sense."

"It doesn't?" He found himself trying to hide from those blank white eyes. "Tell me what you really see."

Asorlok sighed. "Fine, if that's what you want. But I don't know what, if any, good it will do." Once again he scanned the images and text that were just as much a confused jumble to the one who recorded them as to the one presently viewing them.

"Death. I see death. The young titan is the bringer of it but suffers from it as well in the end."

"Thank you."

"You don't sound too surprised." Asorlok sat back in his chair, watching his sister roll up the parchment as carefully as how she'd originally unfurled it.

"Should I be?"

"Are you going to tell me what it means, then, because somehow I think you know and just don't want to tell me."

"Neither you nor the rest of the pantheon—not yet."

"So is it about Vearus?"

"Most likely." Asorlok waited for her to say more, but she only placed the rolled scroll to her side. Out of sight and now presumably out of mind.

"And just what might that be, exactly? It sounded pretty important."

"All of what Omni recorded is important."

"But we're just talking about this part," he pressed. "And you had me read it too, so you're not going to be spoiling anything by filling me in on it."

"When the time is right. And thank you. You've helped me see more than I had before."

"I have?" He wasn't sure that was the case, unless he missed something in their conversation.

"Yes. More than you might know."

"Which you're not going to share with me."

"I believe I already have. You did just read from the scroll."

Asorlok shook his head in defeat. "I don't know how Dradin puts up with you sometimes." Rising from his seat, he asked, "And how long are you going to keep this from the others?"

"Until the time is right," she repeated.

"And it isn't right now. Not even if that *is* Vearus in the image and he was bashing statues and dealing with silver serpents."

"See that you're careful about not jumping to conclusions. A little knowledge of something can often do greater damage than good. Which is why, until the time is right, the others will be kept from knowing anything more than they already do. I trust you will respect my wishes and keep this all to yourself."

"I wouldn't know what to tell them even if I wanted to."

Saredhel nodded her approval.

"So then we're done here?"

"For now. When I have something more for you, I'll let you know."

"I'll be waiting for that answer." He made for the door. "I'm trusting it will be clearer than mud when you give it too."

"You will be enlightened, I'm sure." Her voice followed him down the hall as he hurried to the portal and back to his own realm, away from all the shadowy talk and murky possibilities.

• • •

"Thank you," Shiril told the Lady of Magma standing across from her.

"Lord Rheminas wanted to make sure you received it," said the black-haired titaness. When she'd first arrived, Shiril wasn't sure what to make of the visit. A Lord of Earth had alerted her to the arrival but said nothing else.

The Lady of Magma was alone and unarmed, which was also a bit odd. At first she thought it was a delegation, but quickly put away such notions. If Rheminas wanted to tell her something, he'd most likely do so in person. He hadn't been shy about sharing his intentions before. The necklace was another matter.

"It's quite the gift," she said, observing the fine craftsmanship. It had been presented on an orange cushion the Lady of Magma extended her way.

" 'Something unique for someone quite unique' is what he said."

"Well, you can tell him I appreciate it." Shiril chose her words carefully.

She wasn't used to having so many visitors and was even less used to them sending her gifts. Of course, Rheminas was more than a simple visitor nowadays. And if this token of his affection was any indication, he was thinking similar thoughts. She still wasn't sure how she was supposed to react to such things. Everything was happening so fast: the battle on Thangaria, the birth of the triplets, the interest from Rheminas. It was a whole new world, and she had yet to find a comfortable place for her feet to tread.

"I will make sure he gets your reply." The Lady of Magma smiled knowingly.

It was clear she knew or had a fairly strong suspicion about what was going on between Shiril and her lord. There was a twinge of concern and fear with the revelation, but Shiril brought it under control. What did it matter? She was free to do what she wanted, just like any of the other gods or anyone else in the cosmos. Yet part of her, some deep-rooted aspect that still loved her old life and the order that had surrounded it, kept a small piece of her concern and doubt alive. Finally, feeling awkward she'd left her visitor holding the cushion in front of her this whole time, she reached out and retrieved the necklace.

"Was there anything else you wished to convey?" The Lady of Magma brought the empty cushion to her side. It was a subtle way of asking if there was a return gift or word.

Shiril hadn't been expecting the necklace and so wasn't ready with anything in exchange. Not that she would have necessarily given something in return. Again, this was all so new. She wanted to step carefully and keep from overcommitting or doing something she'd later regret. Again, she longed for a clearer path to tread.

"No. If I have anything further for Rheminas, I will let him know." It was a fair and clear-enough answer and spoken in a way that was polite yet firm.

"Very well." The Lady of Magma gave a bow of her head. "Good day, Your Highness." She removed herself from the audience chamber.

Once alone, Shiril took in the necklace more carefully. She was drawn to the brilliant fire opal. It had been polished in such a way that the small oval resembled churning lava. She was fascinated by the design and enjoyed the bronze chain itself. It was clear Rheminas had invested some effort in it.

What wasn't clear was whether the necklace would have any strings attached to it or was given without any expectations; that would have to be worked out in the future. Given his recent behavior, she was confident he'd return, allowing her to clarify matters then. For the more she got to know him, the more he surprised her. To think he was capable of such sentiment . . . and other things . . . was truly unexpected. And she liked that surprise. In fact, she was liking more and more about him the longer she thought about him and shared more of herself with him.

In some ways, it was freeing, but in others those old concerns still lingered. None of the rest of their generation—the cousins—had taken a mate, and certainly not from among their own number. There had been some issues when their parents married and brought them into the cosmos. How many more, she wondered, with the recent birth of the triplets, would news of her and Rheminas' actions produce? And he was the son of Khuthon, who now sat as the head of the Dark Gods. And Rheminas was a Dark God himself, whereas she was still aligned with the Gray Gods. And Rheminas was his father's son in many ways . . . Would that play out in her life as it had in Asora's?

More questions and few answers. But she'd have them soon enough. If anything, her parents had instilled in her a great patience. She'd learned what she needed eventually. For now she would take each day as it came. And until things settled down across the cosmos and the triplets came of age, the rest of the pantheon would no doubt be doing much the same.

"A unique gift from a unique person," she told the necklace.

CHAPTER 15

S hador slowed his horse to a stop in the empty landscape. There was nothing but dead rock piled into hills with a few scraggly bushes managing to find root. All of it cloaked by the night. His main focus was on a dark cave mouth a stone's throw from him where Rilas was supposed to be awaiting his arrival.

He'd ridden farther than he'd originally felt comfortable venturing on his own, but it was where the map brought him. It was also a likely place for a trap, and so he kept himself ready for anything. He'd worn common attire and drawn his hood to better hide from any prying eyes. The mail shirt under his tunic and the dagger concealed at the back of his belt would help even any remaining odds.

"I'm here." Shador spoke in the cave's direction. "I've come alone."

Nothing.

Tensing, he gave the terrain another pass of his eyes, then tried once again.

"Show yourself," he shouted.

"You've really come alone?" A voice issued from the cave. He couldn't see what might lie inside. It could be deep enough to easily keep a company of men from view.

"Hopefully not foolishly so."

"You made good time." A black mass emerged from the cavern's dark bowels, taking on a humanoid shape as it drew near the cave's mouth. To Shador, who'd never really seen an Umbrian up close, he didn't really know if this one was of any particular note. All he saw was black skin, hair, and eyes—a basalt statue carved from living pitch. From what he could discern, the Umbrian was both unarmed and wore no armor. Shador wouldn't put it past him to have something hidden on his person, but for all initial appearances, he seemed to be holding to his word.

"You said you had something important to offer." Shador dismounted.

"I don't do this lightly, you understand." There was a ring of truth to Rilas' words. Shador could feel the other's gaze finishing its inspection.

"Nor do I. But when you profess to know something no one else should, I'd like to find out how and why."

"The scepter, you mean." Rilas closed the distance between them. "I have my sources."

"The palace?"

Rilas was impossible to read. "You came because of the scepter. How I learned of it isn't important. What is, is how I can help you get it."

"And why should I believe an Umbrian's word?"

"Because at the moment we both want the same thing: Gurthghol and the pantheon kept out of Altearin."

"I'm just holding the seat until Gurthghol's return." Shador made sure to sound as humble as possible. It came to him more naturally now than ever before.

Rilas laughed, revealing his black teeth behind the curl of dark lips. "And something tells me the longer he keeps from returning, the happier you'll be. We both don't want the pantheon sticking their noses into things, and having a Lord of Darkness on the throne is better than any god or Lord of Chaos."

"Because it brings you closer to your dream of returning to the former days." Shador could see where this was going, and in a way it made sense. Wasn't he, after all, attempting a similar thing? "You know it's never going to happen. The planes aren't going to return. Altearin is forever."

"One would have said that about Gurthghol a few days ago too. Seems things are more subject to change than we might like to think."

"So what do you want?"

"To help you get the scepter."

"That's it?"

"As long as you stay out of Umbrianic affairs, what you do isn't any of my concern."

"And you *are* aware of just *what* that scepter can do?" Shador watched Rilas carefully.

"Yes. The same as you."

"And you'd *trust* me with it?"

"No." Rilas was blunt. "But I'd prefer it in a titan lord's hand over some god's. Because I know *you'd* use it in keeping the gods at bay."

"And you're really willing to help me get it rather than try to take it for yourself?"

"I realize it may be hard to believe. Yet you must have had enough faith to see you here."

"Maybe I wanted to see the face of the Umbrian who actually wanted to side with a Lord of Darkness rather than try to destroy him." The words birthed a small grimace across Rilas' face.

"Not so much an ally but a means to an end, as I've said. It's a simple working arrangement both of us can accept until we can go our separate ways."

Shador continued poking holes in what he was hearing. While none of this was entirely natural, what had been these last few days? And if Khuthon was looking to lead a charge into Altearin, having that scepter would make an excellent deterrent against him or any other god—or divinity—following his example.

"And *who* would you have help me get it?"

"I'd get it for you."

"*You'd* get the scepter and then bring it to *me*? Why would you even think of letting something like that go once you had it in your possession?"

"I believe I already answered that."

Shador gave the Umbrian another hard stare. "You're serious."

"I wouldn't have asked to meet with you if I wasn't."

"And how would you plan on getting the scepter? It's being held in Thangaria, and it's watched over by Tularins."

"I trust you've heard at least something of my people—how we're deeply in tune with the cosmic element of darkness."

"And how is *that* going to help?"

"Come now, Shador. Every Lord of Darkness knows how to use shadows for their travels."

"Some more than others. But Thangaria isn't Altearin. You'll be out of your depth."

"We both would be . . . by ourselves. But *together* . . ." Rilas let the sentence finish itself in Shador's thoughts.

"You need me." Rilas finally broke the silence. "And I'm willing to help."

"For the price of your autonomy? That's what this is all boiling down to in the end, isn't it?" There were probably other things still cloaked here and there, but the chief focus was clear enough.

"A price, I think, you'd be willing to pay." Rilas was right. He'd no interest in taking on any Umbrians. He'd have enough on his plate to deal with in the days ahead. If he could somehow get some assurance they'd be content to live in whatever pocket of life they kept for themselves, it might actually be worth it. That was, if he could trust this Umbrian.

"Assuming you *could* get it, how would you keep the pantheon from knowing the scepter was taken? I'm not fool enough to raise the pantheon's ire any more than I have already."

"You'll see." Rilas' confidence actually made Shador almost believe him. Almost.

"So are you doing this for yourself, or are the rest of the Umbrians behind you?"

"I can only speak for my city," said Rilas, "and they won't be a problem. I'm confident I'd be able to convince the others to refrain from getting involved—that is, if I can be assured of you honoring *your* commitment to *me*."

"Quite a risk for your supposed enemy," said Shador.

"But worth it if you honor your part of the bargain."

A quiet calm ate up the moments between them while Shador finished his mental hole poking. He didn't see too many issues that needed tending. All in all, it was a pretty straightforward proposition. Easy to gauge and easy to verify—on the major fronts. Though the actual retrieving of the scepter still had some finer threads to tidy up. But should Rilas fail him or try to betray him to the pantheon or anyone else, he could see a few ways to turn even that into a possible advantage. So was it worth the risk? Or rather, was it worth the reward?

"Part of me just wants to see you try and fail, but if you actually succeed . . ."

"So then we have an agreement?" pressed Rilas.

"You've intrigued me, I'll give you that. But—"

"You want to know the specifics of the plan before you can fully commit."

"It would help."

"I'll tell you what I can." Rilas paused. "I trust it will suffice. You and I both know that at some point you'll be called before the gods to answer for your recent actions."

"Most likely."

"When they summon you, I'll join you on Thangaria. And while they are dealing with you, I'll have a free hand to take the scepter."

"Just like that?" Shador still wasn't entirely convinced. "And do you even know where it is?"

"I'll find it."

"The palace is rather large, you know."

"But I can slip between shadows to speed up the search. And I'll be looking for the room that's the most heavily guarded."

Shador nodded his approval. "Yes, it would have to be protected, so that narrows things down, I suppose. But you still haven't said how you'd take it without being noticed."

"You'll have to trust me on that part."

"Your leverage," said Shador.

"My plan. And you'll need me for it. You couldn't do it on your own, even if you tried."

Rilas was right. And what did he have to lose at this point? The plan wasn't that far fetched, and if he was occupied with the pantheon when something went awry, he would appear blameless. In fact, if it all went wrong, Rilas might get taken out, and anything else he might know about or be plotting would no longer matter. It wouldn't be an equal form of compensation, but it was something to consider.

"All right," said Shador. "I'll humor you. But don't get cocky, and don't even think about betraying me."

"I'll be ready as soon as they announce the summons," said Rilas. "See that you are too."

"Oh, I'll be ready, don't worry about that. Now, if we're done here?"

"I think so." Rilas took his cue, returning to his cave.

Shador watched him out of the corner of his eye as he mounted his horse and turned back the way he'd come. This was all still so bizarre, but he wasn't about to turn down a legitimate opportunity, no matter how it was presented. Though all these coincidences in timing and connections were beginning to have him wonder just how deep and thorough a cleansing he was going to have to make of his own personal circle. Spurring the horse on, Shador rode back to his keep at top speed.

• • •

Rilas had hurried back to Ulan following his meeting with Shador. Once more ensconced in his throne room, he parsed every word they'd said, making sure he didn't miss anything. He'd done as good a job as he could knowing what he did, but it wasn't enough for what would come next.

While he'd hated every minute of the meeting, he had forced himself to stay and speak, hoping it would be enough to bring the titan to his side. And while it seemed to have worked, for all his talk Rilas didn't know how he was going to deliver on what he'd promised. Thangaria wasn't simply a house one could rob. This was the seat of the divine council—the pantheon itself.

He was disliking all of this more and more. He was already acting on the assurances of one whose motives were slightly uncertain, to say the least. And now there was the connection to Shador, who also might be playing him in his own game. How was all this going to help him again? He'd had a working idea at first, but now even that was foggy.

Contemplating the seal, he said: "I wish to speak with you."

There was a shifting in the darkness, and Bron appeared. He still maintained the pretense of being a Lord of Darkness, but Rilas no longer cared about the masquerade. What he craved now was greater clarity on the next steps.

"I trust you made contact with Shador?"

"I did, and he was open to having me help."

"Like I said." Bron sounded quite pleased. "He's hungry for the scepter at any cost."

"I told him I'd be able to help him get it, even sharing the same plan you told me."

"And that gained his trust?"

"Just like you said it would. But can it be trusted?"

"Hasn't everything I've told you proven true?"

"So you're saying you're infallible?" It wasn't so much a question as a mild accusation.

"My master has seen the future, as I've said. The pantheon will be calling Shador before them. They'll want him to answer some questions. Which will allow for the perfect diversion to claim the scepter."

"Which is just what I told him. Only you haven't told me *how* I'm supposed to get the scepter. Tagging along with Shador to Thangaria isn't that hard. Even sneaking into the palace isn't impossible. But how can I take something that will be heavily guarded without their raising an alarm or even knowing it's missing? You've never told me that part."

"This will be all you need." Bron withdrew a slender silver rod from under his cloak.

"Tularins aren't stupid," he growled. "That doesn't look a thing like—"

"This rod, once placed against the scepter, will change into an exact replica. It won't be able to do anything the real scepter can, but it will fool anyone who sees it—god and divinity alike."

"How?" Rilas took a renewed interest in the object.

"It's nothing that need concern us at the moment."

Again he tried peering under Bron's hood. "I'm assuming you're going to want me to do that twice?"

"Yes." The same hand already holding the rod dove back under the cloak and emerged with a second rod—a twin of the first. "One for the pantheon, and then one for Shador. Just don't lose them. They aren't the easiest to come by right now." Bron offered the rods to Rilas. They were nearly as long as his arm.

"And how do you expect me to carry those unnoticed?"

"Take hold of them."

Rilas hesitated before he finally wrapped his hands around the cold metal. He felt the rods shiver—almost as if they slithered into his grip. As they did, the thin cylinders shrunk in size until they were more in line with Rilas' proportions, making them look like nothing more than common batons or the shafts of a mace. He was amazed at how lightweight they were. It was as if they were rolls of parchment instead of metal.

"Now," Bron continued, "you should be ready to act when the time comes. Just remember who gets the *real* scepter."

"I take it there's a word or phrase to make them work?"

"Just to activate them, which they already have been. All you have to do is hold the rod next to the scepter, and it will do the rest. So make sure you don't have them touch any other metal objects—except each other—until then, unless you want them duplicating something else."

"Should I assume you know just where they're keeping the scepter too?"

"My master knows that terrain fairly well."

"I bet."

"I'll pass along instructions before you leave."

"You know when I'm leaving already?" Rilas wasn't too surprised, given their previous encounters, but it was unnerving to hear nonetheless. "So when will they call for Shador to stand before the pantheon?"

"Soon enough." Bron began fading from sight. "Once I've passed on the instructions, I'll wait for your summons when you have the scepter in hand. Until then, we have nothing further to discuss."

"And then you'll leave me alone?"

"My master only wants the scepter." Bron was now only a wavering outline and voice. "Once he has it, we'll trouble you no more."

Confident the titan had truly left him, Rilas lifted the two rods, examining each in greater detail and dreaming of a better day to come.

• • •

Shador made sure he'd returned the saddle and riding gear *exactly* where they had been before. The horse itself was left to finish its meager snack in the stable. He'd seen to its grooming and requirements himself rather than rousing anyone else. He already had reason to be more cautious than normal, given what Rilas had shared about what he knew of Shador's desires. He didn't need anyone else poking their noses into things.

"You're up early." Twila's voice spun him on his heel. Her flowing dark gown gave the impression of her being cut from the starless night. He'd thought he'd made an unobserved departure and return. Apparently he'd been mistaken.

"So are you." He tried to sound as natural as possible. "I thought you'd be more tired after our dessert."

"You too. But when I woke and didn't find you beside me, I thought something might have been wrong." It sounded innocent enough. And why wouldn't it be? It was an honest and simple excuse, but after his meeting with Rilas, he couldn't help but wonder what those who crossed his path might be hiding just below the surface.

"What could have been wrong?" he asked. "We had a lovely dinner and discussion and the dessert was nice."

"Just nice? You sure nothing's wrong?"

"Everything is going as it should," he replied, moving out of the stable. "I just needed some air."

"And so you wound up in the stables?" The question didn't sit well with him. There was something off about it—something accusatory that made him feel the need to be on the defensive.

"Not every question you might have needs to be asked." He tried couching his warning in as soft a tone as possible. "I still need to speak with Erdis to officially set things up in the capital." Twila remained close to his side. "Then I can work from there instead of here at the keep, and I'll be closer to what's important for what comes next."

"I don't think he'd object to anything."

"He shouldn't. But there's still a protocol to maintain. And you know how much Erdis enjoys his protocol."

"I have an idea." Twila locked arms with Shador. "But then what happens after that protocol?"

"Then, my dear, we rule." It still exhilarated him to imagine the freedom and potential the possibility allowed. "And all with a cover the pantheon can't touch."

"You mean once you have the scepter?" Twila's question wiped the smile from his face. He hadn't told anyone else about it, only her. And yet Rilas had heard of it and was already offering his help to retrieve it. "You really think you can get it off of Thangaria?"

"I believe a way is possible, but that's all I'm going to say for now." He hoped Twila took the hint.

"I'll be looking forward to hearing your plan."

"I bet you are," he said, but his mind was already elsewhere, pondering just how much more he should share with her and when—if ever. At least until things were completed with Rilas. That would be long enough, he supposed. She was a fair ally, after all. He couldn't have moved as quickly as he had if not for her help. But like many things in life, things can and do change . . .

"So do you feel up to some more dessert for an early breakfast?" she asked.

"I thought you took your fill last night," said Shador.

"Did you?"

He couldn't help but laugh. "I guess I could do with a little more."

"Me too." She pulled him closer as they picked up their pace toward the main residence.

CHAPTER 16

Asorlok sat in his private room, resting and thinking. He couldn't help but dwell on the thoughts that came after his visit with Saredhel. He'd actually seen the Omnian Scrolls. He'd even read from one of them. But why did Saredhel have him do so? What could he have seen that she couldn't? And what *did* he see exactly?

Even now he was still so uncertain. Had the male titan been meant to represent Vearus? The child was far from grown. Who's to say how he'd even appear as an adult? And maybe he'd take more after his mother than Khuthon. But he did have red hair, and his father had made a trip to the Abyss once before, which caused their family some grief. Would his son follow his father's example?

But again, what had he seen? A warning, yes. But for what and for who and for when? It was all so confusing but also slightly terrifying to imagine what the full implications might be. But was it tied to the Great End in any way? He didn't think so, else Saredhel wouldn't share it with him. She'd made clear in the past her intention of keeping the scrolls from them in full. She only warned she thought she saw how the cosmos would end. Or, in the very least, how the cosmos they knew would end, and that was it. No details and no further information, only that at some point it would all end—they themselves and all the worlds as well. It would all be gone.

But this was never shared with any sense of grand urgency, nor with the hint of some agency being able to hinder or spread it more than she knew. It simply was. And since Asorlok didn't see any way around it and already was predisposed to seeing the end of all things ushered in, he didn't really pay it much mind. But then recent events took over and brought it all back into the forefront, stirring new thoughts into contemplation . . . birthing a revisiting of old stratagems . . . and possibly allegiances . . .

Closing his eyes, he concentrated on the cosmic element of death. It was something he'd studied and dedicated himself to for centuries, allowing him a familiarity with it that few, if any, sought. For in Nuhl was the element given sentience, just as in Awntodgenee was the cosmic element of life. As such, the full measure of death was allowed to enact its will as far as the ancient pact between it and Awntodgenee allowed.

Asorlok brought an image into focus in his mind's eye of a Tralodren engulfed by his patron's hungry black tendrils. The smoky strands would strangle the life out of all things, crush the very rock into lifeless dust. This was its will—its desire—for all things in the cosmos. Asorlok watched as the planet he helped bring about crumbled into small lifeless chunks even as the moon cracked and disintegrated like a stale biscuit.

He watched the stars blink out one by one, leaving nothing but cold, lifeless darkness. He had seen this before. Nuhl had shared parts of its plan and desires with him—revealed to him how it would all unfold in time—for Nuhl was insatiable. It could never be satisfied with only one planet or even system or galaxy but was always craving more, reaching for more.

Asorlok had accepted this long ago. He embraced the truth that all things are going to meet their end at some point. And by embracing the truth he had sought to master it. For if one could master death, one could be master over all. Nuhl had promised as much to him already, sharing how he'd be the last thing left alive when it was done. It was meant as a reward, and Asorlok had taken it as such until the events of these last few days . . .

His eyes still closed, Asorlok's thoughts shifted to the pantheon—his brothers and sisters, nieces and nephews. One by one, he watched them die. While they might have been born gods, their bodies still weren't immune from aging, even if their spirits were immortal. All grew older and older until their flesh dried on their bones and then blew away like crumbled leaves. And then the rest of their bones followed, dropping into a gray mound of fine powder. He should have been unmoved by the imagery. This was the way of all things, after all—the greatest of truths— but instead it didn't sit right with him like it once did. Conflict had arisen where there should have been none. And there was something else . . . something behind the unease: fear.

A knock at the door shook him out of the vision.

"Yes."

"Forgive the intrusion, Majesty, but I bring news," said the voice behind the door.

Asorlok motioned with his hand, and the door opened of its own accord. Behind it stood a humble Telborian priest.

"Go on."

"A new council has been called."

"So soon?" He was surprised Asora was up to the challenge—and also the others, who had their own duties and concerns across their realms.

"I'm told there is much to discuss and your presence was requested as soon as possible."

"Then I'm sure I don't want to disappoint. It'll be the first time Khuthon gets to take his new seat."

"Again, I apologize for the interruption. Had it been anything else, I would have—"

"No, you did well. And it was time I had a change of venue anyway. Even if it's just Thangaria." He rose from his chair. "I'll leave you to make known my departure to the appropriate people."

"As you command, Majesty." The Telborian removed himself from the room.

• • •

"This council will now come to order," Ganatar informed the gods once again seated around the large table in the council chamber.

Khuthon had taken his new place on Gurthghol's throne, leaving his previous chair at the table empty. In keeping with the old rules for councils, once more the gods had adopted weaker guises instead of coming in their true forms. While things had changed in many ways, this didn't warrant an exception, unlike the last council. In similar manner, no weapons or armor were seen among them. Nor were any other servants or soldiers permitted. The fighting was over. Such measures helped afford a semblance of normalcy to the proceedings.

"I trust the time away has allowed us all to return and deal with the matters before us with a greater sense of unity," Ganatar continued, beginning the council. He, like the rest of the gathered gods, appeared close to his true form, adopting more or less formal but not too regal attire.

"Yes." Khuthon sought to emulate a statesman rather than a god of war. "Unity is key to moving forward."

"And in which direction would you have us move?" Dradin was perhaps the plainest of those assembled, keeping to his simple green robes and staff.

"I'd say we look to the matter of Gurthghol," Khuthon returned calmly. "We can't afford to waste any more time."

"Like you have on the matter?" Perlosa sniped.

"Actually"—Khuthon was unreadable as he addressed his daughter— "I haven't let the matter rest. And a recent search of Altearin—"

"You sent troops to Altearin?" Ganatar bristled. "Even after we decided against it in the last council?"

"Did we?" Khuthon asked Ganatar. "I don't recall a vote."

"Even with his absence, it's still Gurthghol's realm. You had no right or authority to do so."

"Had I tried to get it, I would have been refused."

"And for good reason." Olthon shared Ganatar's concern. "You've just conducted what might be perceived as an act of war."

"I sent a delegation. Nothing more." Khuthon remained calm, reassuring. "A *small* delegation."

"For what purpose?" Dradin studied Khuthon closely.

"Altearin is a wad of kindling waiting for the right spark," he replied. "Gurthghol kept things in line but the longer he's absent—"

"Or the longer you don't sit on its throne, you mean," Olthon fired back. "You aren't content with just taking his seat at council. You'd really have his realm too?"

"I would have order, which maintains the peace." Khuthon glared back at his sister. "I trust *you* could respect *that*?"

"Then you should have come to the council," said Ganatar, "made your desires known, and then—"

"And then we would have been in the dark as to the rebellion that's already flared up." Khuthon stepped over his brother's objection. "Shador has declared himself regent of Altearin."

"Shador?" Rheminas gritted his teeth. His gray cloak made him appear as if he was covered with ash. "The same Shador who's been playing god behind our backs?"

Khuthon nodded, making sure to make eye contact with everyone around the table. "He's tried to tie it all up in a neat bow, but it's clear it's a revolt." He made sure to put as much concern in his voice as possible. "If we don't act quickly, the roots will only grow deeper. And who knows, it might even tempt others to try the same in other realms."

"And you learned all this from your delegation?" Dradin continued his studious stare.

"Yes. I sent them there to inform the leadership I was the new head of the Dark Gods, only to find the one who should have been eager to work with us while we sort things out had quickly claimed the throne instead."

"What did he say exactly?" asked Panthora, who, as in many previous visits, wore a hide-and-leather gown, keeping her dreadlocks in a ponytail.

"That he was voted to the position by a majority of the lords." Khuthon was careful with this part of the news. He had to present it just right or risk losing the foundation he was building.

"And all the lords got to vote?" asked Ganatar.

"That's how I understood it."

"That's not a coup then." Ganatar sat back in his seat. "He's been duly elected."

Khuthon snorted. "You think it was a *fair* vote? It's just a smokescreen. He wants cover for his life. Now that he's lost his patron—*temporarily* lost his patron—he's left open for what's due him."

"You're worried over a Lord of Darkness giving you trouble?" Aero was finding this all hard to believe. "Are we really afraid of a lone, beaten titan lord? Since when have you been so worried about the actions of just one man—divinity or not?"

"Since Cadrith Elanis." Asora's response chilled the air. Khuthon wasn't expecting that, but it helped turn things again in his favor, letting him continue building momentum.

"It's also about the principle of the matter," he continued, pressing the conversation forward. "If he's allowed to get away with what he's attempted, it could send the wrong message to others at this time when we need to shore things up."

"He might not be the most noble of persons," Dradin began, "but if what he said is true, then he hasn't done anything wrong in being named regent. And there is the matter of Altearin being Gurthghol's realm. The council is limited in what it can do in one another's realms."

Khuthon was quick to retort. "I think Gurthghol would understand if we took any needed action."

"Not when it was one of the first rules he established when he brought us together to form this council," said Olthon.

"Agreed," added Ganatar. "Shador's been elected to a proper position. We should respect that if it truly is the will of the lords of Altearin."

"And if it isn't?" Khuthon let his gaze swim between all gathered.

Ganatar remained unmoved. "All we have is your opinions and assumptions—far from solid evidence upon which to base any actions."

"It's just bad precedence," he returned. "*We* should decide who gets to watch over the realm, just like we did with Gurthghol's absence on the council. It's a matter for *gods* to decree."

"And why do I think you already have a candidate in mind to watch over Altearin as well as Gurthghol's seat?" Endarien crossed his arms, a less-than-thrilled expression soaking into his face.

"If he was elected, then where's the harm in his taking temporary rule?" Causilla asked of the others. "Shouldn't they be allowed some say in the matter? It *is* their realm, after all."

"Were *they* allowed a choice when Gurthghol first came to rule over them?" Rheminas hotly retorted. "No. Father's right. Precedent needs to be maintained. We're gods, and *we* rule over the realms. The time of the titans and titan lords ended with the rise of Vkar. A *god* must sit on Altearin's throne." His tone cooled as he added, "Until Gurthghol's return, of course."

"Vying for the seat yourself, are you?" Perlosa's smile was as frigid as it was sarcastic.

Khuthon ignored it, pushing all the sentimentality he could muster into his voice. "I know some of you have your doubts, but think of the long term. What might happen to Vearus and his sisters? Already there'll be less for them than there was for us in *our* generation. And now we seem to allow a realm to govern itself after one of our own spent so much time and effort to create it in the first place?"

"So you'd have us face another war?" asked Olthon.

"I'm saying we need to deal with this matter before it becomes more trouble than we'd like."

"Then it seems the easiest way for resolution would be to ask Shador to come and explain the matter to us directly." Dradin's comment shattered Khuthon's rising confidence.

"I've already made the facts clear." He swiftly attempted regaining his previous ground.

"*Your* facts," Ganatar clarified, "from your *own* perspective."

"And you weren't even there yourself," Causilla added. "It all came from your men."

"In speaking with Shador," Ganatar continued, "we can hear his side and see the whole picture so as to better rule on the matter."

"You mean put him on trial?" Panthora wasn't comfortable with the idea.

"No," said Ganatar, shaking his head. "We simply ask him to come to the council and give a report of his current elevation. We'd not hold him guilty of anything nor be looking to judge him. All we'd be seeking is information."

"And you'd withhold judgment about his cult on Tralodren too?" Rheminas' eyes narrowed. "There needs to be a reckoning for that. We can't just—"

"We have to determine this matter first," advised Ganatar. "Once we know things more clearly, then we can see what else we'll be required to deal with and how." While it wasn't what Rheminas wanted to hear, he kept his mouth shut.

Khuthon wasn't about to do the same.

"And you think he'll tell the whole truth?" He did his best to hide his irritation, but it still managed to leak out around the edges of his statesman-like veneer.

"I expect him to appear and give his report," Ganatar returned. "He might have been found guilty in other matters, but this is another altogether, and if we're to be wise and fair to Gurthghol, we should stand on what protocols we can. For the council's sake as well as any." Sensing a consensus on the matter, Ganatar seized the momentum. "Who agrees to calling Shador to stand before the council?"

All save Khuthon and Rheminas lifted a hand.

"Then it's agreed," Ganatar continued. "We'll summon him to give an answer. Now, what else is there to take up?"

"The scepter," said Perlosa.

"I agree." Khuthon was eager to try for the second item on his agenda. "We need to be sure it's well protected and made ready for any future attacks. A weapon like that needs to be well guarded and maintained."

"And it is," said Ganatar. "The Tularins are doing a fine job keeping watch over it here."

"But are *they* really suited for such a task?" he pressed. "They're loyal, yes, but are they strong enough to stand against any threat put before them?"

"Like another god?" Olthon lobbed the question Khuthon's way.

"We have to be open to the possibility—"

Panthora cut off Khuthon. "You really think one of us would be so driven as to take the scepter and turn against the pantheon?"

"It wouldn't be the first time one of our own has turned against us," Rheminas answered the goddess. "*Sidra* comes to mind."

"Exactly." Khuthon leapt into his son's logic.

"So now we need to be *fearful* and *distrustful* of each other?" Olthon soured on the developing discourse. "Is *that* what you'd like to sow among us?"

"It *would* be wise to take precautions," Perlosa put forth. "While we doubt anyone *here* would try to take the scepter for themselves, there are *others* outside our ranks who may covet it."

"But it's on Thangaria," Causilla stressed. "This is a *sacred* place—a *secure* place. Why *can't* it be kept here? The Tularins have kept watch over Vkar's essence all these years with no loss, why not the scepter?"

"My thoughts exactly," said Endarien. "This is the best place for it."

"Agreed," Aerotripton spoke up. "There's no better place for it." The others around the table also shared his sentiment.

Khuthon tried to think of a way to change the tide before he lost any remaining ground.

"Since it seems we've reached an agreement on *that* matter," Ganatar said, closing the discussion, "perhaps we can get on with some other matters the council was called to address."

Khuthon silently fumed. He'd been so close. This wasn't shaping up as he had hoped, but he wasn't going to surrender. He still was head over the Dark Gods and would make that work as best he was able by pushing for the rest of his agenda as the council continued.

• • •

Shador was working on balancing ledgers in his private study. Twila had apparently been pretty liberal with those gold bars in securing his support to the regency. He wasn't entirely upset about it, since he realized he was in a position to remedy any shortages, but he made yet another mental note on matters of finances for the realm. They needed to keep some semblance of balance and order, and spending chests of coin like they were water wasn't any way to endear themselves to Erdis and Mergis, let alone the rest of the lords and even the pantheon.

Taking a break to sip some wine, he heard a knock at his door.

"Yes?"

"Visitor, my lord—one Atticus Worin."

"The jeweler? Send him in." Shador rose as the same bearded titan he'd seen not so long ago made his entrance with a small wooden box in hand.

"I made better time than I thought." Atticus approached.

"Much better than I could have hoped. May I see it?"

"Of course, my lord." Atticus handed him the box.

Shador noticed the lid was on hinges, allowing him to lift it with ease. Inside the tiny crate rested something truly splendid. "I like the black diamonds. Dominant but tasteful." He lifted the new necklace off the purple cushion upon which it rested. The pendant was a diamond-studded oval. Black diamonds outlined the lip, with one larger one in the center. The rest were a mixture of blue and white diamonds that sparkled in the light. Shador took hold of the latticed silver chain, noting the strength and craftsmanship of the material.

"The pendant opens by means of two concealed latches." Atticus motioned to where they were. Shador enjoyed their hidden nature; they were clearly meant to be secure and secret. Yet another request Atticus more than achieved. Opening the latches revealed an area just large enough to place the other necklace inside, its chain nestled along the perimeter of the pendant to keep it from tangling.

Eager for a final proof, Shador fished out the other necklace from his pocket and neatly set it inside. "A perfect fit," he told the grinning Atticus.

"It won't even so much as rattle once inside," he replied.

Shador closed the pendant and redid the latches before giving it a shake. Nothing. It was one solid piece. "It's perfect. You've more than earned your pay."

"Thank you, my lord." Atticus bowed.

He was donning the necklace when there came another knock at the door. "Lady Twila, my lord."

"Come in," he replied.

Twila had Aris once more at her side, who curiously sniffed Atticus' pant leg as Twila made quick note of the new necklace.

"Something to celebrate my recent elevation," Shador hurried to explain before she could think or say anything else. He turned to Atticus. "You outdid yourself, Atticus. Please see the Swarthin attendant on your way out for your payment."

"It was an honor to have worked on it, my lord." Atticus took his leave, allowing Twila a closer inspection.

"I thought you were worried about all that gold we spent?"

"We'll get it back," he replied. "This is more about presentation. I figured it was an item fit for a regent."

"That mean you have something for me?"

"When we can make things more official, I will." He covered himself quicker than he would have thought possible, but experience, it seems, was proving a fast teacher.

"Well, you might not want to wear it before the pantheon just yet." Shador's eyes narrowed. "What do you mean?"

"I just intercepted a Tularin," she explained. "He told me the pantheon had summoned you to answer some questions."

"You intercepted him rather than let him come directly to me?" He'd been willing to let things go up until now, but this was crossing a line. One he had to make sure wasn't going to be crossed again.

Twila instantly saw her error. "I'm sorry. I thought the fewer who knew he'd arrived, the better it would be."

"Next time, you can leave such concerns to me," he advised. The deed was done. And she'd been warned. There was little he could do about it.

Aris nuzzled his right leg with his nose, causing Shador to stroke the midnight fur of his head. "So what else did he say?"

"That was all. You've been summoned to stand before them three days from now."

"A good thing you weren't slow in bringing me the message. I wouldn't want to be late."

"I'm sure it wouldn't be too hard to find an excuse to—"

"No. I need to go. They can't touch me. It's time they understood that." He let his gaze linger, letting her catch the implications of his underlying message. "Erdis is with me and Mergis isn't about to risk trying anything. The pantheon needs to know of that solidarity—needs to know what they risk destroying if they try to remove me from power."

"Then I'm coming with you." He wasn't expecting that.

"They'll only want to speak to me; they won't even give you an audience. You'd be wasting your time."

"I'll be the judge of that."

"Don't you have enough to keep you busy with your own affairs?"

Twila drew closer. "I thought *you* were my affairs."

He was going to say something more but was interrupted by Aris' growling. The barghest had turned his attention to a deeply shadowed corner of the room. From out of that darkness a humanoid form emerged. The shape continued refining itself until all could clearly see it was an Umbrian. Twila reached for the dagger she kept hidden in her left sleeve. Shador braced himself until he recognized the Umbrian's features.

"It's all right," he told Twila.

"It's far from all right." She kept the dagger at the ready. "You have an Umbrian in your private quarters."

"Yes, I do."

"And you're just going to let him stand there?"

"He's here with some news, I take it." Shador kept focused on Rilas while continually petting Aris to keep him from tackling the incarnate outright. "We agreed to keep each other informed on any further developments."

"You *agreed*? And when was this?"

Both Rilas and Shador ignored Twila's question.

"Though I was expecting another Swarthin, not yourself," he told his guest.

"It seemed the best option, given what I have to say," said Rilas.

"What's going on, Shador?" Twila was truly surprised. "You *know* this Umbrian?"

"Well enough to know he wouldn't be here for no good reason." Shador took some pleasure in seeing there was something he'd managed to keep from her. Assuming her surprise was genuine, that meant she wasn't the source of any leaks about the scepter.

"True," said Rilas, taking a step forward and ignoring the growling barghest. "It seems our window to act is now open."

"You heard the news of the pantheon too."

"More or less."

"How?" Twila huffed. "I only just—"

"Are you sure it's wise to talk in front of her?" Rilas nodded at Twila. "The smaller the circle—"

"*I* can be trusted," she shot back. "As to *you*—"

Aris gave a harsh bark.

"He's a friend, Aris," Shador assured the barghest with some more petting over his tense neck and upper back.

"A friend?" Twila's eyes became slits as they searched Shador's face.

"More an ally of convenience," Rilas corrected.

"Rilas. Twila." He introduced each to the other.

"From Gurthghol's harem, wasn't she?"

Twila sneered at Rilas' questioning gaze.

"He had good taste," Shador added, taking special note of Twila's hard glare and tight-pressed lips. Yes, he was rather enjoying seeing her unsure in her footing. It gave him hope for being able to do more of it in the future.

"What are you planning?" she growled. Her charm had evaporated like so much smoke in the breeze.

"To secure my place for good."

"By using an *Umbrian*? They hate *all* the Lords of Darkness. He'll turn on you if given half a chance."

"Not when we have a common goal."

"Which is?" Twila crossed her arms.

"Keeping the gods out of Altearin."

"And the Lords of Darkness out of our affairs," Rilas added.

"You're good," said Twila, "but not that good. Even if you can get through a council meeting with the regency still intact, they could still try to take Altearin whenever they want."

"Not if we had that scepter, remember?"

"Yes, but that's under lock and key in Thangaria. How do you plan to—the Umbrian. So that's where you went the other morning."

Rilas bristled. "Are you *sure* she can be trusted?"

"Can you, Twila?" Shador faced her with a boldness she clearly wasn't expecting.

"I'm more worried about *him*," came her predictable reply.

"If you're going to Thangaria, there won't be a more opportune time," said Rilas.

"Don't you think they'll miss it?" Twila stated the obvious.

"No," Rilas continued. "I'll make sure of that."

"How?" she pressed.

Rilas stared Twila down. "With nothing that need concern you."

"I'm still going with you," she declared. "You'll need me—now more than ever."

"For what, exactly?" Rilas kept up his needling.

"To keep you honest, I think." Shador couldn't keep the crooked grin from showing.

Rilas apparently had the same challenge. "I wouldn't be here if Shador didn't already trust me. *You*, on the other hand, can be a liability."

"Or a distraction," Shador quickly added when he saw Twila's mouth about to snap open for a retort. "To our enemies, my dear, not us." While it might have smoothed her features, it didn't extinguish the blaze behind her violet eyes.

"You might not be able to join me in Vkar's Hall, but you could help provide some distraction, if needed. At the very least it would give them someone else to watch, splitting their attention and perhaps allowing Rilas a greater chance at success."

"All right." Rilas sighed. "It's not ideal, but I can work around it."

"What else do you need to prepare?" asked Shador.

"I'm ready now," said Rilas.

"Then meet us back here in three days. We'll be waiting for you with a griffin—"

"I won't need a griffin, just you to hold to your part of the deal." Shador watched Rilas' form fall to the shadowed floor like water pouring onto a hard surface. One moment he was there, the next gone, blending into the surrounding shadows.

"This had better work," said Twila. "We've invested too much to squander it on some—"

"We need that scepter, Twila. It's the last piece of the plan, remember. Get it and we'll both be set for a long time to come."

"You're right," she relented. "But why did you keep it all from me? I could have helped."

"How? *Rilas* reached out to *me* and barely trusts me as it is. You just heard what he thinks of you."

"Yes but—"

"It's going to work out. Don't worry. We'll be fine. And I really do need to finish these ledgers." He motioned to the books on the table he'd been writing in before Atticus arrived. "So if there wasn't anything else you needed . . ."

Twila looked as if she was about to try to say something more but at the last moment relented. She tried making the frustrated sigh sound like a pleasing exhale, but it didn't fool him.

"Of course." She made to leave the room but stopped halfway, turning her head over her shoulder. "Will I still get to see you tonight?"

"We'll see."

She hid her disappointment well, but it was the best answer for the moment.

"Come, Aris." The barghest eagerly followed after his mistress, once again leaving Shador to his budgets.

CHAPTER 17

The last three days had gone by quickly, but Shador wasn't worried. Instead, he stood before a long mirror in his dressing room, admiring his rich black robes and hooded cloak. The subtle black-on-black designs only made their appearance known whenever he moved just right for the light. Other than this, it appeared the regent was covered in a swath of night. He'd polished his black diamond-studded onyx circlet especially for the occasion but refrained from taking any additional adornment. He wanted to strike the right balance of legitimacy and humility.

As planned, he'd been preparing himself at his keep, allowing few visitors, which kept those like Mergis and others away. Mergis had already given him an earful of what he thought of this upcoming meeting and why Shador couldn't afford to get above himself. There was some other advice accompanying this, but Shador paid it no mind. He had his plans, and they were more than sufficient for what was needed.

"You ready?" Rilas poured out of some nearby shadows.

Shador still wasn't comfortable with the ease in which he did so—and unannounced—but let such concerns pass.

"Right on time." Shador feigned congeniality.

"Just make sure you keep them talking."

"Oh, I'm sure they won't need any encouragement there." Shador made his way for the door. "They'll probably spend the first half of our meeting lecturing me."

"And where's Twila?" Rilas followed Shador's lead.

"Waiting at the griffins."

"She isn't going to get in my way, is she?"

"No. She's going to be watched closer than she might realize, so she won't dare anything that might show our hand."

The two of them traversed the empty hallway and went out another set of doors that brought them to a small courtyard with two griffins saddled and prepared for departure. Beside the griffins stood Twila, who wore a new deep purple robe for the occasion. Traced with a black scrolling design along the hem and cuffs, it made a fine complement to her black hooded cloak.

She kept her hood down, displaying just how much extra effort she'd taken in adorning herself for the journey. Like Shador, she wore her onyx circlet, marking her as a Lady of Darkness, but she also added a set of dangling onyx earrings with some polished fluorite. The hue from the gems was matched by her eyeshadow and lips. Combined with the dark complexion all Lords of Darkness shared, it made for an intriguing mix. Shador approved. It was striking and memorable, which was no doubt what she was hoping to achieve.

"So good of you to arrive on time." Twila greeted Rilas from the back of her griffin with only thinly veiled sarcasm. The Umbrian ignored her as he approached Shador's griffin. The saddle was clear above his head, making the already-dominant creature even more so in comparison.

"I'll wait as long as I can, so make sure their full attention is on you," said Rilas, watching Shador mount the griffin.

"Well?" Shador peered down at the incarnate.

In a heartbeat Rilas blended his form into a flat shadow and seeped into the darkness under the griffin's saddlebag like ink. Once this was finished, Shador gave his griffin a small kick, and both he and Twila ascended into the clouds.

It didn't take them long to reach the capital, where they found the appropriate portal to Thangaria. Not surprisingly it was the oldest portal in the realm. The titanic empire had expanded from Thangaria, putting the world of Ladon in its sights long before Gurthghol merged it with the planes of Umbrium and Anomolia into the present realm. Instructions had been given to activate the portal when they were sighted, allowing them continuous passage up to and then through the portal itself. Shador wasn't about to waste any time, providing every part of the plan as smooth a path as possible.

Shador took the lead through the disk of light, Twila right behind him. And before he could take two breaths, both he and Twila had brought their griffins to land on the other side of the mystical gateway. The former titanic home world had been destroyed with the death of Vkar, the first god, turning it into a field of floating debris, where this portal and the palace remained on the largest of the rocky chunks.

He calmly kept to his griffin as the gruff-looking titanic mystics who manned the Thangarian portal—or rather, what remained of it—gave both of them a hard stare. One did not just appear on Thangaria—even if summoned. There were certain protocols. And unless you were a god, you didn't have the luxury of avoiding any of them.

"State your name and business," the first mystic said in Titan, the official language all would be using from here on out. He, like his companion, kept his white hair short. Their brassy skin contrasted the somber shades of their robes.

"Lord Shador, and this is Lady Twila," he replied. "We're from Altearin. I've been summoned to the council."

The other took them in from head to boot with his green eyes. There was a healthy respect among most titan lords for the mystics. It was from them that the first titan lords emerged, after all. And they did have a hold of cosmic power in some ways equal to that of the lords, who'd focused on a single element for their mastery instead of wielding all of them, like the mystics did. For a moment Shador feared the mystic might have enacted a spell or ability of some sort which helped further discern his intentions. But just as quickly the fear passed with the other's soft nod.

"All right. You're expected. But only you."

"What?" Twila snapped before getting herself under control.

"She's part of my testimony," Shador calmly returned. "Depending on what we get into, they may wish to speak with her as well." The other titan paused, considering the matter. "And if they do," Shador added, "I'm sure they'd appreciate having her closer at hand rather than up here."

"Fair enough," the mystic relented. "You're free to go. You'll meet your escort after landing."

Shador brought his griffin back into the open sky. Though there really wasn't much in the way of air here, just a thin grayish atmosphere the gods had been able to salvage around the palace and this portal which allowed beings like himself and Twila the means to continue breathing. The griffins had a curious ability of surviving longer without such comforts. One of many traits that had so endured them to the titanic heart—especially after they'd embraced a more imperial outlook.

While the palace wasn't far, always in sight of the piece of planet holding the portal, it was still surrounded by other debris which needed navigating. The expansive cloud of it went on for miles. The former seat of the Thangarian Empire was nothing but floating pieces of lifeless rock. Here Twila and Shador dodged and ducked the bobbing asteroids and clouds of dust. Finally the large stone island that served as the pantheon's seat came fully into view. They made their griffins veer for the palace's courtyard around Vkar's Hall. After their ears had popped, they heard wings flapping their way.

"The pantheon has been expecting you, Lord Shador," said one of the five fair-skinned Tularins stoically. "You will be escorted inside. *Only* you." He gave Twila a passing glance. "Your guest shall have to remain outside the hall." Twila was about to speak up when Shador shot her a hard look, strangling any rebuttal in her throat.

"Of course." Shador dismounted. "See to the griffins," he told Twila and made his way toward the hall. "I won't be too long."

She dismounted, keeping her eyes on the saddlebag on Shador's griffin. Four Tularins had left to escort Shador to his meeting. Two in front and two behind, as if he were a criminal about to stand trial. The one that remained with Twila went from griffin to griffin.

"I'll see to some water for your mounts."

"Thank you." Twila plastered a smile on her face. "You'd better not fail," she told the saddlebag. After the Tularin had departed, a dark shadow sank from under the bag and onto the cobblestone, where a puddle of it swelled before slithering for the hall.

• • •

Once again the gods gathered on Thangaria, this time to hear from Shador. And in keeping with the nature of the event, the pantheon assembled in a room common to such venues. It had once been Vkar's audience chamber. Now it served all the gods.

They sat on golden thrones arranged in a semicircular dais opening to the room's two large doors. In the middle sat the leaders of the three factions: Ganatar, Dradin, and Khuthon. To their left were their siblings and the Race Gods, to their right, their children. While each took a guise, all had decided to appear in their true form, making sure they put on the best appearance and presence for the proceedings.

Lit by the crackling braziers placed on either side of the semicircle's mouth and two more below where the three head gods sat, the room was devoid of any further decoration. Indeed, it was the most drab in the hall, and the faded and broken mosaics and frescoes were in need of repair. For if Vkar's Hall was meant to be a shrine, then this was the shrine of that shrine—the very room in which Vkar and Xora had met their ends at Sidra's hands. It therefore made for a fitting place to face another possible threat to the pantheon.

"Are we ready?" Ganatar asked of the others, noting everyone's response carefully. Seeing they were, he instructed the two Tularins at the doors to open them.

The hooded Shador glided into the room with careful steps. "Most esteemed council, I've come at your request." He bowed low.

Khuthon watched him carefully. Given his introduction and demeanor, he could see the would-be regent of Altearin was going to play things as smoothly as possible. He wasn't expecting anything less, actually. He knew Shador was smart and had laid out some strategies in keeping with that understanding.

Ganatar took the lead as the doors clanked shut, securing the chamber. "Are you aware of why you've been summoned?"

Shador peered up at the god of light, squinting slightly at the slight glow the god often exuded from his person. "I was told you wished to discuss recent events on Altearin—namely my election to care for the realm until Gurthghol returns."

"That and a few other matters," Khuthon flatly added.

"I'll do my best to relay what I can. But I don't see what I've done to warrant a trial."

Yes, he was keeping things quite smooth. Khuthon admired his effort.

"This isn't a trial," said Dradin, "merely a venue for us to hear what has happened in Altearin and what might be in store in the days to come."

"I see." While Shador didn't smile, Khuthon was sure he could hear it hidden away in his voice. They'd already confirmed his continued safety; why wouldn't he be happy?

Ganatar began the questioning. "Could you please explain for us what led up to the events that have you now sitting on Gurthghol's throne?"

"Gladly. The other lords and I heard of Gurthghol's . . . sudden departure after the battle here on Thangaria and knew that without him Altearin would quickly fall into—you'll pardon the phrase—chaos. Perhaps a better description might be 'fragmented sects.' We needed to keep the realm united, at the very least, for our lord—and in the meantime, for our own well-being."

"So you strong-armed your way to the seat?" Khuthon insinuated more than inquired.

Shador calmly directed his darkened cowl at the god of war. "No. It was decided among the most senior-ranked Lords of Darkness and Chaos that one of us was best suited to help keep things from unraveling and a vote should be taken." Shador shifted back to Ganatar. "It seemed the only fair way at the time."

"And Mergis, the other viceroy appointed by Gurthghol, agreed to this?" Ganatar continued.

"It was actually his idea. And he had the opportunity to stand for regent as well, but he didn't get enough votes."

"So you're saying you have the support of both the Lords of Chaos *and* of Darkness?" Olthon was clearly intrigued.

"Yes, Your Highness. And a rare thing too, which surprised me as much as everyone else."

"I'll bet," Khuthon muttered.

"Following my election I was informed by Khuthon—or rather a delegation sent by him—that he'd been elevated to the rank of head of the Dark Gods. I passed on my congratulations and informed the delegation of my own recent elevation, which I assume has been passed on to you, since I'm now standing here having to answer for it."

"So how long do you plan on ruling Altearin?" Rheminas cut straight to the chase.

"As I've said, I don't have any desire to be there longer than I have to. It's something of an unfortunate necessity—one I don't take lightly."

"And did you think of contacting the pantheon to see what might be done rather than acting on your own?" Rheminas continued.

Khuthon was pleased. It was good seeing his son engaged in the process. While he might have a natural tendency of being a bit too suspicious at times, in moments such as this it helped serve Khuthon's plans rather nicely. It also helped having another to pepper Shador with the right questions rather than trying to do it all himself. He could come across as adversarial to a point but couldn't really cross too many lines if he wanted everything to work out as he planned.

"No," said Shador. "We had thought the matter could be easily resolved with us, and truth be told, after the recent events you might have had other pressing matters to attend to. And Altearin hasn't always been that high on the pantheon's list of priorities."

"So you took a god's seat on your own initiative?" Rheminas' eyes narrowed.

"It could seem that way, I suppose, but it wasn't the intention."

"And what is your intention for Altearin now?" Olthon helped cool the room with a less belligerent manner.

"I intend to keep Gurthghol's policies intact and act as if he's still here for as long as we can. I will be required to make some choices, but for the most part, if we keep to day-to-day things, it will be like he never left. As I'm sure many of you might be aware, he entrusted many of the duties to Mergis and me long before his recent absence. He never did have that great a love of the daily details of running a realm."

"I was under the impression he had a trusted chamberlain as well," said Asora. "Where is he in all this?"

"Erdis? Yes, a very loyal and honest Kardu. I've spoken to him and he agrees with Mergis and me that we should work together for the good of the realm and all in it."

"And he did this *freely?*" Rheminas emphasized the last word quite heavily, to Khuthon's delight.

"Oh yes. He has no interest in seeing things fall apart any more than you or I or Mergis does. This is our home; we don't want to lose it."

"And what of his army?" Khuthon leaned forward.

"I'm afraid I don't understand the question."

"The army you now have control over," he again accused more than explained. "Gurthghol held on to that as his own. Now that you're regent, it would fall into your hands. So what are your plans for it?"

"To defend the realm, as always." Shador humbly returned Khuthon's hard glare. "But since we don't have anything of a threat looming over us, I hope we'll be able to be at peace for some time."

"It's better to have this put out in the open, rather than continuing to beat around it," Causilla began. "There's the obvious coincidence of you taking Gurthghol's seat just after losing your cultists on Talatheal."

Khuthon wasn't expecting that but wasn't going to stop the line of questioning from continuing either. This might work even better and faster than he first imagined.

Shador paused, considering Causilla carefully before addressing the rest. "I'm aware of how things might appear."

"And of how you wouldn't even be here if not for your present rank?" Rheminas was growing more aggressive by the moment. "You tried to put yourself forward as a god. You can understand why some of us aren't pleased with where you are now."

"What has happened in the past is in the past." Shador did his best at remaining the humble servant. And for the most part, he succeeded. But Khuthon wasn't having any of it. And it was time to push the offensive just a little more . . .

"Is it?" He raised an eyebrow. "Your cultists get destroyed and then, lo and behold, you suddenly become a regent, which grants with it certain privileges and protections from any further reprisals. One could look at it as a means of seeking to build up even more power."

"Or to take revenge," Rheminas added.

"Again, what was done in the past is in the past," Shador repeated. "I can't change it."

"Yet you don't apologize for it," said Ganatar.

Again Shador paused. Khuthon could almost see some worry collecting in the corners of his eyes. "I won't deny what I did. That can't be changed. I let myself get carried away in something I had no business doing in the first place."

"Was that an apology?" Rheminas glanced Ganatar's way.

"More like an excuse," offered Khuthon.

"But would you do it again?" asked Endarien. "We already know you're capable of it, but would you repeat it if given the chance?"

"Forgive me"—Shador dropped his chin to his chest to accentuate the humility in his voice—"but haven't you allowed everyone on Tralodren free will to decide what they want to do and whom they want to worship?"

"As the creators and defenders of Tralodren we have discretion to act as seems right and proper for the continued good of the world," Ganatar explained.

"And what was I doing, then, that threatened that good?" Shador ever so gently pressed.

Oh yes, he was very good. Khuthon was growing more impressed with him by the moment.

"We're deviating from the matter at hand," Dradin said, seeking to right the conversational cart. "The matter is what has happened in Altearin. The concern of some is that you've crossed a line that should not be crossed. Something that has never happened before has taken place and done so without our sanction."

"I only acted in the best interest of our people and the realm overall, as I said."

"That may be so," said Olthon, "but in taking on the rights and authority of a ruler of a realm—which are the domains of gods alone— you've entered into an area that is unprecedented and untested. And while it's admirable what you've sought to do in honor of your lord, you can't keep that seat forever."

"I am well aware of that, Your Highness."

"So then you must have a plan for if the worst case develops," Ganatar continued.

"If Gurthghol shouldn't return, you mean?" Shador sounded as if he were grieved to even contemplate the idea. "I'd never wish for such a thing, but if it did occur, we'd handle it as best we could."

"And how might that be?" asked Endarien.

Shador paused. "If it ever would come to such a situation, then I suppose the best course would be to seek the pantheon's aid and intervention. As I've already stated, I'm not looking to replace my lord. Should the worst occur, it would fall upon unique situations to bring about a solution." It was an interesting ploy. Khuthon hadn't thought he'd use it but had planned for the occasion just in case.

"Are there any other questions?" asked Ganatar.

No one said anything further.

"Very well." He motioned to the Tularins and they opened the doors. "Please wait outside while we decide how we will proceed on this matter. We'll summon you once we've reached our verdict."

Khuthon waited until the doors had shut. "He's lying."

"He was duly elected," said Ganatar.

"That's what he *says*," he continued, "but if we take some troops and—"

"We're not going to bring about another war," Olthon adamantly returned.

"Then if we allow him to go, we've just let him off his leash." He let his voice raise ever so slightly. He was building his case, and proper presentation was a large part of it.

"Have we?" Olthon wasn't so convinced. "We've given him parameters in which to operate—clear expectations and standards. And ones to which he has agreed."

"You've shown him how much he can get away with," Khuthon growled. "And he's going to make sure he uses every possible avenue he can to do so."

"And so what is *your* solution, Father?" Perlosa's question grated him more than usual. "That you lead a force to conquer Altearin and make it your own instead?"

Khuthon's growing ire burned into Perlosa's cool visage. Her previously agreeable mood of their last encounters had fled, leaving her as she'd always been. He wasn't hopeful for a change and wasn't surprised seeing things shift back to normal. Asora, though, might have thought differently.

"We need unity now more than ever," stressed Panthora. "I fail to see what we lose by allowing Shador to serve that purpose for the time being in Altearin."

"Only if he would be appointed to the seat," Rheminas tried to make clear to Panthora. "He wasn't elevated like you were but was—"

"Elected by the lords of the realm," Ganatar interrupted. "To go against their wishes, no matter how unprecedented, would be standing against what we enact here—what *Gurthghol* brought about in the first place."

Leave it to Ganatar to stand on order and rule of law. Not surprising but still a burr in Khuthon's side and something more he'd need to overcome with the others. And so the discussion continued—back and forth between various views and gods. All brought up their own thoughts and concerns, making the matter extend into a much more vigorous debate than any had expected.

But through it all Khuthon wove his words into the conversation, pushing his ultimate end and desire. He was hopeful he'd win out in the end if he remained consistent and worked all the angles to his advantage. It was a gamble in some ways but one he was willing to make. The rewards far outweighed any risks and efforts to achieve them, and so he pressed on through the verbal fray, mentally focused on his forthcoming victory.

• • •

While the gods debated, Shador had emerged from the chamber with the same humble façade he'd worn before the council. It wouldn't do to shed it just yet. The Tularins were the eyes and ears of the pantheon, and he needed to keep up appearances.

"Please remain here until the council has reached its decision," said a pale-faced Tularin.

"Of course," he politely replied, wondering how serious of a threat they could pose if he decided to disobey their wishes.

While he'd done his best before the gods, he wasn't entirely sure how much time Rilas needed. You could only defend yourself so long before it hurt more than helped your case. He was surprised they'd let him get away with what he'd said about his cult, but at the present there wasn't really anything they could do. He was a regent and, like they said, was afforded some protections. It certainly had chafed Rheminas. It had taken all he had to keep from laughing at the god's vexation.

So far the guards hadn't been summoned, and there wasn't a commotion in the halls. It seemed Rilas remained undetected. Hopefully, he was closer to where he needed to be. He didn't know how long the gods needed to debate, but he didn't envision it taking hours. What time Rilas had was limited. He'd better make full use of it. Shador wasn't going to stay here any longer than he had to.

• • •

Inside the same hall a shadow flowed throughout the corridors without any notice. Those few Tularins Rilas did pass weren't considering the ground, allowing him to slip by without any trouble. So far what Bron had told him was proving true yet again. The ease of his progress was encouraging, though he knew he'd have to slow his pace once the scepter was in sight.

But it was the light that was proving the greatest challenge. It came through random windows and fat globes of white glowing illumination hanging from chains descending from the ceiling or elsewhere across the walls like torches. Every time he got too close, he winced, barely able to keep his eyelids parted beyond a tight squint. And yet he somehow forced himself onward, closing his eyes entirely when needed for a momentary respite. He was finding it helped to use the darkness he was traveling as a screen, which diminished some of the threat, but not all. And he wouldn't be able to do that all the time—especially when he reached the scepter.

He'd taken on a humanoid shape though remained in his two-dimensional form for total ease of movement. Silently, he slid through the broken halls and battered walls, following Bron's directions. It took some turns and twists amid the ancient interior, but he had a sense of making progress. It didn't help the place was built for a god and titans, which made his slow speed seem even slower, but thankfully the corridors thus far hadn't been so highly populated. Only a handful of Tularins occupied the area.

And then he rounded another corner and came upon just what he'd been seeking: a fully restored hallway where two Tularins stood before a massive iron door. A set of glowing globes of light shone on either side of the doorway like torches.

Rilas slowed and squinted, making sure he wasn't seen, and then sunk into the puddles of shadow littering the floor. He used the moment to refresh his vision and focus his thoughts. He'd need both clear for what came next.

A few heartbeats later, he worked his way up to and then under the Tularins' feet, gliding right under them and then the door behind them.

So much for keeping things secure. There hadn't even been so much as a mystical ward keeping him from entering. Once more Bron's words about their defenses proved true.

Inside was a rather empty and unimpressive room. It might have been a personal chamber at some time but was long ago stripped of its contents and left to become a storage room instead. Only this chamber wasn't like a normal storage room. Its walls were lined with sections fenced off with iron bars. Behind them were an assortment of chests, crates, and barrels.

Thankfully, the light wasn't as overpowering, emanating from only a handful of smaller white globes lining three of the four walls. There were no windows or any other doors, save the iron one under which he'd just passed. His attention was focused on the center of the room, where a square block of bars formed a central cell. The top of the bars were as tall as a titan but covered with a flat iron roof.

A Tularin stood watch on each of the cell's sides. They were like statues, faithfully focusing on what lay ahead of them, yet oddly not on the cell's contents. Rilas hadn't believed that part when Bron told him, but yet again the titan's words were verified. Behind the Tularins, inside the cell, was a ten-foot stone column. On top of it he could make out the scepter's silver sheen. The cell's locked door was on the side opposite the room's entrance. But Rilas wasn't going to need any keys to get beyond it.

Once again he slid across the floor, mimicking the pockets of shade. Upon reaching the cell, he slid between the bars. Twisting around the column like some sort of snake, he ascended to its top and stopped.

Listening intently, he held his breath. Nothing. The Tularins still kept their winged backs to the cell and him. Blinking the fresh tears from his eyes, he focused on keeping his lower body a two-dimensional swirl of shadow around the column while restoring his torso to its full dimensions. This allowed him to lean over the top of the scepter without actually touching it.

And that's when he saw just how plain it really was. While it still held a fine sheen, the silver was devoid of any markings or further embellishment. It was elegant in some ways, yes, but didn't possess anything that screamed for greater attention or investigation, which was probably the idea. If this really was something capable of bringing a god low, you probably didn't want to advertise the fact too boldly.

Completing his inspection, he didn't see any sign of traps or warning devices but couldn't be entirely sure until he actually removed the scepter. He retrieved one of the rods from under his cloak and brought the tip of it down on top of the scepter. Instantly, the object transformed into an exact duplicate. If he didn't know he held the fake one in his hand, he'd be hard pressed to tell one from the other.

Carefully, he took hold of the real scepter with his left hand while placing the fake one down in the exact same position with his right. He studiously considered his efforts. When no alarm was raised and he was confident in the look-alike's presentation, a small weight lifted from his shoulders. Retrieving the last rod from under his cloak, he touched the top of the scepter with it. Again the rod became the scepter's twin.

Smiling, he put the real scepter on his right side under his cloak, the fake one on his left. Once both were firmly attached to his belt, he became a flat shadow once more, uncoiled from the column, and hurriedly exited the cell.

Making his way out from under the door he decided to slide up and into the ceiling instead, better keeping himself from any additional eyes he might have missed the first time around. He wasn't about to press his luck. While this brought him closer to the globes of light, it also had the added benefit of masking him behind their mass and glow. Now, he just had to work his way back to the griffins and wait for Shador—assuming all went well with him.

• • •

Twila tried finding something interesting to occupy her mind. For a short while she had conjured some darkness between her hands, playing with it like a child might a wad of dough. But it was more entertaining watching the nearby Tularin's reaction to the experience. But he soon enough recovered from the spectacle, bringing her diversion to an end.

Left to her own thoughts, she soon found herself pondering the possibilities. It wasn't hard to imagine things all falling apart. They *were* dealing with an Umbrian, after all. And most wouldn't want to help a Lord of Darkness. And yet both he and Shador had seemed ready enough to join forces. It irked her discovering such a collusion was possible beyond her notice. She wondered how many more secrets Shador was keeping from her.

And then she noticed the dark patch off in the distance. At first she thought it was a common shadow. But this shadow moved, speeding along the ground and in her direction at a steady rate. It slid right beside the Tularin, who diligently kept his vigil over Twila and the griffins. But for all his supposed diligence, the Tularin entirely missed the shadow slinking over to Shador's griffin and then under its saddlebag. She had to force herself to keep from laughing.

Feigning boredom, which wasn't hard to do, she went and leaned against Shador's griffin, near the saddle. To her delight, the Tularin didn't seem to care.

"Did you get it?" She kept her voice low, speaking in Stygian for good measure.

"Yes," came a whisper from under the saddlebag. She had to keep her surprise in check. This Umbrian had just stolen something from the very heart of the pantheon's palace, and he was still breathing. It was more than amazing.

"Any trouble?" she asked.

"No."

"Did you see Shador?"

"No, but I wasn't really looking for him."

"Then we could be here for a while. The pantheon isn't always so quick to make up their mind—especially with no immediate threat on the horizon."

"Everything all right?" Twila was shocked to find the Tularin hovering nearly face to face with her. His curious eyes searched her own, causing a momentary twinge of fright.

"I'm fine." She quickly recovered with as innocent an expression as she could muster. She knew she couldn't rely on her usual charms. As incarnations of the very cosmic element of good, Tularins weren't ones to be as easily swayed or tempted as others might have been.

"I was just talking to myself. Guess I'm just getting a bit bored." She smiled politely. The Tularin gave the matter some thought, then let her be.

"Hurry up, Shador." She crossed her arms with a sigh. The last thing she wanted was to press their luck, and the longer they stayed out in this courtyard, the more it felt like that was just what they were doing.

CHAPTER 18

"Then it seems a vote is in order," Dradin concluded after the dust from their passionately protracted discussion had settled.

While Khuthon and Rheminas hadn't relented in their opposition, it wasn't enough to sway the others to their side. Eventually their arguments weakened and fell flat. He'd been hoping for more but knew when to stop and reconfigure his approach. And he did have more than one iron in the fire as it was. He didn't want to risk one in order to gain the other at the moment. It was better to let things play out and find a new angle to work. He'd find one soon enough.

"Don't say I didn't warn you," Khuthon informed the rest, making sure he had something to pick up again later when needed.

Ganatar ignored him. "All in favor of leaving Shador in charge until we can decide how best to move forward on the matters with Gurthghol?"

The result was a near majority; only Khuthon and Rheminas withheld their vote. He was surprised by Asorlok, but again, he wasn't going to press the issue. He'd only just assumed his place as head of the Dark Gods. If he started demanding or arm-twisting too soon, it would severely weaken his position, and right now, during this transition, he needed an image of strength to be front and center.

"Send for Shador," Ganatar instructed the Tularins at the doors, who opened them and invited the Lord of Darkness back inside. Once he'd entered the circle he stopped, looking into Ganatar's face through his slightly squinted eyes.

"It has been decided you may keep your current position in Altearin for the time being, but if there should be any change in the situation that needs to be addressed, you are to cede the matter and all rights to the pantheon."

"I understand, and it shall be done."

"Further, in your role you will also abide by the rules of this council and acknowledge that Khuthon holds the seat of rule over the faction Gurthghol has sided with. This doesn't mean you're to be treated as Gurthghol's representative on the council, nor sit with the pantheon in council, but you will have the right to rule over Altearin for the present time."

"I will look to do the best at representing what Gurthghol would have wished." The words were as feigned as the humility in which they were spoken. Everyone could clearly see it, but Khuthon let it slide. He was already laying the groundwork for his next plan.

"As to the other matters of your activities on Tralodren," Ganatar continued, "it has also been decided you've already received your punishment with the decimation of your former followers. Provided you do no such thing again while holding the regency of Altearin, no further actions will be made. However, should we discover you continue to engage in activities from which you were forbidden, then appropriate action will be taken."

"I understand," said Shador. "And I thank the council for their wisdom on the matter. You can rest assured, I won't squander the mercy you've shown me today."

"Not if you want to keep the regency." Khuthon's voice was a low growl just loud enough for Shador to hear. To his credit Shador didn't gloat, keeping himself from marring that humble-servant veneer.

"We will be keeping an eye on things," added Dradin. "It is quite possible there might be something that develops that could reveal Gurthghol's whereabouts."

"I have nothing to hide," Shador assured them. "I meant what I said before. I only wish the best for Altearin."

"As do we," Ganatar agreed. "Restoring order is a chief focus until everything that yet remains to be dealt with has been taken care of. You're free to go. May you watch over Altearin well."

"Thank you." Shador made a deep bow from the waist before silently departing both council and room.

Ganatar waited until the doors were closed before beginning the next topic on the agenda. "I believe the only other thing we need discuss is the possible changes to Thangaria's defenses. With the scepter resting here, among other items, it's wise to consider what might be lacking."

"Yes," Khuthon said with renewed energy. "And our last confrontation helped to reveal our present weaknesses."

"And how *do* we stand on the defense of Thangaria?" Ganatar asked Khuthon.

"I'm still working out what might be done, but given how rare the attack was and what forces are always stationed here, I'll need a bit more time to fine-tune a recommendation."

"Why not keep what we have?" Olthon inquired. "We haven't had need of any greater force before. And, like Khuthon said, this last attack was so rare—"

"And deadly," Rheminas broke in. "We can't afford such a surprise again."

"And so you'd keep a standing army here to stop your fears from materializing?"

"To protect what's left of our heritage," Rheminas quickly returned. "Now that the last of Vkar's essence is gone, all that remains is this palace and the small chunk of planet it rests on."

"I never thought you were the sentimental type." Shiril shot Rheminas a curious gaze that stilled his tongue and temper. Khuthon noticed he seemed to take an interest in her necklace for some time before coming back to himself. He couldn't see what was so interesting about it. The fire opal wasn't anything remarkable, and the bronze chain didn't stand out in particular.

"There's more to this place than history," Rheminas informed Shiril. "It's a symbol of the pantheon being unbeaten in the cosmos. Now more than ever, it exemplifies how we've withstood any threat that's ever risen against us."

"And so you'd turn it into a military base?" Olthon's brow wrinkled. "We have Tularins who are sworn protectors and curators. They're more than enough to keep the first line of defense, and should they need more, they'd be able to summon us, like this last time."

"But this last time we had some warning," said Asorlok. "We might not be so fortunate next time."

"Next time?" Endarien raised an eyebrow. "Is there something you want to share?"

"Things can happen faster than you might think—even unexpectedly," he replied.

"I don't see how things could get by us if we have Saredhel to warn us," said Aero. "She helped warn us of what came before and how to deal with it, and she'd do so again."

"As helpful as she has been up until now," Asorlok continued, "she still isn't infallible. And her visions aren't always clear when they might need to be. It wouldn't be unwise to put in place some extra protection, just to be sure we're ready to pounce on any potential threat."

"Why do I sense this breaking down over party lines?" Asora asked Asorlok.

"Doesn't just about everything else?" Rheminas shared a sardonic twist of his lips.

"I'd been hoping we could be more united moving forward—that recent events would have helped guide us to that end." Asora sighed. "But it seems old habits are hard to break."

"I don't like it," said Drued. "Why all this sudden press for change? I understand you have enemies, but who can really stand against you—besides the recent event, that is. And why even attack this place to begin with?

"There's nothing here, like we've been saying. Nothing left of Vkar. Nothing left of anything but an old palace. Why spend time and resources defending something that doesn't need any more than it has? The only reason the last battle was here was because we chose it to be."

"Before we put forward any new action, we have to see how we stand in our own realms," Endarien added. "I can't really commit to anything until I know how Avion fares. I still have a lot to look over, as I'm sure all of you do with your realms. It will take some time to get through all of it. It would be foolish to overcommit when we don't even know what might be at hand."

"How long would you need?" Dradin inquired.

"I'm not sure. More than a few days . . . I have to get a good run on my troops, check my own inner and outer defenses, tend to some matters I've been letting slip for a while . . ."

"A month?" Dradin probed.

Endarien paused. "I suppose I should be ready by then."

"And the rest of you?" Dradin scanned the other gods. "Would a month serve you as well?"

"It would help give me time to get the babies into a workable pattern, among other things," Asora offered, followed by the rest of the gods softly chiming in with their own thoughts on the matter.

"Very well." Ganatar rose from his throne. "Unless anyone else has anything further, I think we can adjourn until then."

"Good." Khuthon joined the others in standing. "I think I've had enough of these discussions for the time being. I can't remember us ever having so many councils so close together as these have been."

"Stay away from Altearin, Khuthon." Ganatar's face became as stern as stone.

"If action is required—"

"You'll leave it to the council."

"I'm aware of the verdict," came Khuthon's sardonic reply. "I *was* right here when you sought to tie my hands on the matter."

"The council was established to keep the peace," Ganatar continued. "It would be a terrible service to Gurthghol if we abandoned that purpose now."

"I'll keep that under advisement." Khuthon watched Ganatar make his way from him. So absorbed was Khuthon with the departure he didn't hear Asora draw near.

"Are you planning on visiting tonight?" Her green eyes sparkled. "I've enjoyed seeing you more often, and I know the children would love—"

"There's still too much I need to do."

"Are you sure it can't wait?" She stroked his chest with her hand. "I can have some roasted—"

"No." Khuthon cast aside her hand, along with the light previously dancing in her eyes. "There's just too much to do, and you have the babies now too. We have . . . responsibilities. And I should be returning to mine." He never saw Asora's shoulders sag with her sigh.

• • •

Shador focused on keeping one foot in front of the other. He didn't want to appear to be hurrying from Vkar's Hall, nor did he want to be too slow. A happy medium would see him through the journey. The four original Tularins had accompanied him up to the entrance and left him to find his way back to Twila and their waiting griffins.

He was still trying to keep from processing everything at once, focusing on one part at a time. He was still alive and had the pantheon's blessing to keep the regency of Altearin. It was just what he wanted. He worked hard to keep from bursting into a jubilant shout and run. He was nearly beside himself. He'd won. He'd actually won on his own terms. To say it was invigorating was to acknowledge water was wet.

He hadn't seen Rilas but didn't really think he would, skulking about as he was throughout the palace. Whatever time he'd been afforded had reached its end. And Shador wasn't about to try to play for any more. His only hope was Twila would have something to relay. If not, well . . .

The Tularin guarding Twila greeted Shador once he'd reached earshot. "I trust your meeting has ended?"

"Yes," he returned. "We've finished."

"Then you're free to leave," he said, motioning Shador to the griffins, as if he'd forgotten the way.

"Thank you." He didn't waste any more pleasantries and headed straight for his mount.

"You okay?" Twila followed him with her eyes.

"Fine. Everything is just fine. How about you?"

"It couldn't be better." Twila gave Shador's saddlebag a gentle pat.

He climbed into the saddle. "Then I guess we should be getting back to Altearin."

"So how did they take it?" Twila took to her own saddle.

Shador paused. "The regency? They let me keep it. Indefinitely." Anxious to get flying, his griffin started flapping its wings.

"Just like that?" She was amazed. Her griffin too started making some gusts.

"More or less." Shador gave the command, and his griffin took to the air.

Twila followed. "So then we—you really did it."

"Let's just get back to Altearin before we celebrate."

• • •

Twila fell silent, considering the saddlebag where Rilas had hidden. She'd continue eyeing it all the way back to Altearin and the palace. The trip itself seemed to pass like a puff of smoke. The stop at the portal, the final questions by the mystics, and then the flying through the portal and back into Altearin again was a blur. Once back at the other side of the portal with their griffins on the ground, she finally allowed herself some delight in the venture.

"What are you smiling about?" asked Shador as he dismounted.

"We did it. We *actually* did it."

"You're surprised?"

She stopped and considered. "I guess I am. I wasn't sure we could trust your new ally."

"Meet us in the throne room," Shador informed his saddlebag, then turned to face the capital. The portal being outside the heart of the city meant they'd have a walk to reach the palace, but it would be pleasant. Almost like a triumphant processional of old through the twisting streets.

"So what do you plan on doing with the scepter once you have it?" she asked when she'd decided they were safe enough from any ears and eyes, Umbrianic or otherwise.

"Let me get it first, then we can see what comes next." He'd been more guarded of late, keeping her from enjoying her usual review of developments. She wondered if it wasn't tied to something else she wasn't seeing.

Did he have a new partner to share his bed? Was he looking to ease her out once he took his full place as regent? Those were two rather troubling thoughts and possibilities—ones that would be explored more closely in the coming hours. If she was losing her grip on her position, she'd need to act quickly to restore it.

Eventually they entered the palace and made their way through the ancient corridors and various guards and statuary until arriving at the throne room. It was here Shador stopped and faced her.

"Ready?" The smile reminded her of old times. For a moment her concerns were set aside, fresh hope of a brighter future flooding her mind again.

"If you are," she replied, motioning for him to continue forward.

Shador didn't miss a beat, pushing aside the thick door and marching into the throne room. The empty throne room.

Twila closed the door and waited. They both waited . . . and waited. Finally, Shador moved for the throne. "Show yourself, Rilas."

At once the shadows of a nearby wall slithered in their direction. As they did, the Umbrian's shape formed itself from among them, stopping before the unimpressed Shador.

"I had to be sure I wasn't seen." The excuse felt as flimsy as the shade from whence he'd come, but Twila held her tongue.

"All right," said Shador, "but you're here now. So where's my scepter?"

"Right here." The Umbrian retrieved it from under the left side of his cloak. Shador clasped it instantly, admiring its every angle. Twila noted his pleasure. She could relate. To hold such potential in your hand . . . it had to be something indeed. She was looking forward to savoring it herself in time.

"Doesn't look like much," Shador quipped.

"But it will certainly pack a punch," said Rilas.

"And they won't notice it's missing?" Shador inquired.

"No. You're safe with it."

"Are you going to tell me how?"

"My leverage, remember?"

Twila doubted the Umbrian's smile was sincere, but it seemed to satisfy any of Shador's concerns.

"And you'd just hand it over?" She still found that part the hardest to swallow. "You don't want to keep it for yourself?"

Rilas turned her way, dark eyes hooded. "No."

"I find that rather interesting," she continued.

"We had a deal, Twila," said Shador. "And he's honored his part quite well, I think."

"And you trust him?"

"I'd say this is proof, wouldn't you?" He lifted the scepter for emphasis.

"But just *how* did you take it without being seen?" Twila wasn't about to let the matter drop.

"I'm good."

"But you didn't just leave nothing behind when you took it," she continued.

"If he had, there would have been an alarm." Shador stepped in, seeking to reduce the rising friction between her and the Umbrian.

"But how did you—"

"I don't see where any of that concerns you."

Twila scowled at Rilas' rebuke. She was about to snap something back when Shador inserted himself again.

"You did well and held to your bargain."

"And I trust you'll hold to your side?"

Twila couldn't read anything into Rilas' question, further frustrating her and increasing her dislike of him.

"Oh yes, you'll be given more freedom. Just don't take it all at once. We can't move too fast, too soon. As long as things happen gradually, none will be the wiser, and the gods will leave us all alone."

Rilas appeared satisfied. "Then I'll leave you to your spoils."

"Not going to stay and celebrate?" The sarcasm nearly dripped off Twila's tongue. She couldn't help it. This upstart incarnate clearly had a way of getting under her skin. The sooner they both were done with him, the better.

"Not with titans." Rilas faded from sight.

She turned to Shador, amazed. "You're really going to let him go?"

"We had an agreement, Twila."

"And you have no idea how he got it. Aren't you the least bit curious?"

"Not as much as you, obviously."

"But he could have just left an empty spot when he took the scepter."

"And so what if he did?" He gave the scepter another practice swing. "I was watched the whole time, as were you. We won't be suspected—even if it *is* discovered missing. And Rilas wouldn't leave any trace, because he'd know I'd hold him to it. The agreement was rather balanced that way—protecting *both* our interests. Sometimes you're too paranoid for your own good."

She bit her tongue, swallowing back the choice words that screamed for release.

"And don't worry. You'll get to share in the success, like we said."

And there she had it: confirmation of her place in all this. She was still where she needed to be and able to continue as she had been. Things were right and moving forward as they should and without any impudent Umbrians inserting themselves into the picture.

Twila coiled herself around Shador's chest and waist. "Does that include getting to hold it?"

"Maybe." He brought the scepter to his side, then shot her a look she knew all too well.

"Sounds like you could do with some persuasion." She traced her finger behind his ear, twisting a tuft of hair around it for good measure. "I can be pretty good at that."

"Then you're welcome to do your best."

CHAPTER 19

Rilas took a deep breath and held it, carefully going over everything one last time. He wouldn't have the luxury of second—or even first—thoughts once he summoned his guest. He'd seen to Shador well enough and had returned to Ulan without any trouble. Back in his throne room, he was still amazed it had all gone so well. But there was just one more thing that needed doing. One task that would make all of these last few days—the efforts and risks he'd taken—worth it.

"Be ready," he told the darkness in the room. His trusted warriors had hidden themselves in it, prepared for just the right moment. "We can't let him have the first move."

He took up the metal emblem on his lap and spoke to it once more. "I'm ready to meet."

Taking another slow breath, he waited. A few heartbeats later, there was a violet slash of light in the room. From It entered the cloaked titan. As before he maintained his guise as a Lord of Darkness.

"Do you have it?" Bron asked as the slash of light faded behind him.

"I do." Rilas took hold of the true scepter under his cloak.

"You did well." Bron admired the scepter as Rilas turned it in his hand. He enjoyed the heft of it. It felt right in his grasp.

"Better than Shador thought, I'm sure." Rilas descended the dais toward the titan. "And none the wiser that he got nothing out of the deal either."

"You've helped weaken both the pantheon and Shador," Bron continued. "You should be pleased."

"So what now? You've been so willing to share the future before; what's next to come?"

"I've told you all I can. The rest is up to you."

"What about Shador and the pantheon?"

"They'll find new distractions to keep them busy. Now if you would"— he held out his golden hand—"my master is awaiting my return."

"A shame to have to give it up." Rilas extended the scepter headfirst to the titan's waiting grasp.

"It'll be put to good use."

"Maybe," he said, pulling the scepter back rather sharply. "But not as good as what I have planned." Just as rehearsed, Rilas' men emerged from their hiding places. Each was armored and armed for a hard-pressed fight. He was sure Bron wouldn't let the matter go with anything less.

"Rilas?" There wasn't any fear in the voice, only a small twinge of annoyance.

"I'm sorry, but that scepter's too valuable to just hand over."

"You're making a mistake."

"I don't think so."

"You don't even know how to work it."

"I can learn."

"Not fast enough." Bron flung his hands forward, and half the men around him were slammed into the ground. The sound of breaking bones filled the throne room. The remaining men rushed him, but the titan was too fast and vanished before they neared.

"Keep a sharp eye!" Rilas ordered. "He could—"

He was silenced by a strong hand on his throat.

"You're being rather foolish," said his former ally from behind.

His other hand went for the scepter, yanking it free amid Rilas' grunting protests. He wasn't going to give up so easily. Rilas flattened into a shadow, dropping out of the titan's hold.

While the action might have saved his life, it didn't keep the scepter from Bron. Rilas watched him place it under his cloak. With Rilas free of his grip, his remaining men were able to inch closer with their spears leveled.

"You can stop your pretending," said Rilas. "Your *master* isn't anyone but yourself. I don't know what you may have been planning, but *I* did the work and *I'm* going to keep the reward." He motioned for his guards to close the remaining distance.

"I was told I could let you live." Bron barely gave the advancing warriors a passing glance. "But if you proved troublesome, I was to eliminate any loose ends." He reached back under his cloak. "You might not know how to use the scepter, but I do." He raised it as if to strike. "If you want it so badly, I'll be quite happy to give you a taste."

"Take him down!"

The guards rushed Bron even as Rilas melted into the darkness. The titan held his ground. The guards shoved their spears forward. But instead of piercing him, they found their spear points curving and bending back on themselves. Left holding twisted shafts, most had little else to defend themselves with when the titan attacked.

With another wave of his hand, all were flattened to the floor. In the next instant Rilas appeared on top of Bron. He'd wrapped his legs around the other's neck and pummeled his face with frenzied fists.

Enraged, the titan attempted to dislodge him. In the process the scepter was brought right up to him. Switching tactics, Rilas clamped both hands upon it, liberating it from Bron's hand. An eyeblink later he leapt for the floor and ran to the back of the room near the door.

"I'm asking you to be smart," he said. "You leave the scepter with me, and no one else will know."

"*I* will know and my *master* will know."

"Then you're just going to have to live with that. Unless you want me sharing the news with Shador and the pantheon about what you tried to do."

He'd reached the last of his contingencies. If Bron didn't take him up on the offer, then he'd have to go toe to toe. And given what he'd seen so far, he wasn't any keener on the option than he was before they reached this impasse.

"You wouldn't expose yourself by telling them. And you're just as guilty in the plotting. So you wouldn't be risking only yourself but your city—and maybe all the Umbrians across Altearin."

"You'll find we're more resilient than you think." Rilas tapped into the cosmic element of darkness and forced it in the titan's direction. A swirling black mass enveloped him in a dark cocoon.

The cocoon trembled and pulsed. Like a beating heart it expanded and shrank in size, back and forth. Rilas retreated a few steps as the process intensified. Finally, in a massive burst, the liquid darkness sprayed in every direction and blended back into the blackness that had spawned it. Where the cocoon had existed stood Bron.

"There is one greater than any cosmic element," he said. "Greater than any god or anything in the cosmos, and you'd be a fool to risk his wrath."

"I wouldn't be the first," said Rilas.

"And what now? You try to attack me again? That doesn't seem to be going so well."

"I let you leave with your life."

The titan laughed. "I'm taking that scepter."

Rilas again reached into the darkness, tapping deeper into the very heart of the cosmic element. This time the darkness coalesced into a titan-sized figure with black half-plate armor and a long sword in hand. Rilas willed it to attack.

Bron punched the elemental in the face. The creation didn't move. He tried again. Again the attack failed. The darkness elemental slammed his sword hand into Bron's face, and the titan toppled onto the floor.

Rilas watched the elemental bring down his sword. The blade barely missed a leg but allowed Bron room to maneuver to his feet.

Once righted, he summoned a violet blade. The glowing sword sliced through some of the armor but did no real harm. The counterattack, though, was deadly.

The elemental jabbed below Bron's left arm, drawing blood. A second attack slashed across his chest. The third strike cleft into his hood and neck, knocking Bron to his knees. A swift kick from the elemental toppled the titan. Blood spilled onto the dark floor from his wounds.

"You can tell your *master* if he wants the scepter, he's going to have to come get it himself," said Rilas.

The elemental finished the job, separating the titan's head from his neck. Freed from the hood, the head rolled into view. Rilas observed the golden skin and silver hair. The purple eyes stared into space while a circlet of pure amethyst studded with peridot, emerald, ruby, and diamond caught his eye.

"So much for you and your master. And now I have a new trophy." He laid hold of the head by its hair. "And I know just where to put it."

The guards were slowly forcing themselves to their feet. Some of them were more wounded than others, but they'd recover. And if they had been killed, it wasn't too much of a loss. Crafted from the realm, they'd return to it soon again, ready for the rest of their eternal lives. He'd been hoping for a cleaner resolution that hadn't involved killing Bron, just in case someone else really was pulling the strings, but what was done was done.

He doubted there'd be any real reprisals—planned on it, in fact. Even if Bron really wasn't his own master, the one behind the shadows wasn't going to risk stepping into the light. Of that much Rilas was confident.

He'd won. He'd played Shador and had beaten Bron. And none knew he now held one of the most powerful objects in the cosmos.

"It's time to celebrate," he said, lifting the scepter overhead. "This day marks the beginning of a new era for Ulan and every Umbrian everywhere." Facing the nearest able-bodied guard, he continued, "Summon the lords of the city. There's much that needs saying."

CHAPTER 20

Khuthon's eyes marched over a map of Tralodren—the Northlands were of great interest. Alone in the simple room which served as his private study, he took careful note of all the terrain and where the boundaries crossed. The various tribes of the north—the Nordicans in the south and the Jotun kingdoms in the northern reaches of the lands—had been established for quite some time.

He was never one to be content with just one strategy and often had several things he was plotting at once. It kept him active and prevented boredom. Most often he had a plan in place for things outside Tralodren and one or two that focused on the planet and its population. Usually, such plans were tied to his creation—the giants—but he wasn't above using the younger races when and where possible.

This new plan centered on the Northlands, a region he hadn't taken too much of an interest in for some while. It was time to advance his influence and bring about more of his control over those lands. Recent events and the monthlong break everyone would be taking before the next council were a good cover to keep everyone distracted from what was going on elsewhere. And if he did things just right—kept his hand out of view just enough—it would seem those in the Northlands were acting on their own and would be free to do so as long as things stayed within reason. And he'd make sure they would, until the final moment.

It was also an opportunity to teach the Jotun some lessons. They'd been giving too much ear to his daughter over the generations, and he'd have them come back to him—fully. *He* was their creator, not Perlosa, and it was to him they should show their honor and respect. He'd allowed for their split worship of both him and Perlosa, but now that he had a chance to do something about it, he was going to take it.

Khuthon pulled out a small metal figurine from a nearby wooden box and gave it a thorough inspection. The figure was made of copper and resembled a Jotun warrior. The giants of the Northlands had long been a force to be reckoned with but had become satisfied in recent generations to keep to their own land rather than claiming any more beyond their current borders. It was time to change that. Any weapon, no matter how great, if never used will rust and fall to ruin. And if they were his creation, they needed to do a better job of reflecting that truth to the rest of Tralodren.

Khuthon placed the small figure in the center of the Wolf Lands, a territory to the southwest of a land called Valkoria, the southernmost land in the Northlands. Another figure was added to the center of the Bear Lands. The third he placed in the center of the Plains of the Panther. He reached for a nearby chalice, drained it in one gulp, then studied the map again, searching out every possible counterattack or further avenues he would exploit.

Picking up one more figure, he placed it beside the marking designating the keep belonging to the Knights of Valkoria. These too had become an annoyance to his plans and desires in times past. And with the shamans gone thanks to Gurthghol's actions with Vkar's throne, Khuthon was eager to fill the void. It was only going to be him, Perlosa, or Panthora. The tribes never really allowed much else, even with the shamans at their greatest influence.

The knights were also a possible snare in his general plans with the Jotun. For with the shamans gone, the Jotun would be able to face the

Nordicans on equal footing. The Nordicans had no real mages to speak of, and the shamans were their only real defense. The other priests were too weak and too small in number. The only exception was the Panians and their knights and priests: a martial force who'd trained for generations for a fight. But Khuthon wasn't going to give it to them—not on their terms. No. He'd wipe them from the map before they knew what hit them and swoop in to claim his prize before anyone—whether mortal or god—knew what happened. Smiling to himself, he slid the figurine on top of the keep's icon, then took a step back to admire his work.

Not bad for the first wave.

• • •

Panthora contemplated the map of the Northlands. She was alone in her study. Her only company was the collection of lanterns shining their brilliant light around the wood-paneled room and the table on which the map rested. There was a bookcase to her left, but it wasn't filled to capacity. There were some old scrolls and a few thick tomes, but mostly there were maps and small wooden boxes.

She wasn't much of a scholar, even in her former life on Tralodren, but wasn't a stranger to planning. And she'd been doing much of that of late—especially following her visit with Asora. With another council weeks away and nothing further on her courtly agenda, she could take more fully to the rest of her plans.

Moving to the bookcase, she took one of the small boxes back to the table. Opening it, she studied the bronze figurines inside. They were men mostly—and humans, Nordicans specifically. Some were wrapped in hide and fur; others donned what would be considered modern attire by those presently inhabiting the Northlands.

Shifting back to the map, she considered Valkoria, the southernmost of the clump of four landmasses grouped into the Northlands. She put her finger on the Hymir Mountains. With the finger of her other hand she pointed to a place called Hosvir, the capital of the Panther Tribe. She noted the distance between the two locations.

Reaching for the box, she pulled out the figurine of a youthful Nordican. He wore the leather armor belonging to a lower-ranking Knight of Valkoria. The panther motif worked across it had been crafted in fine detail.

"Soon," she told the figurine. "Soon we'll get to meet face to face." She placed the figurine in a spot between the two locations she'd pointed at earlier, studying its placement carefully.

"Soon."

• • •

Saredhel sat at her desk studying the seventh and final Omnian Scroll. She had meant what she'd said about Asorlok helping her see new things. And for that she was thankful. But Asorlok had been truthful too. There was something beyond their previous discourse, and he and the others of the pantheon had a faint inkling of what it might be, at least as far as what she had seen fit to pass on. But as with so many other things when it came to the matter, she wanted to be sure of what she saw and understood before sharing it.

Such was the case with what she now viewed. The seventh scroll only had two visions, but they were important ones. These were the last two Omni had recorded. And each spoke of what was most likely to occur in what had become known as the Great End. In the section where the second vision was recorded was a black landscape with a hawk-nosed, cloaked figure holding out a large broken hourglass with both hands. This was the bottom half of the glass, and it was spilling sand at a rapid rate.

Then in an image immediately to the right, this same figure was wrapped in a collection of black tentacles, obscuring it from view. This was followed by the third and final image Omni drew of the vast cosmos—filled with stars and planets.

As with the rest of the scrolls, there were blocks of text accompanying the illustrations. And while she'd read these sections around these last three images many times over the years, she did so yet again, taking in what was said once more, expecting some further enlightenment.

It took me some days to fully recover from what I had seen in the last vision. And as the days progressed I thought perhaps my time of seeing such things was finally at its end, but then I experienced one final vision—perhaps the most strange and terrible of all.

I rose at night to fetch a drink of water when it was as if the whole of the world and all reality tied to it—vanished. I was once again surrounded by blackness and found myself fearing that perhaps I had returned to the place where I left off with the previous vision. But something was different this time.

There was a hooded man to my side, observing me. His cloak was as black as the darkness around him, and he nearly blended in perfectly with the rest of the blackness encompassing him. Only he wasn't entirely solid of frame—I could see through him as if he were made of fog rather than flesh.

His piercing blue eyes latched on to me from under his hood, burrowing straight into my spirit and head. When I asked who he was and what he wanted, the other simply brought out a large broken hourglass from under his cloak and turned it over, dumping what remained of the sand between us.

As the last of the sand fell, I watched as the blackness around us suddenly became alive and dissolved into a collection of writhing tentacles, which enveloped the other who stood across from me. When it did I saw the open span of the cosmos that had been hidden behind the tentacles.

When I looked back to my side, the other figure had disappeared, along with the swarm of tentacles. All that remained was the small pile of sand that had once flowed from the broken hourglass. I watched this sand slowly spread out across the cosmos as if borne on some silent breeze. When finally all the sand had run its course, I found myself again in my chambers at night.

With this experience fresh in my mind, I went to record it. It would be some time before I took my rest, and it would be some further days until I was once again entirely at peace after such an experience. But this was thankfully the last of my visions. It remains also the most puzzling of them to decipher. Perhaps those after me will be better able to make sense of it. And maybe they'll even be able to find a way to keep some of those other troubling visions from occurring.

Sitting back, she chewed on the lines some more as she put her thoughts in order. When she was ready, she took up a fresh piece of parchment and began to write.

• • •

Shiril stood before a cluster of large diamonds jutting from the tunnel's rough walls. These were as big as a human's head and blazed with a soft blue light, serving as the only source of illumination in the dark environment. This was one of scores of networked tunnels acting as the guts of her palace. And just as this tunnel was studded with glowing diamonds, others were lined with shimmering jewels and even raw chunks of precious metals, each of which possessed a soft glow all their own.

"I don't think I'll ever get over the sight." Rheminas came up beside her. He was dressed in a black tunic with brown pants and black boots. This more subdued attire meant he wasn't trying to stand out but rather to blend in—especially if his visits would be growing more frequent.

"I haven't." Shiril kept her attention on the glowing gems. "And don't think I ever will."

"I wasn't talking about the diamonds." Shiril tilted her head and saw Rheminas sporting his now-familiar mischievous grin. "I'm happy to hear you liked my gift, though." He noted the necklace. She'd developed a habit of wearing it just about every day. "I figured you'd enjoy the fire opal. It reminds me of you."

"How so?"

"A cool exterior keeping back a molten core." Her stoic face revealed she was at a loss as to the analogy. "You might not see it, but when you tap into it—well, you know the result." Again he smiled and she couldn't help but blush.

"I didn't expect you back so soon." She started moving down the tunnel.

"You're hard to stay away from."

Shiril turned around. Rheminas' mischievous smile had only deepened. "I wasn't even sure you'd come back."

"Why not?" Rheminas made a move for her.

"I—it was all so sudden . . . and then there's the concerns as well."

"About what?"

"It shouldn't have happened."

"And yet it did."

"It wasn't right."

"It wasn't?" He raised a bushy eyebrow. "Look me in the eye and tell me that."

Shiril stared intently into Rheminas' yellow eyes and tried grabbing ahold of the words she'd just said, but they now seemed so far away, drifting further all the time. Instead, all she could offer was an anemic sigh.

"We're just too different."

Rheminas traced the back of his hand down her neck and shoulder. "Maybe not as much as you might think." A part of her delighted in the warm touch. It brought back more than a few memories of when that same hand had last caressed her.

"I haven't been able to stop thinking about you since our last encounter. But if you really don't want me here, I'll go." It felt like glaciers skidded past them in the silence that followed. A silence that seemed to grow only more oppressive and immobilizing with every breath.

"Would you really have me?" she asked at last.

"Oh yes." Rheminas' eyes widened in delight.

"Then we probably should—"

Rheminas had pulled her to himself and smothered her lips with his own before she could say anything further.

She didn't pull back. Though it hadn't been that long ago when she'd last felt the heat of his lips soaking into hers, a part of her had been craving the experience again. And now that it was here, she wasn't so quick to let it depart. Instead she savored it, allowing the fire of Rheminas' body to excite her—seep deep into her—and there kindle the flame it had once before. An inferno that was welling up from within—like tapping into some hidden shaft of magma . . .

"Would *you* have *me*?" Rheminas searched her face. There was a strange vulnerability in his gaze she found even more attractive. She couldn't do anything but consent.

She ran her hand through his thick orange hair. "What if the others find out?"

"Since when did you start thinking about what others thought?"

"It's just . . . we're the first in so long to—"

"And who says anyone will have to know anyway?" He pulled her closer. "Besides, the secrecy only makes it all the more enjoyable."

For the moment she couldn't argue with the logic. Instead, she drank deep the searing nectar of her lover's lips—becoming more inflamed with every rapid heartbeat. When they'd finally paused for breath, she whispered into Rheminas' ear: "Let's not waste a moment more."

He was only too happy to oblige.

• • •

Asorlok was enjoying a modest meal, alone as usual. Fine red linen covered the wooden table. Atop the linen were silver candelabra filled with tall white candles. They striped the long table's center all the way to the head, where the god of death sat. He ate off pale bone china, drank his red wine from a clear crystal goblet, and used ornate silverware polished to a fine sheen.

The meal was a simple affair. Roast beef with some vegetables. He'd finished with most of the meat and was about to clear off the remaining vegetables when the door opposite him opened. He watched one of his priests enter—a titan from the early days of Tralodren. He was carrying a letter.

"My apologies for the interruption, but this just arrived." Asorlok took note of the envelope. It was sealed with a stylized eye staring back at him from the midst of some lavender-colored wax.

Saredhel.

"Thank you." He took the letter in hand. "You may go. All of you," he informed the handful of other priests—these mostly humans with a handful of elves among them—who had been silently tending to his needs. All bowed and quietly made their departure.

Once alone, he took a knife and broke the seal. He shook the clumps of wax onto the table and opened the letter. It wasn't long but could finally provide him an answer.

He read the missive eagerly.

> *You came to me seeking answers, and as I promised, I have sought diligently for them. In the Omnian Scrolls and elsewhere I have endeavored to be as thorough as I could, knowing what I shared would be taken to heart perhaps more than you might realize.*
>
> *You asked me to vouch for Nuhl's character. I can't. You think you need such knowledge to help make a decision you've already made but are trying to keep from yourself.*
>
> *What I can say is this: Nuhl will be true to itself. You must be true to yourself.*

Taking his goblet, he swallowed some wine before returning to the letter. He'd repeat this pattern for some time—sipping wine, reading the words, and finding his answers.

● ● ●

Bron materialized in the Expanse a few yards behind his master. Once again his lord was focused on the Fade—or rather, what lay beyond it in the Void, too far away for Bron to fully discern. But his lord was more able in such things, having been a Lord of both Space and Time before assuming his current rank. Not that Bron was at a loss as to what it was that held his master's attention. He, like all the other Lords of Space, was well informed on what presently resided in the dominion of absolute nothingness. And like the others, it had been made quite clear to him that they should have nothing to do with it.

"Back so soon?" His master continued his gazing.

"It went faster than I thought," he replied, approaching.

"Then it went well?"

"By now Rilas should be standing over the body of my adopted guise. Once he gave me the opening, it was easy enough to exploit."

"He tried wrapping you in that cocoon of darkness?"

"As you'd foreseen. It provided the perfect cover to send in my replacement and return to you."

"And the scepter?"

Bron reached under his cloak for the object. "In your possession, as it should be."

His lord peered over his shoulder. "Seems my trust in you was well placed."

"Thank you, my lord." His lord held out a hand. Bron was prompt in relinquishing the scepter. "It was just as you said. He was too clouded by his greed and lust for power to even consider I might have another rod to make a copy."

"They'd be foolish to attempt to use it, but still . . ." His lord's attention returned heavenward. Bron joined him, imagining a plum-skinned enthroned god hovering in the midst of the all-consuming darkness. The white throne upon which he sat was more akin to a tombstone amid that hungry ocean of nothingness.

"Even *if* he's a god, he won't last forever up there."

"He's seated on the throne. That will keep him longer than you could imagine. I'm sure he's already finding that out. It was probably a bonus to the punishment. They knew he'd die a slow death. They probably thought to destroy the throne in like fashion. But I've already prepared against that possibility."

His lord made for a larger palace in the distance. It was one of many the Lords of Space had built over the years, which aided in obscuring his master's movements from any prying eyes—from either the pantheon or elsewhere.

"It's a good trap." Bron respectfully followed from behind.

"Yes, and it also gives us the perfect cover in which to operate. I have the scepter, and now the throne is back within reach. They've given me everything I need and don't even realize it."

"They will soon enough."

"Until then we'll have to make sure we lull them into a false sense of security. Let them focus on these new gods and look to their own affairs. In short order a calmness will descend, a dulling to the true reality, letting me grow stronger until everything finally is in place. And by then Gurthghol will be ready to see things from my point of view. But until then we'll wait."

"As you command, Lord Vkar."

APPENDICES

APPENDIX A

A BRIEF HISTORY OF TRALODREN'S NORTHERN HEMISPHERE

THE FOUR HISTORICAL DIVIDES

Tralodroen scholars (primarily Patrician Dradinites) have made four basic divisions when it comes to documenting the history of Tralodren.

The first two divisions are unrecorded and recorded time. Unrecorded time is the span of years that came before the first known written documentation was put down by the ancient ancestors of the mortal races who now inhabit the planet. Because of this understanding, it is widely held that recorded time is the beginning of not only written history, but mortalkind as well. Before recorded time, there is nothing but legends, myths, and uncertainty: the creation, the reign of the gods, and the dranors. Most of this insight comes by way of the Kosma and Theogona, two ancient texts written before the days of mortalkind. And while outside of other oral histories and tales, they are the only two resources most tend to trust to hold any degree of truth, though even that in recent years has been decreasing among some scholars and sages.

The second two divisions are formed by dividing recorded time in relation to the Divine Vindication. This watershed moment in history separates all recorded time into two distinct historical periods: all that came before is BV (before Vindication), and all that came after is PV (post Vindication). In addition to these divisions, there are a few others that have been used in times past and make their appearance in this summary. These are:

- **Cosmic Timeline (CT)**, used primarily by the titans for their main timekeeping. It is said to start at the beginning of the cosmos and then work its way up to the modern day.

- **Before the Great Shaking (BGS)**, used by most to define what took place before the worldwide event known as the Great Shaking. Anything that took place before this event used this demarcation.

- **After the Great Shaking (AGS)**, the timeline that followed the Great Shaking and would be used for a long while, all the way up to the configuring of the new divisions brought about by the Divine Vindication.

- **Tralodroen Time (TT)**, a time system created and used by the dranors that starts at the beginning of Tralodren (which was also their own beginning) and continues from there. It includes mortalkind, which is often thought of as a continuation of the dranors in various ways.

UNRECORDED TIME

The Beginning
The Thangarian Age
The Pantheonic Age
The Titanic Age
The Fiendish Wars
The Dark Decade
The Wars of Liberation
The First Rebirth
The First Great Decline
The Second Rebirth
The Dranoric Age

The Great Shaking
The Third Rebirth
The Second Great Decline

RECORDED TIME

The Shadow Years
The First Age of the Wizard Kings
The Second Age of the Wizard Kings
The Third Age of the Wizard Kings
The Fourth Age of the Wizard Kings
The First War of Magic
The Second War of Magic
The Third War of Magic
The Divine Vindication
The Age of Ash
The Age of Recompense

UNRECORDED TIME

THE BEGINNING
(Timeless)

This was the beginning of everything. Myths and legends speak of two powerful and unknowable forces causing the existence of all things: everything that was, is, and ever will be was created from just these two entities.

THE THANGARIAN AGE
(1–1519 CT | 10,000–8481 BV)

Myths also speak of a time when the titans came to power. They ruled a great empire spanning many worlds, centered on their home world, called Thangaria. As the empire grew, it came to be ruled by the first gods, Vkar and Xora, who would later give birth to the pantheon.

THE PANTHEONIC AGE
(Began 1519 CT | 8481 BV)

Following the fall of the Thangarian empire and the death of their parents, the children of Vkar and Xora took power and ruled instead, forming the pantheon. It was during this age that the gods created Tralodren and many of the races which came to live on the world. Each god also increased their realms, power, and influence, which they continue to do into the modern day.

THE TITANIC AGE
(1524–2314 CT | 1–790 TT | 2588–1798 BGS | 8476–7686 BV)

The first powerful empire on Tralodren was ruled by titans who had migrated from Thangaria. They were the rulers of the world before any other race could dominate the planet. At first a peaceful people, they soon grew jealous of the gods and wished to be like them, then greater than them.

Mighty in nature and ability, they ravaged Tralodren in their battles with the linnorms in trying to forge their dreams of greater glory into reality. Ultimately, this drive would unleash some of the darkest times Tralodren has ever known and alter the course of the planet and its population forever.

THE FIENDISH WARS
(2314–2330 CT | 790–806 TT | 1798–1782 BGS | 7686–7670 BV)

The time of the titans and their rule on Tralodren ended in a horrible series of wars brought about by their foolish actions to try to free some fiends from the Abyss who might aid them in their fight against the gods. Instead, their would-be allies quickly turned on them and proceeded to conquer all of Tralodren before warring among themselves in an effort to secure their new domains.

THE DARK DECADE
(2330–2340 CT | 806–816 TT | 1782–1772 BGS | 7670–7660 BV)

Named for the ten years during which the fiends ruled unopposed on Tralodren after establishing their territories during the Fiendish Wars. It was known as a time of societal darkness and decay that threatened to wipe all that had been accomplished into ashes and memory.

THE WARS OF LIBERATION
(2340–2350 CT | 816–826 TT | 1772–1762 BGS | 7660–7650 BV)

After a decade of darkness and oppression, the gods aided the people of Tralodren and brought about a time of liberation that would take another ten years to complete but would free the inhabitants from their fiendish masters while also removing the titans from Tralodren as judgment for what they unleashed upon the gods' creation with the start of the Fiendish Wars.

THE FIRST REBIRTH
(2350–2650 CT | 826–1126 TT | 1762–1462 BGS | 7650–7350 BV)

While the people were free from their wicked masters and had nothing more to worry about from the titans, they were far from living in peace and plenty. Tralodren had been greatly ravaged; large swaths of its landscape had been burned and ruined, poisoned and corrupted. Worse still, there were plagues, famine, and hidden evils others would later find left behind by the fiends. Most of the cities were ruins or ash, the towns and villages decaying rubble.

Adding to this were the roving bands of monstrous races still seeking what mischief and pillage they could find. It would take some time to rebuild, which the population would do—slowly at first but in time recovering some momentum and a sense of greater hope and peace growing ever brighter on the horizon.

THE FIRST GREAT DECLINE
(2650–2750 CT | 1126–1226 TT | 1462–1362 BGS | 7350–7250 BV)

Although many were looking to a more hopeful future before them, it wouldn't turn out as bright as they'd thought. As more titanic ruins were explored, some dranoric magi unleashed a rapidly spreading plague which took its toll not just on people but also on wildlife. It would come and go in cycles throughout the next century, pushing back the gains that had been made across the races and nascent nations. And while the negative effects were finally stopped, it would take some time until the populations once again reached the point where they had been before this terrible onslaught arrived.

THE SECOND REBIRTH
(2750–2825 CT | 1226–1301 TT | 1362–1287 BGS | 7250–7175 BV)

Poetically named for the various revivals and recoveries of populations and resources—and a sense of greater self-reliance and collective goals among the populace—this period of time helped raise society back to levels higher than had been seen before even the First Great Decline. The accelerated birth rate was suspected as some sort of boon given by Asora to help jump-start the people again and keep them from losing ground. The surplus of grain, fruit, and vegetables also helped people in having healthy children and being able to feed them and their new livestock, whose numbers also increased.

THE DRANORIC AGE
(2825–4112 CT | 1301–2588 TT | 1287–0 BGS | 7175–5888 BV)

Soon enough, the dranors would rise to greater power on Tralodren, taking the place once held by the titans of old. And sadly, like the titans, they too wound up as despots in the end. Because of this, according to the Patrious and Kosma, the gods cursed them to a slow extinction and caused them to bring forth elves, humans, dwarves, gnomes, and halflings in their attempt to escape it. But like the titans before them, they sought to wage war against their creators rather than repent and possibly free themselves from their curse.

Finally, the gods would have no more of it. Seeking to stop them from taking any more foolish actions akin to what the titans did in their rebellion, the pantheon decided to put an end to the race and their empire entirely, thus saving the other races from any further corruption and oppression in the process.

THE GREAT SHAKING
(4112 CT | 2588 TT | 0 BGS | 5888 BV)

In a single moment the dranors were wiped from the face of Tralodren, their spirits shuttled to the Abyss. And then the world was shaken; all of Tralodren was changed. The lands cracked and reeled, sliding into the now-growing ocean. Other parts were swallowed by magma and otherwise faded from existence along with the ancient race and the cities that dotted their once-massive empire.

The lands that remained were ravaged fragments of their former selves, washed by wild surf, gnawed by earthquakes, and consumed by hungry fires. Lava and lightning took care of the rest, as massive storms birthed from the event plagued the world for days. Finally, when the terror did subside, there was an empty calm upon the world, a sense of relief mixed with a growing uncertainty of what now awaited those blessed enough to have survived . . .

THE THIRD REBIRTH
(4112–4357 CT | 2588–2833 TT | [1–245] AGS | 5888–5643 BV)

Much to their own surprise, pockets of survivors of the terrible divine judgment of the Great Shaking found themselves alive and trying to find a way forward on their greatly altered planet. And this they did, in a slow but progressive fashion, even as the aftershocks and turmoil of such devastation echoed across the world for a few more years, until finally things fell into a kind of stability that would become the new reality for the ensuing millennia.

THE SECOND GREAT DECLINE
(4357–4521 CT | 2833–2997 TT | 1–164 AGS | 5643–5479 BV)

After some centuries the land had been established and the people had started making new progress on fleshing out and improving their lives and civilizations. However, as new groups would mingle and grow, so would diseases among them. The result was a series of cross-contaminations that took a toll on various populations, setting them back a few notches from their previous achievements. This in turn birthed fighting and small skirmishes, as with perfect timing, the monstrous races made new inroads and fought with increased linnormic and draconic attacks. All these events combined to whittle away any gains made with the earlier population growth, setting up another period of years darkened in their outlook.

RECORDED TIME

THE SHADOW YEARS
(4521–8845 CT | 2997–7321 TT | 164–4488 AGS | 5479–1155 BV)

This was a time of societal darkness, as those who'd survived the Great Shaking had to rebuild and repopulate the new world presented to them, being unable to reclaim or re-create any great civilizations until the arising of the origin cities.

The Time of Beginnings
(4521–6880 CT | 2997–5356 TT | 164–2523 AGS | 5479–3120 BV)

These years are fragmented in terms of recorded documentation, growing more detailed as time progresses. Encompassing the span at the very dawn of history for mortalkind, these were the centuries when the origin cities came to power, and all the other creatures, nations, and races that called Tralodren home began to flourish.

The Imperial Wars
(6880–7000 CT | 5356–5476 TT | 2523–2643 AGS | 3120–3000 BV)

As the races grew in number and territory, they began to rub up against each other with increasing friction. In time, fueled by ambition, greed, and other dark traits, a period of global warfare soon erupted. Each nation either tried to defend itself from being taken over or was the one trying to do the conquering. The wars destroyed all the origin cities save Remolos, which was rebuilt and has remained inhabited to the modern day.

The First Great Unrest
(7000–7500 CT | 5476–5976 TT | 2643–3143 AGS | 3000–2500 BV)

Taking advantage of the rubble and bedlam the Imperial Wars caused, a great wave of murderous migrations exploded from the lands beyond the Boiling Sea. From here came jarthals, ryu, and their offspring, along with more monstrous races who took over lands and ransacked ruins, slaughtering at will. The wave of death and violence spread from the south all the way to the far west and the extreme north. The whole expanse of their carnage-laden migration served as the seedbed for what would in modern days become the tribes, clans, and pockets of goblins, hobgoblins, ogres, giants, and lizardmen that now live across most of the Northern Hemisphere.

The Whispering Years
(7500–7750 CT | 5976–6226 TT | 3143–3393 AGS | 2500–2250 BV)

Here the available recorded knowledge grows scarce, and any insight into this era is dim and fleeting, like straining to hear whispers in the wind. All that's known for certain is it was a time very like the Years of Perdition, and all was depressed, in poverty and ruin. Further, the people were very faithful, looking to do penance to the gods for a release of the hardships many suffered during these years.

The Years of Restoration
(7750–8400 CT | 6226–6876 TT | 3393–4043 AGS | 2250–1600 BV)

This time period was a shorter version of what had happened in the Time of Beginnings: rebuilding and repopulating the lands and world that had been ravaged by the Imperial Wars and then the First Great Unrest.

This was when new kingdoms arose, independent cities emerged, and nations began to define themselves anew. There were still a few minor skirmishes here and there, but the general trend was of an upward nature. In time much of the scars healed and smoothed over, setting the stage for a new era dawning over the horizon.

The First Great Ascent
(8400–8845 CT | 6876–7321 TT | 4043–4488 AGS | 1600–1155 BV)

On the heels of the Years of Restoration, the improvements didn't stop once things were restored. Indeed, many new discoveries were found, and the knowledge of all was increased, from the lowest of peasants to the greatest of kings. Progress in architecture, art, and the sciences soared at this time. In addition, a number of social and political matters were addressed so as to help bring about what's been called "Tralodren's Golden Age."

THE FIRST AGE OF THE WIZARD KINGS
(8845–9095 CT | 7321–7571 TT | 4488–4738 AGS | 1155–905 BV)

For the most part what marks this age is the rise of mages. People began to understand the nature of magic, and many found they had the ability to wield it. While just fledglings in skill, well below even what present-day apprentices can master, they grew in understanding and recorded what they learned. It was during this time that the Tarsu, the first school and organization of mages, was founded. In time they would give birth to the rise of the wizard kings. During this age, however, they were scholars and scavengers of lost knowledge and magical insight.

The First War of Spoils
(8845–8903 CT | 7321–7379 TT | 4488–4546 AGS | 1155–1097 BV)

As the Tarsu began to teach students, others began to rediscover the dranors and sought out their ruins with fervor. Lost treasure, hidden secrets, and forgotten mysteries from long ago all caused a massive campaign funded by merchant, faith, and king alike to try to gain as many of these artifacts and riches as possible. While not a true war in the sense that no one fought battles against one another for these so-called "spoils," the drive to get them was equal in pitch to the energetic din of combat. Eventually, this craze died down as many of the known sites were picked over, and very few—if any—new locations were found to keep the flame of looting burning.

THE SECOND AGE OF THE WIZARD KINGS
(9095–9345 CT | 7571–7821 TT | 4738–4988 AGS | 905–655 BV)

When true mages started to appear, it marked the beginning of this age. More skilled than their previous teachers, they had begun to approach the talents of most mages in the present age. The Tarsu also became more political at this time, gaining much influence from the royal, rich, and highly esteemed citizens who had joined their ranks.

The Second War of Spoils
(9198–9257 CT | 7674–7733 TT | 4841–4900 AGS | 802–743 BV)

As with the First War of Spoils, new discoveries of ruins and secreted wealth led to searching for artifacts, riches, and tempting insights into greater magical power. However, this time it became a more wide-scale event, as many kingdoms, headed or influenced by Tarsu members, pushed the issue for their own gain. As with the previous collection of spoils, this craze burned out when the trickle of locales dried up and was picked over.

THE THIRD AGE OF THE WIZARD KINGS
(9345–9595 CT | 7821–8071 TT | 4988–5238 AGS | 655–405 BV)

It was during this age that mages first ascended into wizard kings, taking up ruling their own territories as kings and queens and starting to amass followers and subjects as a true ruler would. Seeing their rising power, many turned to them for aid instead of the gods and their priests. This caused a decline in the faithful and worship of the pantheon in favor of the wizard kings—who took this growing attention to rise closer toward a divine rank with each new generation of devotees.

The Years of Perdition
(9360–9510 CT | 7836–7986 TT | 5003–5153 AGS | 640–490 BV)

This was a chaotic time with the rising of wizards and the fracturing of faith and society. Poverty and other calamities came upon the land, forcing many into crime and other vices that further added fuel to the fire. The Gartaric Knights were created to combat these troublesome matters. For forty years they waged a massive campaign, gaining support all over Tralodren in a war against crime and injustice. These wars led to a massive recruitment and decreased unrest on a large scale, helping cement the knighthood into one of the oldest and most respected institutions in the world.

The Great Apostasy
(9510–9635 CT | 7986–8111 TT | 5153–5278 AGS | 490–365 BV)

While the Gartaric Knights were respected, not many people held to the old ways as had their ancestors before them. As more and more people turned from the gods to the wizard kings, the temples and priesthoods faltered, shrank, and then faded. Many smaller shrines and places of worship were converted to serve the wizard kings instead. With the increase of this new godlessness of the masses, many faithful saw a great threat on the horizon and dreaded the day when it would fall upon them, taking out the last bastions of fealty to the pantheon.

Fenningway's Crusade
(9535–9545 CT | 8011–8021 TT | 5178–5188 AGS | 465–455 BV)

Alarmed by the falling faith of his peers, a zealous gnome named Josiah Fenningway organized a militia group to combat the rising tide of the wizard kings. His plan was to turn people back to the truth and the gods, but it was a short-lived venture.

After preaching his messages and gaining more successes against weaker wizards, he was killed in 460 BV (9540 CT | 8016 TT | 5183 AGS) in a reprisal attack by a more powerful wizard queen who had grown tired of his efforts. For five years his followers traveled all over the world spreading his message, but they met with little success. At the end of this period they had either lost their zeal, been killed, or been silenced by fear.

THE FOURTH AGE OF THE WIZARD KINGS
(9595–9845 CT | 8071–8321 TT | 5238–5488 AGS | 405–155 BV)

During these centuries the wizard kings rose to their greatest heights. With such mastery of magical power and insight, which raised many to the rank of a divinity, they turned an envious eye toward each other in plotting for still more. Kingdoms and empires were their playthings, for no ruler dared touch them; all feared their power and ire. Faith in the gods reached its nadir. Temples were turned into houses for the glory of the wizard kings, and cults had begun to spring up around them, seeking to deify these mages for their great accomplishments and mere presence. Other rulers and some brave souls, however, would soon rise up to challenge the continual crushing domination under the wizard kings' heels.

The Second Great Unrest
(9595–9630 CT | 8071–8106 TT | 5238–5373 AGS | 405–370 BV)

Hard times became even harder when the wizard kings began to purchase large armies comprising the monstrous races that had made up the First Great Unrest and unleashed them on their enemies and weaker mages. All over the world these mercenary armies battled for their magical lords. Only by the efforts of the Gartaric Knights, other faithful warriors, and the remaining priests did the armies eventually shatter, and a fragile peace was able to return.

The Elven Cleansing
(9620–9700 CT | 8096–8176 TT | 5263–5243 AGS | 380–300 BV)

This period was named for the bold actions of the Elyelmic emperor Dinous, who began a pogrom of slaughtering all mages and magically inclined individuals in the Republic of Colloni. It was a bloody affair but effective in ridding Colloni and its territories of any magical taint. Those who were not slaughtered in this campaign fled to more tolerant lands.

Dinous' War
(9705–9820 CT | 8181–8296 TT | 5275–5390 AGS | 295–180 BV)

Seeing the success of his war, Dinous made his case to the other nations, offering to join forces to attack all the mages and wizard kings wherever they resided. Not all of these leaders took him up on the offer, but those who did waged a massive war against the wizard kings and the lower-ranked mages who followed them.

The war had found much success, when in 186 BV (9814 CT | 8290 TT | 5384 AGS), Dinous was killed by a fiery sphere falling upon his palace. The attack stilled the efforts of the other nations over the next six years as all learned the true threat of what they were facing and how they could all be next should any of their sworn opponents choose to make them an example.

THE FIRST WAR OF MAGIC
(9845–9875 CT | 8321–8351 TT | 5488–5518 AGS | 155–125 BV)

This first series of battles were fought sporadically and took care of many of the lesser mages and weaker wizard kings across the world. With their knowledge captured by the victorious wizard kings, these conquerors grew even more powerful. No one dared interfere with these battles, as they feared to back a losing mage or, worse yet, risk the ire of both warring parties. So the wars continued, the numbers of mages fell, and the power and prestige of the victorious wizard kings grew.

THE SECOND WAR OF MAGIC
(9875–9945 CT | 8351–8421 TT | 5518–5588 AGS | 125–55 BV)

The battles increased in frequency, duration, and intensity as more-skilled wizard kings began to raise massive armies to fight their foes. Cities and kingdoms were pushed aside in these battles like so much rubbish, and the victors grew ever more powerful. Many people were displaced, whole terrains were decimated, and new hardships, such as famine and disease, began to cover the world in a sickly shroud. To all who lived through these years, it seemed as if hope itself was dying.

THE THIRD WAR OF MAGIC
(9945–9995 CT | 8421–8471 TT | 5588–5638 AGS | 55–5 BV)

Finally, all the fighting had winnowed away all the lesser mages till only a handful survived to battle for supreme rule over all. Continents were shaken, whole populations were slaughtered, and the world looked as if it were destined to become a terrible, hellish waste. The wizard kings didn't care. Each battle brought them closer to their goal of total supremacy.

Eventually, these remaining wizard kings made their final press for total control of the areas in which they lived. As these plans for dominance grew, so too did the carnage they spawned. The battles they unleashed were something Tralodren hadn't seen since the time of the titans and greatly displeased the gods. Seeing that nothing would change without their intervention, they brought about the end of the fighting and set their focus on dealing with the real root of the issue (as they saw it).

THE DIVINE VINDICATION
(9995–10,000 CT | 8471–8476 TT | 5638–5643 AGS | 5 BV–0 BV)

The pantheon had decided that Dradin's gift to the dranors—that is, magic—was being abused by mortalkind and so ordered Dradin to revoke it. Dradin followed their declaration, causing the minds of mortalkind to forget what they had once known and greatly weakening their ability to manipulate any form of magic.

While not revoking his gift entirely, Dradin's actions pleased the pantheon. Over a period of five years, the abilities and skills of those who had once been able to wield magic faded away. Magic itself grew harder to cast and spells increasingly less powerful than they'd formerly been.

And along with this was the loss of knowledge from dranoric texts and elsewhere. It was harder for mages and others to obtain these for any new insight, and even these same texts tended to be lost in a number of surprising ways, ranging from raids by monstrous races to fire, flood, and even mysterious thefts.

At the end of the five years, no elf, human, dwarf, halfling, or gnome could wield or understand the nature of magic. So it was that the ages of the wizard kings and the wars of magic they brought to the world finally ended.

THE AGE OF ASH
(10,000–10,373 CT | 8476–8849 TT | 5643–6016 AGS | 0 PV–373 PV)

This was a bittersweet time on Tralodren. The world was torn from many wars and had to heal. People returned to the faith of their ancestors, rejecting the ways of the wizard kings, which had left them disillusioned and their lives and lands ruined. Over time the nations were rebuilt, and all returned to the state of peace that had been in existence before the horrible wars and the wizards who had caused them came to power.

THE AGE OF RECOMPENSE
(10,373–10,900 CT | 8849–9376 TT | 6016–6543 AGS | 373–900 PV)

The start of this age is assumed to begin with the return of magic to Tralodren in 373 PV (10,373 CT | 8849 TT | 6016 AGS) via a handful of mortals who once again came to understand the workings of magic, despite Dradin's efforts to remove it. The pantheon was concerned, but— once they found out that Dradin had nothing to do with this event—they allowed it to continue under a wary eye. It was agreed that if wizard kings should ever again arise, even under the hindrances placed upon them by Dradin, then serious action would be taken.

Slowly at first mortalkind was awakened to their latent ability as knowledge and insight were increased across the globe. Added to this was the growing influence of the Tarsu, which had remained together through the Divine Vindication and the Age of Ash. As their ranks swelled, once more they sought ways to further spread the awareness of and acceptance for magic.

These efforts would take some time, since many were still against the mages and any sort of return of magic in general, fearing a return to the dark days that they'd so recently clawed themselves out of. But as the generations passed, so too did some of the fear and ill will among those who were magically inclined, to the point that even academies were opened across the Northern Hemisphere for wizards' education. And this happened seemingly without major opposition from priests, rulers, or even much of the general populace.

But magic wasn't the only thing growing across the world. Trade and commerce would explode, built on a solid and secure foundation and favorable conditions brought on by years of peace. And along with the increase in trade and commerce grew the power of the people and organizations and nations who controlled those channels and resources. It was speculated by one scholar looking back on the timeline of this era that the gods must have wanted to provide a recompense to those who had previously suffered through so much. And thus his commentary inspired the name of this period.

The Great Silence
(10,753–10,760 CT | 9229–9236 TT | 6396–6403 AGS | 753–760 PV)

This event is better marked and known by those who followed the shamanic religion. For in one day they lost contact with the power of their worship, forever silencing it and their shamans. In the ensuing seven years some sought answers, while others slowly changed their beliefs or stopped believing in anything altogether. It would mark the end of anyone on Tralodren being able to access something that was first discovered and adapted some ten thousand years before.

As to the reasons why it occurred and if the shamans would ever regain their power and abilities, there are no end to the stories. Some hold it to be a punishment from the gods for straying from their worship; others say it had something to do with the takeover of Arid Land by the Elyellium; still others think that the shamans finally wore out or even used up whatever power or abilities they had been tapping into for so long. None know nor will ever know for certain, which makes the loss all the harder to accept for those who once knew the shamanic religion, beliefs, and practices so intimately.

APPENDIX B

RECORDING THE HISTORICAL RECORD

Whereas later and more modern centuries have seen many different historical accounts, each as varied as their audience and intended purpose, ancient Tralodroen history has been maintained and kept by two main sources: the Theogona and the Kosma.

THEOGONA

Date of Creation: 2335 CT | 811 TT | 1777 BGS | 7665 BV
Timeline Covered: 1–2335 CT | 1–811 TT | 2588–1777 BGS | 10,000–7665 BV
Created by: Tralodren-based titans

The Theogona was created by titans who had fled the growing power of the Lords of Tralodren leading up to their time of calling in the fiends onto the planet. They were a mixture of Cosmin, Pantheonists, and defectors who truly feared for their future and, with the rise of the fiends, sought ways to document what they could of their history so they might leave behind some sort of record.

Given the various views and ideologies of those who composed it, there are naturally some points of view or topics that tend to get highlighted more than others. But when it was compiled, efforts were made to smooth and balance things out to present a more whole and uniform presentation of the historical account. If this was going to be the last remaining voice of their race, the compilers reasoned, they'd want it to be as accurate and thorough as possible.

In the years after the titans' removal from Tralodren, other scribes and scholars worked on copying the material, which has continued to be the case even until the present time, thus ensuring that the work and the information it conveyed would never be forgotten. As such, the Theogona is considered the foundation of history, even if viewed by those in later centuries as a collection of myths and legends.

Combined with the Kosma, it offers some of the only insights into the times not just of the early days of Tralodren but what came before and led up to its creation. Naturally, with such insight, it's highly favored among priests and those given to such matters while, since the Divine Vindication, having fallen out of favor with the general population, who look to more modern historical accounts for a sense of place and purpose in the cosmos.

Even so, many wealthy people and those of status often will seek out their own copy for their libraries. And while the history is still of interest to many, it's seen more as a collection of stories and tales than actual history. A summary, perhaps, but not something that should be entirely believed without critical thinking and skepticism to help pull out the real kernels of truth amid the fanciful dressing.

KOSMA

Date of Creation: 3920 CT | 2396 TT | 192 BGS | 6080 BV
Timeline Covered: 2335–4521 CT | 811–2997 TT | 1777 BGS–164 AGS | 7665–5479 BV
Created by: Dranoric sages; later added to by other sages and scribes of mortalkind

The Kosma was inspired by and follows the Theogona, which provided a summary and ongoing historical record for what took place before the coming of the dranors. When Marat's push for greatness turned dark and corrupted, and the dranors found themselves lost, dying, and cursed as a race, those still not taken with Marat's fantasies desired to create a history of their own race and nation—both the good and bad, highs and lows—picking up from where the titans left off and their story began but also including what they could of the other nations and races who shared the planet with them.

The work was involved, compiled from other sources and information along the way, but after about fourteen years of effort, a collection of eighty dranoric scribes, sages, and scholars finished a document they hoped would not only preserve something of their existence but also, when combined with the Theogona, help continue the story of creation and life.

It also helped that for a time into the Shadow Years, when recorded time was established, sages, scribes, and scholars—mostly from mortalkind—added to the story of the planet and peoples after the Great Shaking. While it was a general overview, given the chaotic nature of what followed this catastrophic event, when combined with what was already written, it provided a thread for future generations to follow.

And in this it has done well. Many scholars and even priests cite the work for certain references and information used in conducting research or composing their own works of history. Bards and other storytellers have even been known to mine its depths for inspiration or hints of tales they can take and make their own. It also helped form the foundation of the modern understanding of the present ages and even how one is to write historical documents in general, forming the foundations of the modern templates for scribes, scholars, and sages.

Finally, it has also contributed to parts of the modern religions on Tralodren, since they use the document in part to help flesh out certain elements in their own histories as well as provide a foundation upon which to solidly anchor their ancient texts and sacred tomes.

APPENDIX C

PANTHEONIC COUNCILS

The following is a list of the various councils the gods have had and what was discussed and decided during them.

The First Council (1519 CT | 8481 BV)

The gods assembled for the first time and laid out the framework for how the council would function. It was also the time of the creation of the factions—Light, Gray, and Dark Gods—and the sharing of the plan to create Tralodren.

Borders and boundaries of the new order were established, reparations were made, and prisoners were returned. Titans were also given the option of moving to new domains or realms if they liked but would not be allowed to move elsewhere for a new permanent residence after that.

The Second Council (1521 CT | 8479 BV)

Over a year following their first meeting, the pantheon took up the next matter of reform while still plotting out their creation of the new Tralodroen solar system. It also saw the reformation of the Imperial religion to Pantheonism as well as the creation of the Pantheonic Dispensation model, which introduced the concept of the chosen, those who would get to stay with the gods on their realms after death. The basic structure of the afterlife was also defined and Sheol established as the seat of judgment for everyone passing through to their final destination. It also introduced the creation of the Galgalli to serve as the enforcers of the pantheon's judgment on various matters.

The Third Council (1522 CT | 8478 BV)

The foundation of the Tralodroen system was established, along with their basic domains. But things were stalled on the final aspects of Tralodren, prompting them to meet again in hope of finding a resolution.

The Fourth Council (1523 CT | 8477 BV)

Unity on Tralodren's final design was reached, and the races to inhabit it were finalized. The idea of having the titans live on the world was also presented, allowing them the choice if they so wished. Ultimately one half of the remaining mortal titans decided to take up the offer, these mostly being Cosminian in their religious outlook.

The Fifth Council (1524 CT | 8476 BV)

Often called the Tralodroen Council, for this was when Tralodren and the Tralodroen system were created. It also created and established Galba's protection over the throne, the Grand Barrier, and the final rules of all future meetings of the pantheon.

The Sixth Council (2150 CT | 626 TT | 1962 BGS | 7850 BV)

This council called for the punishment of the titans for their warring across Tralodren and attempt to take Vkar's throne for their own. Their king, Ralgor, was killed and the whole titan race cursed with sterility, which could be reversed if they repented of their ways.

The titans who remained with the gods in their realms weren't so cursed, for they had maintained a good and healthy relationship with them and thus would remain the only titans in the cosmos who would be left to reproduce.

The Seventh Council (2335 CT | 811 TT | 1777 BGS | 7665 BV)

This council was called to decide on how to deal with the fiends on Tralodren. They first sought help from the Lords of Evil, who scoffed at the idea. This prompted the Lords of Good and angels to enter Tralodren by a portal created by the dranors, in the same way the Lords of Tralodren had allowed the fiends entrance, and attack them on their own terms.

The Eighth Council (2350 CT | 826 TT | 1762 BGS | 7650 BV)

Called to decide the final fate of the titans who remained on Tralodren. They were sent to the Abyss. The portal that brought the Lords of Good and angels to the planet was also dismantled and decommissioned to prevent it from being abused in the future. The races created by the fiends were allowed to remain in hopes they might be redeemed.

The Ninth Council (3960 CT | 2436 TT | 152 BGS | 6040 BV)

This council was called to deal with the rising threat of the dranors who had strayed far from their former way. Under the direction and inspiration of the increasingly deranged Marat, they were seeking to turn on everyone on Tralodren and even attempt to take on the gods themselves. Their punishment was to decrease in population and from there start to give birth to what would later be called mortalkind.

It was also the time when a final decision maker was elected who would have the power to end ties and debates. This would fall to Ganatar.

The Tenth Council (4058 CT | 2534 TT | 54 BGS | 5942 BV)

The dranors were judged and removed from Tralodren by means of and in conjunction with the Great Shaking. The gods also spared some of the other races, who were left alive and alone to begin the repopulation of this new world and the rebuilding of their own nations. To aid in this endeavor, the gods also reset the mortals' lifespans, giving them more of a chance to repopulate the world. It also saw the judgment of anyone living on Tralodren's moon, sending a Galgalli there to make sure all dranors and life did not survive.

The Eleventh Council (7000 CT | 5476 TT | 2643 AGS | 3000 BV)

Following the results of the Imperial Wars, it was decided that something had to be done to help bring unity and restoration to the races on Tralodren—namely, mortalkind. And since the brunt of the battles and trouble dealt with the humans, elves, and dwarves, the gods called for a council and there decided to choose three candidates from these races—one for each race—to help guide them in a special role as emissary for their race to the gods. The idea was to elevate this candidate to the rank of god of that race to bring about the unity and healing that was needed.

Each would be answerable to the gods and council for their actions and efforts, but that would be their sole focus, since up until now the gods had not been able to bring about such unity or peace among the races, nor were they able to stop the warring—some of their number even encouraging it.

And while Olthon, Causilla, and Asora pushed to find a representative for the gnomes and halflings, no suitable candidates were found. It was later argued that Olthon was fairly well liked and universally worshiped among the gnomes and could do some good there. Causilla had some inroads with the halflings, and it was assumed she would be able to make some more in the ensuing years—perhaps even adding in Asora along the way.

Among the three other races, some suitable persons were found. Among the humans, a Celetoric warrior and shaman named Panthora was selected. Among the dwarves, a wise and dedicated warrior who took the name Drued was chosen. And among the elves, it was decided, by a narrow vote, that Aero Tripton would be elevated, since he clearly showed himself to be able to inspire and lead his fellow elves. And he already had the workings of a religion he could tap into among his followers.

Each of the three was given a realm carved out from Civis, both so the gods could watch them more closely and to prevent any fighting over their prospective abodes. The council also hid the fact that they had to use some of Vkar's essence to bring the initiates into their new rank, letting them think they were the ones who did it instead. In doing so, they kept the secret of such things lest the new gods were tempted and sought to increase their power and station over time.

And so it was that this council closed with the elevation of the new gods, who began at once working to bring about order and peace to the fractured societies and peoples across Tralodren.

The Twelfth Council (9995 CT | 8471 TT | 5638 AGS | 5 BV)

The pantheon decided that Dradin's gift given to the dranors—that is, magic—was being abused by mortalkind and so ordered Dradin to revoke it. Dradin followed their declaration, causing the minds of mortalkind to forget what they had once known and greatly weakening their ability to manipulate any form of magic.

While not revoking his gift entirely, Dradin's actions pleased the pantheon. Over a period of five years, the abilities and skills of those who had once been able to wield magic faded away.

At the end of the five years, no elf, human, dwarf, halfling, or gnome could wield or understand the nature of magic.

The Thirteenth Council (10,373 CT | 8849 TT | 6016 AGS | 373 PV)

A council was called when magic returned to Tralodren after so long an absence. And this learning and usage of magic was done in spite of Dradin's previous actions to hinder its growth and use. At first it was alleged Dradin had something to do with magic's return, but once they found out Dradin had nothing to do with this event, they allowed it to continue under a wary eye. It was agreed that if wizard kings should ever again arise, even under the hindrances placed upon them by Dradin, then serious action would be taken.

The Fourteenth Council (10,753 CT | 9229 TT | 6396 AGS | 753 PV)

The gods assembled to deal with the return of Nuhl and its efforts to threaten Tralodren and even the pantheon itself with another attack. This time that attack came through the agency of Cadrith Elanis, the last wizard king of Tralodren, who had been groomed for such a task. However, while the gods were successful in routing the enemy, they lost Gurthghol in the process, along with Vkar's throne. With Gurthghol's absence, Khuthon petitioned to take over as head of the Dark Gods, and so in a way continued where he'd left off after surrendering the position to Gurthghol following the Second Dynastic Wars and the formation of the pantheon.

The Fifteenth Council (10,753 CT | 9229 TT | 6396 AGS | 753 PV)

Following on the heels of the fourteenth council, the gods assembled to deal with the matter of Gurthghol's realm and Shador, a Lord of Darkness who maneuvered his way into a place of power in Altearin as a regent acting on Gurthghol's behalf. This both kept him safe from reprisals for having a cult on Tralodren and also gave him power over the realm, since the gods were limited in what they could do with him and his supposed rule over it.

In the end Shador was allowed to stay, leaving a new status quo in place, and the rest of the gods would work to sort out and establish their own affairs—both personally and in their own realms and planes.

APPENDIX D

THE DIVINE FACTIONS

The Tralodroen pantheon is made up of sixteen gods who form a familial dynasty organized around three parties or groups that tend to split the vote of their council fairly evenly between them. This council is chaired by three chief gods. Of these three, Ganatar is considered ruler and final decision maker, earning the title "king of the gods."

The three main parties that compose the council are:

THE LIGHT GODS

Leader: Ganatar
Purpose: Devoted to regulated development, ordered progression, and enforcing and spreading the basic tenets of civilization
Members: Ganatar, Olthon, Causilla, Asora, Aerotripton, Drued, Panthora

THE DARK GODS

Leader: Gurthghol (Khuthon after 753 PV)
Purpose: Support unregulated development and progress and the

protection and promotion of the natural ebb and flow of such cycles while allowing the natural order to dominate all
Members: Gurthghol, Asorlok, Khuthon, Rheminas

THE GRAY GODS

Leader: Dradin
Purpose: Fully support neither the light nor the dark outlook but ensure there is a choice between the two positions and value free will and its protection very highly
Members: Dradin, Saredhel, Shiril, Endarien, Perlosa

RACE GODS: A SUBGROUP

There is a subgroup of deities who rose from mortalkind to divinity following the Imperial Wars. These were the leaders of the three main races fighting the wars on Tralodren at that time: Aerotripton (elves), Panthora (humans), and Drued (dwarves). Collectively called Race Gods, they've merged into the Light Gods, joining them in their efforts and thus tipping the scales of power to favor the Light God agenda more often than not.

The Race Gods were also given the ability to heal those under their charge (these being their respective races)—something no other god, save Asora, can do. This means Aerotripton can heal elves, Panthora can heal humans, and Drued can heal dwarves when their priests petition them to do so.

APPENDIX E

THE DIVINE LINEAGE

The following is a basic introduction to the structure of the family of gods and their relationships to each other. It only covers those of the divine family, omitting the Race Gods, who have no direct relations to anyone in the pantheon.

THE FIRST GENERATION OF GODS

These are all the children born to Vkar and Xora, who were the first gods of the cosmos. The siblings are listed from oldest to youngest.

Gurthghol | god of chaos, darkness, dragons, entropy, and linnorms
Ganatar | god of law, light, justice, the minotors, and order
Dradin | god of knowledge, learning, literacy, and magic
Asorlok (twin of Asora) | god of afterlife, death, and journeys
Asora (twin of Asorlok) | goddess of health, healing, and life
Khuthon | god of giants, the jarthalian races, strength, tyranny, and warfare
Olthon | goddess of peace and prosperity
Saredhel | goddess of fate and time

THE SECOND GENERATION OF GODS

These are the children of the first generation of gods and the grandchildren of Vkar and Xora. They are all cousins and are listed from oldest to youngest.

Causilla | goddess of the arts, beauty, and love
Endarien | god of air, birds, the sky, and weather
Shiril | goddess of earth, metals, and minerals
Rheminas | god of fire, magma, revenge, the ryu, the sun, and volcanoes
Sidra | ruled over nothing; instead sought to gain power from Nuhl, whom she worshiped
Perlosa | goddess of ice, the moon, snow, and water

THE DIVINE FAMILIES

Here the gods are broken down into families, with a list of partners (whether spouses or consorts) and the children they have had together.

Gurthghol + Marona (a titaness)
   Sidra

Ganatar + Olthon
   Causilla and Endarien

Dradin + Saredhel
   Shiril

Asora + Khuthon
   Rheminas, Perlosa, Vearus, Meesha, and Talaya

Chad Corrie has enjoyed creating things for as far back as he can remember, but it wasn't until he was twelve that he started writing. Since then he's written comics, graphic novels, prose fiction of varying lengths, and an assortment of other odds and ends. His work has been published in other languages and produced in print, digital, and audio formats. He also makes podcasts.

ChadCorrie.com | @creatorchad

Scan the QR code below to sign up for Chad's email newsletter!

Enjoy podcasts? Chad also produces the following:

Cauldron of Worlds
Corrie Cast

Further information about the world of Tralodren can be found at Tralodren.com as well as on social media (@tralodren). Chad also produces two monthly podcasts delving into the setting, stories, and what's happening in general with current and forthcoming works as well as sharing additional insight and information:

Tralodren: Behind the Scenes
Tralodren: Legends and Lore

All these podcasts can be found on his website and wherever else podcasts are available for listening and/or subscription.

Tralodren.com